D1642707

LITANY OF SORROWS

Peter J. Marzano

Best wishes to all

Swan Publishers
Durham, Connecticut

For information visit: www.litanyofsorrows.com.

Publisher's Note: This is a work of fiction. References to historical people, real places and events are used fictitiously. Any names resembling characters, places and incidents are a product of the author's imagination. Locales and public names are sometimes used for atmospheric purposes. Any resemblance to actual people, living or dead, or to businesses, companies, events, institutions or locales is merely coincidental.

Editing and layout by Rita M. Reali
(https://persnicketyproofreader.wordpress.com)
Cover Design © 2021 Peter J. Marzano
Final cover assembly – Al Esper Graphic Design
Cover Photo – soldier by shutterstock.com
Cover Photo – nun with rosary cover artwork by Andrew Sokol
Cover Photo – Italian church and cattle car by Peter J. Marzano
Published by Swan Publishers, Durham, Connecticut
Printed in the United States of America

Ordering Information:
Quantity sales: Special discounts are available on quantity purchases by corporations, associations and others. For details, contact the Special Sales Department at the web address above.

Litany of Sorrows / Peter J. Marzano – 1st ed.

ISBNs
Paperback: 978-1-7366827-0-8
E-book: 978-1-7366827-1-5

"The essence of government is power;
and power, lodged as it must be in human hands,
will ever be liable to abuse."

– President James Madison

1751-1836

Virginia

Dedication

To my uncle Vincenzo Marzano, born in Reggio, Calabria.
A soldier in the Italian Army during World War I,
he fought and died for Italy in the cold and snowy Italian Alps.

***

To my uncle Frank Marzano, born in Greenwich Village, NYC.
He served in the 157th Infantry Regiment of America's 5th Army, in World War II
and fought in Africa, Sicily, Italy and Germany. Two days before his unit freed Dachau,
he was gravely wounded. He survived and was awarded a Purple Heart.

***

To my uncle Robert Finbarr Burges, born in Cork City, Ireland.
He immigrated to the U.S. as a child in 1928 and joined the American Army in
WW II. Upon returning from war, he discovered his wife of two years had left him.

***

To my father-in-law, Harry Coyle, born in Jersey City, New Jersey. He joined the
U.S. Navy after Pearl Harbor, serving in the Pacific on a PBY Catalina.
Upon returning from the war, he graduated from Manhattan College and worked at
Catholic Charities in three cities devoted to building low-income housing.

***

To my neighbor Gene Ammann, born in Germany in 1922. His family moved to NYC
in the 1920s. In WW II for the U.S. Army, he flew P-51 Mustang sorties from
England over France. His best war story: Escaping two German Messerschmitts chasing
him in France, he flew so low he hit a mound of dirt. Upon landing back in England,
he found his propeller tips bent, and a crop of radishes in his air scoop.

To my friend's dad, Juanito "Bob" Rohan, born in the U.S. Virgin Islands.

He was a sergeant for the American Army's 92nd Infantry Division, an all-black

combat group known as the "Buffalo Soldiers." In WW II he was a forward artillery

observer in the 600th Field Artillery, Battery A, fighting in Italy along the Gothic Line

against Germany's Wehrmacht General Field Marshal "Smiling" Albert Kesserling.

Post war, Bob served as a New York Port Authority Policeman. Retired for many years,

Mr. Rohan is an active and healthy 100-year-old as this book is published.

***

Finally, to my dad, Louis Vincent Marzano, born in NYC in 1908, months after the

family arrived from Calabria, Italy. Too old for World War II, he left his executive role

on Wall Street to work in the Brooklyn Navy Yard. From 1941 to 1944, he helped

weld the mighty USS Missouri battleship... upon which the Japanese surrendered.

Acknowledgments

Thanks to my dear wife, Kathleen, for her support in allowing me to focus on the book by going lightly and limiting my "honey-do" lists.

Thanks to Kathy and dear friends Cathy Tolk, Bill Loudermilk, Pat McGarry, Al McConaghie, Leo Rohan and Tom Mensi for reading early drafts.

Thanks to my beta readers, including Chris Kopyt, Susan Ciani, Bill McGrath, Greg McLaughlin, Nancy Robitski and Denise Stemmler – all career educators – who provided excellent reviews to chew on.

A special thank you to my award-winning editor, Rita M. Reali, for her editing skills, guidance and exchanges we shared. Our conversations were interesting, enlightening, painful and encouraging – in that order.

Thanks to our children, Peter, Tricia, Kathy and Shawn for their encouragement, and to our eleven grandchildren for brightening each day with their smiles, for their effort in school, sports and music, for playing word games and chess games with me online, keeping me challenged and balanced and allowing me to enjoy life from a wonderful perspective as a grandparent!

Thanks, Shawn for your book savvy and guidance. Your own experience as an author helped so much.

Donation

Ten percent of the profits from the sale of *Litany of Sorrows* will be forwarded to the **Adenoid Cystic Carcinoma Research Foundation** (ACCRF) to help find a cure for this uncommon cancer that affects the lives of hundreds of thousands of people around the world. It will be sent on behalf of our daughter, Shawn Elizabeth George, who suffered from the disease.

Author's Note

S ummer 2019 was a particularly difficult time for my wife and her four siblings. When August arrived, their father, Harry Coyle, a 94-year-old World War II veteran, was in the final weeks of his life.

Harry joined the Navy days after Pearl Harbor, like so many other young men. He served proudly as a radioman and gunner on a PBY Catalina, performing search-and-rescue missions for American pilots, and patrolling the South Pacific for Japanese warships.

The hospice staff at the VA Hospital in New Jersey kept "Pop" comfortable in his final week. Our children and grandchildren all visited, saying goodbye to their grandfather and great-grandfather. During my last visit, I leaned over to kiss Pop. Barely able to speak, he whispered, "Have a good life." Four days later, he was buried on Staten Island, in a military funeral attended by Naval officers. The "Greatest Generation" had lost another good man.

After the burial, my wife and I stayed at her brother's home on the New Jersey shore. During dinner we reminisced about good family times. The August night was stuffy, hot and humid. Despite the air-conditioning, I became uncomfortably warm and restless around 4 AM.

As dawn approached, a lengthy dream came to me. Recollecting it fully upon waking, I grabbed a pencil and wrote a dozen pages of notes. What followed was several months researching details of World War I and World War II, including how the WW I Treaty of Versailles terms were not well enforced... and how divisive politics, extreme nationalism, revenge, religious prejudice and the fear of communism ignited Europe and the rest of the world into World War II. My characters all had their place and roles during the period.

I started writing *Litany of Sorrows* in mid-September 2019, four months before the Covid-19 pandemic hit. While I was writing, we all heard divisive politics and rhetoric during a national election, watched impeachment hearings and saw individuals die from prejudice and hate. I listened to elected officials spout fake theories, witnessed an assault on our nation's Capitol and saw millions die from the coronavirus.

How unique, sad and sorrowful these last 21 months have been.
– *Peter J. Marzano*

Introduction

L *itany of Sorrows* is a work of fiction. Its characters are integrated with historical facts, places and individuals of the period. The story begins with Katrina's deepest sorrow, then flashes back to 1912, when Otto von Richter and Valentina DiBotticino meet and marry.

Decades later, their young adult son, Karl, falls badly skiing in the Italian Alps, and is nursed to health by attractive Katrina Amorino, whom he met a year earlier on the slopes. He eventually returns to Italy and convinces her to live with him, but before she arrives, he's drafted into SS Officer training.

Katrina eagerly awaits Karl's return, but the SS attack Jews on Kristallnacht. Her hopeful love is dashed and then crushed as she learns of his horrific role in the Final Solution, and his return home one night.

Years pass. Karl has a final and critical Nazi SS task in Berlin as the war ends. Returning home, he learns his parents have died, and Katrina and their child are missing. During his search for them, his conscience, corrupted by Hitler's false promises of a pure national race, emerges and begins to haunt him. Despite coming face to face with the horrific reality and guilt for what he has done, his anger and rage remain and are easily triggered by frustration.

Now, Katrina must look past her mistakes and move on. But how can she? The story flashes forward to 1951, Katrina's search and an un-expected end.

The story presents immature love and want, self-centeredness, distraction, politics, religious bias, indifference, Jewish genocide, and adoption. It reminds us how mistakes of judgment have lifelong effects, upon ourselves and others, and sadly upon next generations. We are also reminded of the horrific destruction of war and genocide, and the pain parents and children suffer when separated – even years later.

Note: The *Historical Background* section at the rear of this book offers the reader insight into the period - how the fledgling German democracy post WWI moved to a dictatorship, how Hitler re-armed Germany and prepared for war. It highlights how the Treaty of Versailles was ignored, Germany's effort to grab adjacent territories it had lost, its blitzkrieg attack on European neighbors, and then battling Russia, and how it declared war on the United States just days after Japan attacked Pearl Harbor.

LITANY OF SORROWS

CHAPTER ONE

Katrina's Search... Fall 1949

Before and during World War II, Giovanni Cardinal DiBotticino held considerable political strength in the Vatican, and had made good deals for the Church, deals of all kinds. He quickly became a favorite of Giuseppe Sarto, Pope Pius X, when he first entered the seminary in Rome because of his family's business interests. Most knew, upon his ordination in 1910, it was only a matter of time before business relationships and politics in the Vatican would lift Giovanni to the positions of monsignor, bishop and, eventually, cardinal.

During his different assignments in Rome, then Brescia and again at the Vatican, Giovanni accomplished things few others in the Roman Catholic Church could have. In fact, the joke among Vatican City clergy was "DiBotticino can move mountains, cutting them with his family's quarry equipment, if necessary." And, given his family's deep financial resources, including the ability to finance construction of new churches and the repair of old structures, Giovanni Cardinal DiBotticino was well known, even beyond Italy. A few openly commented, "Giovanni could have been a Medici."

By fall 1949, Katrina's relationship to the now-deceased cardinal no longer wielded any power. And so, as she began searching for where her baby son had been placed through adoption, her visits to Church officials in Brescia, Milan and Genoa, while referencing the cardinal, failed to develop any leads.

In January 1950, Katrina's husband suggested a sizeable donation directly to the Vatican. It quickly cut through the Church's red tape and, within the month, the agency in America that had handled the adoption and placed her son with an American family was identified.

Katrina had no intentions to reclaim the boy. She had let him go because she wanted the best for his future. Profound guilt and sorrow continued to pain her heart deeply. They gnawed at her conscience and pushed her to reconnect with him. She wanted to let her child know how much she loved him. She wanted his forgiveness. And more than that, she wanted her son to know about his history – about his grandparents, the von Richters and Amorinos – and his German and Italian heritage, including the history of the DiBotticinos.

But none of Katrina's effort to find her son was for his father. As far as she was concerned, he could sit in hell for eternity. Over the years, she had grown more bitter toward him for raping her years earlier. Her inability to relax now, even in bed with her husband, remained rooted in how badly he'd brutalized her that night during the war.

Now, Katrina prayed each day, thanking God for her understanding, patient, kind and gentle husband. His emotional support, especially his daily words of encouragement, helped her deal with her sorrow.

And now, she needed to find her son. Making sure he'd been properly placed, loved and well supported financially would resolve years of anxiety, and give her much-needed emotional peace.

CHAPTER TWO

Otto and Valentina Meet

I t was the week before Christmas 1912. Valentina DiBotticino had spent the last three days skiing at St. Moritz with her three girl-friends from Brescia. The weather in the Swiss Alps had been perfect all week, and the light, fluffy powder from last night's snow fall made the slopes perfect again for today's skiing.

Emboldened by her skills and today's surface conditions, she flew at top speed down the mountainside. On her last run for the day, she unknowingly passed Otto von Richter.

Intrigued first by her ability to handle the steep slope at such a high rate of speed, the tall young German followed her. The woman, her long hair flying in the wind, turned off the main slope onto an even steeper trail – one with a skull-and-bones warning sign at the entry point.

Otto followed, but couldn't catch her. After two jumps and a few breathtaking minutes of expert maneuvering, she reached the bottom of the run.

Seconds later, the handsome, dark-haired German ended his run as well, coming to a brisk stop alongside her. He purposely let one of his skis slide across hers. Then, politely, he said in Italian, "Excuse me, miss. I'm so sorry for stopping so close to you. May I apologize further by buying you a drink this evening at the lodge?"

Valentina pulled off her ski goggles and hood to take a better look at the young man. As she did, Otto was captivated by her beautiful deep-blue eyes, long dark eyelashes and fair skin.

His attempt to speak politely in Italian was nice, but Valentina knew right away he wasn't Italian. She didn't mind. She thought the tall skier was cute. In a flash, she upgraded her opinion. *He's handsome...*

and... well, curious! Why not? It's my last night here, and I'd like to tell my girlfriends I met a tall and handsome, dark-haired German.

"*Sì. Mi piacerebbe,*" she replied in Italian. Yes. I would like that.

After brief introductions, Otto and Valentina agreed to meet that night in the lodge.

Wintertime in the mountains was wonderful, and this season was no exception. Only last year, operators of the local ski areas, including here at St. Moritz, began using car engines, pulleys and long ropes to help skiers up the hillside to increase the frequency of their runs. Almost every mountain was using these car engines this season, and the sport received a sudden boost in popularity.

The ski lodge had been beautifully decorated for the Christmas holiday. Snow had been falling for the past six weeks; the deep base and light powder made the mountains perfect for skiing. A slow-moving warm front with humid air drifted across the Alps and had warmed the temperatures to just below freezing. Large fluffy snowflakes drifted to the ground on the breezeless night. As her girlfriends readied for dinner, Valentina said she had a dinner date.

"Oh, and who is the lucky guy?" they asked.

"He's a skier staying in the first slope-side cabin."

"Does he have any friends?"

"Good question. I'll see you all later tonight and let you know."

Otto and Valentina approached from different directions. They smiled upon seeing each other through the snowflakes. Her heart rate unexpectedly increased as the broad-shouldered skier approached. *How perfect the setting! And the Bavarian-style lodge with its steep roof looks magnificent draped in snow.*

His smile widened as they met, and he opened the carved wooden door with its colorful stained-glass inserts. They stepped inside and sat near the stone fireplace and its roaring fire.

The interior of the lodge was decorated in brilliant red materials and lush green pine branches for the season. Otto suggested a cocktail of dry vermouth and a splash of scotch; she agreed. He began making small talk.

He impressed her with his von Richter family history, dating to the 1200s – with the Duchy and Kingdom of Württemberg.

"We have a complete history of our lineage written in our two-hundred-year-old Lutheran family Bible," he told her with pride, adding he was the eldest of four, and once again mentioned his strict Lutheran upbringing.

Valentina, raised Catholic, dismissed the religious difference. She wouldn't let it be a hurdle to a relationship with the handsome young man.

"I live in my family home in the village of Friedrichshafen on Lake Constance. The Bodensee, as locals call it, is the third-largest fresh-water lake in Europe and touches the shores of Switzerland, Austria and Germany. We sail in summer, and ski as much as possible in winter. When you look south from our backyard, you can see the Alps. As the eldest son, our old Bavarian house – the envy of many in our village – will be mine someday."

Otto took a sip of his cocktail and continued. "I started working at a foundry part time as a teenager, and now I'm a full-time apprentice."

He continued talking about the different parts they made at the foundry.

Valentina smiled. It was interesting, but the detailed explanation became too complicated for her to follow. *Maybe he should be a watch maker?*

He concluded saying, "I'm impressed with your skiing skills. Perhaps we can ski together tomorrow? I've added metal edges to my wooden skis. I'll let you try them if you're interested."

She nodded. "I'd like that."

Valentina began telling her family story, as all DiBotticinos did, by telling of the Crusader who fought in the Siege of Acre, and how, fearing for his life, came to Brescia, Italy, to hide in the mountains.

"A bounty was placed on the head of all Templar knights when Pope Clement V declared the end of the religious Templar Order on the morning of Friday, October thirteenth in 1307. They were made outlaws of the Church, and many were purposely killed. It's why everyone fears Friday the thirteenth."

Otto's eyes widened in interest.

"The Templar Knight learned all about stone cutting while he was in the Middle East. When he landed in the mountainous area north of Brescia – at the southern foot of the Italian Alps and just west of Lake Garda – he began cutting and quarrying the limestone. The knight lent his family name to the limestone deposit, and the quarry expanded over the last six hundred years. By the way, my oldest uncle, Uncle Vincent, still has his sword, Templar tunic and chain-maille mesh armor hidden in a wooden box. We consider it sacred."

As they finished their cocktails, Otto suggested dinner and Valentina agreed.

He continued to impress her during dinner. She listened intently and her dreams expanded. She quickly became hooked on the muscular German.

After the main course, Otto asked about her father and his business.

"By the late eighteen eighties, our family's quarry business had become extraordinarily successful because of the fine quality of our stone. But the efforts of my father, Luigi, the youngest of the five DiBotticino brothers, made it grow beyond expectations. My father is an outgoing man – and an aggressive salesman with a wonderful approach. His reputation precedes him when he travels from city to city and church to church in Italy, France and Germany, and as far away as Belgium and Poland. People are attracted quickly to his witty, warm and vivacious nature. And, of course, my skilled uncles and cousins always provide timely deliveries, whether it's statues or a column or simple building blocks for foundations or walls. And my sweet father always promises a small gift at no additional cost. It might be a cornerstone for a church or building, or a carved grave marker if a customer's loved one recently passed."

She paused, smiling.

"Everyone appreciates his generosity."

As the plates were being cleared, Otto ordered a flan dessert with two spoons.

"I have a younger sister and two young brothers. You?"

"My parents were blessed with my brother, Giovanni, and a few years later, me. That's all. Giovanni's carving and chiseling skills, like my uncle Tommaso, were exceptionally good even as a youngster. When he was twelve, he expressed an interest in the priesthood. When Gio turned eighteen, he entered the seminary in Rome to study. He was welcomed there because the pope and cardinals knew our last name. Most of the Doric, Ionic or Corinthian topped columns inside the basilica are carved from our stone, and a few statues inside the Vatican were carved by my ancestors. The soft beige tone and absence of deep veins and faults in the stone made the stone from our quarry so desirable."

To finish the evening, Otto ordered a small plate of cheese and shelled nuts, with two glasses of twenty-year-old French brandy. He wanted so much to impress Valentina – and he knew it was working.

As the evening grew late and Valentina politely covered her third yawn, they finished their brandy and left the lodge, exchanging chaste side-to-side kisses as they parted company.

Valentina virtually floated back to her room, feeling warm and filled. She fell sound asleep before her friends returned.

For his part, Otto felt certain he had found the woman of his dreams. As he lay in bed, he knew he would marry Valentina.

They met the next morning, as planned, but spoke only briefly. She apologized, saying her girlfriends wanted to leave early. Otto was disappointed they wouldn't ski together.

Before departing, they agreed to meet again, in St. Moritz, the last weekend in January.

Otto and Valentina saw each other several more times that winter and into the spring. Their fondness for each other grew quickly as they enjoyed skiing together. By April they considered making their relationship more permanent.

CHAPTER THREE

Otto and Valentina Marry

I n May, while enjoying their last ski runs of the season, Valentina and Otto became engaged and planned to marry at the end of the year.

Valentina invited Otto to the annual DiBotticino family gathering in June, where she would announce their engagement. Almost everyone in the town of Botticino was family; many relatives from Brescia attended, as well, as did a few cousins from as far as Lake Garda and Lake Iseo.

Their day in the foothills of the Italian Alps was beautiful. The unspoken rule was for everyone to arrive by noon time, as the church bells finished chiming. Confirming her aunts, uncles and important cousins were there, Valentina announced the celebration of her parents' thirty-fifth wedding anniversary, which this year fell on the same day as the gathering. Next she introduced Otto, standing beside her, and without pausing announced they would marry in December in the Old Cathedral in Brescia.

Being a proper Lutheran, a bit stiff in his manners, and not openly demonstrative, Otto struggled with the family cheers, hugs and kisses. But as the hours passed, he relaxed and warmed up to the day's celebration.

A new barrel of Tommaso's homemade wine was opened after the announcements. The pastor from the cathedral, Father Alfredo Pucci, was there at the party and told Tommaso he would use his homemade wine at Mass again this coming year. Anticipating the request, Tommaso had already set aside a thirty-gallon barrel for the priest's use, which he promised to deliver to the cold cellar of the Old Cathedral, the *Duomo*

Vecchio. But he knew, like last year, most of the wine would never make its way to the sacristy to be used for Mass.

Later in the day, Valentina's aunt brought a hearty cheesecake out to the center table. Then to Otto's surprise, everyone began to sing, celebrating his June birthday, and moments later, the men and women danced the tarantella. As evening approached and darkness fell, the old men finished their *Scopa* card game and took their last gulps of grappa. Everyone hugged and kissed and said goodbye as they left for their homes. It was a happy and satisfying summer's night in the DiBotticino compound. And Otto knew he had chosen the right girl to marry.

Unfortunately, a similar visit for Valentina at his family home on the lake in Friedrichshafen was never set up. In fact, when he suggested a lakeside get-together at the family home, his sister, Hilda, had a lot to say about his committing to marry an Italian Catholic.

"Otto, you should know those Italians are unsophisticated – there is virtually no industry in Italy. And the Catholics! You know very well Luther was right about the pope, cardinals, bishops and priests being corrupt, selling indulgences. You must change your mind and avoid that woman you've been seeing."

His younger twin brothers, Heinz and Helmut, standing next to Hilda, voiced similar objections.

"Otto, you should marry a good Christian-raised Lutheran woman with a Germanic heritage. We believe Father wants you to keep our von Richter family heritage intact and purely German," Heinz said.

Helmut nodded his agreement.

Otto's elderly father, Kristofer, heard from Hilda about Otto's plans, but knowing the power of love, kept silent on the matter.

Despite the pushback from his siblings, Otto said he was deeply in love and planned to continue with his plans to marry Valentina two days after Christmas of 1913.

For Valentina and her small family, excitement filled the air. Her parents were thrilled to have the tall, handsome German join the family. And Stella, Valentina's mother, thought bringing some height into the family was a good idea, especially since her own husband, Luigi, stood a mere 5'5".

In late October, Otto told the plant superintendent he would be getting married in late December during the factory's slow period. He was in the last months of completing a three-year apprentice program at the Ravensburg Foundry, Milling and Machining Company.

"Congratulations, Otto! That's wonderful news! When you return from your honeymoon, you will be promoted to a journeyman position, with full company benefits."

Otto and Valentina married in the Old Cathedral in Brescia, with Father Pucci presiding. A large reception followed in the church hall. It was cold outside, but several massive fireplaces kept the large room warm. Almost two hundred attended, including several Botticino customers and two high-ranking clergy from Milan who braved the day's blustery wind and wet snow.

None of Otto's family attended. In fact, his siblings never even replied to Valentina's handwritten wedding invitations. Sadly, Kristofer died a month before the wedding. Otto believed his father would have made the trip were he still alive. Valentina felt hurt and sad for her husband.

Being avid skiers, they honeymooned in the Alps. They picked Innsbruck because while they each had skied there in the past, they never skied there together. Months earlier they'd invited their respective friends to meet them there for their honeymoon week to celebrate. The light powder Innsbruck offered was terrific, and the New Year's Eve celebration was exceptional. The skiing that whole week exceeded the couple's expectations. By week's end, everyone was exhausted, and filled with wine, food and great memories of the extended marriage celebration.

On their last morning, Otto and Valentina bade farewell to their friends and returned to her parents' home for a last goodbye. She wanted a few more days with her parents, and Otto understood. Stella, knowing they would be returning, planned a surprise.

Valentina's brother, Father Giovanni DiBotticino, unable to attend the wedding because of impromptu meetings with the pope and a cardinal at the Vatican, would be there to greet them when they returned.

Like many Catholic families of the time, parents expected one or more of their children to consider the priesthood, become a monk in an abbey or, if it was a young girl, to enter a convent. Giovanni, the pious young man with the extraordinary stone-chiseling skills, had decided at a young age to join the priesthood to honor his parents and the family. Everyone in the family was happy for Luigi and Stella, and proud of Giovanni for his interest in serving the Church. The exception was his uncle Tommaso, who seriously believed the family would be better served with Giovanni – the most talented of the next generation of DiBotticino sons – applying his skills at the stone works than as a priest. Carving and chiseling stone had come naturally for him and, by learning to deal with the imperfections of the stone, he unknowingly prepared himself for his role in the priesthood with the virtues of patience, understanding, acceptance and forgiveness.

Valentina was thrilled to see her brother upon her return home from their honeymoon.

She shared with Giovanni how she loved Otto and said, "But Gio, I'm anxious about moving to his hometown in Germany and being accepted by his family."

Her brother comforted her. "I can see how much Otto loves you and I'm sure his family will come to accept and love you."

The next day, as they prepared to say goodbye, Valentina hugged and kissed her parents and brother. They packed their bags in Otto's 1910 Fiat Tipo and headed for Friedrichshafen. Giovanni stayed another day, then returned to the Vatican, driving a six-cylinder Aquila borrowed from a local businessman in Rome.

Driving long distances was tough. Roads across the Alps and those back to Rome in many stretches were merely muddy wagon tracks, and in the snowy Alps, treacherous at times. Having two or three spare tires was crucial for a long trip – and having the strength and ability to change them – was just as important, as was carrying extra gasoline in cans.

Upon returning to her husband's village, Valentina found the lakeside home beautiful. She was delighted with its gorgeous setting on the Bodensee and distant views of the Alps. And now, with the sudden passing of his father only a month earlier, he was the sole owner of the von Richter family residence on the lake.

Otto promised Valentina an addition as their family grew. For now, with his father's passing, the Opa suite was empty, and the size of the house perfect for several children. Sadly, Valentina soon learned how Otto's siblings resented his inheritance. As much as they said they valued traditions, they resented the family home going to Otto and the Italian Catholic.

Otto was everything Valentina expected from him as a husband and provider in the months following their marriage. Warm, kind and considerate, and even shy at times, he treated her like a princess, making sure her every need and want was met. He earned enough to meet their needs and even saved some money from every paycheck. Marriage was all the young couple had expected.

Life was good for the young couple, but off in the distance a political storm brewed. Several European countries aligned themselves with other countries, forming treaties and forging military alliances. Britain and Germany were competing in a military buildup on the high seas, with the construction of large battleships. In mid-1914, Great Britain's attempt to organize a political conference to resolve increasingly hostile disputes in other countries failed to materialize. Germany feared being crushed militarily by a Russia-Great Britain-France alliance, and aligned with Austria-Hungary. A flashpoint event occurred with the assassination of Archduke Ferdinand and, within days, Germany declared war against Russia. Two days later, on August 3, Germany declared war on France and quickly moved its armies westward through neutral Belgium with a plan to attack Paris.

Weeks after the declaration of war, a large group of men from Friedrichshafen and Ravensburg, feeling the need to stand up for German interests, joined the Army. Otto and his cohort of volunteers left for war in late September 1914.

In the final months of her pregnancy, Valentina struggled emotionally after her husband left. She knew the war and its consequences could somehow change their lives forever. She just didn't know how right she was.

CHAPTER FOUR

Karl Arrives and Otto Returns

Baby Karl was born November 10, 1914, seven weeks after Otto left for war. He proved to be a blessing for Valentina, as she had plenty of time to provide extra motherly care.

Little Karl walked before he was one and noticeably bright by the age of two. By his third birthday, his motor skills allowed him to easily manipulate wooden building blocks, read simple words and retell several fairy tales. When he turned four, Valentina bought him a child-size mandolin and had him begin music lessons. She hoped he someday would play his grandfather's full-size mandolin, as music had always been important to the von Richter family.

Valentina continued to teach Karl, exposing him to simple math, printed multiplication tables, puzzles and memory games. She enhanced his language abilities, speaking to him in both German and Italian. The toddler took to both languages without hesitation.

Valentina hoped to visit her parents' home in Botticino, certain Luigi and Stella would love to hear little Karl speak Italian, but she held off going because of the war. She grew increasingly anxious about her husband, as she had received no letters from him since the war started.

Otto's years of fighting in the trenches were hard, and hand-to-hand combat with bayonets was particularly horrific. Finally, after countless advances on enemy positions, he was shot just above his knee. Had it not been for a fellow soldier immediately securing a tourniquet on his thigh, Otto might have bled to death lying between trenches. But the fast action saved his life and medics carried him to a nearby tent for medical treatment.

The bullet shattered Otto's kneecap, damaged ligaments and tore through his quadriceps. Multiple fragments in his thigh bone, just above the knee, made his recovery long and painful. Nevertheless, he still had his leg and he felt grateful to be alive. He looked forward to going home to his sweet and beautiful Valentina.

During his recovery, Otto received one of the countless letters Valentina had sent. It found Otto at the hospital in Munich in May 1918. In the letter, Valentina referred to their son Karl's recent third birthday on November 10, 1917.

Otto cheered at learning he had a boy, but he cried at reading of his sister Hilda's untimely death. He left the hospital six months later, a week before his son's fourth birthday.

When he finally returned to his lakeside home, family and friends greeted Otto as a war hero. But within a week of his arrival, special news about the war reached Friedrichshafen. It was not what people wanted to hear. The German chancellor had signed an armistice agreement with France and Great Britain on November 18, 1918, effectively giving up and putting an end to the war.

Why did so many Germans need to die? What was accomplished? What was gained by all the fighting? What will happen to Germany now? Otto wondered.

Otto avoided discussing his experiences, which weighed heavily on his psyche. Memories of the brutality haunted survivors from both sides. In his first year back home, his lingering pain and inability to walk comfortably crushed his once- happy spirit. Otto's outgoing personality, and his cuddly warmth with Valentina, disappeared. His injury prevented him from returning to work at the foundry, and his inability to ski and race downhill with Valentina left him despondent. Although he was re-covering slowly, he was in such pain at times, he often wished they had cut his leg off above his knee.

During her husband's difficult days and long months of recovery, Valentina remained a loving wife. She worked at Karl's school. When she returned home from work, with young Karl in tow, she would cook Otto his favorite meals. She did anything she could to please him. But home remained a sad place. His painful recovery diminished the strong

14

emotions and physical attraction between them. What remained was their love for and pride in their child.

It took another two years before Otto's ravaged thigh muscles finally healed and his leg pain subsided. Despite a limp, getting around the house was no longer a problem. He could put his full weight on the leg, and his attitude about many things improved. He finally began to speak about his days in the trenches, and the limp became a badge of honor for having served his country. He also felt more comfortable being with Valentina again.

Otto finally believed it would be possible for him to return to work, but he'd have to find a job where he could sit a good part of the day. Before long, the superintendent at the Ravensburg factory heard Otto von Richter wanted to return to work. Inside of two weeks, he made changes to his staff, and then visited Otto to discuss his return to work. Otto appreciated how accommodating they were.

The next week he began work and handled two jobs: Scheduler, coordinating production of upcoming projects, and Assistant Buyer, ordering raw materials for those projects. Both were desk jobs, requiring minimal walking. It was perfect.

Upon hearing the good news, an old friend and fellow factory worker offered to pick Otto up each morning on the way to work, about seven miles away. Otto accepted his friend's offer as he still couldn't operate his car's clutch. Once again, the bread winner in the von Richter home, Otto's sense of self-worth returned, and Valentina delighted in her husband's return to work.

CHAPTER FIVE

The Factory

T he Ravensburg Foundry, Milling and Machining Company, noted for its size and diverse capabilities, produced a wide variety of steel products. The combined length of its three buildings totaled just over nine hundred feet, end to end.

One exceptionally large overhead crane with a 100-ton capacity was located inside the main foundry building. It facilitated the pouring of molten metal into molds, and the moving of the heavy cast metal pieces. Another crane similar in size carried metal parts from the foundry area into the milling and machining shop areas. A third crane moved parts to the end of the building and extended another hundred feet outside into the yard.

A rail spur from the town's main railroad line entered the three connected buildings at each end and, once inside, split and ran straight through to the other end. Rail cars would bring iron ore into the foundry for smelting, as well as coke and coal to the two huge furnaces. Steel ingots forged in the primary furnace subsequently became available for new parts as the molten steel poured into molds cooled. Large pieces coming from multi-piece molds typically had scale and burrs where molds joined together. The milling and machining areas processed the parts into final products. The workers deburred the edges of the metal parts, drilled holes or applied further heat to bend and reshape the metal, allowing a piece to become a part fitting into a final assembly. The world over knew German workers possessed extraordinary machining skills.

In his assistant-buyer role, Otto evaluated blueprints and plans to estimate quantities of raw iron ore needed to cast molten metal into parts. He had the foundation for understanding his job, having worked there years earlier as an apprentice. Combining his buying responsibilities with his role as project scheduler, he successfully planned the quantities of raw materials, and the factory produced and shipped finished products in the shortest amount of time.

Within twelve months, Otto advanced to become the head buyer for the entire factory. He continued to oversee project scheduling for the foundry's production, and the flow of the foundry's unfinished parts into finished goods. Otto then took on one more responsibility: forecasting the manpower needed to complete factory orders.

Recent orders caused a shortage of men to complete the work. Otto responded by creating a human-resource plan to forecast the man hours required, then synchronized the manpower to raw materials flow and production. His plan even included vacation hours and time off for unexpected family needs.

By the end of his first full year of responsibility for hiring workers, a reliable volume of manpower became available to do the work, alleviating workflow choke points. He performed like the conductor of an orchestra, waving his baton and keeping every part of the symphony in sync.

Otto was well liked by managers in the factory complex because his changes relieved many daily pressures. As 1932 began, the factory owners, the von Court brothers, recognized his work ethic and leadership by promoting him to plant superintendent.

In his new role, Otto assumed responsibility for all production and the business' bottom line. The accompanying generous raise proved favorable for the von Richter family, bolstering its reputation within the village. Otto's brothers suddenly seemed to appreciate Valentina more – as her brother Giovanni, the priest, had predicted years earlier.

Meanwhile, day-to-day conversations among factory workers centered on the politics of the day. Renewed and elevated interest in nationalism became a hot topic. Otto and his workers, like millions of others in Germany, still held strong negative feelings regarding the Treaty of Versailles, feeling it badly mistreated Germany. But beyond Ravensburg, complicated politics in Munich and other large German cities caused unrest in the young Weimar Republic.

In January 1933, a series of negotiations supported by former chancellor Franz von Papen and prominent conservative businessmen convinced Hindenburg to appoint Adolf Hitler as chancellor. With Hitler and his Nazi Party in power, they held enough political power to push back against the Communists in the Reichstag. The Enabling Act passed months later allowed Hitler and his cabinet the right to enact laws without the involvement of the Reichstag. His master plan was set in motion, and now as dictator, he quickly made his move to re-arm the country.

A key element of Hitler's war plan was to build an aggressive mobile war machine. Ideally it would move German ground forces into other countries swiftly. New orders placed at the Ravensburg factory in the second quarter of 1933 came as a surprise and increased at a new record pace.

Work in the factory intensified for Otto in his new position, and his long hours and late-night arrivals home prevented him and Valentina from enjoying their interest of late afternoon sailing, or watch their son Karl ski on winter weekends. And sadly, they stopped hosting dinner guests at the lakeside home.

Concerned about Otto's long working hours, Valentina felt her husband's temperament change from work pressures; he'd return home exhausted, and often unhappy, snapping at the simplest questions. Pleasant small talk between them stopped. She pined for the days when they had raced each other down snowy mountainsides.

Noting subtle changes in Germany's economy, he and his senior managers recognized something extraordinary was happening. Manufacturing of parts for heavy machinery rose significantly, not just in their Ravensburg factory but throughout the country, despite limitations and provisions in the Treaty of Versailles.

By mid-summer, Otto began returning to work after dinner, and occasionally he even stayed overnight at the office. Planning for raw materials and human resources had become so demanding, it consumed all his time. New orders for vastly different parts came to the foundry every day. By the end of 1933, work and output increased more than 300 percent from the prior year. Otto improved workflow and purchased wisely resulting in saving the factory seventeen percent in material costs.

He paid suppliers quickly, taking advantage of the small two percent discounts offered.

In the factory the pressure of the increased workload ruffled the old timers' feathers, but they appreciated the overtime. And when a huge bonus found its way into his end-of-year paycheck, Otto was all smiles.

As 1934 began, Otto, stressed even further, never returned home for supper, except for an occasional day on weekends. The Ravensburg foundry's ability to produce top-quality parts on time placed it above other small factories in southern Germany. Suddenly a key part in the plan to build Germany's war machinery, the foundry received even more work orders.

Provisions in the Treaty of Versailles prohibited Germany from constructing tanks. To circumvent this limitation, factories of all sizes throughout Germany built tank parts in secrecy, telling foreign inspectors the parts were for tractors and other farm machinery. The largest tank-production efforts took place in the major cities of Nürnberg, Kassel, Brunswick, Magdeburg and Berlin. Eventually, tank-part manufacturing and assembly grew more dispersed. Parts foundries and machining factories sprang up wherever good access to railways and newly developed high-speed roadways became available.

During the mobile war machine buildup, political favoritism inserted many unqualified Nazi Party members into the raw-goods procurement and production process in larger factories, which created issues for mass production. Small factories and parts manufacturers became more vital and integral to the plan. Under Otto's leadership, the Ravensburg factory benefitted as it significantly increased production.

By the end of summer 1934, manufacturing tank bodies, turrets and treads was a huge focus of German foundries and factories. In September, the growing list of parts manufactured by the Ravensburg foundry included treads for tanks and halftrack armored vehicles. An exciting new war strategy called *Blitzkrieg* had been approved by Hitler and adopted by Wehrmacht field generals. Blitzkrieg offered Germany's military a speedy means to roll across the European countryside virtually unimpeded, thereby surprising and crushing the enemy.

Peter J. Marzano

CHAPTER SIX

Karl's Career Begins

In the end of the summer of 1934, Otto's son, nineteen-year-old Karl von Richter, finished his second year as an apprentice at the foundry. A strong rising star, his prior two years were deemed sufficient, and management waived the requirement for him to complete the four-year program. Given the growing number of new people working in the factory, and coupled with his father's position, Karl became the manager of all newly hired employees.

Karl's management style mimicked his father's. At times he was soft and encouraging. Other times he used a strong tone and pushed hard on the new workers to get things done. He had no patience for slackers and felt confident confronting employees one to one, telling the person what he expected, and what the job required. He made good use of his diverse team to assist in various departments, wherever the workload was heaviest.

His team focused on unexpected issues and choke points in production and helped get departments through difficult projects to achieve goals. Before long Karl received additional responsibility within the factory. Otto felt proud, seeing his young son manage teams effectively with men twice or even three times his age.

Taller than Otto, Karl's strength came from factory work, and his athleticism from skiing. With skills well above average, he challenged the best slopes in the Austrian, Swiss and Italian Alps. Like his parents once had, he enjoyed skiing on winter weekends. In the past four years, he would get away for a weekend whenever possible with friends and head to the Alps. Unfortunately, because of Otto's leg injury, Karl and his father never skied together.

20

By 1935, Germany's pent-up nationalism emerged like a phoenix from the ashes of World War I. A feeling of strength and vigor spread quickly across the county. The Nazi Party, strong and united, continued to grow in the hearts and minds of citizens. Hitler sought to annex more land to Germany. The economy was fully recovered, and secretly engaged in building a variety of war machines. As Karl heard the latest stories from friends and factory workers about Germany's renewed strength, he was emotionally moved and, for the first time, embraced his German heritage. Young and highly impressionable, Karl became enamored with the emerging ideals of Nazi Nationalism, anti-Communism and anti-Semitism. Those strong feelings captured his soul and became a focus of his conscience and his manhood.

The Ravensburg Foundry, Milling and Machining Company found itself positioned perfectly among German factories. The complex was set up to handle the growing heavy workload. The rail line that ran into and through the building successfully managed and transported high volumes of parts and components of the heavy assemblies. Ravensburg's skilled staff enjoyed their work and displayed positive attitudes. Favorable leadership from plant superintendent Otto von Richter helped them to consistently deliver parts on time or ahead of schedule.

The Ravensburg factory owners, Wilhelm and David von Court, agreed to invest more capital into the facility to meet increasing demand; they purchased land adjacent to their buildings to increase the size of their yard for storage of parts and finished goods. Otto was happy to be in a good industry at the prime of his career. And best of all, his son Karl worked there with him.

In 1936, employment and production at Ravensburg expanded again. Now more than two thousand factory workers produced parts and components for a growing assortment of armored vehicles, including the newly designed tank, the Panzer II. Rumor had it if they did well, they'd have a strong chance to produce parts for the upcoming Panzer III, a much larger tank.

Being considered for new work, Otto proposed to the foundry's owners the construction of a 100,000-square-foot annex building, as a final-assembly facility. The new building would be added at one end of the complex, and sit over the existing rail line. He proposed two additional rail spurs inside to accommodate moving fully assembled tanks and armored halftrack vehicles. The von Courts again agreed to spend the capital, knowing it would enable the factory to bring in more parts work and allow them to win a contract for the final assembly of Panzer tanks. Confident of the financial return, they made the investment.

When word got out, the factory workers grew excited, knowing the new facility could bring in more work, and additional profits for the business – not only now but after Germany had won the war.

Construction of the assembly building began immediately. Karl was tasked to oversee the construction team, in addition to his own workload. Even before the huge annex was completed, production requests from the German Arms Minister increased twofold. These new orders again put a strain on the workers. Otto and his management team switched the work crews to twelve-hour shifts; formerly optional Sunday work became mandatory, and all vacations were forbidden. The factory had new lighting installed and now functioned around the clock.

The new workload left factory buyers scrambling to secure raw materials. At the same time, small components, sometimes delayed by other factories in the supply chain, held up final assembly of tanks and other armored vehicles in the new annex. Karl watched his father's leadership and temperament as work volumes and pressures increased. Seeing his father in action motivated Karl to grow, establish goals and achieve success.

But Karl, annoyed at the attitudes of some workers, developed a tougher approach. His style was less forgiving than his father's. That became a noticeable difference between the two. Nevertheless, Otto saw this as a positive and believed Karl would someday achieve great things. He knew his son would make ample use of the many lessons he learned in the factory – especially in the areas of building and construction, and his ability to manage subordinates.

CHAPTER SEVEN

Karl Sees Katrina Again

O tto promised his son a long weekend off from the factory. After all, it was December, which meant prime skiing weather. With his father's approval, Karl headed off for a four-day vacation in Vipiteno, in the Italian Alps. He skied there last winter and longed to return. He unexpectedly got the nod from Otto to bring along two school friends who also worked in the factory. The three of them were ready for a good time, and happily leaving heavy conversations about German nationalism and the worries and concerns of a factory far behind.

Late in the day on December 28, 1936, while navigating a black diamond run with his friends, the edge of Karl's ski clipped a broken branch sticking up through the snow. He took a bad fall, tumbling hard and smashing his foot against a tree.

Minutes later, another skier saw him and helped Karl, carefully sliding him down to the base. His handsome features grimaced in agony as he was transported to the local hospital, Ospedale Vipiteno, just off Via Santa Margherita.

Karl had initially refused pain medicine offered at the mountain base, but after arriving at the hospital, he desperately needed the relief it promised. The next morning, a surgeon using a newly acquired x-ray machine, observed a slightly fractured and dislocated bone in his ankle. After some maneuvering, the surgeon reset the bone with a sudden sharp whack from a cushioned hammer.

Karl saw stars and let out a roar heard on the next floor of the hospital.

That afternoon as he lay in bed, reflecting on his father's war injuries, an extremely attractive nurse walked in. Tall, shapely and slender, she had long, almost-black hair, olive skin and beautiful, sparkling blue eyes.

That's her! The girl I saw on the ski slopes last year. She was a terrific skier. Yes, I think we had a drink, too. How beautiful she is! And how lucky I am to find her again, and be in her care. It must be fate!

"Nurse, do you remember me?" he asked.

"No. Should I?"

"Yes, we skied together last spring. We raced downhill. You're… uh, uh, Francesca, right?"

"No."

He shook his head. "I must have hit my head when I fell."

The nurse studied his features for a few moments. "Oh, yes. Of course. Now I remember you. We had a pleasant chat one night over a glass of wine, and we exchanged addresses. I wrote to you… twice, but never heard back."

"I'm so sorry, uh…."

"Katrina. It's Katrina Amorino."

"Ah, Katrina, it's been a very busy year."

Just then Karl's two friends walked into the room.

"Karl, we stayed last night, hoping you could leave today, but the doctor says you'll need to be here at least another week to let the fracture begin to heal. We need to leave now and head back to work. One of us will come back to get you next week. You look like you're in good hands with this beautiful nurse."

As his friends spoke to Karl, Katrina remembered that night… and having felt attracted to him. She was beginning to feel the same way as she looked at him lying in the hospital bed.

As his friends turned to leave, she told Karl, "My shift is over, and I'm headed home now. I'll be back tomorrow. Maybe we can chat more then. Get some sleep."

The next day Katrina made her rounds, then returned to sit with Karl during her lunch break. Karl reintroduced himself, emphasizing his heritage. He talked about his parents' lakeside home, and the new place he had just bought for himself in a nearby hamlet called Langenargen. He shared how his parents similarly met on the ski slopes, how his father had survived a war injury, recovered and became the superintendent in the factory where he worked. Then he described his line of work and how exciting it was for him to work with his father.

Katrina shared about her formative years in Lecco, as the daughter of a baker. She said, "My parents met in Rome. My mother gave my father her address… at least he wrote to her. They fell in love, married and moved to Lecco, where my father started his bakery. As I said, at least my father wrote to her… not like you."

She sighed. "Karl, I thought we had a moment like that last year when we met. I gave you my address that night, but you never wrote. I remembered this morning I even wrote to you a third time, but you never replied. I was so disappointed.

"The summer my parents met, my mother had considered becoming a nun. But after meeting my father, she decided not to go into the convent." She paused a moment. "Karl, for the last six months, I've been seriously thinking of entering the convent."

Karl wasn't sure what that meant. His ankle started to pain him, and he lost focus on what she was saying. He interrupted her.

"Katrina, could I have some more pain medicine?"

Slightly annoyed, she left the room. Another nurse returned with a shot to reduce the pain and put him to sleep.

***

Karl's ankle fracture proved to be worse than expected. It was another two weeks before he could put weight on it. During this time, he had several more conversations with Katrina, mostly focused on their shared love of winter sports. In one conversation, Karl finally admitted he had lost her address.

In response, she looked at him and said, "I mailed you three times and included my return address. Where did those letters go?" He had no answer.

Katrina thought he was attractive but her recent thoughts about the convent confused her. She wasn't sure where his thinking was, nor hers.

She decided his being on the pain drugs clouded his thinking, so she wisely decided to put off any more serious conversations.

When the day came for Karl to be released, Katrina helped Karl to the front door of the hospital, where his friend waited with the car. She gave him a hug and a peck on both cheeks. "Stay in touch this time."

Standing gingerly on crutches, Karl awkwardly returned her hug and promised he would see her again soon. As they looked in each other's eyes, they both felt a connection.

As his friend drove Karl back to his small house in Langenargen, the conversation quickly focused on the buildup of the German military, and recent news: the formation of an official Rome-Berlin Axis coalition.

Karl was supposed to rest and allow his ankle to heal completely for another four weeks. But stubborn and feeling somewhat better, he returned to the factory a week later, using one crutch. He saw the factory was remarkably busy with more new orders. He saw a clear difference in just the few weeks he'd been away.

Hitler's master plan to develop vast numbers of mobile war machinery was well underway. The broad complexity of the Wehrmacht mechanized buildup was beyond the comprehension of most German citizens, but inside German factories, production of tanks, ships and airplanes continued to grow, month over month. In some locations, the German SA and SS gathered up men and women and pressed them into service in the factories to help with the growing production demands.

Wehrmacht generals were planning movements here and there across Belgium and France, and eventually Poland, Czechoslovakia and Hungary. The SA and SS continued to grow in number and power. At the same time, concentration camps were constructed to hold groups of laborers; some of these camps held political prisoners. The camps under construction would hold massive numbers of Jews, Slavs, Hungarians, Poles, Gypsies, homosexuals and other deplorables and eventually exterminate those seen as outcasts to the future German Arian society.

Hitler's war-planning effort had become a broad and massive movement. Otto and Karl were fully engaged in driving the factory to its full capacity – perhaps even beyond its capabilities.

CHAPTER EIGHT

The Sketch is Approved

I n the first two months of 1937, projects coming into the Ravensburg foundry reached their highest numbers ever, and women began joining the work force. The annex operated at full capacity.

Another rail spur built alongside the foundry facilitated even more raw material deliveries. Trains dropped off semi-finished pieces daily to be further milled and drilled as finished parts and assemblies for tanks and armored vehicles. Trains also brought huge, twelve-cylinder water-cooled gasoline engines produced by the Maybach Company for installation in Panzer I and Panzer II tanks being assembled there, at the Ravensburg complex.

Months later, the factory's focus shifted to producing exclusively Panzer III tanks and, shortly afterward, larger 21-liter Maybach engines, capable of producing 650 horsepower, began arriving for installation.

An additional 50-ton capacity overhead crane was installed to lift engines into the open tank bodies. A completed tank turret, including the long gun barrel, was lifted, placed and installed atop the tank's body. As final assembly was completed, an overhead crane lifted the finished 23-ton Panzer III tank onto a flatbed rail car, to be shipped wherever it was needed.

Six months earlier, before the tank-assembly work arrived, Otto developed a team of workers to make mechanical and electrical connections inside the tanks in the final-assembly area. Initially, six tanks were being completed every day.

Heinz Guderian and several Wehrmacht commanders credited Otto for the high production levels, high quality and low failure rate of assembled vehicles.

During this last increase of production in the assembly area, Otto, who had been sleeping on a couch in his office, built a bedroom upstairs in the factory. Valentina, who'd been bringing Otto his meals, suggested he build a kitchen in the facility, to provide food service for the factory workers.

Otto liked the idea and set up a cafeteria. He thought it would be best at the far end of the building, allowing workers to see their finished products being placed onto rail cars. He was right. Despite the extremely hard work and long hours, seeing finished tanks move from the factory on rail cars motivated the workers.

Paralleling the factory's continued growth in the past year were Karl's management skills. Being responsible for directing the work of hundreds of men in the milling and machining shops wasn't easy. Both were critical points in the quality of the parts; Otto knew he could trust Karl's sharp mind and keen eyes to get things done right.

While inspecting the tank treads being milled there, a persistent flaw in the foundry's molten pour came to Karl's attention, because of the rework it required. At the same time, he came across an old sketch of a Soviet tank tread design and noticed several small but key differences. Thinking it through, Karl considered a change in the current German tread design that might be an important improvement. He spoke with his father at lunch one day, explaining the issue and suggesting a change that had three additional benefits over the current German tread design.

"The tank tread would be stronger but lighter. It could be assembled faster, and the improved tread would shed mud, snow and ice easier," Karl said.

Otto liked the idea but knew they'd need approval from the high German command for the tread drawings to be changed, and new molds made to create new treads.

"Karl, sketch the new design and write your full explanation, including a financial assessment and operational evaluation regarding how the tread can be replaced in the field," Otto instructed his son. "I'll send it to Berlin once you give it to me."

Two weeks later, two German officials arrived unannounced and asked to speak to the plant superintendent. They were directed to the upstairs office. Without knocking, the two men opened the door and walked in. Otto was deep in thought, trying to resolve a new supply issue. He turned, wondering who the men were. A moment later, Otto's face lit up with a broad smile.

The shorter of the two was Oswald Lutz, the German soldier who had put the tourniquet on Otto's leg that long-ago day in the muddy trench during World War I. Lutz smiled in return and they hugged.

"I stayed in the service after the war," Lutz told his old friend. "My responsibilities grew and eventually I became responsible for motorization of our troops all in the shadows behind the Treaty, beginning in the late 1920s. Now I have become the general responsible for the Wehrmacht's Panzer troops."

Lutz introduced his companion, Fritz Todt. "Fritz is an engineer; he was appointed by Der Führer as Inspector General for developing and improving our roadways starting in 1932. He has been able to stay apart from most of the politics and internal power struggles of our Führer's inner circle, but he reports directly to Hitler. His position as a technical expert has enabled him to oversee many types of projects. When your note arrived, we were in a meeting. I asked Fritz to look at the new tread design and his immediate reaction was positive. He had a few questions and wanted to meet the person who drew the sketches and laid out the benefits. Is Karl von Richter any relation to you?"

Otto nodded, then called to his secretary. "Monika, find my son and bring him here right away."

While they waited, Otto and Lutz reminisced about their time in the trenches and about the tourniquet. Then he began the story with the singing on Christmas Eve.

Lutz chuckled, and then his face grew serious. He turned to Todt. "Otto was the one who started all the soldiers in our unit singing carols that night… and of course he was the loudest of all the German soldiers."

Otto replied, "I couldn't believe it when Oswald bravely climbed out of the trench, put his gun down and walked toward the enemy line while singing *Silent Night*. Then the English soldiers started to climb out of their trenches as well, singing the same song. It was an unforgettable sight."

Otto and Lutz laughed heartily together, sharing the memorable scene, then abruptly stopped their laughter as they recalled the cold, wet trenches, the hand-to-hand fighting and the killing with bayonets. Both took deep breaths and lowered their heads.

"If only it all ended that night. But we were all reprimanded and we began the fighting again the next morning." Lutz said softly, looking sad. "Too many of our friends perished." It was a poignant moment for both men.

Just then, Karl came flying through the door. "What's up, Father? I'm terribly busy!" he exclaimed, not realizing guests were in the office. Upon seeing the two men, he quickly added, "Oh, excuse me, gentlemen. I'm sorry for my outburst."

"That's alright," said Lutz.

"Son, slow down a moment."

After introductions were made, Todt asked Karl how he had come up with his idea about the tread design.

"The goal is to be more efficient and economical in the milling and machining areas, as well as on the assembly lines. The pouring of molten steel into the molds for the current treads leaves too much after-work. My new design results in a lighter tread, and the new shape of the ribbing on the flat side makes each one stronger and enables it to shed mud, snow and ice more readily. The new shape would make them easier to install and, in case of damage to a set of treads in the field, easier to replace, enabling a vehicle to continue its mission quickly."

Lutz and Todt nodded in approval. Karl turned to look at his father. Otto was all smiles as the buttons practically popped off his shirt.

Todt asked a few more questions and Karl responded easily.

Lutz turned to Otto. "My old friend, here is the situation. In two weeks' time, Adolf will change the draft's guidelines. Young men who are first- and second-level engineers working in factories will no longer be exempt. Your son will need to enlist purposely or get drafted. Adolf is also insisting we get more local German women into the factories as we move young men into the battlefield. To supplement the workforce, we plan to use slave labor in factories from among the Jews and Slavs we've gathered up. Yes, Otto, we'll be doing more of that, too, the gathering of the Jews, in the coming months and years. The Jews and communists have caused a lot of issues for our country in the last decade.

"We have a plan to take over Austria, and we also will move to occupy Czechoslovakia. War will begin with fronts in Belgium, France and Poland. Now, Otto, this must not be repeated beyond this office, but the Fuhrer's master plan even suggests a false alliance with Russia, followed by a massive attack against them. We will have the Russians on their heels!"

Karl watched the officer intently. Lutz's eyes were bright with excitement as he spoke of the lofty goals of the Fatherland.

"So, Otto, I propose a deal for you. If you implement this new tread design here in Ravensburg, continue to handle all the orders coming in, double your tank-tread production and commit to a final-assembly rate of ten Panzer III tanks a day, I will personally see that young Karl is taken care of, such that he will never be on the front line of fire. Fritz will take Karl under his wing and he'll have a productive service during the war. His reputation will precede him for his contribution to the German war machine's success. We need young men with good ideas and good work ethics to be in key positions to lead our country to victory."

Wow! Karl thought.

Then Todt turned to Karl. "You will become my right-hand man in a few months, and when you do, I'll expect much from you. But first, you will have to go through some training. Wrap things up here with your father and you'll hear from me within a week."

Moments after Lutz and Todt said their farewells and left the office, Karl turned to his father.

"I must go back to Italy to see Katrina, the woman who was my nurse. If she is still single, I will propose marriage. She's been on my mind since I left the hospital. I'll need some time off. Perhaps no longer than a weekend."

Otto nodded. "You can leave in two days. Make sure your files and records are updated. Hand your work schedule and list of tasks to Ulli Kempf. He's your best assistant and I trust him."

CHAPTER NINE

Karl Looks for Katrina

K arl was quick to put everything in order and a day later he headed to the hospital in Vipiteno, Italy, in search of Katrina. He had his fingers crossed, hoping she hadn't found another man yet. He wished it were a skiing trip, but he wasn't sure he'd ever ski again on his weakened ankle.

When he arrived at the hospital, he was told at the front desk that nurse Katrina Amorino had left her employment two weeks earlier. Her new nursing position was at the hospital in Chiavenna, further south and closer to Lecco, making it easier for her to visit her parents more often.

Karl immediately decided to head to Chiavenna. He realized he would be gone longer than he'd told his father, but this was important. Katrina had been on his mind since his skiing accident. She was the girl of his dreams: a slim, athletic skier with fair skin, dark hair and those bright, sparkling blue eyes! He hoped that, although he'd only sent one brief letter after he left the hospital, she was still available.

As he drove down from St. Moritz to the north side of Chiavenna, Karl found himself near the hospital. As he crossed the street, he recalled Katrina's warm care, and especially how her beautiful hair smelled so good as it crossed his face when she would fix his pillows. He wondered whether she had done that on purpose. He entered the hospital lobby and asked for Nurse Amorino. He was told she was at lunch and would return in 10 minutes. He took a seat in the lobby and waited. After 15 minutes, he walked back to the front desk and asked again when Nurse Amorino would return.

The old woman at the information desk looked at him, then said firmly, "Young man, she walked right past you five minutes ago."

Karl felt his cheeks flush. "Sorry, I'm tired and must have had my eyes closed!"

She looked at him, disbelieving his comment.

"Please, would you call Nurse Amorino and ask her to come to the front lobby."

The old lady again looked up at Karl and, waving one hand, said, "What's the matter with you? Open your eyes. Nurse Amorino is standing right over there with the other nurses."

Karl looked up, and there across the lobby, several nurses stood speaking to each other. A charity event was being held in the hospital lobby the next night, and the nurses were planning how to decorate and where the band would be situated. This time, Karl saw Katrina. She was even more beautiful than he remembered.

He turned and walked toward the group of nurses. A moment later, the approach of the tall, handsome German caused the conversation among the nurses to stop.

Katrina looked up. "Is it your ankle again? I'll be right with you. Just wait over there."

Karl went back to the chair and sat down again. The nurses whispered; one giggled at her abrupt comment; another asked who he was.

Meanwhile, as Karl sat, the little old front-desk lady called to him, "Hey, sonny, now I know what's wrong with you!"

The nurses' meeting broke up three minutes later and they headed back to their stations.

Katrina approached Karl… slowly. He stood up and reached for her hand to kiss it.

But she pulled it back. She said in a flat tone, "Well. It's been another year. You wrote once. What brings you here now?"

"I have a lot of explaining to do. Instead of doing it all here in the lobby, can we have dinner together?"

"I'll finish in four hours. We can meet at my favorite restaurant, Crotto Giovanantoni. It's old and quaint and only a few blocks from here."

He went back to the car and drove to the restaurant on Via San Giovanni. It was just a minute from the hospital. He parked in front and practiced for a few minutes what he would say to Katrina, and soon fell asleep.

She arrived on time and noticed him sitting in his car. She smiled, thinking of when he was asleep in the hospital bed. She knocked on the window of the car.

Startled, he sat up, got out of the car and gave her a polite hug.

As the sun set, a shadow from the nearby mountain cast itself across the restaurant. They stepped through the dark entryway, but the atmosphere inside was perfect, as each table was lighted with a colorful candle dripping on an old Chianti bottle. Katrina ordered a glass of the house red wine and he ordered white. Karl began with apologies; she accepted. They exchanged small talk over a shared antipasto and then dinner.

He said he lost her address yet again, right after he wrote to her the first time.

She gave a look of disapproval. "Karl, I wrote back to you three times after you sent your letter, and each of my letters had my return address. You could have written or come back to find me sooner. Where have you been for the past year and what's been going on?"

He explained about the increased workload at the Ravensburg factory. "I'm at the factory much of the time, and we sometimes stay overnight there. If I don't go home to Langenargen for a few days, my mail is kept at post office box, waiting for me to pick it up. If too much accumulates, my friend at the post office forwards it to my parents' home in Friedrichshafen where I grew up, but I haven't visited their house for months."

"Wouldn't your mother have seen the letters? Don't you work with your father? Wouldn't he bring your mail to work?"

"Yes, but due to the workload at the factory my father doesn't go home much, either. Lately it's like we both live in the factory."

But Karl knew where her letters were: right on the corner of his desk. He had opened one. And then, well, work was his priority, and there was no need to pay attention. That is, until Lutz and Todt visited this past week, bringing a sudden sense of urgency to reconnect. Katrina was strong willed and maintained the upper hand in the conversation the entire night. All Karl could do was backpedal and be apologetic, and he did.

Katrina liked Karl while he had been her patient. She seriously thought there might be something between them as he left the hospital. But now, she wasn't sure. The thoughts of entering a convent were on her mind again.

"Katrina, are you dating anyone else?"

"I saw someone a few times. It never became serious, and he left for the Italian Army six months ago."

Karl was relieved, then broke the news. "A general call of men into the military will happen soon in Germany. I know I will be drafted. The good news is I'll go into a special unit because of my father's connection with his friend and Fritz Todt, who runs a construction company called Organization Todt. I'll have to do some initial training, then I'll be inspecting factories initially and then construction project management. And although I haven't written, you have been on my mind every day. I must admit even though we've been apart, I've fallen in love with you. It happened while you were my nurse. You are so beautiful and caring, Katrina. I remain impressed with your skiing skills and athleticism when we first met two years ago." He reached for her hand. "I've wanted a beautiful woman like you for my wife, and I'd love to raise a family with you – a family of skiers."

Taken by his words, she smiled. *Could it be he is the one? He is very tall, and so handsome! I am so attracted to him. I wonder if he's a good lover.*

Katrina felt a sudden rush and found herself aroused.

They continued to talk non-stop through dinner, she about her duties at the hospital and he about his newly approved tank-tread design. Dessert was simple, a sweet sparkling wine, *Muscato D'Asti*. Katrina thought, again, of being with him in bed.

"It's late, Karl. Where are you staying tonight?"

"Frankly, I was hoping to stay with you. Perhaps on a couch. Otherwise, I'll sleep in the backseat of my car. It's not safe driving back through the mountains tonight."

She smiled. "Come with me."

35

Smiling back, Karl stood, took the last swallow of his wine, and put down enough money to cover the meal and a generous tip.

As they left the restaurant, she took Karl by the hand and led him outside. They had walked scarcely 100 feet along San Giovanni when she opened a door to a stairway leading up to her small apartment.

Her apartment was comfortable and warm. They wasted little time on small talk. Katrina led him to the bedroom. They quickly shed their clothing, then Katrina and Karl boldly allowed their passions to run loose.

Satisfied well beyond expectation, as she fell asleep, she thought, *Maybe I've been wrong about the convent. Maybe this big German is the one meant for me.*

Karl was equally pleased with the evening. Katrina was far more than he ever experienced.

The next morning, Katrina woke first and looked at Karl still asleep. She pulled back the curtains, letting the sunlight in. The sun's rays shone against the tiny specks of dust in the air. She stretched, and then looked back at his naked body lying in her bed. Last night was so good. She slipped on her thin nightgown and sat next to him. *Maybe he's the right one after all these years of worrying and wondering. I feel so good.* She kissed him awake, eager to make love with him again. He accepted.

Thirty minutes later, they were eating breakfast in the same restaurant where they had enjoyed dinner last night.

"Karl, I would like to spend more time with you. I need to get to know you."

"Okay! Then let's get married! Let's do it here today with your nurse friends as witnesses!"

Disappointed by his flippant response, she frowned. Katrina had expected a thoughtful reply discussing how they'd spend time together to build a deeper and more complete relationship.

He didn't know what to say. The conversation stopped. Silence. She knew he wanted to be married and have her as his wife. Karl, still immature in some ways, was ignorant to a woman's view of how relationships developed.

Katrina knew she would need more time, but it wasn't enough to keep her from saying "No" to starting a relationship. *What a good lover he is, and the journey of getting to know each other could be good. I'll let him think of another alternative.*

"I have a few months before I'm drafted into the Army," he said, knowing well it was a lie. "Please come and live with me in my home. It's in a tiny hamlet called Langenargen, on a beautiful lake, south of the village where my parents live. Stay and get to know me. You can get a job as a nurse in Friedrichshafen, not far from my place. We will have time together when you arrive, and after my initial training, I'll be back for a few months and it should give us enough time to get to know each other. If things continue well between us – and I expect they will – we can get engaged and married. It can be a nice family affair – your parents can come from Lecco and stay with my parents on the lake. They all can go sailing, too. Maybe your father the baker would like that?"

Karl then finished his appeal to have her come live at his home with his best suggestion. "My parents have close ties to the administrator of the local hospital. My mother and his wife are close friends. You'll have a job in days after you arrive."

She smiled, then nodded. "I like your idea. We have lots of time to get to know each other."

As he continued to speak, he felt Katrina run her foot up his leg beneath the table. Within a minute, the two stood up from their half-finished breakfasts, left the restaurant and returned to her apartment. Although she was scheduled to work that morning, she knew it could be some weeks before she saw Karl again. Katrina's goal was to ensure he remembered her.

They enjoyed the rest of the morning playfully exhausting each other. It was past noon before they woke up.

"It could take twenty to thirty days before I would arrive at your house," she told him as she dressed in her nurse's uniform.

"I look forward to your arrival. If I'm already away in training when you arrive, go to my parents' house. My mother, Valentina, is Italian, like you. She'll help you get settled, including getting you an interview at the hospital. You two will get along well. She was also an exceptionally good skier years ago, before my father's injury."

Karl knew Katrina and his mother would take to each other quickly. He put his shirt back on and said, "My initial training should be quick. I like my idea of having our wedding in my parents' lake house."

Katrina rolled her eyes, but turned toward him and smiled, feeling emotionally lifted. "Karl, it's been a wonderful night and a morning I'll never forget. I'll consider your marriage proposal once we've spent a few months together. I don't think you'll have anything to worry about." She gave him a hug and a memorable deep kiss as he left to return to the factory in Ravensburg.

She went to the window and, brushing the curtain aside, watched him drive away. *Maybe I won't be an old maid, after all. I need to let my parents know right away. I'll visit them in Lecco this weekend to explain. I'm sure they'll be as happy as I am.*

Katrina arrived at the hospital around the corner minutes later. As she entered, her fellow nurses looked up and gave her the silent stare as she walked toward them. She innocently smiled.

"So, Katrina, where have you been all morning? It's past noon and we're almost finished decorating and planning for tonight's event."

Another spouted, "I sure hope you were with that guy since last night. He's gorgeous! I saw you two going into the restaurant last night."

Katrina laughed. "Fat chance! We had a drink and then he left. I ate dinner by myself. But I think I had something bad and was sick all morning. How are we progressing for the event? Did the caterer confirm the time they'd be here this evening?"

"Katrina, Layla and Isabella saw you walking together last night. They said you were holding his hand as if you were pulling him along."

Stella continued, "I stopped to pick up pastries and bread at the restaurant before work this morning. You were in a back corner, having breakfast. You seemed fascinated with each other, and I saw you lean across the table to kiss him. And that, my dear friend, was over four hours ago!"

The other nurses giggled.

Caught in her lie, Katrina blushed. "Well, he was really good, and I just needed some more of him this morning before he headed home."

They giggled again, then told Katrina in her absence from this morning's decorating meeting, she'd been selected as the main speaker to welcome all the guests at tonight's charity event.

***

As Karl drove through the Alps, he smiled. He'd just made the best decision of his life and captured a terrific woman to be his wife. And although she was a northern Italian – and one of those Catholics – so was his mother, and that was good enough for him. As he drove along, he noticed several ski runs without snow. *It's been over a year... I hope my darn ankle will someday heal completely, so I can chase Katrina down the slopes again... maybe like my parents did when they first met.*

CHAPTER TEN

Karl's Draft Letter

Upon arriving at the factory, Karl jumped back into his work, not even telling his father he had returned. He found his assistant manager, Ulli Kempf, checking on the load of iron ore that arrived by railcar overnight. Karl asked Ulli if he had reported its arrival to Otto. He had not, so Karl took the clipboard and went to his father's office.

Surprised to see Karl, Otto welcomed him back and asked how things went.

Karl gave him a big smile. "Father, I've found a beautiful woman who reminds me very much of Mother. I plan to make her my wife. I'm sure you will like her."

"Wonderful! Before you go, a letter for you came in early this morning from Fritz Todt. I opened it since you were away. He wants you to go through SS officer training right away, and then afterward you can work with him. Todt's note says you'll receive a letter from Himmler – a draft notice – in a few days. The draft notice will say you need to report to the Waffen-SS Officer Training, Junkerschule at Bad Tölz right away. Go find Ulli and start giving him the rest of your responsibilities, beginning today. Work with him one on one the rest of this week and next."

Otto handed him the open letter. "I'll try to be home for dinner with you and your mother on Sunday afternoon."

At the chilling news, Karl swallowed hard. His brow furrowed as he read. "Damn it! Father, I expected to have at least another two weeks before I left – maybe even three."

"Son, I also got a note this morning. From Lutz. He said he might be back again in two days to talk with us. Your idea about the tank tread design has made quite a stir when it was reviewed at other manufacturing plants. Lutz said he likes how we have things set up here in the factory in the machining and milling area. Apparently, we're producing at a higher rate than other factories our size. He'll bring someone who wants to take a closer look at how we have the factory and assembly line laid out."

The next morning Oswald Lutz returned to the factory, a day earlier than expected, this time with Heinz Wilhelm Guderian, the principal advocate of aggressive tank warfare. Lutz toured Guderian around the facility, spending the better part of two hours examining its layout, watching molten pours in the foundry, milling and machining in the shops, and observing the heavy lifting in the assembly area.

As they walked the production floor end to end, Guderian told Lutz, "This isn't the largest factory, but for its size it appears to be the most efficient I've seen producing Panzer tanks and track-based armored vehicles."

Lutz nodded in approval as Guderian continued.

"If we can be this efficient in other factories, we can increase tank production fifty to seventy-five percent. We need a huge surge in production capacities to meet the war plans laid out by Der Führer and to implement my strategy of overwhelming our enemies with tanks," Guderian said. "We'll need to produce tens of thousands of tanks. We need good factories. This factory is managed well, and we need to replicate elsewhere how it's organized and run."

Lieutenant Colonel Guderian had become chief of staff to the Inspectorate of Motorized Troops under Lutz in 1931. The role positioned him in the center of Germany's development of its mobile warfare and armored vehicle forces. In the early 1930s, he advocated having a distinct Panzer tank division capable of rapid deployment. His *Blitzkrieg* strategy depended on using tanks and other swift-moving mechanized vehicles to create an overwhelming approach to ground war, by overrunning the enemy's position quickly and decisively. Guderian initially needed to convince Lutz; when he did, the two tirelessly pushed the idea with Hitler for a strong Panzer tank force. Guderian advocated Blitzkrieg among German field generals and commanders, while Lutz handled the politics within Hitler's inner circle.

Lutz eventually convinced the Führer, and Blitzkrieg became accepted as the blueprint for Germany's mechanized offensive strategy by the Wehrmacht field generals.

In the meeting that morning, Lutz told Otto, "Listen closely my friend. My longtime associate, Heinz, likes what young Karl has proposed on the improved tank tread. It's been accepted as our new tread standard, and Heinz wants him on his staff. Second, he wants Karl to identify any other changes on the tanks or armored vehicles he thinks need to be made. Third, Heinz wants Karl to visit every other German factory where our Panzer tanks and armored vehicles are being made, to be sure we're as efficient elsewhere as you are here. He believes your son can help him achieve that goal. Congratulations. The Führer will know the von Richter family name and your son Karl's name, and what you've done to advance our war efforts. You and your factory workers should be proud of your exemplary contribution as we prepare for the coming ground war to restore our country to its rightful position in Europe and the world."

Lutz's words brought the suddenly quiet Otto to tears. His lifelong work and his leadership in the factory had culminated in his being recognized in this rewarding moment.

Guderian nodded to Otto, who in turn nodded to Lutz.

"Thank you, my friend, for acknowledging my son and me, and thank you, yet again, for the tourniquet in the trench long ago."

Otto's comment made Guderian and Lutz smile.

Lutz said, "Otto, we have had a destiny to be together in war. Let us now continue to fulfill Der Führer's dream to make Germany great again."

After the two left the office, Otto sent Monika to find Karl, who arrived a few minutes later.

"Father, what now? I was with Ulli, giving him the schedule of raw material deliveries scheduled to the foundry in the next six weeks."

"Son, sit down for a moment. Your modified tank-tread design has been approved across all German factories making treads. Heinz Guderian wants you to assist with seeing that those changes are implemented immediately. He wants you in the field doing factory inspections.

You'll work for him, not for Todt. Guderian has said many production improvements are required at other factories and he wants you to lead the effort."

"How soon, Father? Do you know?"

"According to Lutz, Guderian wants you in Munich in ten days. You have one week before you have to leave."

"It's fantastic that my design will be integrated into all the tread factories across Germany!"

Just then, Monika came into the office with the morning's mail. "Karl, I'm glad you're still here. This envelope just arrived for you; it's marked 'Special Delivery.' "

He opened it and his stomach sank. The draft notice promised by Fritz Todt had arrived.

April 22, 1937

Good Day, Herr Karl von Richter:

Greetings from Reichsführer SS Heinrich Himmler, Waffen SS Commanding Chief

1. *You will report immediately to the Waffen-SS Officers' Junkerschule in the town of Bad Tölz.*
2. *You will bring only yourself, no other clothing, no valuables, no photos of family, friends or girlfriends.*
3. *You will be evaluated for strength, endurance, speed, intelligence, math and reading comprehension for your future role in the SS or the German Army upon completion of your training.*
4. *You will train for no less than six months.*
5. *Upon completion of training, senior officers will decide your role in the Waffen SS, Army or Navy.*

Failure to report within eight days from the post mark of this letter will cause your name to be brought to the attention of the local SS authorities.

Best wishes for a successful career.
Heil Hitler,
Heinrich Himmler/Frau Dausch/mfhs-68

Karl read the letter and his heart jumped with excitement; another moment passed, and his stomach sank.

"Father, what am I to do? During Lutz's first visit, Todt implied he wanted me to work with him. This morning Lutz told you Guderian wants me to work for him. And now this. Who am I to listen to? And what about Katrina?"

"It looks like Todt quickly submitted your name to the SS Officer training school. I suggest you get yourself trained in the SS school first. It will be a good move. You won't find yourself on the front lines or in trenches like I was in the last war. My guess is Lutz would prefer you work with Guderian to inspect and improve the efficiency of factories after your SS officer training."

"What about Katrina? She'll be coming here to live. I knew I would be going to training, but the letter says, 'training for six months.' I expected to be back a few weeks after basic training and get married to her. Now she will be at my house alone."

"Son, don't worry about Katrina. At your age, women come and go. You may think you like her... or even believe you love her, but you really don't know her yet. You might find another woman next month or in six months. Right now you need to focus on your own future and the position you can attain in the Army. If you can get into the SS as an officer, you'll be much better off. Karl, help Germany win the upcoming war. If this girl is as smart as you say she is, she'll be patient and wait for you."

Surprised by his father's comments, Karl's thoughts drifted to his last morning in bed with Katrina.

Just then, Monika walked back into the office without knocking. "Otto, your wife is here."

"Valentina? Here?" He shook his head, annoyed. "Now what does she want?"

"She said yesterday was a special day... and you missed it by not going home last night."

As Monika finished speaking, Valentina entered Otto's second-floor office with its glass walls that overlooked the factory floor. She looked at her husband in silence for a moment.

He looked at her, having no clue why she was there.

"Otto, dear, I thought it would be nice to celebrate my birthday today, especially since you forgot about it yesterday, and never bothered to come home last night. So, I decided to bring you your favorite apple strudel. It's a day old. I couldn't be sure if you'd be home tonight. And with that blank look on your face when I walked in, I'm sure I wouldn't have seen you tonight, either."

While Otto felt bad for forgetting her birthday, Karl couldn't care less about his father's oversight as he stood with his draft notice still in his hand. *My best choice is to commit to the SS Officers training school. Unfortunately for Katrina, it'll finish well after her arrival in Langenargen.* His mind drifted further. *I'm sure she'll get along fine without me, being bilingual. She can spend time with Mother; maybe they'll speak Italian. Mother will get Katrina a job at the hospital, and she can work extra hours without worrying about my waiting at home for a meal. It'll also give Mother a chance to teach her to cook my favorite dishes.*

"Karl. Karl, dear. Are you with us? Or are you elsewhere? Please, have a piece of your father's favorite apple strudel… even if it is a day old."

"Yes, Mother. Happy birthday."

Karl's mind raced. He realized setting a marriage date would be impossible. He'd envisioned a quick marriage after her arrival, knowing it would make his relationship with her more acceptable to their families, friends and neighbors. But marriage wouldn't happen soon.

Acknowledging the timeline of his coming weeks and months, Katrina's image became a distant foggy thought… and then was gone. In fact, with his emphasis on SS school, if Karl were asked about Katrina, his first response might have been, "Who?" It wasn't the first time Karl had moved aside his relationship with her, as his priorities emerged and waned quickly. But sadly, and unknown to Katrina, she now sat in the distant last row of his brain as she made plans to join him.

He stood and handed his empty plate to Monika. Then, looking at his parents in silence, he left the office. Now he was setting his parents aside like Katrina.

Karl returned to his office, and sent word to have Ulli come see him. He assessed his long list of responsibilities. He knew Ulli wasn't ready to take on the full brunt of the factory's scheduling challenges. As he waited, his mind drifted and then focused on preparing to enter SS Officer school.

Ulli arrived, and an hour later, Karl's concerns for production in the factory moved to the rear of his brain… near where he'd compartmentalized Katrina. He was concerned only about himself and about the challenges the weeks and months ahead would bring.

Later that same afternoon, Otto sent a telegram to Oswald Lutz on behalf of his son, to resolve the conflict of his being steered in one direction by Fritz Todt, another path by Guderian, and now being drafted into the SS Officer training school.

The next morning Lutz telegrammed back. *Once your son has completed the SS Officer training and is selected as an officer, he can join my team directly under Guderian.*

Reading Lutz's response, Otto reaffirmed his promise to increase production at the factory.

As Karl transitioned his work and prepared for the SS school, he gave neither thought nor concern for Katrina. He never let her know the draft letter demanded his immediate departure, or that he'd be in training for six months. He simply wasn't concerned about Katrina, nor her arrival. Over the next few days, Karl heard more about the SS organization from several suppliers visiting the factory, and he daydreamed about starting the training.

Work at the factory intensified after Lutz's first visit. Approval for updated tank treads increased demand – but first, new molds needed to be created. Otto focused on meeting his commitment to Lutz, giving no thought to a young single woman invited by his son to his home in Langenargen.

Meanwhile, in the lakeside home, the thought of a young woman and a future daughter-in-law thrilled Valentina, who began preparations to welcome Katrina into the von Richter family.

CHAPTER ELEVEN

Katrina's Move

Six hours south of the Ravensburg factory, Katrina Amorino's day at the hospital in the small town of Chiavenna, Italy, had just ended. She put away her patients' charts, changed out of her uniform and left the hospital. She stopped at a small grocery store for bread, milk, onions, peppers and eggs, then headed to her tiny apartment.

Inside, she changed into something soft and more comfortable, started the kettle and sat to say a brief prayer remembering deceased family members. Then she added another prayer, for guidance in her upcoming move. Just then the kettle whistled. She poured the piping-hot water over the loose black tea and let it sit for a few minutes before adding a splash of milk and grabbing a crunchy almond biscotti as a prelude to her dinner of fried peppers and eggs tossed over reheated linguini, fried in the same pan.

The draft of a letter she'd started yesterday sat in front of her on the small kitchen table. It announced her resignation from her nursing position, and asked for a reference from her supervisor. To gain favor, she offered a 14-day notice, allowing the hospital to find a replacement. *It's fair to do this. They've treated me so kindly. But I can't wait to be with Karl again! He made me feel warm and wanted. And he truly was magnificent!*

The following day, Katrina headed to the hospital for her regular shift with some anxiety. After signing in at the desk on her floor, she began going through the daily transition to take over the patients in her wing when she spotted her supervisor at the end of the hall. Katrina's stomach flipped in an anxious moment as she waved, then called to the other woman. "May I please see you when you have a moment?"

Her supervisor approached. "What is it Katrina? I have a few minutes; let's walk over to my desk."

Katrina thought it'd be later in the shift when she broke the news. "I have something to tell you." With tears in her eyes, she announced softly, "I'm leaving the hospital to move to Germany. Here is my notice. My letter explains the details."

Her eyes filled more and, as her supervisor read the letter, she cried too. "Oh dear. Of course, we'll do everything we can to accommodate your transition, Katrina. There's always a home here if you decide to return. Thank you for the lead time. But no one could ever replace your wonderful sweet heart. We'll give you a glowing recommendation for your next opportunity. You're everything a good person is, and what a good nurse needs to be. God bless you and thank you for your service here."

Knowing she was loved by her supervisor and the other nurses, Katrina, still crying, felt a strong rush of emotion. *I'm so sad to leave, but it won't be long before I'm with Karl, and that will be wonderful.*

Less than a week after Katrina gave her notice, a new nurse was hired. Katrina graciously guided her replacement through the tasks of the hospital wing and shared her daily activities. Meanwhile she continued to pack, looking forward for her move to Germany.

The night before Katrina was to leave the hospital, her friends surprised her with an evening out.

Living in the Italian Alps shielded most people from the heavy politics of the day. Naïve in some ways, Katrina simply didn't know about anything happening in Germany. Sadly, she didn't fully grasp how her decision to leave Chiavenna, for a German man whom she hardly knew, had set her on a regrettable path that would echo across the rest of her life.

***

Before departing, Katrina made a surprise trip to her parents' home in Lecco, to share her news. When she announced she was moving, Dino and Lucia were stunned and virtually speechless. They couldn't believe their only child was going to live with a man she hardly knew – in Germany.

Katrina glowed with naïve excitement, but her parents were more aware of what was happening in the world.

Her father's short temper flared as he tried to explain it to her. "First, getting involved with a German is undoubtedly a mistake in your judgment. Next, working in an industrial German city will inevitably put you in harm's way. And, worst of all, a young German man's life will be at great risk when the next war begins – and it soon will."

"What war, Father? There's no war going on."

"Katrina, of course you don't see what's happening. You've been up in Chiavenna, inside the hospital all day, treating patients. But we hear what's going on. There's been economic unrest in Germany ever since they lost the war. And since that crazy fellow, Hitler, took over as chancellor, right-wing politics are thick and explosive. There are many changes people don't see. I hear from travelers coming through the Alps from Germany, and even a few from Austria, there may soon be another war. People say Germany is re-arming itself and already breaking many of the terms of the Treaty of Versailles."

Lucia shushed Dino, and he quieted down. Her parents loved her immensely and her mother understood Katrina's newfound love. She spoke calmly. "Dino, maybe there won't be a war. Katrina dear, your father is expressing imagined concerns, and we fully support your decision."

The heated conversation suddenly cooled, Dino turned and walked away, mumbling to himself. "Just wait, you'll see what I mean."

Katrina stayed two days and went to church with her parents on Sunday morning. It was uncommon for Dino and Lucia to attend Mass because of their work at the bakery, but they wanted to wish her well and be with her in church before she left them.

After Mass, they headed home for one of her favorites – fusilli and meatballs, with freshly grated pecorino cheese and her father's slightly overdone crusty bread. After their afternoon meal, she hugged and kissed them and returned to her apartment to check her mail and pick up a few last things.

Before Katrina began her long drive to Karl's house, she recalled how he had given her a note with addresses: his house in Langenargen, and his parents' home in Friedrichshafen, which she recognized as his old mailing address. She checked to see the note was there in her wallet, then began the six-hour drive through the mountains.

She was on her way at last!

Her trip to Langenargen took two hours longer than expected. She needed to drive slowly in some areas, with icy and snow-covered roads, and she stopped several times, including once to switch out a flat tire. Fortunately, a truck driver came by within moments and made the change for her. Despite the delays, her plan to be at Karl's place before he arrived home worked. She reached the hamlet and made the last turn onto FriedhofStrabe.

She drove past the church and cemetery where the grave markers cast long shadows in the late-afternoon sun. She slowed. In another hundred feet she pulled up to the cute house, and she could smell the nearby lake water. She stepped from the car, stretched and walked to the water's edge. *How beautiful the Bodensee! And look! The Alps are even more beautiful!*

On the note with his Langenargen address, Karl had written, "My sailboat is stored in a nearby boat yard on Obere SeeStrabe." She looked at the Bodensee again. *Maybe we can take Karl's boat out tomorrow if he comes home early.*

Upon entering the house, Katrina found it mostly bare, fitting the profile of a bachelor. After a few minutes' inspection, she went outside and brought in the rest of her belongings, as well as some of Dino's dried sausage and two-day-old pastries. As Katrina prepared *pasta e' fagioli* for dinner, she looked around. *I can brighten things up a bit in here with some warm-color fabrics as curtains and I can sew some couch covers.* She couldn't find a welcome note, which upset and saddened her.

She lit a fire in the fireplace, expecting Karl to arrive around 6. By 7, the meal on the tiny stove was cold. Disappointed he hadn't yet returned home, she put the food in the little refrigerator and continued to wait for his arrival. At 8, tired from her eight-hour drive, she stepped outside. It was crisp and cool. She walked down to the water's edge again, and as her eyes adjusted, the broad vista and star-filled night over the lake amazed her. Living in the mountains, she'd never seen such an open view of the night sky. She took a deep breath and let it out slowly. Smoke from nearby fireplaces filled the air.

She went back inside and added a log to the fire, hoping Karl would arrive soon. She retrieved her favorite blanket, the one her mother had crocheted for her, and reflected on the evening she and Karl had spent together, and how much she enjoyed her time with him in bed that night and the next morning. Within a few minutes, she fell asleep. She dreamed of Karl and her skiing together with a little boy, their son, on a snowy hillside alongside them.

The next morning, a ray of sunlight came through a window and landed across her face as she lay on the couch. As she woke, a moment passed as she wondered where she was. Then it all came back to her, and she wondered where Karl was. After a cup of tea and a piece of toast from a loaf of her father's bread, she washed, brushed her long hair and changed. She planned to visit Valentina this morning and wanted to look her best, but couldn't find an iron or ironing board anywhere in the house. She pulled out her own tiny Hotpoint electric iron and used it on the wooden kitchen table. She started a list of things the house needed. It made her feel good to help bring some needed order from a woman's perspective into Karl's life.

About 11 a.m. Katrina drove to her future in-laws' home, on the edge of Lake Constance.

While cleaning the floors, Valentina heard a knock at the front door. She quickly went to open it. "Yes, may I help you?" Only a second passed before Valentina realized this young, attractive blue-eyed woman must be Katrina.

"Good morning, Mrs. von Richter. I'm Katrina Amorino. I've come to stay with Karl. I'm sure he's told you about me and our intention to marry. He gave me your address and suggested I visit you."

"Welcome, dear. It's so nice to meet you. Please come in. Excuse the mess. I'm cleaning and had no idea you would be coming to visit today. I'm so embarrassed! Would you like a cup of tea? Let me put these things away and freshen up. I'll put the water on and be back in two minutes."

"Yes, of course."

Valentina put the bucket and mop outside the back door and went into the bedroom while Katrina took the few minutes alone to look around. The kitchen area opened to the living room where several indoor plants, sitting on wide windowsills, held back cute, colorful curtains. The massive stone fireplace boasted a beautiful carved mantel. Over it hung a map, which didn't look like any country Katrina knew of. A thick book, perhaps the family Bible, sat on the shelf next to the fireplace. An old mandolin with a broken string leaned against the wall in the corner. The colorful home, with its shelves filled with knickknacks, seemed so cozy. She realized Karl's place needed a womanly touch.

As Valentina returned, Katrina took the liberty of shutting off the whistling tea kettle. Valentina poured the water into two small, colorful china cups. Quiet at first, neither woman knew what to say next. They again exchanged smiles and relaxed.

"I arrived in town late yesterday and drove to Karl's house. He has a lovely home but it's nothing like this! Your home is magnificent."

"Thank you, dear. Otto's family has owned this home for over two hundred years. He's made a few changes to modernize it. I'm so happy our bathroom is inside now and we have a lovely tub and shower. Isn't indoor plumbing wonderful!"

"Soon after I arrived, I prepared dinner, but Karl didn't come home last night. I assumed he was working late with his father? He had told me during his last visit he's been working long hours at the foundry. I'm sure he's alright. Did your husband come home last night?"

"Oh dear. Didn't Karl tell you?"

"Tell me what?"

"Karl received a draft notice to join the Army. His father and I are so proud he was selected to go to officer training school. He left three weeks ago."

There was an awkward pause, and Valentina's eyes looked away.

"I'm sure he intended to let you know, but maybe in the confusion, he was overwhelmed and didn't send word... or maybe he did and it was delayed in getting to you."

Katrina's heart sank. "Oh, no! How terrible that we missed each other! I gave notice at the hospital and then went to tell my parents in

Lecco about Karl and that I'd be coming here. Maybe his letter arrived at my apartment while I was away. I forgot to check the mail before leaving yesterday."

Katrina lied, saving her future mother-in-law the embarrassment of a careless son. She'd checked the post office one last time just before leaving Chiavenna, and there was no mail for her. Katrina recalled how Karl never sent any letters, except one, in the year after they met again in the hospital. This was a bad way to start her new life, but she quickly resolved to put her concern behind her. She had already convinced herself she was in love with Karl. Now she would simply wait for his return in a few weeks. She smiled at Valentina.

The rest of their conversation was smooth and pleasant. Katrina had brought along her letter of recommendation and offered it to Valentina to read.

Understanding Italian, she looked it over and said, "I have a close friend whose husband works at the hospital here in Friedrichshafen. I'm sure she'll arrange an interview with him for you within a week or two. He's the administrator there and makes all the decisions."

As they chatted, Valentina told Katrina about Otto's family, much of which Karl had already told her. Katrina patiently listened and even asked a few questions. Over another cup of tea, Katrina briefly shared how her parents met at a fountain in Rome.

Valentina asked Katrina to stay for lunch, and she happily agreed. Valentina shared her stories. She related her and Otto's initial meeting on the ski slopes, the snowy night and dinner at the St. Moritz lodge. She talked about Otto's war injury and his suffering, the long time to recover and his joy at finally returning to work. Valentina mentioned how Otto and Karl had similarly began their careers as teenage apprentices helping their fathers in the foundry.

When Valentina mentioned how Otto's factory had grown busy with the recent demand for more war machines, Katrina grew nervous, recalling her father's words. Germany's gearing up for a war would no doubt affect the lives of tens of millions of people beyond its borders.

She finished her lunch and her fourth cup of tea, then excused herself for the bathroom. Her head swirled with all she had heard about tanks and other types of war machines. That afternoon's conversation exposed Katrina to the details of the coming storm. Nevertheless, the two women bonded.

When Katrina returned, Valentina asked her to stay for dinner, but she gracefully declined. She wanted to be alone; she needed to think things over. After a pleasant goodbye and a warm hug from Valentina, Katrina headed back to Karl's house. Yesterday she had felt it would soon become her home. Now she needed to reassess her situation. The entire premise of her going to live with Karl and get to know him had been undermined with these new facts. *Father knew what was happening. I should have listened to his guidance. But that angry tone of his never sounds like guidance.*

The next day, Valentina drove to her son's house, arriving just before noon. Katrina, still unpacking her clothing and ironing her nurse uniforms, answered the door. "I've been to my friend's home earlier this morning, the one whose husband runs the local hospital. She rang him and he set an interview for you tomorrow morning for a nursing position. He told her, 'we always need experienced nurses.' "

Valentina assured Katrina everything would go fine, and she'd undoubtedly get the job right away. Then she apologized for keeping Katrina so long the day before. "With Otto working at the factory so many hours, and sometimes staying overnight, I've been so lonely. It's so nice, having someone to talk to, especially a future daughter-in-law."

Katrina smiled as Valentina shed a happy tear.

"Dear, please come for dinner this evening. Otto will be home tonight, and I know he'll want to meet you."

Katrina accepted. "Can I bring anything?"

Valentina waved away the offer. "It's not necessary. Just bring yourself. Why don't you come at five thirty? Otto might have to go back to the factory afterward." Valentina didn't tell Katrina she had demanded her husband come home that night to meet their son's fiancée – and Otto wasn't happy about leaving work to do so.

Otto arrived home thirty minutes later than scheduled, but Valentina had anticipated that and the veal in the frying pan was ready. After the brief introduction with few words shared, Otto turned to a list he brought home and began reading it. Karl's replacement, Ulli Kempf, had received his draft notice that morning, and Otto had scrambled all day to find Ulli's replacement.

The meal and dessert included his favorites: Weiner schnitzel and warm apple strudel.

As they ate, Otto repeated his debate with a foreman that day. "France and Great Britain's tough terms in the Treaty of Versailles have set up an almost impossible situation for our country to recover economically. That young Hitler, the head of the Nazi Party and our chancellor, will bring Germany back to its glory and rightful position in the world."

Trying to lighten the conversation, Valentina said, "Otto, did you know Katrina's parents are bakers who make pastry and breads, including the crusty rye bread with caraway seeds on our dinner table this evening. Katrina brought it with her as a gift. She thought you'd like it."

Otto shrugged. "So? Uh, yes, it's okay."

He never engaged directly with Katrina, nor did he express any concern about her efforts to find a job. Within a minute of finishing the last piece of veal on his plate, Otto pushed himself back from the table, stood and excused himself. He said he needed to pass on the strudel and get back to the factory to finish the day.

"My entire office staff is working late tonight to calculate end-of-month production and cost numbers. I need to go over everything before Monika types it up for my meeting with Lutz tomorrow morning. He's coming in again."

"Dear, aren't you going to show Katrina the family Bible and strum a few bars on your father's mandolin before you go?"

Otto frowned. "Maybe another time. Goodbye, Katrina." He left, neither acknowledging nor kissing his wife goodbye.

"I apologize for his abrupt manner," Valentina said. "Otto's not always been like this. The foundry, milling and machine factory are doing great, but new production quotas keep him working overnight, now four or five nights a week."

Nodding, Katrina said she understood the pressure he must be under. She thanked Valentina for the delicious meal, and said she needed to get a good night's sleep for her interview the next day. As she readied to leave, Valentina gave her a plate with leftover veal, dumplings and strudel.

On the drive home, Katrina reflected how she'd just seen a grown man in a crazed state. She understood the pressure Otto felt to fulfill the production responsibilities. As a nurse, she saw evidence of high blood pressure in the redness of his face and neck, especially as he became more annoyed speaking about the Treaty.

The buildup of tanks Otto spoke about sounds bad. It seems the situation in Germany will get worse. And from listening to him talk about German leadership and the production of war machinery, it makes me think this Adolf Hitler is stirring people up with his speeches. What kind of leader promotes extreme right-wing nationalism against minorities, blaming them for its problems? It seems like he's demanding Germany ready itself for war.

The next morning, within minutes of meeting her, and after reading the detailed reference letter from her prior supervisor, the interviewer decided to hire Katrina. She asked Katrina to remain in her office; after a brief consultation with the hospital administrator, the woman offered her a job.

"Miss Amorino, your skill level is well above that of the new nurses we typically hire here. The administrator has agreed to a nice starting salary with a generous increase in your hourly compensation after the first month."

Grateful, Katrina accepted the offer to begin work the following week.

CHAPTER TWELVE

Karl Returns from Officer Training

Work at the hospital was exceptionally good for Katrina; she quickly fit in socially with the rest of the nurses, and her techniques of patient care – especially how she comforted those who were struggling – was admired. As promised, she received her pay increase after thirty days.

After three months, the administrator of Bodensee Hospital came to her directly. "We are so pleased with the quality of your work, I'd like to promote you to nurse supervisor, responsible for a wing. It means a nice increase in your pay – along with increased prestige within the hospital."

Valentina heard the good news later that day from her friend, and brought supper to Katrina as she returned home from work that evening.

"I'm so grateful to have you in my life, Valentina," Katrina told her.

She couldn't yet put her finger on why, but there seemed to be something uniquely special about Valentina.

As months passed, her confidence at the hospital grew, but so did her anxiety about Karl's absence. Each day when she arrived at Karl's house, she wondered how – or even if – her relationship with him would ever develop.

Finally, just over six months after Katrina arrived in Langenargen, Karl returned home from SS Officer training school. A rainy Sunday in late October, Katrina arrived home from work. Upon coming inside, she saw logs roaring in the fireplace and dinner ready to be put on the table set for two. From behind the door, Karl surprised her with a huge hug and kiss.

"I'm finally home! And look at all this delicious food I've pre-pared for you!" The truth was, he'd first visited his mother, who had cooked the food, and Karl brought it back to his house to reheat for their supper.

Karl's unexpected arrival was a delight. Plenty of kissing accompanied the hugging. But as things settled down, Katrina's anger surfaced.

"I'm upset with you, Karl. Your lack of letters during your train-ing is unacceptable. You knew full well I left Chiavenna to start a new life with you, but there was nothing here to welcome me or acknowledge my arrival. A small note saying where you were going, or how long you might be gone, was not only appropriate, but would have been a sign of your concern for me. But I found *nothing*. Was I that far removed from your thinking that I didn't warrant your writing a simple note? Or a letter from the training school? You seem so inconsiderate, Karl. Frankly, that worries me."

Karl said he was sorry. And although he seemed to listen to her, he didn't really hear what Katrina said. Instead, excited to be home, he was more interested in telling her about his adventures at SS school, and what had happened to him in the months since they had last seen each other. He began by saying his transition from the factory was difficult. Then spoke about how the SS Officers school and the change to military life challenged him.

She listened but remained upset. After all, she had made a big change, too.

He told her how each day at training started early with intense calisthenics before breakfast. His mornings focused on weaponry, then studying infantry tactics and maneuvering. Karl felt the tactics for ma-neuvering Army ground forces were equally applicable to tanks and halftrack armored vehicles, and he wrote a note suggesting such to his teacher. He then told her how proud he was when the class started using equipment from the Ravensburg factory. Karl went on to tell Katrina how the SS instructors placed emphasis on physical aggression. "I loved every moment of it." He continued.

"The school put us in battle simulations, firing artillery right over our heads. It allowed us to get used to the shock, noise and concussion of the cannons firing. The training helped many of us get past our fears, but regrettably, some young men cried, and others became shell shocked from the artillery and were removed from officer school right away.

"We spent three weeks in a concentration camp, learning how to deal with and manage the Jews and Slavs we gathered for slave work in nearby factories. Or even possible elimination for some of the weaker ones. I got to meet Theodor Eicke, the camp commander at Dachau. He told us how the concentration camps were being built and set up. One day I spoke to him at length. I told him I'd met Fritz Todt and had been told I could work with him someday. Eicke invited me to go with him to a newly constructed death camp. There, I saw how the gas chambers and furnaces were being set up to handle Jews, Slavs and others they plan to exterminate. I mentioned how we use blast furnaces at the foundry to smelt iron ore into a molten state. I recommended he consider injecting oxygen into the furnaces at the death camps to heat them up faster and reach higher temperatures. He said he would look into my idea."

Hearing Karl's horrific description, and seeing his matter-of-fact attitude, left Katrina speechless and without appetite, even though the food smelled delicious.

In her silence, he continued, explaining how ground-war strategy develops and is put into action. "After a blitzkrieg using fast-moving tanks and armored halftracks to occupy the open land of a conquered territory, emphasis is put on urban fighting – it's when the war moves to the inner city to crush the remaining resistance."

As he spoke, his animated expressions showed he had become energized and emotionally ready for battle. Then as Karl finished telling her details of his SS training, he paused, lit a cigarette, and relaxed.

Katrina couldn't believe what she was hearing, and seeing in his comportment as he described the military movements. *Is this the same man I had the most wonderful time with eight months ago?* Karl made her uncomfortable and nervous.

"Once Germany is fully armed, perhaps by next year, we'll attack the Western front and then push and create an Eastern front. Eicke gave me a lot of insight into how the next several years will look as Germany takes over Europe, eliminates Jews and other undesirables. He says a strong possibility exists we will end the treaty Hitler just signed with the Soviets, and then push our way into Russia and change the way of life for those Marx-loving Communists." He puffed out his chest with those last words, and took a few steps with a bit of swagger.

Katrina had seen Otto ultra-focused on manufacturing for Germany's rearmament. Now she saw Karl in the same warlike state of mind. But worse than Otto building machines of war, Karl spoke of gathering people into camps and making them slaves – or killing them outright.

Karl abruptly said, "Get the food on the table. I'll be right back." He grabbed two bottles of white wine and brought them to the table. Sitting again, he reached into his pocket and pulled out four pills he'd been given in SS school. He swallowed them with a full glass of wine.

Only a few minutes passed before he finished the first bottle of wine by himself. He opened the second bottle, poured a glass for Katrina, and continued to drink as she served the dinner his mother made for them.

Katrina was confused. She wasn't sure who Karl was. She watched him devour his meal, without conversation. She quickly caught on, and decided to just put the wine glass to her lips, but not drink any. She watched Karl finish the second bottle. His appetite was ravenous. Katrina heated another dish for him, leftovers from the night before. She knew he'd soon fall asleep from the wine and a full stomach.

Finished at last, he got up, went to the couch and fell into a deep sleep before the fireplace.

Shaken by the details of his stories, and his silence during dinner, Katrina's head spun in disbelief. She threw a blanket over him, put two more logs on the fire, and went to bed disappointed.

She didn't sleep well, and the next morning awoke much earlier than usual. Still tired, Katrina decided to leave right away, shower at the hospital and get into her nurse's uniform there. She left Karl a note to say she'd be home at 4:15 p.m., and suggested they go to his parents' house for dinner at 6:30. That would give them time to be together, relax and reconnect. Katrina called Valentina from work at 7 a.m., thanking her for the dinner she prepared last night, and to ensure Valentina knew she had suggested dinner at their place to Karl.

A knock at the door woke Karl at 8. He stood up from the couch still fully dressed from last night. "Good morning, Mother."

"Son, it's wonderful to have you home. How was your dinner and evening with Katrina? She's a beautiful woman. I hope you spent some time with each other catching up on things. She's done very well at the hospital and she is well liked there.

"Katrina called earlier this morning. I've made your favorite breakfast. Here, it's in the wicker basket. Come and sit and eat while it's still warm. Katrina said you'll be coming to dinner tonight. Let me start a pot of coffee for you."

Karl sat at the table, took a few bites and lit a cigarette.

"I'll make sure your father is home tonight. He stayed at work again overnight. I called his office before I left to come here, but there was no answer. He's been sleeping in the bedroom next to his office. Karl, your father has been working so hard. He must be sound asleep to not have heard the telephone."

Karl began telling his mother how she should be proud of his many accomplishments at school. "I earned a marksmanship medal in the use of rifles, and two more medals on math skills and the use of logic."

Then he spoke about the trip to Dachau and the new camp being constructed. As he spoke, his eyes opened wide.

"You can't believe the size of the facilities, and they've started building several concentration camps four times larger – to hold tens of thousands of people. Hitler wants us to use the people as laborers from countries we conquer, while sorting out the Jews, Slovakians, Gypsies, homosexuals and others. We'll use the few healthy workers we come across and eliminate the others. Our country should be cleaned up and free of Jews, Communists and the other deplorables and troublemakers within five years."

His mother leaned back in her chair, disbelieving her son's glib talk of ethnic cleansing – he was talking favorably about genocide. "But Karl—"

"Mother, I also scored first in my class for aptitude to lead fellow SS officers and soldiers in my last test two days ago," he interrupted. "As a reward, I've been selected to lead a small unit of twenty-five junior SS

61

officers, like myself, in an event against Jewish store owners this Wednesday. Because of the preparations and planning for the event, which will happen simultaneously in several cities, I need to return to Berlin this morning for final orders." He grasped her by the shoulders. "Mother, your son will help make Germany great again."

Shocked by his comments, Valentina didn't know what to say. She still couldn't fully grasp the details about the concentration and death camps, but his statement about eliminating Jews reverberated in her mind. His comment about organizing to start trouble and disrupt Jewish businesses and synagogues later in the week never even registered.

"When I spoke to Katrina this morning, I agreed to have dinner for you both at our house tonight. I'll make sure your father will be there. He'll want to see you. Can't you please stay for dinner?"

"Thank you for breakfast, Mother. Seeing you is so refreshing. But I must leave shortly to catch the train in Friedrichshafen to Ravensburg and then go on to Berlin. Maybe I can stop to see father briefly at the factory."

"Karl, dear, what about Katrina? You did tell her you'd spend time with her when you returned from Officer Training school. Didn't you? You need to get to know her if you two are to marry."

"Mother, she'll have to wait, like all the other women in Germany. We have a war to fight and a country to cleanse."

Karl stood and went to the bedroom to change while Valentina tearfully cleaned up from the breakfast. As she readied to leave, he returned to the kitchen dressed in his starched SS military uniform. He bent to hug and kiss his mother goodbye.

Valentina returned to her car and openly cried. She struggled with what she'd just heard from her son.

Otto says it's okay to fight the British and French again because of a bad treaty, but rounding up and eliminating people isn't right. It's immoral. Otto certainly wouldn't like what Karl talked about. What is this Hitler fellow doing to Germany?

As Karl gathered a few old shirts and pants, he spotted a note Katrina left him on the bed. She reminded him of their time together in her apartment. How much they enjoyed the time with each other. She said she hoped they could spend more time like that together again as soon as possible. Her note moved him. He regretted not making love with her last night, and he wrote back on the note.

K – Nice seeing you. Sorry I fell asleep last night. We did have a good time at your place. Unfortunately, I must leave this morning for Berlin. We plan to storm through several cities, creating trouble and mischief against Jewish storekeepers later this week. I've been selected to lead a small troop of soldiers to start a riot in Berlin. If we're lucky, we might even burn down a few synagogues. Read the newspaper this weekend. See you at Christmas.
Your husband-to-be, Karl

Valentina called the hospital and left a message for Katrina that Karl was leaving that morning, and invited her to come for dinner anyway.

When Katrina left work, she bought a bottle of Gewürztraminer and headed to Valentina's. Meanwhile, Otto called home, saying he needed to stay at work and would miss supper, and wouldn't be home again tonight.

During the meal, Katrina and Valentina expressed how upset they were over Karl's abrupt arrival and departure. They also spoke in hushed and worried tones about his involvement in concentration camps.

"The rumors of Germany starting a war are scary," Katrina said. "Worse, and to be honest with you, I'm concerned about having the time to develop a proper relationship with your son."

What she didn't say was she was afraid she'd gotten herself into a bad situation. Karl was a virtual stranger, and she saw no easy way out of her entanglement with him.

***

For Otto, every day at the factory grew more complicated. With more new parts being made at the foundry, the milling and machining areas were choked for floor space. With changes and modifications to each type of vehicle, final assembly was often delayed due to the wire harnesses, made at other locations, not arriving fast enough. The storage yard holding unfinished tanks was filling to capacity. It held finished tanks that had yet to ship, because the German central command made weekly changes on which war front to ship finished tanks. The logistical complexity grew daily.

Otto proposed the factory's owners acquire the adjacent parcel of land and knock down two old buildings to create a larger storage yard that could accommodate more Panzer tanks, halftracks and other mobile war machines.

Otto knew losing Karl's skills to the SS eight months earlier had hurt the production line in multiple ways. And unfortunately, news came that morning that Ulli had been killed in action. That hit Otto hard. Ulli, a good kid with lots of common sense, listened well and often felt more like a son than Karl. He couldn't put his finger on it, but, to his annoyance, Karl was often brash and contrary. Ulli had never been like that.

***

On the evenings of November 9 and 10, 1938, Karl and hundreds of other SA paramilitary forces carried out their plans against the Jews while regular German police looked on without intervening. At one point, three of them entered a butcher shop. Karl smashed the front window by lifting and hurling the wooden butcher block through it, and then, with the others, threw all the Kosher meat onto the floor. Then they set the store on fire.

In all, during the *Kristallnacht pogrom*, Nazi Party members and military units damaged or destroyed more than seven thousand Jewish businesses and over 250 synagogues in several cities across Germany, Austria and Sudetenland – the part of Czechoslovakia where German-speaking people lived.

When Karl returned to his barracks days later, he wrote to his father, proudly sharing what he'd done, and boasting of his new nickname, "Butcher."

Distraught at what he read when the letter arrived, Otto brought the letter to Valentina; she wept. Learning the details of what Karl was doing as an SS officer made her stomach turn. Otto – and Valentina to a much lesser extent – supported nationalistic feelings against the French and English, but both felt hurting Jews was wrong.

A few days later, Katrina approached her future mother-in-law to again discuss Karl's activities. Valentina broke the news about Karl's participation in the crimes against the Jews during Kristallnacht. Still terribly upset, the letter from Karl caused Valentina to share a secret with Katrina – one she'd kept from Otto for all their years of marriage – about her mother's childhood and heritage, and where Stella grew up before moving to Venice.

Katrina listened and understood the deeper meaning of what her future mother-in-law revealed.

Neither Katrina nor Valentina had any idea how deep Karl's involvement in activities against the Jews would become. They didn't know he would eventually work alongside those responsible for the construction of concentration and death camps. Worse, they had no way of knowing how skilled the man they both loved would become at slaughtering Jews.

The following Monday, during the factory's daily morning coffee break, Otto told one of his senior managers, "It's one thing to fight a just war with men and machines against other men and machines. But upsetting and killing the Jews is wrong. More than a hundred of them were killed during Kristallnacht, and thousands of businesses destroyed. The outright killing of innocent people due to their religious preference is against our Lutheran Christian beliefs."

December seemed to pass quickly. As the finals days before Christmas approached, both Katrina and Valentina grew more and more hopeful for Karl's promise to return home. Together they decorated their homes, making Katrina feel closer to Valentina. Both prayed their homes would help Karl re-center himself on the family and spiritual purpose of Christmas. Valentina hoped Karl's favorite Christmas ornaments would spark childhood memories of home and of his grandfather, Kristofer Ulrich von Richter.

But Christmas Eve and Christmas Day 1938 turned out to be huge disappointments. Karl never came home, and he never sent word he couldn't make it.

CHAPTER THIRTEEN

Promised Promotion

Spring and summer passed quickly. In late September, Katrina received a promotion that had been promised earlier in the year – and it was more than she expected. The administrator, delighted with Katrina's work and organizational skills, rewarded the young nurse with an assistant administrative position at the hospital with an excellent salary – almost three times what she'd earned as a nurse in Italy. There was some truth that his wife, Valentina's good friend, helped him decide to make the move.

Katrina visited her parents for two days in the fall. She shared stories of Otto and Valentina, and their 200-year-old family home on Lake Constance. She also told them the hospital administrator and his wife were delightful people.

Dino and Lucia expressed delight at their daughter's success, an extraordinary professional advancement for a woman at the time.

"That's wonderful, Katrina," her mother said. "I'm enormously proud of you. I always said you have a lot of talent besides skiing. What about Karl? What's he up to these days?"

Katrina looked down at her hands. "My fiancé is very busy in the German Army," she said simply. Embarrassed, she left it at that. Deep down, she hoped his assignment would have changed by now, and so she never mentioned Karl's work with Eicke in the camps.

"And is Germany preparing for war, Katrina? There's news that Germany has created havoc with its Jewish citizens. The news says Jews are being gathered in camps and held against their will."

"Father, we understand many of those people are communists and troublemakers. We see none of that in southern Germany, where I work in Friedrichshafen. I'm told it's all isolated incidents being overblown by the news media."

Dino shook his head. "My daughter, you need to wake up. The Kristallnacht incident wasn't isolated, as you say."

The rest of her visit was awkward; Katrina felt her father really didn't care much about her career. But Dino's primary concern was that his sweet daughter was living in another country, and rumors from people visiting his bakery made him worry for her safety.

Katrina returned to Langenargen, focusing on her new job as she drove. Her work and the promise of a promotion kept her fully engaged at the hospital. She would soon be making more money and, with the hope of saving as much as she could, she turned a blind eye to the reality of Karl's SS assignments. She naïvely hoped the bad things happening in northern Germany were temporary and would soon resolve themselves. She wished all the noise and rumors would just go away. She longed for a return to the evening she'd spent with Karl in her apartment so long ago and those feelings she so enjoyed.

The next morning, Katrina proudly walked through the hospital's front door wearing a smart-looking dress she'd picked up while shopping with her mother in Lecco. Hooked on the prestigious job and its generous income, her desk was immediately filled with tasks long overdue since the departure of the prior administrative assistant weeks earlier. By 4:30 that afternoon, she found herself exhausted from the items on her lengthy to-do list.

Her father's words suddenly echoed in her mind: *"Is Germany preparing for war, Katrina? The Jewish are being gathered in camps and held against their will."*

***

Work at the factory reached peak efficiency when Otto hired Gunter Schmidt to replace Ulli. With more space in the newly expanded yard, another rail spur was added. Gunter's duties included keeping track of rail cars with parts and assemblies coming in daily, and the newly built Panzer III tanks with the Maybach engines being shipped out to various war fronts daily.

Otto's work now kept him at the factory 24 hours a day, seven days a week. He never slept at home and wasn't even visiting his wife. The love they'd shared, complicated by the demands of his work, all but disappeared. The intensity of preparing for war divided them, and the onetime joys of watching their vivacious son ski, no longer bonded them.

Increasingly, they found themselves at cross purposes. Otto hoped the Wehrmacht would achieve an overwhelming win using his factory's mobile war machines. But Valentina wanted peace and prayed daily. But they still shared one thing: a mutual anxiety at Karl's horrific activities of building camps. Their son was now a willing participant in genocide.

Even before Otto began living full time at the factory, he'd turned to Monika for comfort. Wanting comfort herself, she willingly obliged. Valentina somehow knew.

Meanwhile, Valentina's health became a question. She had not fully recovered from a spring chest cold. The illness and cough lasted into the fall.

Katrina urged her to visit the hospital, as her coughing had lasted so long. But Valentina stubbornly resisted. And both knew it wasn't just a chest cold.

CHAPTER FOURTEEN

1939 – 1941

O ver the next 36 months, Germany embarked on a series of blitzkriegs and land grabs. In the last week of August 1939, Germany signed the Molotov-Ribbentrop Pact – a non-aggression treaty – with Russia.

A week later, Germany invaded Poland from the west and Russia invaded eastern Poland, agreed upon in a supplement to the secret pact. Germany also renounced claims to portions of Lithuania, appeasing the Russians.

In May 1940, Germany invaded and, in just eight days, took control of Belgium, Luxembourg and the Netherlands. By May 25, German Panzer IV tanks outflanked the Maginot Line, pushed deeply into France and rolled through town after town. They couldn't be stopped.

From May 26 through June 4, the British Expeditionary Force, having assisted France in its attempt to hold back Germany's advance, retreated to Dunkirk. Some 338,000 English soldiers were rescued by an armada of 800 vessels. Britain lost 68,000 soldiers in the campaign to help France, and in the melee of its retreat, left behind all of its tanks, vehicles and equipment.

On June 14, 1940, two million Parisians woke to loudspeakers announcing a curfew, and saying German troops would be entering and controlling Paris that evening. With the surrender of Paris, an armistice was signed between Germany and the new French "Vichy" government officially allowing the occupancy. The next day, the German soldiers marched, victorious and proud, on the Avenue des Champs Elysees up to the Arch de Triumph, and the Gestapo immediately went to work with interrogations and arrests.

On June 22, 1941, Germany, in a surprise move, invaded Russia in a massive action called Operation Barbarossa, quickly advancing over a thousand miles to the outskirts of Moscow. Germany also continued to build concentration and death camps, collecting and imprisoning Jews from the countries they conquered.

Later that year, Japan bombed Pearl Harbor on December 7. And Hitler, having had an extraordinarily good relationship with the Japanese foreign minister, followed Japan's lead by declaring war on the United States on December 15. The German military command in Berlin had believed the U.S. would respond against the Japanese and make the huge mistake of spreading itself too thin by joining its Allies in Europe. They felt the Allies would attack Italy, the underbelly of the Italian-German military Axis. Hitler, believing Italian dictator Benito Mussolini was weak, felt Germany should take control and manage the Italian Army by synchronizing Italy and Germany's combined war efforts. He wanted full military control as far south as Calabria in southern Italy, and even Sicily and North Africa, to prepare against a U.S.-led Allied invasion.

***

SS Officer Karl von Richter was working among several new death camps when he was recalled to the Wehrmacht's Berlin command center. Fluent in Italian, he received orders to go to Milan with two Wehrmacht generals to discuss strategies and defensive plans with Italian generals. Realizing he could stop and see his parents and Katrina beforehand, Karl flew from Berlin a day early.

Karl arrived at the Friedrichshafen airport late in the day two days before Christmas 1941. He ordered the pilot and one of his staffers to stay with the plane overnight. His other staffer secured a local police car and drove Karl to his parents' home.

His parents' house was dark and cold. Going inside, he found his mother in bed, suffering. Bedridden for the last two months, Valentina didn't see Karl enter the room, but she suddenly felt a presence. Unable to turn over, her deeply sunken eyes looked up. *It's my son.*

He paused momentarily, surprised at seeing how terrible his mother looked. Then he noticed the fireplace's remaining ashes barely smoldering, and no wood in the room. He grumbled, then went outside to gather the few pieces he could find, but the uncovered wood pile was damp, which made restarting the fire difficult. He found some kindling and, although smoky at first, it finally flamed. He waited another twenty minutes while making sure the fire stayed lit. He expected his father to be home soon.

Karl gazed again at his mother. There was a tear on her cheek, but she had fallen back to sleep. Devoid of emotion, he left the house and had his assistant drive him to Langenargen.

Upon arriving on the small street, Karl noticed curtains in the windows as he walked up to the house. He knocked and immediately stepped inside. He saw colorful knickknacks, several crocheted blankets on the couch and, in the bedroom a colorful floral bedspread covered the bed. Pleased with what he saw, he started a fire and looked around for something to drink. He spotted an unopened bottle of 1938 Brunello, and a two-armed brass corkscrew. He removed the cork and poured himself a glass. Before he took a drink, he reached into his pocket, grabbed six Pervitin pills and put them in his mouth. After he finished the glass, he began guzzling the wine straight from the bottle.

Ten minutes later Katrina turned in to the street. As she drove toward the house, she saw a police car parked out front and, looking closer, a uniformed German SS soldier at the wheel. As she approached the front door, she smelled burning wood in the dense air and noticed the glow of the fireplace through the window. She opened the door and saw Karl with a big grin, sitting in a chair in his starched SS uniform and highly polished knee-length black boots. Standing to greet her, he seemed taller than she remembered.

"Hello, Katrina. You're looking well."

"Karl! What are you doing here?"

"I've come home to spend the night with my wife."

"I was just at your mother's. She barely whispered to me that you stopped to see her. Karl, she's extremely ill, but she refuses to go to the hospital. I believe she's got lung cancer. If she doesn't get help at the hospital in the next day or two, she will die from her illness."

He ignored her words. "I need to be in Milan in the morning to straighten out our military communications with chubby little Benito and his Blackshirt gang. But I came here tonight because I want to be with you. The next generation of the von Richter family must be established. I need a son."

"Karl, it's been four years since you've visited me – or your parents. We haven't had a single letter from you. Your father heard rumors of your activities, but we never knew where you were or what you were up to. We didn't even know if you were alive or dead.

"And, except for one night and one morning in Italy, you and I haven't spent any time together. I'm not your wife. We aren't married. We barely have a relationship, and I won't go to bed with you as an order."

She walked to the side of the table, then turned to look directly at him again. "Did you hear me just say your mother will die if she doesn't go to the hospital? Karl, look at me. What's happened to you?"

Karl looked at her blue eyes, then lifted the wine bottle by its neck and took another gulp. "Katrina, now it's your turn to listen to me. You've been living in my house. I'm guessing you have a cushy position at the hospital because my parents are your future in-laws. So, tonight, you and I are going to play husband and wife. Do you understand? I want a son."

He flipped another handful of pills into his mouth, followed by a long swallow of wine that drained the bottle.

Katrina watched him, stunned. It had been years since she'd seen him.

His behavior is so different. He's aged. His face looks different, his eyes are sunken, he's thin and scary. His stare! My God, he looks like the devil, and that skull on his uniform adds to his wicked appearance. He's the German war machine personified. And he seems taller, more muscular and stronger looking than I remember. It's like he's a complete stranger.

Suddenly, Karl grabbed her arm and yanked her into the bedroom as if she were a rag doll. He threw her down onto the bed, climbed on top of her, grabbed both wrists, pinning her hands above her shoulders. He laughed as she struggled to free her arms. Holding her hands, he pulled up her skirt.

Katrina twisted and struggled to push him away, as he unbuckled his pants. It was a game to him. Karl forced himself on her brutally. He hurt her badly, and she felt the pain as he penetrated her. He hurt her, then he hurt her again. High on amphetamines, he was a mad man… a drugged mad man.

Soon afterward, Karl rolled off her and fell asleep.

Katrina, heart still racing, retreated to the living room and cried. Angry and violated, she couldn't have imagined Karl being anything like that when they first got together in her apartment. *It was so different in my apartment. This man is a completely different person than the young skier I cared for and fell in love with. He must be on some kind of drug to behave like such a maniac.*

She went into the bathroom and washed herself. Still not feeling clean, she washed again, and then again. She hurt all over. When she dried off, she got into comfortable clothes and fell into a fitful sleep on the couch.

When she woke at 5, he was already gone.

In the bathroom's small mirror, Katrina noticed black-and-blue marks on her face and forearm where he had grabbed her. She looked down at her thighs; she was scratched and bruised. She was beaten up and sore everywhere. Katrina went into the bedroom, tore the sheets off the bed and threw them into the garbage. She washed yet again, dressed in her uniform and, instead of heading to work, drove to check on Valentina. She cried on the way, recalling how brutal Karl had been. *My God, how could this have happened? I've been waiting for a different person to return. What am I to do now?*

Katrina knocked at the door. Getting no answer, she let herself in. As she entered the living room, she saw last night's fire in the living room fireplace had gone out completely. Not even an ember glowed under the ashes. The house felt cold. Karl hadn't bothered to say goodbye or reload his mother's fireplace with wood this morning before leaving for Italy. Worse, it looked as if Otto had not come home again last night. Anger churned within Katrina. *Otto should come home at night to care for his wife. I've called and left him several notes with Monika, letting him know Valentina has been so ill.*

Katrina went straight to the gas stove, lighted a burner and put a kettle on. She walked to the bedroom door and called out, "Valentina, it's Katrina. Would you like a cup of tea?"

No answer. In the bedroom, she saw that fireplace was out, as well.

Katrina walked to Valentina's bedside. "Valentina. Valentina. It's Katrina. I'm here now." She touched her arm. It was cold. She put her fingers on Valentina's wrist to find a pulse. Nothing. Poor Valentina. She had died sometime during the early morning.

Katrina sat on the foot of Valentina's bed. Tears rolled down her face. "Oh, Valentina, my dear Valentina. What a terrible night for both of us! Dear lady, I'm going to miss you."

In the final weeks of her life, Valentina told Katrina many things about her childhood and her upbringing at the DiBotticino quarry and stone works. She talked about her mother, Stella, and her childhood, and her mother's secret, imploring Katrina to never repeat it to Otto or Karl.

The two women had cried together several times over the past week. Each of her visits added to their mutual trust. It had reached the point where all they had was each other, and the two loved each other as mother and daughter.

After several minutes, Katrina wiped her eyes and returned to the kitchen. She turned off the whistling tea kettle and reached for the wall phone to call work. She told the hospital operator where she was and why. She asked for her supervisor and requested an ambulance to pick up Valentina's body. Then Katrina called Otto.

The assistant secretary, Ingrid, answered. "Oh, Katrina, hold on a moment, Otto and Monika are walking in right now."

Ingrid handed the phone to Otto. Katrina gave him the sad news and shared how long she had been ill, and how she had tried and tried to reach him, even leaving messages.

Otto teared up and began to weep. Guilt weighed heavily upon him for not being there last night, or stopping at the house for the past four weeks. He quickly recognized his absence had contributed to her death. His affair with Monika had been going on for almost two years. He knew he was at fault.

Katrina knew exactly where Otto had been that night, and she knew Valentina knew it, too.

For the next two hours, out of respect for Valentina, Katrina helped make the arrangements with the local undertaker, and for services at the Lutheran church. Afterward, Katrina returned to the hospital. The rest of the day she went through her nursing responsibilities, emotionally detached, and still hurting from the physical pain Karl had caused her.

That evening, she headed back to Langenargen, but the drive there made her anxious. She knew now she needed to abandon the hope of a life with Karl. He now was such a different man than he'd been when she nursed his ankle injury. She recalled spending the night with him in her tiny apartment... it had felt so good. But now the trauma of being raped dominated her thoughts.

Six weeks after her rape and Valentina's death and burial, Katrina found herself experiencing morning sickness. She missed her period and, when another month passed, she felt other changes. She was pregnant.

The summer months arrived with warm and more humid weather. As Katrina's belly grew, she learned to deal with the physical challenges of being pregnant and working. Although she wasn't working as a nurse any longer, in her role she still trained new nurses, showing them daily tasks, and it became quite uncomfortable for her.

Katrina prayed about her situation, stopping in the hospital chapel each day during her break. She knew Germany was at war. Leaving her job now and going to Italy was not a good idea while she was pregnant. She would have to wait.

CHAPTER FIFTEEN

Otto's Demise

L ate that summer, a strong feeling swirled among the factory workers that Otto might be replaced. The rumor started after Oswald Lutz visited with Albert Speer, the new Minister of Armaments.

The rumor mill caught wind that another World War I veteran running a larger factory – twice the size of the Ravensburg factory – with better production metrics would take over. Curiously, no one had heard of him before.

Weeks later, when the new man arrived, he initially reported to Otto, but everyone knew he would soon replace him. The next day, a member of Otto's team discovered the new man was a Nazi bureaucrat, a friend of Speer, with no prior experience at any other factory. The rumor about his prior experience came from a faked news-release flyer, drafted for Speer as a favor by Goebbels, and dropped purposely on the factory grounds by Speer during his visit. Only two weeks after the Nazi started, Otto saw Speer in the factory again, making an unannounced visit. Otto kept himself hidden as he watched Speer walk the factory floor. He joined his bureaucrat friend and together they made a complete sweep of the foundry area, walked through the milling and machining areas and huge assembly building, then outside to the yard, where undelivered tanks were stored.

Unfortunately for Otto, the assembly building and the foundry yard had three dozen brand-new Panzer IV tanks sitting idle, waiting to be finished and delivered to the war front. Delivery had fallen behind schedule because of an assembly gaffe. A German company responsible for electrical wiring harnesses sent harnesses for the newest style "Tiger" tanks. Otto's assembly team caught the error and re-ordered the correct items. But the replacements hadn't arrived in time for Speer's inspection.

Given the delay, Otto expected Speer to appear in his office. But Speer left without speaking to him. Otto went into an emotional tailspin that afternoon. He even lost his temper with some of the workers.

Some presumed Otto was finally feeling the loss of his beloved Valentina. Others said he had been told Karl had died. But a few in the assembly area blamed the political appointee from the Nazi Party.

One of Otto's men said he heard the new Nazi manager telling Speer, "Otto can no longer do his job properly. The harness mistake was all his fault."

Only a day earlier, Otto had discovered the harness order error had been made on purpose by the Nazi bureaucrat. Otto hoped to explain what happened, but now it was no use. The stress of the badly bungled delivery schedule made him crack. He blew his top in front of several workers on the floor, then returned to his office and opened the bottle of vodka he kept in his desk.

The following Tuesday, Speer visited again. In a brief meeting, Speer told Otto, "Herr von Richter, I've been advised you're in over your head in your current position. You are being replaced by Herr Muller. You'll move downstairs to manage the schedules. Your compensation will remain the same for the next pay period. Thereafter, your salary will be reduced to sixty percent of your current income, and you'll no longer be eligible for any bonuses. You are to make the move now. I'll be back in one hour and expect to see you in the office downstairs."

Otto limped out to the yard, grabbed a hammer and started hitting a piece of steel. He struck it repeatedly, not caring that he was causing a scene among the workers.

After 10 that night, Otto went to Monika's house, as usual.

His lover sensed his anxious mood and, as she had for the past two years, quickly took his mind off his work. Then, after satisfying Monika, Otto fell into a deep sleep. During the night he had a dream – he was in the trenches with other soldiers. They'd just been warned to put their gas masks on. Suddenly there was yelling.

"Hurry." "Get them on now." "Quickly, move, everyone move

left!" "Oh, my God. No! No!"

The soldiers in the trench all began to run and push one another. Otto tried to run, but he couldn't. Anxious in his dream, he tried and tried to move in the trench, but couldn't. As his heart beat climbed, his blood pressure skyrocketed. Otto began to sweat. In his dream, he had fallen, and his fellow soldiers, running from the gas attack, crushed him as they ran over him. The pain in his arm gradually migrated to his chest. In the next moment, it felt like an elephant sat on his chest. He woke, opened his eyes and gasped.

Early the next morning, while Katrina was dressing for work, she received a phone call.

It was Monika and she was crying.

"Katrina… can you please come help me?"

"What's wrong?"

"It's Otto. He's dead."

"I'll be right there. Call the hospital. They'll send someone right over to the factory. I'll hurry and try to be there before they arrive."

"No, Katrina. He's here. He's at my house."

Katrina paused, then shook her head as she thought of Valentina. "Give me your address. I'll call the hospital and have them send an ambulance to your place. I'll be there in twenty minutes."

As Katrina finished dressing, she considered her options. *I'll have to get away from here and from Karl, as far as possible. With Valentina and Otto gone, nothing is here for me. Not even my good-paying job is worth it anymore.* She thought again about leaving her job once she gave birth. *Maybe I can live with my parents in Lecco. No. That won't work. Karl would surely find me. I'll have to go somewhere he could never find me or hurt me again. I must protect my baby, too. Maybe I should put my child up for adoption to a couple who could give him or her a loving home and then become a nun in a convent far away.* Then she startled herself, saying aloud, "I need to think this through."

At Otto's burial service, with the Lutheran minister presiding, Katrina stood and watched Monika crying, alongside Otto's two brothers and a few family friends – including the hospital administrator and his wife – and a few of the older men from the factory. Most believed Otto was the ultimate plant superintendent, who died at his desk while working long hours to keep up with the increased production demand. They also recognized how Otto had struggled after Karl left, and again after Ulli Kempf died in the military. They knew something had upset Otto, and thereafter the factory spirit was never the same.

The recent death of his first love – his sweet wife, Valentina – had devastated Otto. His guilt at not being there with her while she was sick caught up to him and broke his heart. He came to believe her being so sick for so long, and dying alone, was all his fault. He hadn't been home in over four weeks, and hadn't been a proper husband to her for far longer. He'd been deeply involved – and sleeping each night – with his secretary.

As Katrina left the cemetery, she reflected on her frequent visits with Valentina, how she'd urged her to go to the hospital for better care, and how Valentina had said, "I know Otto is having sex with Monika." But the worst part for Katrina was her sad discovery while helping his assistant Ingrid make final arrangements the day after Otto's death. She had gone to gather Otto's personal belongings from his office to bring back to the lakeside home.

Ingrid told her, "Otto was recently demoted. All the messages you left for him at the office these last two months, saying, *'Otto, you need to go home, Valentina is sick'* and your last messages saying, *'Valentina is extremely sick and needs you at home right away'* – well, they were never delivered to him.

"Monika hasn't been back here since Otto died at her house," Ingrid continued. "Yesterday I needed to find some unpaid invoices. I went upstairs to find them and came across your messages, over thirty of them, buried under a pile of papers on Monika's desk – all upstairs. It's evidence she shut Otto off from knowing Valentina was so sick. He was wrong to be with Monika, but he had no idea Valentina was so sick and dying at home. It's all so wrong and so sad."

Katrina stared at Ingrid in disbelief. *What kind of woman would withhold information about a man's dying wife? Who would do such a thing?*

"Katrina, there's one more thing you should know. The other day I found a 'special delivery' message from Karl to Otto hanging on a nail above Otto's desk. Karl had heard news from a factory inspector, and his note to his dad was brief. It said, 'Father, a Panzer tank inspector told me he saw you a few months ago. You told him, 'my daughter-in-law will be having a baby soon.' Father, is it true? Is Katrina really having a child? It's great news! I'm sure it'll be a boy. I'm too busy to return to Frie-drichshafen or Ravensburg but will see you soon. Send a return message to me at Command HQ in Berlin. It will be forwarded to me.' "

The revelation that Karl now knew of her pregnancy elevated Katrina's anxiety. She had to seriously re-evaluate her next steps.

***

A few days after Otto was buried, and having learned Karl knew she was pregnant, on September 16, 1942, Katrina went into labor at work. Her healthy baby boy arrived late that evening. The nurses in the hospital were so joyful. Valentina's close friend, the wife of the hospital administrator, suggested to him that Katrina remain in the hospital for several days, especially with the recent death of her father-in-law and no one to look after her in Langenargen. Katrina accepted the kind offer. It was a comfort to her to be surrounded by coworkers and nurse friends, some of whom were like sisters to her. She also knew the generous offer reflected that many in the community believed Karl was her husband, and Otto and Valentina von Richter her in-laws.

When she was asked the following day about the child's name for the birth certificate, she named him Bruno Amorino, after her uncle. She had considered a von Richter male's name, but believed an Italian name would be better if she eventually gave her baby up for adoption.

Over the next several months, Bruno grew, strong and healthy. In April 1943, Katrina gave notice she would move to Lecco and live with her parents. The baby was big enough to travel now, and the warmer spring weather enabled her to drive through the Alps without worry of icy or snowy road conditions.

On her last day at the hospital, she shared a tearful goodbye with her friends. She'd told everyone that besides the loss of both her in-laws, she'd received word her husband, the SS officer, had died in the war. It was a lie, but enabled her to leave Friedrichshafen, Langenargen and the greater Bodensee area with grace. As part of her departure charade, she sought, and received, a glowing reference letter, although she had no intention of ever using it.

Over the next two days, she ensured both houses were cleaned and empty. She left the table set for two with colorful teacups in Valentina's lakeside house. It was how she liked it.

On the morning of her departure, Katrina neatly packed her essential belongings. Little Bruno was tucked into a wicker basket in the front seat, surrounded safely with pillows and blankets. His head and toes touched both ends of the basket. He'd grown, and it surprised her. She made the sign of the cross and started the car. The day was sunny and clear, with white puffy clouds. Some clouds were below her as she drove through the high mountains. The long drive was challenging on the winding roads. A late-spring storm had left almost a foot of snow at the highest elevation on her journey, making her passage treacherous for several hours.

Her route passed through Chiavenna, close to the hospital, her last place of employment. *If only I'd ignored Karl and stayed here years ago. That night I was so nervous. I was drawn to him because of the sex. It was so good, but I made such a terrible mistake!* She looked ahead at the road and said to baby Bruno, "I am so sorry, my little son. My heart is broken for you. Please forgive me."

She arrived in Lecco late in the afternoon and drove directly to her parents' bakery. Coming into town, she saw German soldiers in the streets with rifles, standing beside halftrack armored vehicles. Naïve to many things regarding the war, she wasn't aware Germany had stepped up its involvement in Italy and would soon take control of its military. Lecco was one of the many towns where the German Army set up posts to show their presence and keep order.

Her father's bakery displayed the open sign on the front door as Katrina parked the car. She saw her parents working diligently behind the counter. She stepped inside, walked up to the counter.

"One sfogliatelle, please, it's my favorite."

Recognizing the voice, Lucia turned and saw her daughter.

Tears flowed immediately, and for a few minutes there were non-stop hugs and kisses.

Even a longtime customer, who had known Katrina as a young girl, hugged her.

As things calmed down, Katrina said, "Mother, Father, I have a surprise for you." She went back outside.

Expecting to see a few loaves of German rye bread in the basket she carried inside, they all cried again, thrilled to see a grandchild. After showing him off to a few customers, Dino closed the bakery and they all went home, to their second-floor apartment around the corner.

Later that evening, after a dish of Dino's homemade pasta, his fresh marinara sauce and a second glass of his homemade red wine, Katrina shared all that had happened. She told her parents about Karl's becoming an SS officer and being active in the design and construction of concentration and death camps.

To her parents' shock, Katrina told how he arrived unexpectedly one night sixteen months earlier, high on German Army-issued amphetamines, and raped her. Then she explained about Valentina's illness and slow death, her husband Otto's infidelity for two years before she died, and then Otto's sudden and awkward death at his secretary's house. She added neither she nor his parents had heard from Karl for years prior to her rape, or since. She broke down and cried. Her mother cried, too.

Dino was steaming, and then chimed in with, "I knew that guy was no good for you. I told you so, Katrina, but you never listen to me. Now what are you going to do? How are you going to support yourself and the baby?"

With her father's question still ringing in her ears, Katrina felt her life had reached a new low. She neither wanted nor needed to be treated like a child by her father. She tried to compose herself and then told her parents about officially leaving the hospital in Friedrichshafen.

Dino repeated his 'I told you so' statement, saying he'd warned her getting involved with the German was a mistake. "You always were an emotional child, and now you are a fool to have given yourself to a virtual stranger. I knew it would turn out badly."

Lucia spoke up several times, to temper her husband's hurtful comments, then asked about her plan for the baby.

Katrina shared her saddest thoughts. "I've decided to give him up for adoption. And I plan to go into the convent. I want to be rid of Karl forever and atone for my selfish mistake and my physical attraction to him. I want to devote my life to prayer, helping others and ask for God's forgiveness for what I've gotten myself into."

It had been a heavy conversation and his daughter's last comment upset Dino terribly. Katrina was their only child. She was everything to them. Less than five hours ago, they all were filled with love and elation at meeting their new grandchild. Now their prodigal daughter had been raped, was giving her baby away and was going away, again.

Katrina reminded them Karl's uncle, Giovanni DiBotticino, was a priest. Years earlier he had become a monsignor in Brescia, not far from there. She hoped to contact him with a visit, and maybe he could help with the adoption.

Dino, tired from his long day, felt emotionally exhausted from his daughter's story. He stood up from the dinner table, then leaned down and kissed Katrina on the cheek.

"I love you, and you will always be my daughter. But now I am going to bed." It was only 7:30, but his routine was to awaken at 1:45 and be in the bakery by 2 to start making dough for the day's pastries and bread. Lucia usually accompanied him, but tonight she stayed up with Katrina and the baby.

After Dino was asleep, Katrina shared more with her mother about the brutal rape. Crying, she explained how she resisted repeatedly, and how he ignored her pleas to stop.

Lucia couldn't fathom the depths of her daughter's sorrow. At last, she said, "Katrina, if you do give up the baby and go into a convent, you should go to the convent in Bernalda. My cousin Maria is Mother Superior there. I wrote to her often over the years. She knows you are my little girl. I haven't written in the last few years, but Maria certainly will help you."

Lucia went on to tell Katrina how she had wanted to be a nun, growing up in Bernalda. "My cousin Maria and I would sit in the church wing attached to Holy Angels Convent. We would listen to the nuns sing their prayers in Gregorian chant while we sat just out of their sight. She and I would chant along in low voices. It made us feel like we were in heaven. We talked about entering the convent when we finished secondary school. Then, just before I was going to enter, I met your father and we eloped six months later."

Just then, Bruno awoke and began crying. After Katrina changed and nursed the baby, she gave little Bruno to his grandmother to hold.

Lucia cried as she sang an old Italian song to him.

Katrina's sorrowful heart broke as she watched.

CHAPTER SIXTEEN

Katrina Visits Giovanni

T wo days passed before Katrina drove from her parents' home in Lecco to the Old Cathedral in Brescia. German soldiers and heavy artillery equipment were stationed at intervals along the road.

She was stopped once and asked where she was headed. Katrina showed them the baby in his basket and said she was on her way to the church in Brescia to have him baptized. The Lutheran German soldiers raised the check-point gate and let her by without further question.

As she passed, they warned, "Be careful because the Americans are now in Italy and advancing north."

Thank God. The Americans can't get here soon enough to stop this insanity!

When Katrina arrived at Brescia's Old Cathedral, she parked in front of a building that looked like the rectory. She carried the baby to the front door and knocked. There was no answer. She knocked again, and still no response.

Upset, she turned back when she heard the latch behind her being unlocked and the tall carved wooden door opened inward.

"Yes?" the housekeeper inquired.

"May I please see Monsignor Giovanni DiBotticino?"

She replied, "It's Bishop DiBotticino, and he'll be back late this afternoon. Come back tomorrow."

"I'm sorry but I need to speak with him today. It's urgent."

The baby started to cry. Seeing the desperate look on the young woman's face, the housekeeper decided to let her inside. She showed Katrina to a bathroom, where she could attend to the baby.

When Katrina emerged with the freshly fed and diapered Bruno, the housekeeper offered her a cup of espresso and suggested she sit in a nearby side room to wait.

Two hours seemed like four before Bishop DiBotticino returned. It had been a long day for him. Three months earlier, when he was first elevated to bishop, the pope had tasked the new prelate with keeping the Catholic Church organizationally stable in his diocese. The loss of several priests – who were dragged into the German military – had upset the Vatican. And although Hitler had grown up as a Catholic and was said to still have respect for the Church, many Lutheran German generals and SS officers despised the Roman Catholic Church and its hierarchy.

Nevertheless, Bishop DiBotticino, running hard with his newest assignment, was doing his best to keep Catholic churches open, Masses celebrated regularly and the sacraments available to the faithful.

The housekeeper waited until the bishop had the chance to go to his room and relax ten minutes before telling him a guest downstairs in the rectory's visitors' room insisted on seeing him today.

Tired, the bishop made his way downstairs and upon opening the door, saw the beautiful fair-skinned, dark-haired woman with blue eyes holding an infant in her arms. He thought of the painting in the Vatican, *Madonna and Child.*

Within moments of their introduction, he understood Katrina's relationship to his nephew, Karl. He recalled having seen Valentina and Otto upon their return from their honeymoon. He liked Otto, and fondly remembered his sister's visit to the family stone works during a family reunion, and seeing Karl as a boisterous three-year-old full of mischief.

"Bishop, your sister Valentina and brother-in-law have passed away," she informed him.

His eyes grew misty. "Oh, how sad. God bless their souls. I often hoped to visit them on Lake Constance in recent years, however life as a pastor in Brescia grew more difficult with each passing year. And now, being a bishop during wartime is even more complicated."

Katrina told the bishop, "I met Karl skiing, then saw him again a year later because of his ankle injury. We spent a brief time together, and I decided to move to Langenargen and continue my nursing in a hospital in Friedrichshafen. Unfortunately, our timing was bad. Karl was drafted into the military and had to leave before my arrival. He enrolled in the SS Officer school. But during his training, Karl bought completely into the Nazi propaganda of Germany's needing to expand its land and purify itself eradicating Jews, Slavs and other undesirables. News of his radical views against Jews crushed your sister… and even Otto. Neither of them was happy to hear his assignments. I thought it might be a passing thing, and so I stayed, hoping he'd return to his old self once the war was over.

"Valentina and I grew close in Karl's absence. We spent much time together. Sadly your sister's last few months were difficult. She was ill and her stubbornness in avoiding the hospital led to her decline." Now Katrina teared up.

"Bishop, Karl unexpectedly returned home one evening, high on amphetamines. He demanded we have a child and he raped me; it was the same night of his mother's death. He was brutal and left me severely bruised. We weren't married yet. With Valentina's death, I thought I maybe should be there to help Otto. I learned I was pregnant and decided it was best to remain until I had the baby. The war complicated things."

Listening carefully, the bishop leaned forward as Katrina's story unfolded.

"With the buildup of arms and tanks in Germany, Otto's round-the-clock workload became his albatross. His affair with his secretary ruined his marriage. Valentina knew of his infidelity. Then, only a few months after her death, Otto died from a heart attack while in bed with his secretary. With all of that behind me, this week I drove back to my parents' apartment in Lecco."

When she finished, the bishop leaned back in his chair.

"My dear Katrina, first, thank you for being so close to my sister. You were the daughter she never had. You've been through so much. Karl's behaviors and actions toward you and at the death camps are horrific and sinful. It's sad Otto let his marriage fail. This has been an utterly dreadful situation for you. You've been through so much. How can I help you, my dear?"

"Bishop, I'm so sorry for what has happened to Valentina and Otto, and I believe I'm at fault for my pregnancy. I will never marry Karl nor can I have the child grow up without a father. I wanted to discuss giving up my baby for adoption. He needs to be safe and guided by kind and loving parents. I don't believe I can give that to my child now – or at any time in the future. I've also prayed and decided to enter a convent. I've made many mistakes in judgment and need to atone for my sins. I considered life in a convent at an early age, but never accepted a calling. I found myself torn between a vocation and not wanting to disappoint my parents, who said many times they 'looked forward to someday having a grandchild.' I became a nurse with the idea of getting married or, if I was again drawn to the Church, entering the convent later. But when I met Karl, I was so attracted to him! I errantly gave him my body physically before I knew him. I know I was wrong to do that and it was a terrible mistake. I stayed too long, and everything changed. Now I'm left with the consequences of my choices. I am so sorry for what I've done."

She continued through her tears. "My mother's cousin is Mother Superior of a convent in the town of Bernalda in the province of Basilicata. I would like to go there... to pray... to do penance for my sins and to get as far away from Karl as I can."

"How long have you felt this way... about giving up the baby and entering the convent?"

"I knew, immediately after he raped me, I could never live with a man like that. When the pregnancy was confirmed, I began praying the child would someday have a kind and loving father, not one who helped design and direct a horrific genocide. We first learned details of Karl's activities from German SS officers visiting Otto's factory. His behavior was horrible to think about."

She paused, then continued, still weeping. "Long before I met Karl, I wondered how my life might have been, had I devoted myself to prayer. I love nursing and taking care of people. I became an assistant administrator at the hospital in Friedrichshafen. But I stayed too long. When Karl didn't return right away, I should have left, but I was proud of my job and the money was much more than I could earn in Chiavenna, where I once worked, or in Lecco."

Bishop DiBotticino gave a pensive nod. When he spoke, his words were slow, thoughtful. "I know a family in Milan who have taken in children. After a short while, the child is given to a childless couple. Before the war, the child would have stayed in Italy. Over the past few years, however, we've been sending children to Genoa and then on to America. Is this what you would want for your child?"

"Oh yes, Bishop!" Katrina exclaimed. "He deserves a better life than I can give him here as a sinful, broken woman." She sobbed, filled with shame and self-loathing.

The bishop pulled a small rope behind his desk, summoning the housekeeper. When she came in, he asked her to sit and comfort Katrina. Meanwhile Giovanni sat in silent reflection.

The decision to send the child to Genoa and then to the United States for adoption is easy. And I'm certain Katrina wants to go into a convent to pray and atone for her sins. But can she hope to develop a spiritual life suitable for a cloistered convent – especially given her horrible experience with Karl and then giving up her baby? Clearly her desire to go as far south as Bernalda is to hide. But if Karl survives the war, he will undoubtedly look for her – and their child.

"Katrina, I will sign a note granting you permission to enter the convent in Bernalda," the bishop told her. He intended to send a separate note to the Mother Superior, explaining the situation so she could guide Katrina through her emotional difficulties in the months and years ahead. He understood she was Katrina's mother's cousin, and while that was a nice connection and could help in her transition, Katrina's extremely fragile emotions and presence there could prove upsetting for the other sisters.

"Here's what I want you to do. Return to your parents' home in Lecco for one week. I will make the arrangements for your child. When you return here, bring the baby, and your mother. I will give you the note giving you permission to enter the convent with my blessing when you return. Now go back to Lecco. For your penance, I want you to pray a rosary each morning as you rise and each evening before you go to sleep. As you pray, focus on the image of the Holy Family, and the sanctity and holiness of the sacrament of marriage. Katrina, God loves you and forgives you. He will bless and protect your child. I will see you here in one week."

He reached for the chair's armrests to pull himself up to stand when she spoke.

"Bishop, before you leave, there are two stories I must share with you. It was your sister's last request. We spent special moments together in her last week. First, she shared something interesting about her family history. Did you know your mother, Stella, originally lived in Czechoslovakia and was a Jew?"

"No. I had no idea."

"Yes. Her father was a rabbi named Kirsch Baruch Goldman. Your mother grew up in Czechoslovakia as Devorah Goldman. Her father and a Jewish woman, the town's matchmaker, paired your mother at age twelve with a local merchant almost three times her age. Distraught at the arrangement, your mother gathered what little clothing she had and ran away in the middle of the night. She traveled for ages, lost most of the time, walking in rain-soaked clothing and shoes, sleeping in barns and under the stars. Months later she approached Cavallino, near Venice, and hopped onto a boat that took her to Burano. There she took on a new identity, calling herself Stella DiVenezia, and learned how to sew. Ten years later she moved to Venice and bumped into your father, Luigi, in St. Mark's Square while he was selling statues and blocks of stone to St. Mark's Church. She met him again a few months later on his next trip to Venice, and returned with him to your family compound at the quarry, where they married. Years later, you and your sister came along. Your mother told your sister her story and the secret about being Jewish when it would have been time for her bat mitzvah. Valentina said your mother never told you her heritage story because of your interest in being a priest, and Valentina never told Otto she was half Czech and Jewish.

"Then two days before she died, she told me another story. One night, a year after she and Otto married, your sister went to a dance in Ravensburg with three friends. Otto was away on a skiing weekend in the Alps with friends. All four girls were drinking too much that night. At the end of the evening, by mistake the other three left to return to Friedrichshafen without your sister – she was sick in the bathroom. When she came out her friends were gone. A minute later, a man at the dance offered to take her home. Helpless, she agreed. On the way home, she was so drunk she passed out. The man carried your sister inside, put her on the bed and took advantage of her drunken state. Still drunk, she woke briefly and willingly gave in – mistakenly believing him to be Otto. Only the next morning did she realize it couldn't have been Otto. She was horrified at her mistake. Six weeks later, morning sickness confirmed her pregnancy. Thrilled at the news, Otto shared it with all his coworkers.

"Valentina never told Otto about the incident, nor did she ever mention anything about the man who took advantage of her. Otto never knew the child he raised was the product of her rape that night. She said as young Karl matured, his face looked just like the man who raped her. Seeing him reminded her every day of her long-ago mistake. She said the man, a German Jew, worked as a foreman for Otto. Unknowingly, Otto assigned Karl to work with him at the factory when he was a teenager.

"Valentina said the man had a daughter named Ruth. Ruth and Karl looked alike – as if they were siblings – because they were. Years later, Valentina found out Karl and Ruth began seeing each other as teen-agers and she quickly put a stop to it, by commenting negatively about Ruth's family being Jewish. She knew it was wrong to say that, but used that as the excuse. The emotional burden of the rape bothered her deeply all her life. Valentina was sad they never had other children despite their constant attempts. Not having more children soured Otto's feelings and he blamed her, but she knew it could only have been Otto's fault.

"Bishop, that means Karl is three quarters Jewish. He'd never accept the idea he has Jewish blood. He is a proud German, proud of his heritage that dates back hundreds of years – and a proud ultra-right Lutheran Christian. Karl's activities in the SS against the Jews made your sister even more heartsick.

"A few years ago, when she found out Otto was having an affair with his assistant, she felt guilty for not giving him more children. All those conflicting emotions crushed her spirit in her final months. In her last days she thanked God for her wonderful parents, Stella and Luigi. She told me she hoped to see them soon. On the day before she passed, she said, 'Go see my brother. Tell him everything. Tell him I love him and missed spending more time with him.' " Katrina was still weeping.

91

"Katrina, what Valentina shared with you in her final days is a heavy burden to carry. God had you there at her side for a good reason. She needed to share what had happened. You have a good and gentle heart, and God's plan placed a caring person like you there to listen, to understand and to comfort her. But now, you need to let it go. Valentina was a good wife to Otto and a good mother to her son for many years. The pain of knowing Otto was with someone else in her final years must have been exceedingly difficult for her. Keep Valentina in your daily prayers. She is in heaven now, with God and her parents, and Karl will someday learn the truth of his Jewish heritage."

"It's all incredibly sad, but I have one more thing to ask. Since I am here in Brescia, I want to stop at the DiBotticino family stone works to introduce myself. I want to meet your mother, and let her know Valentina has passed."

"My mother passed away two years ago; she was eighty-one. My father died two years before that. He was seventy-nine. I sent word of their deaths to my sister, but she never responded. For some reason I don't think she ever received my messages.

"As for stopping by our family compound at the quarry, right now there's no one from our family working there now. Several younger cousins, and some of the local men from Brescia who worked there, were drafted into the Italian Army years ago. Two years ago, as the Germans began managing the Italian Army, they conscripted the rest of the men at the quarry. No one has returned since. Two of Uncle Vincent's great-nephews, initially too young to fight, were taken by the Germans to fight. I've since learned from a German lieutenant they'd probably be fighting in the marshes south of Rome against the advancing Americans.

"My father's brother, Uncle Vincenzo, Karl's great uncle, is still at the stone works. He's ninety-six now. Sadly, he sits and waits for the men to return. I've visited him a few times. If you have time, please stop to see him before heading back to Lecco, I'm sure he'd welcome your visit."

Katrina finally stood and gave him a respectful hug. "Thank you, Excellency. Speaking with you this afternoon has lifted a heavy burden. It's like I've gone to confession."

He smiled.

Then, sheepishly, she asked, "Might the church have any spare gasoline available for my car? I'd gladly pay for it."

The bishop summoned the housekeeper and told her to have the maintenance man refill her car from the church's gasoline tank.

Katrina thanked him and bade him farewell, then she took Bruno outside and waited.

The bishop immediately wrote a letter to the family in Genoa. He sealed it and asked the housekeeper to send it. Then, drafting a copy, he put it into a book. Next, he wrote to Sister Maria Cassano, the Mother Superior of the convent in Bernalda, explaining the situation between Katrina Amorino and his nephew Karl von Richter, and mentioned the baby. In the letter, Giovanni wrote:

"I hereby grant permission for Katrina Amorino to enter the convent. I suggest a lengthy period of no less than three years before she is permitted to profess her final vows, Longer if necessary. Katrina is a loving and caring soul and a skilled nurse, but she might not be suited for religious life in a cloistered convent.

He sealed the letter and put it into a special mail pouch to be delivered to the Vatican, using the Church's own mail courier. From there it would find its way to the convent in Bernalda. He wrote a similar copy and put it in his book, alongside the note to have the child sent for adoption.

The DiBotticino stone works was a twenty-minute drive north. Katrina passed a German halftrack as she drove through town, and then headed up the steep hill. Little Bruno was sound asleep when she arrived. She picked him up and stepped through the main door of the building, to see if anyone was there. It was much larger inside than she anticipated. Statues stood on small pedestals, and blocks of stone of all sizes sat on the large floor. A moment later, an old, bent-over, unshaven man shuffled slowly from the shadows to greet her.

The young mother introduced herself as Valentina DiBotticino's daughter-in-law.

Uncle Vincenzo realized after a few moments who she was. "Ah! You must be married to my great-nephew Karl."

Katrina nodded, then expressed her condolences about Stella and Luigi. She said Valentina had recently passed in Friedrichshafen, but in her final months had told her about the family stone works. She wanted to see it while she was nearby, visiting the bishop in Brescia. Just then the baby in her arms started to cry.

The old man's ears perked up. "Do we have another stone cutter in the family?"

Katrina smiled and showed the great-uncle the baby.

Vincenzo smiled and looked at Katrina. "My dear, your baby is beautiful, but what is troubling you?"

Instead of answering his question, she gave a nervous glance at her wristwatch, her going-away present from the hospital staff. "Uncle, I'm so sorry for such a short visit. But it's late and we must get back to my parents' house in Lecco. My father is a baker there, and he eats his dinner early."

Vincenzo stood at the edge of the stone works doorway as she drove away, wondering what brought her to Brescia to see his nephew. He noted no wedding band on her finger, then imagined – correctly – why. Long ago he'd found 12-year-old Karl too bold and boastful for his age, and expected he would someday become a troublemaker. Although he knew no details, his thoughts of long ago were confirmed seeing the mother and her child without a wedding ring. His aged shoulders drooped at the realization.

Katrina's return trip wasn't difficult, although a few kilometers from her parents' bakery she was stopped at the same checkpoint where she'd been detained earlier. Now a different set of soldiers who had been drinking stopped her.

"Hello, pretty lady, come stay with me tonight."

Another said, "Stay with me, lady. I'm a much better lover. I will make you another baby."

Although brief, the exchange made her nervous and reminded her of Karl. They raised the gate and she drove away.

Heading back to Lecco, she pondered if she was doing the right thing for her baby or just being selfish. Conflicting emotions plagued her into the evening as she tried to enjoy a nice dinner with her parents. Her still-unhappy father made no secret of his being upset with her situation with a few stinging comments.

That night Katrina went to bed in tears, still wondering whether what she was doing was best for Bruno.

The week flew by. Her emotions flipped back and forth every day, but always ended with the truth that, given the war, being single and the unknown economy once the war was over, giving up her baby was best for the child.

Katrina returned with the child to the church in Brescia, her mother in tow. Leaving Bruno would be extremely difficult. Her raw emotions made her ill that morning. As the bishop entered the room, she introduced her mother, Lucia.

"Bishop, I sincerely and deeply believe it will be better for Bruno to have a good life with loving parents in America than for me to try to raise a fatherless child, alone, in post-war Italy," she said. "And again, please, with your permission, I choose to enter the cloistered convent in Bernalda."

The bishop nodded in assent. He had already received a reply to his note to the family in Genoa, saying the child would go to America. He excused himself, then returned a moment later with the housekeeper and a second woman.

Katrina and her mother cried as the other woman gently lifted Bruno from his mother's arms. Even the bishop's eyes filled. Watching a mother offer her child up to a better life was not something one learned in the seminary or divinity school.

After the baby had been taken outside, Lucia broke the silence.

"Bishop, thank you for making arrangements for the child. It's a blessing. Dino and I remain concerned for Katrina. We feel this German SS officer's temperament is dangerous; he poses a risk to our daughter. We pray that Bernalda is far enough away that he will never find her. Unfortunately, I've been spending more time with my husband in the bakery and haven't written to my cousin in more than five years. When Katrina shows up at the convent, it'll be a surprise. Can you do anything else to help her?"

"Yes, Lucia, I've already sent a letter to the Mother Superior. It includes my permission for her to enter the convent. Now, on this letter I will give Katrina today is my apostolic stamp in wax as Bishop of Brescia. It gives her safe passage for her travels to Bernalda, and includes permission for her to stay overnight in churches and convents during her journey, as well as being supported with meals where she stays. But Katrina must be careful. There's much military activity in central and southern Italy. The Germans have taken control of the Italian Army and all major roads are blocked."

He turned to Katrina. "You need to anticipate meeting people, German soldiers, who may not understand what you are doing and where you are going. Be wise with your decisions. Listen to the guidance of the pastors of the local churches. I will keep you and your son in my prayers, and please keep me in yours."

Giving the travel letter to her, he took up the book with the copy of his previous note to the Mother Superior, and inserted a copy of this letter in his book, as well. Then, reaching into his cassock, he consulted his gold pocket watch on its long gold chain. "I'm sorry, but I must leave for another meeting. The pope sent a message this morning and I need to review it with the local priests. It seems he has a few more tasks for me up his sleeve. It never stops."

Outside, Katrina cried, becoming hysterical once she got into the car. It was a few minutes before she regained her composure and drove toward Lecco. Neither spoke during the trip home. Katrina continued to sob almost the entire way.

During the past week, she had come to regret many of her past decisions. She was sorry for her passionate feelings, and her first night with a man in her bed. She regretted her time with him the next morning. She was sorry she had left the hospital and her friends to follow Karl to Germany. What was even worse in her mind was when Karl left for SS school, leaving no message to welcome her to his house in Langenargen. She knew then, in her gut, something was wrong, but she stayed anyway, and now she regretted staying, because it allowed her to be there – and be raped – when Karl returned.

Now as she drove back to Lecco with her mother, confusion swirled within her. She again second-guessed herself. *Am I doing the right thing by giving my baby up? Will a life devoted to prayer in the convent help my conscience? Can I ever forgive myself for what's happened? God help me... please.*

Sitting in silence alongside her daughter, Lucia harbored her own regrets. *Maybe I should have supported Dino when he said he didn't like the idea of Katrina's going to live with a German skier.*

Lucia's thoughts then drifted to long ago. *Maybe I should have been stronger when Dino decided to move from Naples to Lecco. It was so far away from my family. Oh, how I missed everyone!*

Then her thoughts turned to Katrina. *Will the convent and prayer satisfy my once vivacious and athletically aggressive daughter? Only time will tell.*

When they arrived in Lecco, Katrina drove to the bakery. Dino stood behind the counter at the bakery with a few loaves of bread, and two dozen pastries set aside for his regular late-afternoon customers. Anticipating their return, Dino made a batch of gnocchi using fresh ricotta, and a pot of garlicky sauce with fresh-picked San Marzano tomatoes and beef braciola. He'd also set aside a few sfogliatelle he made earlier in the day for dessert. Katrina's last meal there would include all her favorites. Despite this, they were silent throughout dinner. When Katrina suddenly felt the need to nurse Bruno, she left the table, went into her room and cried again.

Next morning at 3, Dino began his routine in the bakery. Katrina finished dressing and came downstairs with her mother. Two old ladies from the neighborhood who'd visited earlier in the week came to say goodbye. They brought rosaries and holy water from Lourdes. One splashed holy water from a little bottle onto Katrina's red Fiat for a safe journey. When Dino stepped outside the bakery, Katrina hugged him and told him she loved him, and said he'd always be number one in her life. She promised she would be safe in Bernalda and would see him again someday.

Unable to repress his emotions, Dino started to cry and hurriedly stepped back into the bakery. Katrina hugged her mother. As she started to get into the car, Dino brought forth a dozen freshly baked loaves of bread and three huge boxes full of cookies – and two more boxes with fancy pastries – and put it all in the backseat.

"Katrina, please, beware of the people who will stop you for no reason. Offer them food first." He handed her a small box with his old Italian-made pistol inside. "When you stop, they might want to take advantage of you. Keep this on your seat, and don't be afraid to pull the trigger to protect yourself."

He gave her a thick roll of cash to pay for fuel during her trip. Finally, he handed her the map of the roads to take to Bernalda, and a list of towns and churches along the way, all torn from a book from Lecco's library. She started the car.

"Be sure to use the bishop's letter to stay in safe places overnight. Your mother said he gave you a letter with his seal and permission to enter the convent. Don't forget, you can leave there any time. Write to us if you're thinking of leaving, and if that's your decision, I'll come to get you and bring you home."

As Katrina drove away, Dino turned to Lucia. "We're losing our little girl once again. I had a dream last night. I fear we may never see her again."

CHAPTER SEVENTEEN

Karl in Action

In northern Germany, Karl von Richter's career star continued to rise. He quickly became known as one of the more astute SS officers, with a broad set of skills including field marksmanship, knowledge of factory production, building construction, drafting and product design, as well as managing people. Karl met his newest assignment, to help manage construction workers and oversee construction of three new death camps, with great enthusiasm. These new camps featured gas chambers and gas-fired furnaces. Since rail cars were bringing Jews and Slavs to the camps at an even faster pace, furnaces became the most efficient method to dispose of the remains, given the sheer numbers of undesirables being exterminated. Disposing of ashes made more sense, since at another location, trench after trench was filling with bodies too quickly.

At three death camps, Karl made suggestions about the facilities' layout. His experience in the factory and the need for increased production made him more aware of how a smooth-flowing operation could be run – even a death camp. He received accolades from fellow SS officers and a few generals for the streamlining changes he implemented. One general, Wilhelm Mohnke, hearing about Karl's eye for operational improvements and management style, asked him to join his field staff as a strategist.

***

Facing increasing difficulties with the advancing Americans, several German commanders and SS officers spoke of a bright young man who could view the overall situation with a fresh set of eyes. At Germany's Command Headquarters in Berlin, some believed SS Officer von Richter might see something they had not. Days later, Karl found himself again in Berlin, reviewing strategies being employed. Within two days, he identified two flaws in their logistics and long-range planning. He made other useful suggestions, which the Command implemented immediately. Karl's most important suggestion focused on improving the balance of mechanized mobile assets and to improve fuel distribution supporting the field troops' movements.

The next week, Karl flew to Rome. The German spy network learned the Allies planned for General Patton's American 5th Army to move north on the western side of Italy, and Britain's General Montgomery to move the British Eighth Army forces and a Canadian Army Division north up the east side of Italy, along the Adriatic Sea. In response to the new information, Karl made two suggestions helping the Germans revamp their defensive lines against American, British, Australian and Canadian forces moving north through Italy. He believed the Americans would lose their will to fight and withdraw from Italy before reaching Rome.

His first focused on the Winter Line running west to east across Italy, encompassing the Gustav Line, the Hitler Line (renamed the Senger Line) and the Bernhardt Line. Karl suggested fuel and large stores of ammunition be held in the path of what could be a retreat. Moving back slightly would enable German tanks and large guns to be moved north from fortifications, built the year before by Fritz Todt's construction company, and repositioned to fight again.

Ultimately, after weeks of intense fighting and Allied bombing, the entire Gustav Line from Anzio eastward to Monte Cassino, an abbey founded in 529 A.D., failed, thanks to hard fighting by the Americans' 5th Army, and especially its 157th and 92nd infantry divisions.

Eventually the Allies broke through and continued north to free Rome, but the repositioned Germans badly hammered the Allied forces.

Karl's second major suggestion was to improve defensive positions in southern Rome. Unbeknownst to his superiors, he was a history buff who had studied Latin in his teens. He knew of the development of the road called the Appian Way, built by Appius Claudius Caecus in 312 B.C. The ancient road ran alongside low-lying marshy lands south of

Rome called the Pontine Marshes. Virtually at sea level, these marshes received water from two river sources. Years earlier, in a major civilian program, Mussolini had attempted to drain the marshland, overrun with mosquitos and malaria.

Karl suggested the marshy land be re-flooded. "If the American forces break through our first defensive lines and head to Rome, their tanks and other equipment will get stuck in the mud. They'll be forced to halt their advance. We can hold them there so they'll never reach Rome."

General Field Marshal Albert Kesselring, one of Germany's most highly decorated commanders, approved Karl's suggestion and ordered the pumps draining the swamp to be stopped, and river waters released back into the marshy area. With their breeding ground re-established, mosquitos quickly re-infested the swamp, buying the German Army time to reposition itself for the Battle of Rome.

After lending his assistance in Italy, Karl returned to reviewing operations at the concentration and death camps, where he watched the systematic and efficient killing of undesirables. He continued to make process improvements in the camps and was held in great esteem among his SS peers.

Peter J. Marzano

CHAPTER EIGHTEEN

The Convent

Katrina's journey south to Bernalda during the summer of 1943 followed Italy's east coast along the Adriatic Sea. She found refuge in Catholic churches and convents along the way, using the bishop's official letter. She slept in her car a few times, and twice stayed at abbeys, where the dinner meal and wine were better than any restaurant she'd ever been to.

It only took a few days for Katrina to hand out almost her entire supply of bread to priests, nuns and poor people she saw on the side of the road pulling wagons with their belongings.

Once, she gave a family money her father had given her to buy gasoline. She could be generous since a few of the churches filled her gasoline tank at no cost.

In the northernmost Italian cities, she came across German checkpoints. Fortunately, she never had a confrontation like the one with the two drunk soldiers at the checkpoint near Lecco. As she proceeded further south, the German soldiers were mature and gracious. *If only Karl had been mature and gracious to me, we'd have a functioning family, with a beautiful child.* Katrina sighed. She regretted that night. She had struggled so. *The methamphetamine made him so strong and powerful. I had no choice but to give in.*

Her little car proved reliable for almost the entire trip. Late one evening as darkness fell, she accidentally drove into a crater left by an exploded bomb. Struggling to climb out, she walked the dark road to a nearby farm for help. An old farmer, delighted by the beauty of his visitor, brought his cow and ropes and pulled her car out of the hole. She thanked him, gave him a few lire for his trouble and said she was headed

102

to the next church identified on the pages torn from the library book. He suggested she stay at their tiny home, and its being so dark, she agreed.

The next morning as she drove, her thoughts bounced from here to there, recalling events in her life. She smiled when thinking of her father. She remembered playing games with him as a child. He'd make butter cookies shaped as Os and Xes and they would play tic-tac-toe. Whoever won got to eat the other person's O or X cookies. The loser eventually had no pieces to play with. Her papa so enjoyed letting her win. As she got older, she learned to play his favorite card game, *Scopa*. She regretted not spending more time in the bakery, to learn to make bread and pastries. She was still hoarding some of the bread her papa had given her when she left, and treated herself with a bite every so often. It was delicious even hard.

As Katrina continued south, she noticed dust in the distance and saw it was a group of soldiers approaching. It was her first encounter with such a large troop. Nervous, she pulled to the side of the narrow road.

As they neared, she saw their uniforms were different. The soldiers had fair hair and wore berets – a few were smoking pipes. To her surprise, they sang as they marched. One soldier, dressed in a peculiar outfit, played a very strange-sounding device with bags and pipes sticking out of it. The entire group of fifty or sixty men marched in a column, followed by two armored vehicles and a covered truck pulling a large tank with the word "petrol." Leading all the men was a low green vehicle with knobby tires and no roof. A long antenna and machine gun were mounted on the back. A few smiled and waved to her. A few whistled to the song and the odd music. Just then the jeep pulled over and stopped next to her.

The driver spoke in broken Italian. "*Senora, chi sei e dove vai?*"

"*Mi chiamo 'e Katrina. Sto andando a un convento a Bernalda.*" Then she said, "*Aspetti, per favore.*" She reached down to the passenger-side floor. They all reacted, each soldier pulling a gun from his holster and pointing it at her.

To their surprise, she lifted a bag of pastries. "Sfogliatelle! Made by my father in his bakery."

Their eyes widened. They lowered their guns, smiled and took the pastries.

"*Grazie! Mille grazie, senora!*"

In the little English she knew, she said, "Are you Americans?"

"No, we are Scots from Aberdeen way. Young lady, it should be safe as you continue south, but carefully watch the roads for craters. Okay! *Andiamo…* uh, I mean, let's go, everyone."

The bagpipers began playing again and the singing and whistling resumed. The colorful Scots headed north. As they marched away, she smiled at seeing a few in colorful plaid skirts.

Later that afternoon she came to a church, pulled up and parked. Katrina knocked. There was no answer. She went inside, stepping into the tiny chapel, but found no one. It appeared abandoned.

Tired from the day's drive, Katrina decided to sleep in her car. She pushed and tilted the seat back, then bunched some clothing against the window. As she drifted into sleep, she saw baby Bruno. She reached for him and pulled him tightly against her breast. *I love you, my son. I'll always love you.*

Two more days passed, and Katrina finally arrived in Bernalda. After asking for directions to the Convent of the Holy Angels, she drove another half mile and arrived just past 6.

Exhausted, she parked her car, made the sign of the cross and wept. After a minute, she gathered her composure, grabbed her two clothing bags and went to the front door. She gently tugged on the white knotted rope, and heard the bell ring inside. It sounded like a tiny bell to summon an angel.

Within a minute, a small nun came to the door. "Yes, can I help you?"

"Hello, my name is Katrina Amorino. Please, I'm here to see Sister Maria Cassano, the Mother Superior."

"Good afternoon. Oh, excuse me, it's past 6 and I should be saying 'good evening.' I'm Sister Carmella. Please come in. Put your bags down over there and have a seat. Mother Superior is at vespers now. She will be here to greet you in a few minutes."

Ten minutes passed before Mother Superior came to the foyer. She wondered who it could be from Sister Carmella's interesting description.

Katrina introduced herself. Sister Maria immediately recognized her and gave her a big hug and kiss.

"Oh Katrina! For so many years your mother wrote, telling me all about you! You are more beautiful than I ever imagined. I'm so excited you have come to visit. Come with me, dear. You must have had a long journey and I bet you're hungry, too. Let's go inside. You can freshen up. Then we'll have a bite to eat, and you can tell me why you're here."

After washing up in a room off the main hallway, Katrina joined the Mother Superior in a private room, away from the other sisters eating their dinner. In the main dining room, Sister Carmella quickly spilled the news of a beautiful woman with blue eyes showing up with her bag at the front door. A buzz spread among the nuns as they ate. Everyone was curious.

Katrina thanked Mother Superior for welcoming her so graciously, then slowly told her tale. A few minutes had passed before Katrina's tears began to flow – as did Sister Maria's. The Mother Superior asked Katrina to pause, and she rang the bell for Sister Carmella, who arrived promptly – almost as if she were standing right outside the door.

"Two dinners, please, with tea and dessert afterward."

"Yes, Mother." And off went little Sister Carmella to the kitchen.

Over the next two hours, Katrina opened herself completely to Sister Maria. "I so regret my poor judgment and all the mistakes that followed. I hope a prayerful life will let me start again with a clean slate."

Katrina presented Bishop Giovanni DiBotticino's official letter of permission for her to enter the convent. But it was unnecessary. Maria would help her cousin Lucia's daughter any way she could; she didn't require a bishop's note or any official approval. But, having heard the young woman's story, she recognized it would be a long journey ahead for Katrina.

Three days passed before the Mother Superior introduced Katrina to the sisters. Two additional days passed before the new arrival began wearing a postulant's habit and joined in prayers in the chapel. Quickly accepted by all the sisters, her natural beauty amazed them. They all wondered at her presence there, but only Mother Superior knew the full story – and it would remain that way.

A month after Katrina's arrival, Sister Carmella brought in a letter that had come via the church mail addressed to Mother Superior from Bishop DiBotticino. It discussed welcoming Katrina Amorino into the community and shared details regarding her history. He said chances of her successfully following through with the long-term commitment to becoming a cloistered nun were, in his opinion, less than 25 percent. And having heard Katrina the night she arrived, the Mother Superior fully understood the bishop's comments and underlying concerns regarding her life within the convent.

The bishop ended his letter saying the DiBotticino Family Trust would send a dowry after Katrina's first six months in the convent, and finance her stay for as long as she remained there.

Mother Superior set the bishop's note in her desk, not mentioning it to Katrina. She'd already reached a similar opinion on the viability of Katrina's becoming a cloistered nun. In the six weeks Katrina had been there, some days she was happy, performing as a nurse helping older nuns. Other days she seemed sad and would cry for no apparent reason. Maria could see giving up the baby weighed heavily on the young woman. She realized Katrina's litany of sorrows might never leave her.

As December arrived, a dozen nuns decorated the chapel for Advent and Christmas. Three sisters and Katrina retrieved the boxes full of decorations from the convent's basement and set up the Nativity scene next to the altar.

After hanging several items and unwrapping the figures of Mary and Joseph, the oldest nun picked up the Baby Jesus figure and handed it to Katrina.

"Isn't he cute? We always have the newest postulant put him into the crib."

Busy in her own thoughts, Katrina reached for the figurine of the infant. Then, as the nun's words registered, she pulled her arms back. She covered her face with her hands, fell to her knees and began sobbing.

Mother Superior, hanging decorations with several other nuns in the rear of the chapel, heard the commotion. She looked toward the front altar.

"Oh, no, Katrina must have fallen." She hurried to the front of the church.

"Did she fall from the ladder?"

"No, Mother."

Then, seeing the figurine in the hands of the older sister, she knelt on the floor beside Katrina. She took the younger woman in her arms and comforted her, rocking back and forth.

She whispered, "Dear, I know why you are crying. You must trust God. Your child is fine. Now, let's go inside to my office."

She stood and helped Katrina, still sobbing, off the floor. Katrina suddenly pulled back from Maria. Then, loudly enough for all the other nuns to hear, she said, "I've made a terrible mistake letting my baby be adopted. God forgive me for what I've done by letting him go. What a terrible mistake I've made!"

Hearing her words about giving up her baby, the other nuns had their first insight into why Katrina was so upset – and perhaps why she was there in the convent. They looked at each other in sad disbelief.

Maria reached out and pulled Katrina to herself; together they walked from the chapel back to her office. Departing, Mother Superior said to the sisters, "Have Sister Carmella bring some tea and cookies to my office."

They walked back slowly along the corridor as Katrina continued to sob. "I'm sorry, Mother, for making a scene. But it hurts. I so regret what I've done."

"Now, dear, have a cup of tea and a nice almond biscotti, then take the rest of the evening away from the other sisters and get a good night's rest. I'll have Sister Carmella bring your supper to your room. Tomorrow will be sunny. Let's you and I plan for a walk around our grounds after noon prayers and lunch. See you at Mass in the morning. Good night, sweetheart."

Christmas arrived. Katrina recalled decorating their two houses with Valentina, and their disappointment at Karl's not showing up. And despite the infectiously joyous spirit of the other sisters in the convent, she cried.

***

During 1944, Katrina participated in all the activities of community life inside a convent. Her nursing skills continued to be a huge help to the older sisters. Maria let her know how grateful she and all the other sisters were for her assistance. Mother Superior often reflected on God's infinite wisdom and plan that brought Katrina and her skills to the Convent of the Holy Angels in a time of need, as some of the sisters were in their final years.

Over time, Maria had several heart-to-heart talks with Katrina about religious life. In those chats with Sister Katrina – Mother Superior spoke more formally, as she would with a postulant. Each time, Maria tried to gain new insight into Katrina's state of mind. *Are her hopes and dreams focused on being a cloistered nun the remainder of her life, or is there a tiny flame still burning inside her that could someday rekindle itself in a quest for love with a man? Might she eventually move on? I believe Katrina wonders, too.*

The responses she heard from Katrina continued to vary. A wise woman, Maria grew ever more convinced the convent wasn't a forever commitment for Katrina. In response to the irregularities she heard, and recalling the bishop's concerns, Maria prolonged the timeframe for Katrina's steps toward professing her final vows. Her explanation was simple. "Sister, thank you for your work inside the convent. More time and prayer are needed in preparation for taking your final vows."

Katrina, not knowing her path was outside the normal timeframe, accepted it without question.

***

In the fall of 1944, when Katrina finished a long day caring for a sick sister, she knocked at Mother Superior's office door.

"Please come in."

After being welcomed with a hug, Katrina sat and broke down, crying. "Mother, my emotions are all over the place. I'm exhausted. I'm having doubts. I'm just not sure I'm cut out for this life."

"Come, let's go have a cup of tea."

They went to the kitchen, put the kettle on and sat down.

Mother Superior told Katrina a story. "It was the end of May in 1907 in Ciampino, a small town outside Rome, when three young men – friends since childhood – were deciding on their next day's adventure, having just completed their secondary schooling. They came up with the idea of enjoying Rome for a day as if they were tourists. One young man made a list of what he wanted to see, and the others agreed. Their list included the Colosseum, the Trevi Fountain, the Spanish Steps and a visit to St. Peter's. It would be a long walk to get there, but they were young and well fit for their outing.

"The same day of their adventure, a group of five teenage girls arrived in Rome from Bernalda. Recently graduated from their parish secondary school, they were led by a nun who sponsored the trip. The purpose of the trip was to give them a chance to see Rome before they made decisions about entering the convent in Bernalda."

Katrina's blue eyes fixed on Mother Superior's as she spoke. She wondered what this story had to do with her.

Mother Superior smiled. "Your mother and I were two of the girls on that trip. We'd lived next door to each other since we were born; we played and studied and spent all our time together, every day of our lives. We were so excited and nervous to be in such a large city. The night we arrived, we ate and slept at a local convent, and the next day we toured the city.

"That day, the three friends made good time walking to Rome. After touring the Colosseum, they headed to the Trevi Fountain. We were headed there, too, led by the old nun. Once we arrived, she told us, 'Girls, it's customary to make a wish and then toss a coin into the fountain. Here is a coin to throw. Now go and wish for a beautiful life in the convent.'

"Your mother and I were the last in line to get a coin to throw. Coins in hand, we walked to the fountain. I closed my eyes, made my wish and threw in the coin. But as your mother prepared to throw hers, it slipped from her hand. She watched it roll away about fifteen feet... before it struck the shoe of a teenage boy. Seeing the coin rolling straight toward him, the boy started laughing at the girl chasing it. When your mother picked up her coin, she stood up and came face to face with the young man – your father. They smiled at each other, and your father peered into Lucia's eyes. She thought he was so handsome, and he was taken by her beauty. Lucia later told me he said to her, 'Your coin found me even before you made a wish. Now let's go make a wish together.'

"They walked over to the fountain and, together, threw their coins into the water. Then Dino introduced himself, wrote his name and address on a piece of paper and gave it to Lucia. She told me he said, 'You are incredibly beautiful. I wished we will meet again and spend time together. Please write to me. I'm sincere in asking.'

"I had already rejoined the others. Maybe two minutes had passed when I suddenly missed your mother. I looked back and saw her talking with the young man. Then I nudged the nun who'd brought us and said, 'Look. Remember, Sister, I told you this trip might not work for Lucia.'

"On the trip home, Lucia told me she was attracted to the young man with the deep-blue eyes. An hour later, she said she had wished they would see each other again, but didn't say she had his address. Your mother always seemed more interested in boys than the convent. During the next month, I struggled with the idea of being separated from your mother while preparing to enter the convent. I loved her so much.

"Unbeknownst to me, your mother met your father in Naples that August; they spent a day visiting the historic sites of Pompeii and Herculaneum. Your father's fountain wish came true; they fell in love. The next day, she told me she wouldn't be entering the convent. I said when I couldn't find her the day before, I somehow knew. I was happy she had finally decided. I told her I'd met with Sister and set a date to enter Holy Angels convent a few weeks later."

Katrina said to Maria, "I only knew they met in Rome, but never knew the details."

Mother Superior nodded, smiling at her long-ago memories. "Your father was in love; he wanted to marry your mother and he wanted to start a business. He'd spent a month with his nonna, training to become a baker. He left Ciampino for Naples, where he worked as a pastry chef in the Grand Hotel Cocumella in Sorrento, overlooking the Bay of Naples. After several more visits, your parents eloped, marrying in a tiny chapel in Positano. They settled in Sorrento. It wasn't long before your father wanted to open a bakery for himself, specializing in breads and pastries. Then he decided to move to Lecco and open a bakery.

"Lucia wrote to me often, telling me people as far away as Milan, Bergamo and Brescia went to your father's bakery to buy his breads – and especially his sfogliatelle. You arrived soon afterward. Your mother kept me abreast of your activities in school, skiing and when you went into nursing. But her letters slowed ten years ago, and stopped six years ago."

Mother Superior smiled, then took Katrina's hands. "Katrina, you have become a beautiful woman, like your mother. You've got your father's beautiful blue eyes and strong will, and your mother's loving nature. You've seemed like a daughter to me all these years because your mother wrote so many letters to me about you. Perhaps she didn't want to tell me you'd met a man and moved to Germany. My dear cousin, what you've been through these past years is terrible. You need more time to rest and rejuvenate your spirit. I want you to take the next few days away from working in the infirmary. When you're more rested and relaxed, you can again assist the elderly nuns."

"Yes, you're right. Thank you so much, Mother." Katrina stood to leave.

"Before you go, I have good news to share with you. First, your sponsor was elevated to cardinal two months ago. Giovanni Cardinal DiBotticino is already living in the Vatican. And, just moments ago, I received a letter. We've been notified a new priest has been assigned to Bernalda. It says, 'Father Luca Luciano is the new pastor of your parish, and he's also responsible for the care of your convent and your sisters.' "

Maria looked at the note again, this time taking a bit more time and reading it aloud.

"Father Luciano should arrive in town by... well... as I re-read this closer, he's... my goodness! He's already here in Bernalda! And he's coming to visit... what's today's date? Oh my! It looks like he'll be here tomorrow. I somehow missed that!"

"That's wonderful news, Mother. And thank you for our chat. I will pass on supper this evening, go upstairs and go right to sleep."

111

As Katrina walked away with her tea and biscotti in hand, Maria reflected on Katrina's emotions and mood swings. They were difficult, and her sorrows painful and deep. *Please God, I hope guidance from the new priest will help her.*

CHAPTER NINETEEN

Organization Todt

Karl continued working as a consultant, supporting several SS officers running death camps. His newest assignment was at the Ravensbrück camp, which opened in 1939 with nine hundred women.

By 1942, the number of women in Ravensbrück had swelled to ten thousand. Three to four women slept together in each bunk, and bunk beds stood three levels high. Harsh working conditions and cold winter months caused deaths to increase – but not fast enough. The camp bulged well beyond its newly expanded capacity.

The Nazi camp commander initiated a new plan to decrease the number of women with additional hard labor, starvation and by implementing a variety of unethical medical experiments. In August 1942, the new camp commander, SS Captain Fritz Suhren, invited Karl in to look around and give him some ideas.

Shortly after his arrival, and with Karl's advice, Suhren decided to begin gassing and cremating the women held there. But before the new gas chambers and furnaces were completed, the camp's infirmary began killing them with a more complex set of experiments and lethal injections; others were sent to Auschwitz-Birkenau, where the hard labor killed them.

The war delayed the arrival of Organization Todt's construction team members – they didn't arrive until the September of 1944. Karl was invited to return and quickly designed and managed the construction of the new gas chambers and crematorium he'd proposed two years earlier. By mid-December, construction was completed, and Karl began to oversee the effectiveness of the new equipment.

In March 1945, Karl was recalled, and subsequently assigned to the Bendlerblock building in Berlin by Field Marshal General Kristofer von Schultz.

Incredibly, between December 1944 and April 1945, some five thousand women were gassed to death and cremated at Ravensbrück.

CHAPTER TWENTY

Father Luca Luciano

I n late summer 1944, fifteen months after Katrina's departure for the convent, Pope Pius XII summoned then-Bishop Giovanni DiBotticino to the Vatican.

"Giovanni, the Church needs your help. With the Germans expelled from Rome this past June – thank God for the Americans and the Allies – I want you to come and live here in the Vatican. I want you to oversee reconstruction of every Catholic church damaged by the war from Naples south to Reggio, Calabria. Your second task is to ensure every church in that same area has a priest. You must return immediately to Brescia, and identify your replacement there. I will expect you back here in six weeks' time. Once you arrive, you'll be elevated to cardinal to carry out your responsibilities. Go now with my blessings."

Giovanni returned to Brescia and selected his trustworthy associate during the challenges of the past two years as his replacement. Then he returned to Rome and took residence inside the Vatican. Only a week passed when a ceremony was held elevating only Giovanni to cardinal. It was a surprise to many, since normally several men would be elevated at the same time.

Within a day, Giovanni Cardinal DiBotticino began his review of the churches reporting damage, and those lacking priests. Then he made a list of deserving young priests eligible to become pastors. After reading through resumes, Giovanni paired up churches and priests – as to the best fits, based on what he knew about each priest and what the people had written regarding their needs.

Having read notes from a parish in Bernalda with a cloistered convent attached, Giovanni decided to pair it with a conservative young priest whom he felt was a good candidate for a parish pastorate. After reviewing the man's background, Giovanni summoned Father Luca Luciano to his office later that day. Ordained a year earlier, he was the son of a wealthy family dealing in finances and banking. The Luciano family heritage reached back to the 1200s and was tied to the Kingdom of Sicily. Luca Luciano was his mother's tenth child and dedicated by his parents at his baptism to enter religious life.

During their meeting, Giovanni spoke with Luca about his faith and love of helping others, especially those in the Ghetto, and about an interesting note in his personnel file. Luca, a bright student, loved the arts and theater. During his teenage years, he'd sneak away after school and spend time watching actors practicing for the town's plays. One summer evening after a rehearsal, a woman twice his age approached Luca.

The seduction was quick. The secret pleasures they shared for the next two months were intense, and he naïvely fell in love. One evening, one of his sisters followed him, wondering where Luca spent his spare time. She followed him to an actors' rehearsal at the town's theater, hid carefully and then saw him backstage kissing a voluptuous woman while reaching under her skirt. The following day, Luca was sent by his father to the Capuchin Crypt, in Rome. For the next year, Luca lived with the Capuchin Order, forced to study Latin, French and German, and serve in all their ceremonies as an acolyte.

As Luca sat with the cardinal during his interview, he explained what had happened with the actress, including being caught by his sister.

"I need to confess that at times my desire for the woman remains, and it occasionally challenges my chastity. Being found and being sent to the crypt with the Capuchins was a difficult and humbling experience. When those feelings arise, I think of the crypt. I was grateful to be there to correct my sinfulness, but even more grateful to leave the Capuchins when I was accepted into the seminary to train for the priesthood here in Rome."

Giovanni thanked him for his openness and said he would follow up soon. After the interview, Giovanni considered Father Luca's circumstances. He also read about the exceedingly generous donation by the

Luciano family and hoped to take advantage of their generosity once again.

Luca was a good man and a kind priest. His good works with the poor in Rome were notable, especially as a seminarian within the Jewish Ghetto area. The Ghetto was established in 1555 by Pope Paul IV when all rights granted to Roman Jews were revoked. Luca's service for those in need in the community was exemplary in so many ways. Sadly, on October 16, 1943, he witnessed the Nazis round up and capture more than a thousand Jews in their homes, and load them onto a train bound for Auschwitz. Luca was crushed by the event and cried that night in the Vatican. Reading about this, Giovanni felt Luca's heart was ready to serve as a pastor, having personally witnessed the Nazis' imprisonment of the Jews, and despite his youthful infatuation and indiscretion with an older woman.

Two weeks after his interview, Father Luciano received a letter from the cardinal, assigning him to Holy Angels parish in Bernalda. It said in addition to his duties to the Catholic faithful of the parish, he would act as spiritual advisor for a convent of cloistered nuns attached to the church. Father Luca was happy to be given a parish. As for the nuns, he was nervous, but because they were cloistered contemplatives, he felt relieved. With their lives devoted to prayer, there was zero chance he could become distracted or become attracted to anyone.

***

The Holy Angels parishioners greeted Father Luciano's arrival in Bernalda enthusiastically, and many local Catholics returned to church. Luca quickly identified and prioritized the parish's needs, and posted them on the door of the church – an uncommon thing to do.

He took immediate steps to correct building and property issues; and, thanks to increased Sunday attendance and donations, local contractors making the improvements were paid in full and not asked to donate their services. The cardinal approved his idea for a late-afternoon vigil Mass each Saturday, so parishioners could sleep late Sunday mornings. They loved him for this.

Next, Luca focused on the convent, meeting weekly with the Mother Superior. As pastor, he was responsible for the convent's budget and addressed several of its neglected building-maintenance issues. In addition, Father Luciano served the convent by hearing the confessions of the sisters and, after his first month there, he offered to speak with them individually, outside the confessional, if the sister requested. And even as a small group for the few more bashful sisters.

In those open conversations he witnessed the nuns' deep spiritual devotion. He was amazed, and wondered whether he could ever reach the deep level of devotion and prayerfulness these sisters exhibited. Their commitment to their spiritual lives was beyond what he had seen among clergy, even the most pious at the Vatican.

CHAPTER TWENTY-ONE

Rethinking Convent Life

At their last meeting in May 1943, after Katrina relinquished her child and Giovanni had given her permission to enter the convent, Bishop DiBotticino told her, "Katrina, the call of a vocation into religious life isn't easy. And entering a cloistered convent is even harder. Giving up worldly possessions and devoting one's life to prayer is a huge challenge, and it's not for the weak of spirit. And remember, my dear, the sacrifice of being celibate is extremely difficult, especially for those who have experienced life's physical pleasures, as you have."

Giovanni had concluded she was not as interested in a religious life as she was in running away from the crushing experience of leaving her baby, and hiding from the man who raped her. He believed Katrina would eventually change her mind, and not stay longer than three years. Nevertheless, he signed the paper allowing her to enter the convent in Bernalda.

Now, 18 months later, the bishop's words occasionally echoed in the back of Katrina's mind. He was right – her devotion was teetering. Her time with a sweet and gentle Italian boyfriend who became a soldier was tender and too brief. And then there was Karl. Both men exposed her to deep feelings of being drawn to the flesh. At times she still couldn't escape her desires.

It was November 1944, and for the past month, Katrina revisited her reasons for entering the convent daily. Her moments with the Italian were a gentle and precious memory. But she felt especially guilty for her sexual behavior with Karl in her apartment that night and the next morning. She believed it ultimately led to her being raped, the pregnancy and the child. She had asked herself many times if her encounter with him was a simple infatuation, or a mature love from which children should come. Sadly, she knew the answer.

Her second reason for being in the convent was to pray for Karl's soul. She was sorry he had made such terrible mistakes and feared he'd be headed to eternal damnation for his leadership role and participation in the brutalization and extermination of the Jews and others. His role in helping to facilitate the slow, painful deaths of those in the concentration and death camps was horrific. He was so unlike his mother, whose last words with Katrina were a crushing reminder of how bad decisions and mistakes hurt relationships and marriages. She felt so sorry for Valentina, who had to endure physical and emotional suffering at the end of her life, without the comfort of her formerly loving husband.

But now, it was clear. Katrina discovered how deep her painful and guilt-ridden feelings were about giving up her baby. No amount of prayer could fill her emptiness. She felt so sorrowful inside! There was no answer. She felt so alone. Her decision to send her baby away to be adopted had been too hasty. It remained Katrina's deepest regret and sat atop her litany of sorrows.

Now, despite her time in the convent, she struggled even more, day to day. She felt her desire to help others was sincere, but her prayers seemed fruitless, going unanswered. She clearly recognized now she was misplaced in the convent, by her own impetuous choice.

What am I to do? What is next for me?

CHAPTER TWENTY-TWO

Katrina Shares Her Sorrow

One month after reviewing the convent's roof-replacement project, Father Luciano sat at his weekly meeting with the Mother Superior.

"Sister, I need to tell you about how the sisters' spiritual conviction moves me. My efforts to offer guidance to them continues to progress slowly, but I must tell you frankly that, in most cases, my help is unnecessary. The sisters here are blessed with such a deep sense of faith and conviction. It amazes me. No doubt, your guidance plays an important part in how the convent is so spiritual."

"Thank you, Father. I should also share with you the sisters are likewise impressed with your understanding nature. They tell me your soft manner and words have become even more gentle since their first discussions with you."

Father Luca thanked her for the feedback. Then he transitioned the discussion.

"Sister, after hearing confessions last Saturday, I do have one question about one of the sisters – the postulant who hasn't yet taken her final vows. Quite frankly, she has been on my mind quite a bit. She seems to be having a hard time. I'm not exactly sure what it is, but I'm concerned for her. I've sensed a great deal of emotion and anxiety from her."

"Father, I'm not surprised by your comments," she replied with a pensive nod. "When Sister Katrina came here a year and a half ago, it was an unusual situation and she's struggled since she arrived. From time to time her struggle grows worse. Her story is complicated. Her mother and I are first cousins. We need to pray for her. I believe you can help, perhaps by spending some one-on-one time with her. Not in the confessional, but perhaps with a simple walk in the garden."

The next morning, Mother Superior announced at breakfast there would be a small discussion group among six of the youngest nuns, plus Katrina. Father Luca would attend. Each sister would introduce herself, including where she was originally from, and explain her spiritual goals as a teenager.

The meeting took place the following week, with Father Luca and Mother Superior in attendance. As each sister spoke, Luca listened carefully, but he was distracted. He would occasionally glance at Katrina, drawn to her attractiveness, and especially to her deep blue eyes.

Then, just as it became Katrina's turn to speak, Mother Superior looked at her watch. "Oh dear. I'm so sorry, everyone, but we've run out of time. Father Luca, would you be willing to come back again to speak to the sisters?"

"Of course."

"Let me suggest we continue next week with the two sisters who have yet to speak. I'll set that up for next Wednesday after lunch. Thank you, sisters, and thank you, Father, for coming here today."

Katrina was relieved. She wasn't up for the arranged discussion, nor interested in discussing her path into religious life. Her private life before her entering the convent was something she didn't particularly care to share with the other sisters.

On the other hand, Father Luca saw the meeting as an opportunity to help Sister Katrina and looked forward to being with her in an open setting. He thought for days about what he might say. Having sensed her uneasiness and anxiety, he wondered whether she was here against her will, or had changed her mind and had doubts about being there. After all, he'd been forced by his father to serve at the Capuchin Crypt, and satisfy his parents' expectations to enter the seminary. It so happened in the past few years, he had difficult feelings about the priesthood. Was it right for him? He wasn't sure. His assignment to Holy Angels refreshed his commitment to help and serve others by his priesthood. He thought he might have a parallel set of circumstances with Sister Katrina, and he hoped to help her by dealing with his own feelings.

***

It was the beginning of March 1945, and the Lenten season had begun. Mother Superior decided to put off the follow-up meeting until after Easter, because several sisters were feeling ill. She announced the meeting's cancellation at breakfast. Katrina felt relieved at the announcement and secretly hoped it would be forgotten altogether.

Later that same afternoon, a sister in her 80s became extremely ill. She required Sister Katrina's nursing skills and personal assistance the rest of the day and throughout the night. Her advanced age made the situation exceedingly difficult and, despite help from another young sister, Katrina ended up with less than 20 minutes of sleep the entire night. As daylight approached, Katrina felt exhausted. Her hormones were elevated, and her emotions erratic.

Father Luca arrived at the convent's chapel for 7 a.m. Mass and to hear confessions afterward. When the Mass ended, the sisters lined up to enter the confessional before breakfast. Katrina, even more exhausted now, was last in line. When her turn finally came, she stepped inside the confessional. With her defenses lowered, she began by admitting having serious doubts about her religious calling.

She told Father Luca, "My presence here in the convent may not be a vocation at all, but self-imprisonment for my mistakes and wrongful deeds." She teared up.

Surprised at her admission, he leaned in and listened carefully.

Katrina started at the beginning and explained her circumstances: being attracted to a handsome German man while skiing, falling for him while he was hospitalized, sleeping with him at her apartment, quitting her job and moving into his house in southern Germany. She explained how he took SS Officer training, became radicalized, ruthlessly attacked people on Kristallnacht and killed thousands in concentration and death camps.

Jolted by her story, Father Luca felt the young woman's deep pain and sorrow as she began crying in the confessional booth.

"We never married, but he came back to the house one night… he was high on drugs and he raped me. I put up a fight. It was horrible. I became pregnant and had his baby." She cried even harder.

"Then I gave the baby up. I gave away my sweet little baby boy. How could I have done that to an innocent child, Father? What is wrong with me? I pray every day God forgives me for running away from my own child." She sobbed.

Father Luca, taken by her emotionally painful experiences, began to understand. "Sister, please take a deep breath and relax. Everything will be alright. God loves you and He forgives you."

She shook her head. "No, no, He won't. I've made some terrible mistakes. It won't be alright. It will never be alright for my baby. What have I done?" Katrina sobbed more, unable to control herself. Exhausted and overwrought, she became hysterical, crying louder and louder, the sound echoing into the chapel.

Father Luca didn't know what else to say. He opened his confessional door, stepped out and pulled the curtain aside. He reached in and offered his hand to Katrina. She grabbed it and he gently pulled her into his arms, holding her tight. She was shaking and crying. He was crying, too.

Long seconds passed before her heavy sobbing and shaking subsided. He slowly let go of her as she calmed down. Embarrassed, Katrina apologized for her outburst, and Luca apologized for the intrusion and gentle hug.

"Father, I cannot get past being forcibly raped and brutalized by Karl that night. I gave his baby away before coming here to the convent, because I wanted nothing to do with Karl. I know I was wrong to do that. And I need to tell you more about what happened while I was in Germany. Please, Father, I need your help."

"Sister, I want to listen, but I need to be back in the church for nine a.m. Mass. Let's meet tomorrow in the convent's garden after lunch. We can talk then. In the meantime, you look exhausted and in need of sleep. Remember, we are not perfect beings. We all make mistakes. But God loves you and forgives you. Go get some rest."

Katrina nodded, wiping at her tear-filled eyes. "Thank you. Thank you very much, Father."

He left for the parish church, shocked by what he had heard. All through the 9 a.m. Mass, he couldn't keep his mind off Katrina and what had just happened. He understood now why she was so broken, and he decided he'd try to help her get her life back together. As he gave the final blessing to the six old ladies in attendance, Father Luca felt a pull of wanting to know more about Sister Katrina... and even be a part of her life, going forward.

Over the next few weeks, with Mother Superior's permission and encouragement, Father Luca and Sister Katrina spent time together walking in the garden. Their discussions were frank and open. Katrina shared her feelings about wanting to leave the convent. Then he shared what had happened with the woman he'd met at the local theater as a teenager, and about being punished and forced into the priesthood. He said he couldn't forget the strong feelings the woman evoked in him, despite their brief time together. Luca then openly admitted to Katrina his own conflict about the priesthood. What he didn't share was his frequent longing for companionship from a loving and caring woman.

During April, Katrina spoke more openly with Luca as she grew more trusting of his understanding and gentle nature. They each looked forward to their time walking together. The tiny spark that had ignited between them now was an ever-present glow in their hearts and they smiled, looking at each other.

CHAPTER TWENTY-THREE

Karl's Last Assignment

D uring March 1945, sustained aerial assaults by American B-27 bombers destroyed what remained of Germany's key rail lines, causing the Wehrmacht's supply of armaments and fuel to fail. The German offensive could no longer be sustained. Troops and mechanized equipment were pulled all the way back into Germany, and then to Berlin. Pushing west, Soviet Red Army troops led by Belorussian Marshal Georgy Zhukov and Ukrainian Marshal Ivan Konev approached Berlin. From the west, the U.S. Army and its allies pushed east. The war was nearing its end as the Battle of Berlin began.

On April 25, 1945, German SS General Field Marshal Kristofer von Schultz recalled Karl von Richter to the Bendlerblock in Berlin, where German Naval officers had once been headquartered. There he'd be given his final orders.

At 6 on the morning of April 30, German war staffers heard the U.S. Army was advancing into the area southwest of Berlin. But worse, the Soviet Red Army began encircling Berlin with tanks and artillery, tightening its grip on the city, like the jaws of an alligator. They began burning files in the rear courtyard of the building, awaiting final orders to leave.

At 9:15, a radio message indicated the Soviets were about 800 meters east of the Reich Chancellery, waiting for other mobile tanks and artillery units to draw closer on different sides. No one wanted to admit this latest report had caused considerable anxiety among the SS officers and staffers still at the building.

By 10, with files still smoldering in the courtyard, the last half dozen staffers had left. Remaining were a general, three senior SS officers including Karl, two soldiers, Hanz the mechanic, and Fraulein Hilda, the buxom cook. Two other generals had left in the middle of the night, along with eight SS officers and twenty others, all headed west to surrender to the Americans.

Another radio message at 10:15 claimed the Panzer Tigers and Panthers assigned to the battle to protect the city and the Reich Chancellery were running out of fuel. It also said ground troops supporting those tanks were extremely low on or out of ammunition. One of the remaining SS officers told Karl an overnight radio message from General Weidling indicated he couldn't hold his defensive line for the Chancellery building and its bunkers more than another 24 hours.

Karl stepped outside the rear of the building and anxiously smoked his seventh cigarette as he stood with the other SS officer, awaiting their final orders. The time was growing short. In front of them waited two shiny, fully fueled and manned Tiger Panzer tanks. The morning drizzle had become a light but steady rain.

"We can use one of the tanks to pierce the Russian or American lines, then abandon it and hide," Karl told his fellow officer. "But every minute is critical. What's keeping us here? Why hasn't Herr von Schultz given us orders yet?"

Just then, Karl heard his name being called from inside. *Finally!* After another deep drag, he threw down the unfinished cigarette and stepped on it as he headed inside.

The staffer who called to him told the other officer, "Lieutenant, you and Muller are released to go. Karl, you need to go to the general field marshal's office down the hall right now."

What's this all about? Being told it's time to leave shouldn't require a meeting. Hitler flew to North Africa last night, so what are we waiting for?

Karl knocked at the frame of the general's open door. Hilda, the cook, immediately scurried out of his office, half-dressed, making Karl laugh.

"Enter."

Karl gave a salute and clicked his heels.

His commanding officer smiled. "Sit, sit."

Karl found this odd. *It is uncommon to be told to sit so quickly by a general. And what is his smile about? No doubt he's been frolicking with Hilda!*

Karl sat.

The heavyset von Schultz, standing by the leather couch, buckled and zipped his pants. His hair was messy; his still-unbuttoned shirt hung out over his pants. His big toe stuck through a hole in one sock, while his tall black boots sat at attention beside the couch. Von Schultz walked to the oak credenza, reached for a half-empty bottle and poured himself a drink.

It's 10:45 and my general field marshal looks like he's just woken up.

Karl quipped, "Herr General, has my commander just awakened from a good long sleep, or has it been a pleasant morning for you? Or, perhaps both?"

Accustomed to analyzing even the smallest actions of others, Karl enjoyed all the clues he observed. Even slight gestures were clues. But this morning's office scene was extraordinary. *Given the tensions with the Soviet Army advancing nearby, and now the general's casual behavior, there's more here than meets the eye.* It wasn't simply Sweet Hilda, as she was called by the staff, being here to satisfy the general. *Now I'm even more curious about what my general has to say.*

The general tightened his belt one more notch, as he returned to his desk. Karl wondered if he had a hangover. But his slow movement reflected the gathering of his thoughts.

What is about to happen? Something very wrong is going on. "General, please. Why am I here? Whatever it is, tell me quickly if we need to act now! Our time is limited."

The general turned and looked Karl in the eyes. "*Ausgewahlte,* a drink?

His words stunned Karl. "Herr General, what does that mean? Why have you called me 'Chosen One'?"

Karl had planned to turn down the offer of alcohol, having seen General von Schultz already drinking this morning. But now, the other man's comment piqued Karl's interest, and he agreed.

The general reached back to the credenza, grabbed a clean glass and handed it across the desk to Karl. Then he reached for the bottle that held the finest 25-year-old Benedictine liqueur ever produced.

"This Benedictine is straight from France, where I was stationed two years ago," he explained. "I've carried three cases with me and, sadly, it's almost finished. Just like all of us are almost finished.

"Karl, do you know what the D.O.M. on the label stands for? The letters stand for the words '*Deo, Optimo Maximo.*' It means 'To God, most good and most great.' "

Karl nodded. Fluent in German, Italian and French, and a Latin student in secondary school, he knew well the meaning of the phrase. *But why the general's tone? Why his words 'almost finished' like his three cases of Benedictine? And why did he call me 'Chosen One'?*

The general moved to the side of his desk and sat on the edge. He handed Karl his drink, and with his drink in hand, looked Karl in the eye, raised his glass. "Prost!"

"Prost!" Karl replied.

"Karl, what time is it?" he asked after they'd downed their drinks.

"It's ten fifty-five."

"God damn it. Where in God's name were you last night?"

"General, I've been right here, in the building."

"Well, damn it," he shouted, pouring himself more Benedictine, "I couldn't find you. I needed you last night. You should have started this assignment last night at midnight. What is wrong with you, von Richter?"

"Herr General, I am here now. What is it you need me to do?"

The general took a sip, and his tone backed down to a regular volume. "Karl, we are at the end. The Russians have surrounded Berlin and are almost on top of us. The Americans and their Allies will be collapsing on Berlin in another day or two. God damn this headache! What is today's date? Never mind. Well, last night, or maybe it was the night before, Weidling radioed me and said he couldn't defend the city like he should. He said he was almost out of fuel and ammunition. You know what's worse than losing, Karl? What's worse is the God damn Russians are beating the Americans here. The Russians are ruthless. They hate us for Operation Barbarossa. I don't blame them, considering what we did to them."

The general poured another Benedictine for himself and offered more to Karl, who passed, with a small wave of his hand over his glass.

"Karl, two other general field marshals and I foresaw the end of the war. It was clear to us four months ago, with the Americans bombing our rail lines, all was lost. But it wasn't clear to stubborn Adolf with his stupid ideas. Even the few SS officers who tried to kill him here in this building knew it was over long ago. Damn it, we all knew we couldn't sustain the fighting. Our raw materials and resources became so limited. Once those Brits and Americans began bombing the oil fields in Ploesti, Romania, we knew we'd no longer produce the volume of fuel we needed. Our supply chain slowly failed as the rail lines were bombed. Then the Italians removed Mussolini and quit the Axis. None of our soldiers wanted to fight in Italy. Nevertheless, our soldiers fought like hell in Anzio, but we underestimated the resolve of the American 5th Army. Then we lost Rome. The war was supposed to be about making Germany great again, not about making Italy part of Germany. God damn Der Führer and his pudgy puppet, Mussolini.

"Karl, the end of World War I is repeating itself. Every German soldier was war weary back then, and Kaiser Wilhelm decided to stop fighting. Now every German soldier is war weary and we don't have the fuel or ammunition to fight, let alone the spirit." The general shook his head. "Karl, it's over. It's all over."

"Herr General, I completely understand what has happened. But why am I here now? What do you want of me?"

General von Schultz stood. "Karl, you have been selected to lead this mission because of your experience in the field, your linguistic skills and your ruthlessness. You are considered by many SS generals to be the most reliable SS officer who can lead Hitler and a small entourage to freedom. Your extensive Nazi activities, beginning with your leadership on Kristallnacht, followed by your tireless work overseeing construction of the concentration camps, have given you some of the highest credentials among all SS officers. Your distinguished background is extremely well suited to be faithful to Der Führer.

"Six months ago, I developed a plan to extract Der Führer from Berlin. I named the plan 'HOME.' It stands for 'Hitler Optimo Maximo Europa' meaning 'Hitler, most good and most great of Europe.' Like the letters on my Benedictine bottles. My plan is to extract Der Führer from his bunker and bring him – and one or two others – to safety. There are three alternatives for the Führer's escape. The first plan is to escape by air. The two other plans are by land and sea.

"Three months ago, using the SS intelligence unit and several SS officers, we initiated steps to execute that plan. Yesterday, Der Führer turned down the first plan to escape by air. Plan A had senior SS pilot Georg Betz flying Adolf and his new wife, Goebbels and his wife and their six children on a six-engine plane safely to a Nazi-friendly airport in North Africa. It was to refuel there and continue to South America. The Ju390 was designed for long-range flights to bomb American cities."

Ah, yes, the plane with the landing gear built in the Ravensburg factory my father managed. "So, what do you want me to do now? What are my orders?"

General von Schultz poured himself another Benedictine, took a sip and savored the flavor as it went down. "At dinner last evening, we learned the Führer didn't want to fly. It meant Plan B must go into effect. Plan B is to extract Der Führer by land and take him to the sea, where one of our U-boats will be waiting. This time, the extraction, by land and sea, first will be suggested, and then be by force, if necessary. We have a doctor involved who will drug Adolf without his knowledge if he resists. We will take him from his bunker on a stretcher and put him on a path to Bremerhaven.

"It was decided at dinner early last night that you, Karl von Richter, are the 'Chosen One' who will execute Plan B to lead the Führer to safety. Congratulations, Karl. But now you need to hurry. I needed to tell you this last night, and you should have left here at midnight or by one a.m. But Sweet Hilda and I were having a little party. Just the two of us. I've never had a woman like that. We drank and drank, and we must have passed out. I found her unclothed and lying partially underneath me on the couch when I woke up at four to relieve myself. I told her to stay if she wanted. She did and she took care of me again. We were awake for a good while, drank another half bottle and slept soundly for several more hours. We just woke up, maybe fifteen minutes ago. She is such a sweet thing. This morning I gave her all my money. Ha! Too bad for her, since those German marks will be worthless tomorrow." He paused a moment, then walked to the window and looked up at the sky.

"God damn it, Adolf! I can't believe you refused to fly. What an idiot! If the world only knew the real you. Karl, deep down he's a huge coward, and his tantrums are all make-believe to act like the alpha male and make other people think he's in charge. He's only a shell of the man he once was, nothing more than a crippled drug addict. I'm not even sure why we should save his ass."

Karl's head spun from what he had just heard. He leaned forward, placed his empty glass on the desk and asked the general for another Benedictine. The general obliged. Karl downed it in one gulp, and set the glass down hard on the desk. The general poured another for Karl and himself. Glasses in hand, they looked at each other, said, "Prost" and guzzled the last of the Benedictine.

"General, how am I supposed to get Hitler to safety, and what are the details of this plan? If I was supposed to start last night, shouldn't I be going now?"

The general opened the desk drawer and removed a large envelope containing a manila file folder and two extraction plans. Karl slid out the plans and looked at the cover sheets. The plans, marked PLAN B and PLAN C, each had a cover page. Karl took 15 seconds to speed read both.

"Detailed instructions are included. There are several maps. You will find Plan C more complex, with a small addendum. Good luck."

Karl stood, put his right arm forward and upward. He clicked his heels and said loudly, "Heil Hitler! Long live the Führer! Good luck to you, Herr General."

As Karl headed toward the door, the general called out, "Just a moment, Chosen One." He handed Karl a small blue silk purse. "Here, young man. This is for you. Good luck."

Karl thanked the general, put the purse in his deep pants pocket and left the office.

The general sat down, then picked up the bottle and looked at the letters D.O.B. He sighed. He thought, again, about his three cases of Benedictine. Pleased with himself for having created the extraction plans for Hitler, he believed 'HOME' was a great name.

He went to pour another, but the bottle was empty. In the next moment, he became upset again over Der Führer's refusal to fly.

Then the general called out loudly, "Hilda, Hilda, are you still out there in the hallway? Sweet Hilda?"

There was no answer. Turning back to his credenza, he picked up the empty bottle and gazed at it.

I'll never find Benedictine like this again.

Then von Schultz reached into the desk and pulled out a red purse. He opened it, placed the tiny cyanide pill into his mouth and bit down hard.

Peter J. Marzano

CHAPTER TWENTY-FOUR

It's Time to Leave

His watch said 11:25. Already late, Karl planned to sit for five minutes, reviewing the plans and get to the bunker by 12:15. He headed up to the second floor, where he and all the other SS officers were staying. As he walked to his room, he passed by two other officers getting ready to leave the building.

"Why so serious Karl?" one asked.

"I've been drinking with a dead man. I need a cigarette."

"Here's one. Take a couple more. We're leaving in ten minutes. The two Tiger Panzers out back are fueled up and running. Don't be long. It's best we stay together."

Karl went to his room, and stuffed his duffel bag with civilian clothing, underwear and the last of his belongings, including a crumpled photo of Katrina. Then he went downstairs and sat at a small table next to a window in the dining room, just off the kitchen. Time was short, but he wanted to absorb the essence of plans B and C. He laid both sets of plans side by side and reviewed the information. He found directions, maps, U.S. dollars, French francs and British pounds, and passports for Hitler, Eva Braun, Joseph Goebbels and one for himself. No passports were enclosed for Magda Goebbels or any of their six young children.

Plan B looked detailed and well developed, doable but risky. It probably was designed to push Der Führer into choosing Plan A, the flight.

Plan C made little sense. Karl ran his fingers through his hair, shook his head and chuckled aloud. "My general! How could you have come up with this? It must have been too much Benedictine!" Then he laughed again. And yes. There it was. Evidence of a small round stain,

134

the ring from a wet drink having sat on Plan C's cover sheet at some point.

Saving Hitler now is a long shot. He definitely should have taken the plane out of Berlin. Plan B is the better choice. And this Plan C? It's trash.

Initially proud for being chosen to lead Hitler to safety, Karl now grew anxious. This morning's radio messages regarding the advancing Russians, and now knowing the end of the war was upon them, seemed unbelievable. Only yesterday, several SS officers felt the German Army defending Berlin and the Chancellery still could make one strong push back against the Soviets, and perhaps things would end there. But with today's messages, and the general's comments, little chance remained to defend the Chancellery and the Führer's bunker. And now, even getting out alive was questionable.

Just then the two SS officers came through the dining area to the kitchen to grab any food left in the refrigerator.

"Karl, now you have two minutes. We're heading west. If we're caught, it'll be safer to give ourselves up to the Amis than the Russkis we fought at Barbarossa."

Karl stuffed the information back into its envelope. He stood and looked at his two fellow officers. "Gentlemen, I have a final assignment. I'll be using the car to leave. Good luck to you both. Heil Hitler."

As they left the dining area, he saw smoke rising nearby to the east. The Red Army was close. Karl lit up the second cigarette he'd been given, wondering where he could find a few packs before leaving. While he was still looking outside, a reflection appeared in the window. Hilda, standing behind him, touched his shoulder and asked whether she could do anything for him.

Without a word, Karl led her to the pantry. For a few minutes, Hilda let Karl forget about everything. She was good. He thanked her with an American $50 bill from the envelope and cautioned her to leave as soon as possible. Sweet Hilda provided the relaxation he needed to start his final mission. As he left, his watch said 11:48.

Karl headed down the long hallway to the rear stairway. As he neared the staircase, he noticed a full carton of cigarettes on a night table in a bedroom. He grabbed it and three loose packs and threw them into the duffel bag. *A lucky find. A stash of cigarettes and a most pleasurable goodbye from Sweet Hilda.* He was all set. At the rear of the building, an unmarked olive-grey, two-door Mercedes-Benz awaited him. He opened the door, threw the duffel bag in the backseat and slid the envelope with the plans under his seat. As he got in, the staff mechanic came over.

"Sir, I filled the tank and put six five-gallon cans of gasoline into your trunk. There are two rifles, two handguns and plenty of ammunition in the rear seat. So if you hit a mine, you're toast. Sir, one more thing: A radio message fifteen minutes ago said the Soviet Red Army is approaching the Reich Chancellery from the east, north and south, but they've stopped their shelling for the last half hour. It's likely they are re-arming and refueling. Wherever you're headed, avoid bomb craters in the roads and blown-up bridges. Good luck, sir. Heil Hitler!"

As they spoke, the two Tiger tanks' powerful engines growled; the vehicles began to slowly move.

"Heil Hitler. Thanks for the fill-up and ammo. Hurry up and go jump into one of those tanks."

Karl watched the tanks leave, then headed out himself to the Reich Chancellery, where the Führer's bunker lay deep underground. It wasn't far, but based on the mechanic's advice about Russian positions, Karl took the longer route to approach from the west.

As he drove, he reviewed the Plan B strategy. He had confidence in its information, and concluded heading north to the sea, near Bremerhaven, could be achieved. Plan C had them leave Berlin and travel into southern Germany, through the Alps and then further south into Italy. Considering the Italian peninsula was already lost to the Americans and the Allies, it would be crawling with enemy soldiers.

The American soldiers are tougher than expected. All of us have been surprised by them, especially those of Italian heritage. It seemed like they were fighting to win back their homeland. But they're more sympathetic, too, and easier to trick because of their kindness.

Like most Germans, Karl had misunderstood the strong resolve of Americans to win back freedom for the European allies.

Karl opened a pack of cigarettes and lit one as he drove. It was 12:05. As he drove to the Chancellery, he recalled the opening of the new gas chambers and oxygen-injected furnaces at Ravensbrück.

Karl, the heartless monster with no conscience, no feelings of sorrow or empathy and empty inside, felt proud of his work in the death camps, knowing his reputation was unparalleled.

Even a thousand miles away, Italian Blackshirts still spoke of once meeting the infamous Karl von Richter, and of hearing about his diabolical activities in Germany. They called him "Fra Diavolo."

Peter J. Marzano

CHAPTER TWENTY-FIVE

The Chancellery

Now only two streets from the Reich Chancellery building, Karl recalled its role in German history. The building was originally the palace of a German prince.

In 1867 a military alliance of German states was organized as a unified federal state, with a presidency. Prussia's Prime Minister Otto von Bismarck became its chancellor. Four years later, when the North German Federation took over the southern German states, Bismarck became the head of the entire German Empire.

The palace later served as residence for Paul von Hindenburg, who eventually appointed Adolf Hitler, head of the Nazi Party, as the new German chancellor, on January 30, 1933.

In 1935, Hitler constructed a large addition onto the Chancellery building, with a basement. Extra-thick walls let the basement serve as a bomb shelter. In 1943, additional construction expanded and deepened the bomb shelter a level deeper than the original 1935 shelter. The lower bunker, so deep underground, required pumps to remove the water that constantly seeped in. The upper and lower bunkers, connected by a stairway, provided access to the garden behind the Chancellery.

On January 16, 1945, Hitler permanently moved into the lower level of the bunker complex with his longtime lover, Eva Braun. Martin Bormann, Hitler's right-hand man, moved in the same day. Over the next two weeks, several secretaries, a doctor, nurse and telephone switchboard operator also took up residence in the underground complex. At the same time Hitler moved into his bunker, final extraction orders were validated and signed off by the three senior SS field marshal generals residing at the Bendlerblock.

In early April 1945, Joseph Goebbels, his wife, Magda, and their six children took two rooms in the upper bunker, about the time aerial bombings by the Soviets and Americans began over Berlin. Hitler stayed on the lower level, away from much of the noise. He knew the end was near.

The Soviet Army began its Battle of Berlin offensive April 16 as artillery equipment and troops positioned themselves surrounding the city.

Hitler made his last trip from his bunker into the palace garden on April 20, his 56th birthday. On the same afternoon, the Soviet Army's artillery began bombarding Berlin heavily for the first time.

With the end of the war closing in, Hitler married Eva Braun inside his dank bunker in the late evening of April 28.

CHAPTER TWENTY-SIX

The Escape Plans

Making his last turn, Karl saw the Chancellery ahead. He recalled the calendar hanging in the kitchen's pantry.

Today is April 30. Plan B gives me seven days to deliver Hitler to the rendezvous point with the German U-boat on the north coast.

Feeling better about the Plan B timeline, he turned his mind to Plan C.

It's highly unlikely a 760-mile journey straight south into Italy through enemy-controlled territory would be successful. It makes no sense.

He looked at his watch. 12:15. He was twelve hours behind von Schultz's schedule. Suddenly his insides rolled and the queasy feeling of the last ten minutes became more serious. *Is it the sour milk I drank by accident at breakfast? Or those shots of Benedictine on top of it? Am I anxious about extracting Der Führer?*

His forehead and hands started sweating. His insides rolled over again. He pulled to the side of the road and got out just in time to throw up. Besides the bad milk, Karl no doubt felt nervous – the first time in years. He remembered having the same anxious feelings in his stomach just before the Kristallnacht raids began.

Then Karl's mind flashed back to another anxious time he'd long forgotten. It happened at the death camp where he, for the first time, had responsibility for the final phase of construction, and for initiating the new activities.

That day, the unloading of prisoners and the death process began on his signal. It was a mere wave of his hand, as he stood high above the prisoners in the three-story guard tower. From the high perch, he saw the first group of Jews being emptied from the first of three boxcars. Once unloaded, they were led down a lengthy walkway, then separated into two groups – men and women.

SS officers with rifles ordered prisoners to leave their belongings, take off their shoes and glasses, then undress. The soldiers kept saying, "Keep moving. Move to the showers. Keep moving. Move to the showers." The naked men funneled into one yard separated by a barbed-wire fence from the naked women in the adjacent yard, all in full view of each other. Everyone was crying. The 400 Slovakians remained crushed into the other two boxcars, watching what was happening, realizing the fate awaiting them. The process continued that day until all were eliminated.

Karl, still feeling the effects of his morning's nausea, wondered about the people there that day. They were the first group of Jews and Slovakians he'd personally direct to be killed in the improved, larger gas chambers.

He remembered seeing some get sick, and others lose control of their bowels while standing naked in the yards. But the men and women were meaningless to him. His singular focus was implementing Hitler's plan, the Final Solution, to cleanse Germany of these ugly deplorables.

He focused only on the efficiency of getting them gassed and moved to the ovens to be incinerated. It was a horrible scene, and less than an hour passed when the horrible smell began. Karl, the devil incarnate, proudly earned his reputation as "Fra Diavolo" – Brother of the Devil – that day.

He didn't know why that situation had come to mind, except for getting sick himself. *Why that scene? Why now?* He remembered looking down at their faces, one by one, old men and old women, young men and young women.

Had Karl's conscience, muted years ago by Goebbels' anti-Semitic propaganda during Himmler's Nazi SS officer training, suddenly re-awakened? Or was it because now, it was his turn to fight for survival, as he extracted Hitler to escape Germany? Would he survive this daring maneuver to move Hitler to the north coast for the waiting U-boat? Perhaps all his concerns suddenly overwhelmed him and made him anxious and sick to his stomach.

Karl walked back to the car, and got in. He began to process the escape.

With so many American and Soviet ground troops nearby, it will be hard to hide three people and myself. If Adolf refuses, I'll have him drugged, and I can limit it to him, me and one other to help carry him initially. Moving any distance with three people won't be easy. Our best option is just the Führer and me on the run. That's what I'll do. I'll kill the other person with us, and it'll just be Der Führer and me headed to the submarine.

Just one detail stood in Karl's way: He was unaware of Adolf's marriage to Eva.

CHAPTER TWENTY-SEVEN

Heading to the Chancellery

At 12:20 p.m. Karl started the car; only three minutes later he arrived at the driveway leading into the Chancellery. At hearing an artillery shell scream by and hit a nearby building, Karl fretted, shaking his head, and spoke aloud, as if to a ghost companion.

"It's much too late. My arrival and extraction of Der Fuhrer should have happened seventy-two hours ago – and no less than thirty six hours ago. This timing is bad. If Der Führer refused to fly, he should have been drugged then and flown out of Berlin. He would have woken as the plane crossed the Mediterranean. That's how I would have done it. But now I must execute risky Plan B.

"By now the Red Army and American forces have surely encircled Berlin. Escaping won't be easy. The overnight delay by my foolish general is perhaps the biggest mistake of all! What an idiot! All these men in high places – what idiots they all are!"

***

Unknown to Karl, SS Commander Wilhelm Mohnke, responsible for protecting Berlin's central government district, visited Hitler inside the bunker early last night, April 29.

"My Führer, we can hold off the enemy for another twenty-four hours at most," he'd said. An experienced commander, he understood the Battle of Berlin was nearing its end.

Mohnke joined the Nazi Party in 1931 and became an original member of the SS Staff Guard formed in 1933. After Karl's initial SS role in the design and construction of death camps, he briefly joined a Mohnke-led regiment fighting in France. During his temporary assignment, Karl spent time with Mohnke discussing strategy, and playing chess. Karl later joined Mohnke's command as German forces rolled east across Poland. Mohnke commanded the SS Hitlerjugend Division in 1943, and briefly gave Karl command of a tank unit.

Mohnke admired Karl's courage and leadership on the battlefield using pincer movements against the enemy. He wrote to SS Command, suggesting Karl be promoted up the SS ranks 'for having a good and strategic mind.' Karl left Mohnke after his promotion, and Mohnke went on to lead his unit in the Battle for Caen, receiving the Knight's Cross in July, and he commanded his original division in the Battle of the Bulge in December 1944.

Mohnke again returned to the bunker at 11 p.m. "My Führer, we can no longer hold Berlin. It's time to leave. The Russians could be here by noon tomorrow. You passed on the flight, but von Schultz has another plan to move you to freedom in South America. He's been in touch with Johannes Siegfried Becker, who's been operating under the code name *SARGO* in Buenos Aires since 1940. He has a place all ready for you to go and live. We have a U-boat waiting for you at the north coast. An SS officer will be here between two and four a.m. to bring you and Eva and one or two others of your choice to safety."

Hitler, still groggy, having been awakened for the visit, perked up. He liked the idea of leaving in the middle of the night. "Whom can I expect to see?"

"You've met the SS officer once, briefly. His name is Karl von Richter. He's been selected by the SS generals to bring you to freedom. He's the young officer whose father fought bravely in World War I with Lutz, and is credited with the new tread design on our Panzer tanks, improving their traction in bad terrain. He's directed construction of new furnaces at several death camps, and served under me with high honors on the battlefield briefly as a tank commander. He's served you faithfully throughout the war and will care for you now."

Pleased, Hitler smiled. "He sounds like a good choice. Tell von Schultz I'll have a woman even better than his buxom cook waiting for him if he follows me to South America. Becker is a good Nazi. He's done well as SARGO."

After Mohnke left, Adolf told Eva to gather her jewelry and some clothing because they'd be leaving in a few hours. He asked his valet to have the bunker staff line up outside their quarters. Just past midnight, he and Eva finished their goodbyes to everyone and returned to their living room. They packed a few final items and waited patiently for the young SS officer.

Time slowed for Hitler. He became more anxious as hour after hour passed.

Finally, at 6 a.m., a new report arrived from Commander Keitel, charged with protecting the Reich Chancellery. It read, "My Führer, all is lost."

At that news, Adolf exploded into a tirade, screaming and swearing at Keitel, Mohnke and every other general in the SS high command. He screamed so loudly the guards outside Hitler's door could hear him clearly, as did the six Goebbels children several rooms away.

Unfortunately for Adolf, General von Schultz had been lulled to sleep early last night by France's finest Benedictine, and buxom Sweet Hilda. And while a frustrated and steaming Adolf screamed at 6 a.m., von Schultz and Hilda frolicked again, as Karl anxiously lay awake on a cot one floor above his general, wholly unaware of the plans sitting on his general's desk.

***

At 12:24, Karl pulled up to the main entrance of the Reich Chancellery. The morning's rain had become steady now. Two Panzer IV tanks blocked the gate. He turned his attention to Plan B's instructions:

1. Travel northwest to Duhnen.
2. Travel north of Bremerhaven.
3. Row a small boat to the island of Neuwerk.
4. Wait for a U-boat to appear.
   NOTE: It will remain submersed in daylight and surface at dusk until morning light.
5. Send a coded message using the lamp placed in the boat – spell the word "Brazil."
6. You will receive a signal back reading, "Wolf's Lair come aboard."

7. Row to the submarine and board.
8. The U-boat will arrive on May 6, and remain submerged near the island for one week.

This plan is doable, but how many people will the Führer insist upon bringing to the sea? This remains a concern. It makes our journey a challenge of unknown proportions.

The two tanks continued to block the entrance, allowing Karl to revisit Plan C. Those instructions read:

1. Travel south from the Chancellery along the route highlighted in yellow crayon.
2. DO NOT DEVIATE from the highlighted route leaving Berlin, until you are south of Bergwitz.
3. Find safe houses listed along the route, shown on the attached maps as red dots.
4. Arrive in Ravenna, Italy, and go to Punta Marina and secure a small boat.
5. In ten weeks, approximately July 15, a U-boat will appear off the coast.
   NOTE: it will remain submersed in daylight and surface at dusk until morning light.
6. Send a coded message using a lamp – you must secure – spelling the word "Brazil."
7. You will receive a return signal reading, "Wolf's Lair come aboard."
8. Row to the submarine and board.

He shook his head again. *What was von Schultz's state of mind? The highlighted maps are clear, but the driving distance seems impossible. I don't think Plan C is even legitimate. Plan B is the obvious way to bring Der Führer to safety.*

At 12:28, a commander from one of the tanks approached. He said they were waiting for some more officers and it would be two or three more minutes before they left.

Karl continued to mull issues he might face: *How patient will the submarine captain be if we are delayed? Will he be willing to wait an additional week? The U-boat could become a target if it's spotted by American aircraft on patrol. What will happen if it's attacked before we arrive? Maybe Plan C could be a fallback alternative after all, if Plan B fails or we are delayed.*

Karl checked his watch again. 12:34. He lit another cigarette, took a deep drag, exhaled and grumbled aloud. "What's taking so long for these damn tanks to move?"

As Karl continued to process his thoughts about escaping, he realized Plan C's route and timing could allow him to pass Katrina and his son in Friedrichshafen. *Maybe I could collect them and escape with the Führer to the waiting U-boat in Ravenna? We could live happily in Brazil, with Der Führer. This idea could work – especially if the Führer has just one or two people with him.*

It made him think of Katrina and seeing her again. He wondered how tall his son had grown, and was his hair deep brown like Katrina's or darker, like his? Did he have Katrina's blue eyes or his brown eyes? His daydream disappeared on hearing the engines growl and seeing the tanks roll. He took another long drag on his cigarette, then flicked the hot butt out the window. Feeling good from the nicotine, Karl said aloud, resolutely, "I will return to Germany. It may be many years from now, but I will find Katrina and my son, and I'll bring them to my new life in Brazil. For now, though, I must focus on the safety and survival of my Führer. He comes first."

The rain suddenly grew heavy. Karl's thoughts scattered. Looking outside, he admired the handsome Tiger tanks, which had caused so much damage to American forces in Anzio and along the other German defensive lines. He lit another cigarette and listened to the purr of the tanks' Maybach V-12 engines. *Brilliant, powerful engine!* Then seeing the tanks' treads, he smiled. The raised "R" on the treads' edges meant they had come from the Ravensburg Foundry. Karl nodded. *Yes, my idea was a good one!*

As the two tanks moved through the main gate, a dozen people scurried down the driveway alongside several soldiers. The women were crying. Just then, a third tank, a Panther, rumbled down the driveway, with ten soldiers in full gear beside it. He waited for the third tank to pass, then shifted into gear and drove to the rear of the building, toward the bunkers. *Something bad has happened. There must be a new report. The Russians must be awfully close. Perhaps the Führer told everyone to leave the bunkers, so they are not in danger.*

Karl approached the top of the driveway and stopped. He rolled down the window and showed his identification to two soldiers. "I have an envelope for Joseph Goebbels in the bunker."

"Okay. Proceed."

Why are only two guards stationed here instead of the usual four?

As Karl drove slowly, several more uniformed soldiers and an officer walked down the narrow driveway. Everyone's eyes looked glazed over. *What have they seen?* Stone walls bordering each side of the long narrow driveway led to the rear of the old palace. Karl made the final turn toward the palace garden, where the road widened. He pulled to the side for what seemed to be the last tank. The steady rain lightened a bit.

The envelope next to Karl contained not only Plans B and C and their accompanying paperwork, but also the small silk purse von Schultz had given him. Karl's pride led him to believe it might be an Iron Cross medal of honor for saving Hitler. While waiting for the final tank to pass, he reached into the envelope, grabbed the purse and opened it. Inside, a decorative gold box with a porcelain painted cover shone brightly. It looked like one of those vintage Easter eggs designed by Peter Fabergé.

He opened the box. Inside was no medal, but a small, curled note. He unfurled the paper, and a tiny capsule rolled into his palm. The note said,

"Place this cyanide capsule in your mouth and bite down if you are about to be captured."

Captured? Karl scoffed aloud. "We will not be captured! I will deliver Der Führer to safety." He paused and thought.

And I will someday return home to Katrina.

CHAPTER TWENTY-EIGHT

Confusion Outside the Bunker

The last tank passed by. Karl rounded the final bend, arriving in the courtyard alongside the Chancellery garden. There seemed to be confusion among six people running back and forth. Several others ran down the driveway, to catch up to the last tank.

A few yards away, Karl recognized several SS officers. Beyond the edge of the building, something smoldered. He shut off the ignition. The rain held down the rising smoke from whatever lay burning on the ground. As he opened the door, an ugly, familiar stench filled his nose. He flicked his cigarette to the wet ground and stepped on it as he got out. Surveying the scene, he spotted Erich Kempka, Hitler's personal chauffeur, whom he knew from past meetings.

Erich looked up. "Karl! You're just in time to help. Come here. Quickly!"

Karl quickly covered the twenty feet that separated them.

"We need more gasoline."

"Erich, what's happening? What's that burning? It smells like a death camp!"

Kempka looked at Karl with a huge grin on his face. "Surely you must recognize the stench. Word among the SS officers is you've burned thousands of bodies at our death camps. Aren't you known as 'the Brother of the Devil' because of your experience at the gas chambers and the ovens?"

"Yes, yes, okay. But what's that you're burning over there?"

"Come, look for yourself. Look closely. It's Hitler and Eva. Their fate arrived this morning at eleven. Eva bit a cyanide pill, and Hitler shot himself with his Luger. We can't believe he committed suicide! We need to pour more gasoline on their bodies to be sure they're burned to ashes. The rain's getting heavy again – and it's making a mess of everything."

Karl moved in closer.

The bodies lay in a small depression carved out by a bomb that exploded just in front of the bunker's emergency exit, by the ventilation shaft. Hitler and Eva lay there – their bodies smoldering in front of him. He took a few steps forward to get a better look at Adolf. But his features were already unrecognizable.

"Just a few days ago, I wished our Führer a happy birthday and we spent fifteen minutes over there in the garden. We chatted about old times, when the Nazi Party was forming," Erich said. "Did you know he just married Eva yesterday? She was beautiful – only thirty-three years old. Frankly, I have no idea what she ever saw in him. I don't understand why he's done this to her and to himself.

"Traudl, his young secretary, said Mohnke went to see him late last night and Hitler seemed fine. He and Eva lined up the entire staff just before midnight and said goodbye to everyone, including me. Their bags were packed. We all thought they were headed to a more secure location. Then about seven this morning, Mohnke came to see Goebbels, to convince him and Magda to leave with their children. Mohnke didn't realize Hitler was still here. Hitler started screaming at Mohnke at the top of his lungs, loud enough for the guard outside his door and everyone in the bunker to hear.

"Forty-five minutes after Mohnke left, Albert Speer showed up. It was about eight fifteen. He was with Adolf for ten minutes, then left. All was quiet for the next two hours. Not hearing anything from them, Heinz Linge, Adolf's valet, knocked to see if they needed anything. When there wasn't an answer, went inside and found Eva poisoned by cyanide. She was at Adolf's feet.

"Hitler put a gun into his mouth and shot himself. Linge said the bullet badly disfigured the front of Adolf's head. He wasn't even recognizable. We don't know what set him off. But one thing did seem odd: Hitler's gun had a silencer on it."

Karl retrieved a can of gasoline from his car and handed it to Kempka, who poured the five gallons of fuel onto the burning bodies in the depression. As the flames flared, they felt the heat and heard the fat and soft tissue of the bodies sizzling.

"Heinz wrapped their bodies in blankets," Erich said. "Gunsche carried them up from the bunker, but he made the mistake leaving them in the blankets. The wool didn't want to burn, and the darn fire went out. It was a mess. We had to unwrap the bodies, then pour more gasoline to restart the fire. Then it started raining heavily. Gunsche laughed, saying, 'If von Richter were here, the cremation would have been done properly to begin with.' Otto left with Traudl. She's been his new girlfriend since her husband died."

With a grim look of acknowledgment, Karl offered Erich his assistance to finish.

"No thanks. I think we're all done here. Karl, it's over... the war is finally over."

Karl stared at the flames consuming the bodies and listened to the crackling. It was 1:05. Shocked and speechless, he removed his hat and ran his fingers through his hair. The rain, pouring again, ran down Karl's face, masking his tears. He looked down again at Hitler's body; the ugly smoke stung as it drifted into his eyes. Starting to shake, Karl put his hat back on and reached for a cigarette. He tried but couldn't light it, then threw the wet cigarette to the ground.

Why did my Führer despair? He knew I was coming to take him to freedom. Yes, I should have been here ten hours ago. Our leader is dead. Erich is right, now the war will end.

Karl and Erich moved back from the burning bodies. Kempka had enjoyed his role driving Der Führer, and Karl had proudly carried out Hitler's Final Solution – the genocide of the Jews. But now, in these few moments of silence, both men reflected. They glanced at each other but said nothing. The killing perpetrated by the German war machine was over. Hitler's death now freed everyone from the tyranny.

Karl assessed the situation in front of him. *What has the fighting and killing in France, Italy and Russia accomplished for Germany? We have not achieved the promised greatness. And what becomes of those escape plans? The U-boats will be waiting. What am I to do next? Being here isn't safe. I need to leave – and quickly!*

Karl realized he must survive the end of the war. He knew from the mechanic's comments while leaving the Bendlerblock the Soviet Red Army commanders were zeroing in on the Chancellery and preparing for their final assault. Russian intelligence undoubtedly knew Hitler sat in his bunker fifty-five feet below ground.

Karl looked around. Virtually everyone, including the last of the soldiers protecting the Führer's bunkers, had left the area. Suddenly they heard the deep boom and roar of the Red Army's heavy artillery in the distance. A moment later, a whistling artillery shell screamed overhead and landed a few blocks away. The Russian assault on Berlin had just resumed.

Karl looked up at the dark grey sky, and the rain pelted his face. The air, smoky with the stench of burning bodies, was thick and nasty. He turned from the unrecognizable figures to Kempka. "Erich, it's time we leave."

"I'll be with you in two minutes, Karl."

"Make it quick, we're out of time."

As Karl returned to the car, he crossed paths with two remaining SS officers, Georg Betz and Hans Bauer, leaving with portfolios under their arms. Betz, Hitler's personal pilot, and Hans Bauer, Betz's assistant and occasional substitute pilot, looked at Karl. Betz recognized him from when he'd flown him to Rome to assist in developing German strategy at Anzio.

"We pleaded with Hitler to leave in the Ju390 early yesterday. But he turned us down," claimed Bauer.

"So, Chosen One, what the hell kept you? When Adolf turned us down, we understood you were to come and take him away – even drug him, if need be. Mohnke said you were supposed to be here between midnight and three. We stuck around because if he were drugged, we might have put you and him on the plane with us and a few others. Now it's too late. The mess you see over there – well, von Richter, it's all your fault. Der Führer's death and blood is on your hands. Were you drinking last night or screwing some woman – or both? Did you forget to come here?" Betz spat on the ground at Karl's feet, then stalked past him in disgust.

Betz's words struck a nerve. *Betz was no doubt responsible to execute Plan A, the escape by air. When Plan A failed late – and Hitler refused to leave, word must have been sent to von Schultz – but why the long delay into last evening?*

Karl recalled the two empty Benedictine bottles on the credenza.

Perhaps the Benedictine entertained von Schultz and the other two generals who left during the night, or maybe Sweet Hilda and the Benedictine entertained all three. Whatever, von Schultz's failure to give me the orders before midnight is the root cause of this tragedy.

Consoling himself with that thought, Karl got into the car, and pushed the envelope beneath his seat. He started the car, turned it around. His world was upside down. Everything had changed. His concerns about leading the Führer and a small entourage to safety evaporated. Karl's thoughts flashed to his parents and his wife.

Perhaps Plan C is a good idea after all. I'll get Katrina and our child and bring them to meet the U-boat in Ravenna. Now, what's keeping Erich?

CHAPTER TWENTY-NINE

Escaping Berlin

As Karl waited for Erich's return, he re-evaluated the escape. *Von Schultz's plan was defective. I would have: 1) drugged Hitler without his knowledge, 2) removed him from the bunker, 3) flown him to North Africa, 4) refueled, and 5) flown to Brazil. Adolf would have been relaxing in the sun and looking at all the beautiful women sunbathing in Ipanema by June.*

Just then Kempka approached. "Karl, the rest of us are headed to the subway. The rail path will lead us north, where we can disperse in different parts of the city as we exit at different stations. It'll be easier to pass beneath Red Army tanks than to sneak by them on the streets above. Betz told us a larger style of submarine will be waiting off the coast near Bremerhaven. It's our newest class XXI. It's quiet, fast and can easily fit a dozen of us on board. Come with us, Karl. Maybe we can stop in Norway to pick up some of our SS brothers, and travel on to Brazil, just like everyone always planned."

Betz has a big mouth. After the Führer declined to fly, he must have told others a second plan existed. I bet as many as twenty people at the bunker complex know about Plan B and the U-boat in Bremerhaven. With so many people headed to the coast, they'll surely be discovered. Heading south is better. If all those people headed to Bremerhaven get caught, they'll be tortured by the Russians, and our U-boat's location will be revealed. Fortunately, none of them know the code to get aboard. But eventually, as it leaves its current location, it may be discovered and sunk by the British Royal Navy in the North Sea.

Karl glanced back at the smoldering bodies, still struck by the gravity of the situation. Each minute he lingered made it more dangerous. The Red Army's artillery had paused after that single shell was fired. That could only mean they were adjusting their trajectories for a final attack on the Chancellery building. Suddenly, another boom. In a flash, a projectile screamed overhead and hit the corner of the Chancellery, showering the yard with debris. The Russian artillery unit had a forward observer hidden someplace, and he successfully guided his comrades to zero in on the building and Der Führer's bunkers.

As debris showered onto the car, Karl's head spun again. *South? Plan C? It's got to be south – and von Schultz's crazy Plan C with the brandy ring on it.*

"Karl, let's get out of here!" Erich urged, pointing to the final few just leaving.

"Erich, I'm heading south. I'm returning home to Lake Constance and Langenargen. Good luck to you and the others."

He reached beneath the seat, grabbed the envelope and scanned the directions on Plan C's front page. He felt for his holstered and loaded Luger, then rolled down the narrow driveway. Near its end, Heinrich Doose, a member of Kempka's driving staff, held up his hands to stop Karl. He'd been standing with Betz and Bauer earlier.

"Hold on a minute, von Richter. A group of us are going to the Friedrichstrasse station. Betz suggested we use your car to get there quickly."

"Yes. Get the others and I will wait for you."

As Doose ran to tell the others they had a ride, Karl stepped on the accelerator and sped down the driveway. He turned left and headed south, leaving them all behind. He glanced again at the map to read the yellow-highlighted path and the street names.

***

About 8 that morning, in the absence of being rescued by von Richter, Hitler dictated his last will and testament to Traudl Junge. He then summoned Otto Gunsche. "You have been faithful to me. I want you, Bormann and Heinz Linge to stand guard outside my room in the Führerbunker until Eva and I have committed suicide. Then you must see to it our corpses are fully cremated. Do not let the Russians see or parade my body."

At Der Führer's directive, Otto told the other two men to anticipate what would happen, and to wait outside Adolf and Eva's area in the bunker.

A few minutes later, Albert Speer arrived; he entered the Führer's room. Twenty minutes afterward, Speer left, and it grew quiet again. The three patiently waited two hours. Then, wondering what was happening, Linge knocked. There was no response. He knocked again, then entered the room. At the far end of the room, he found the two dead bodies at the couch.

The three were confused, not having heard a shot.

Bormann alerted the staff while Linge wrapped the bodies in blankets for disposal. Then Otto, a tall, strong man, carried Hitler's body over his shoulder up the stairs.

Traudl, traumatized, paid her last respects to Eva, whom she'd so admired. She was alone with her for at least five minutes before Gunsche returned for her body.

Outside, Gunsche pressed Kempka to handle the cremation, then changed into street clothes and left with Junge, mistakenly heading south in the dark day's heavy rain.

***

As Karl proceeded south, he had traveled about a mile when he spotted a couple walking along the side of the road. It was Otto Gunsche and his girlfriend, Traudl Junge, Hitler's youngest secretary. Seeing them heading south together, Karl pulled over.

"Where are you headed?"

"Hello, von Richter. We're getting as far away as we can from the Chancellery right now."

"Get in, I'll give you a ride."

Gunsche opened the door, and Traudl climbed into the backseat. Gunsche put his bag on the floor, then threw in Traudl's duffel bag. It landed on top of her as she was getting settled. The car door slammed and Karl's wet shoe slipped off the clutch pedal. As the car lurched, Traudl, not yet seated, fell awkwardly onto the floor.

For the first few minutes, no one spoke, amid the heavy rain and circumstances of what had just happened at the Chancellery. In the silence, all three reflected on what might have been, had Karl arrived in the early morning hours as he should have.

At last, Karl broke the ice. "Did you know anything about any escape plans for Hitler?"

"I heard about flying him out of Berlin. Adolf and Eva asked the two of us to tend to their personal needs during the escape, and to go and live with them in Brazil. But to our surprise, Der Führer refused to fly at the last minute.

"Then someone was supposed to bring Hitler to a U-boat in Bremerhaven. Wasn't it you, Karl? Weren't you chosen to do that?"

Karl offered no response.

"Where were you last night? Weren't you supposed to show up after midnight? The Führer and Eva were all set to leave. We were going to accompany them. Why didn't you arrive as planned?"

Now he shook his head as a thought flashed through his mind... *Sweet Hilda and the Benedictine.* "It's a long story, Otto. I was at the Bendlerblock building all night, awaiting orders. Late this morning, von Schultz called me into his office. As I approached the door, out walks the half-naked Hilda. Inside von Schultz was pulling up his pants. That's when I found out about my role in Hitler's escape. It was almost eleven. And Hitler and Eva had committed suicide by then." He omitted the part where he'd enjoyed his own five minutes with Hilda.

"Otto, what are you planning to do now?"

"Like I said earlier, we plan to hide tonight, and blend into the general population in Berlin. In a few days, we'll go north to the coast, where that U-boat should be waiting for Hitler."

Karl kept quiet, offering no response. He was thinking.

He continued south on Mariendoffer Damm and then onto Mariendoffer Allee. As he proceeded through the intersection, a Soviet tank rumbled by on a parallel road to their left. Further along, a column of four American tanks sped across a large open park, with soldiers running behind them on the right.

At seeing Soviet and American tanks on both streets, Traudl grabbed Gunsche's shoulder and they exchange nervous glances. But there was more to it.

Traudl, who had grown up nearby, expressed doubts about their direction when she saw the tanks headed the opposite way on the side streets. They passed a few more streets when Karl turned onto Lichtenrader and headed south again.

Karl still wore his SS uniform; his civilian clothes were in his duffel bag in the backseat, as was the change of clothing for Der Führer. "I still need to change," he told the others. "We'll stop for a minute once we cross the bridge over the small branch of the Spree River."

Traudl leaned forward and, grabbing her boyfriend's shoulder again, whispered to him.

At her words, Gunsche's back stiffened. "Karl, stop the car! We're headed south. That's the wrong direction. We should be headed north, toward the coast."

"Otto, have you lost your way because it's raining, and the sun isn't shining? You were walking south when I picked you up, and we've been headed south ever since."

"We should be headed north!"

"Herr Gunsche, are you confused? Shall I find you a compass?"

"Karl, I thought you were headed north, to the coast, like the plan said. You need to turn around and go north. We need to get to the subway station, to avoid the Soviet and American tanks and troops on the road. We need to get to the north coast."

"Listen to me, Otto. If you and Traudl want to escape being captured, south is your best choice. Betz has a big mouth. Too many from the Chancellery are traveling north to the coast. Those heading into the subway tunnels and buildings to hide will be found by the Russians by tonight or tomorrow night – or certainly within days."

Karl had already thought to rid himself of these two. Something about them made him uneasy. Maybe Traudl had whispered too often into Gunsche's ear during the short ride.

"Now you listen, Karl. I said turn the car around. I saw a subway station entrance two blocks behind us."

As Gunsche insisted they turn around, Karl became upset and hit the brakes hard. He pulled his Luger from his shoulder holster and pointed it at Gunsche.

Traudl, on the floor again from the sudden stop, tried to get up.

"Get out now. Both of you. Out! Now!"

Surprised by Karl's sudden demand, and with the Luger pointed at his eyes, Gunsche flung open the door. He reached into the backseat, grabbed Traudl's arm and wrist, and yanked her out of the coupe. He slammed the door, kicked the fender and cursed Karl, who drove away over the small bridge.

The pair began walking to the subway station they'd just passed. Too late, Traudl realized she'd left her pocketbook and bag of clothing in the backseat of Karl's southbound car.

"Otto, we must go back and find Karl. My clothing, pocketbook and things are in the car."

Annoyed and unconcerned, he grabbed her wrist and pulled her along toward the station, unaware of her dilemma.

Karl continued to follow the highlighted route, street by street. He said aloud to his ghost companion, "I can't believe this escape route is working so well." He had no way of knowing a few months earlier, Germany's SS spy organization uncovered the Soviet Red Army's choice of roads into Berlin from the south for its tanks and ground troops. In 1944, a young German SS officer infiltrated the Soviet spy organization called SMERSH. That was the Russian name for three different counter-intelligence agencies the Red Army started in late 1942 to protect the Soviets' war efforts from being infiltrated by German spies.

General von Schultz and another SS spy officer received encrypted radio messages from the German spy each evening at 6. Four months earlier, the encrypted information outlined the Red Army's plans, and their strategic maneuvers to move into and around Berlin. General Helmuth Weidling, the defense commandant of Berlin, and General Mohnke, charged with defending the immediate Chancellery area itself, also received the spy's radio messages.

Two months ago, the Soviets' plan for the Battle of Berlin were finalized regarding specific streets. It let the generals designing Hitler's escape plans make final tweaks in the exact routes to exit the city (north in Plan B and south in Plan C). The escape route, aided by the intelligence, worked.

The intelligence information also was intended to help Weidling and Mohnke thwart the Soviet push into Berlin. But even with detailed information in their possession, attempts to push back the Soviet Red Army weren't working. The German war machine, low on fuel and ammunition, couldn't maneuver as expected. In the last week, as Russians encircled the city, their artillery began shelling on Hitler's birthday – the same day he came out of his bunker for some fresh air. Eventually Weidling and Mohnke could no longer hold their defensive positions. Street battles were consistently won by the Red Army as their tanks and troops moved toward Hitler's bunker under the Chancellery.

The American 5th Army tried to arrive in Berlin at the same time. But the Soviet Red Army moved faster. Like Patton raced Montgomery and arrived first in Messina, Sicily, two Soviet Red Army commanders – Marshal Georgy Zhukov and Marshal Ivan Konev – raced into Berlin with their respective Belorussian and Ukrainian troops. German tanks and ground forces who had the chance, and who recognized defeat, raced westward, giving themselves up to the U.S. 5th Army forces rather than surrender to the Russians.

Karl reflected on all that was going on. *Gunsche's decision to turn around was wrong. My decision to head south is clearly the better choice. It seems the odd alternative has emerged as the best escape route.*

Perhaps more importantly, it gave him the hope of picking up Katrina and the child, and continue to the U-boat waiting off the coast of Ravenna, then to freedom in Brazil. *Despite this terrible situation, I'm still winning. My SS superiors were right. My accomplishments over the last ten years have me ahead of many others. Fortune and opportunity are at my side and will not fail me now.*

He'd arrive at a safe house in the village of Schwarzheide that night. Karl, Der Führer and two others would sleep briefly and continue south. Now it would be just Karl, and he was fine being on his own.

After Karl crossed the bridge, he changed his clothing, but not his boots, and continued along the roads identified in the plans. He followed the yellow-highlighted path, staying on side streets parallel to the main roads. A few times he saw abandoned Russian and German tanks, some blown apart, others still smoldering. After leaving the urban area, and while on farm roads, he saw more American tanks rushing north toward Berlin on the nearby main roads. Troop carriers and fuel trucks followed close behind.

The binoculars in the car were at Karl's side when he noticed dust rising in the distance. He soon saw, far off, a group of soldiers running beside American tanks coming his way on the farm road. Spotting a nearby barn, he turned off the roadway, parking behind it, hoping they hadn't seen him. He shut the car off, took the envelope and hid behind the barn. He watched three American tanks and fifty American soldiers running by.

How great a country is America. Having the fortitude and the resources to bring war machinery to Europe and then fight so hard. It's impressive. Hitler said the Americans had neither the mental nor physical stamina needed to fight for a long period of time on foreign land. But now, seeing those massive American tanks and the soldiers close up, I see Hitler was completely wrong about the resolve of the American soldiers – and the American people who sent them here.

Once they passed, he got back in the car and continued south and approached a village severely damaged in a fight between Russian and German tanks. He slowed down further to weave through a street littered with tanks and halftrack armored vehicles. Numerous German and Russian soldiers lay dead on the street. Broken metal parts of machinery lay scattered all over.

Without warning, the car's front tire went flat. Karl slammed the steering wheel. He got out and saw its sidewall had been slashed. Behind the car, a piece of angle iron, still partially attached to a street sign, lay on the ground, with a rough edge sticking up. It no doubt came from the building next to him, its façade destroyed by a blast during the tank fight. *At least the rain has stopped.* Karl moved the car a bit forward to get out of a puddle, removed the gas tanks from the trunk and got the spare out. The unexpected struggle to loosen the rusty lug nuts rankled his patience. Finished at last, he drove away, careful to avoid other debris.

Another six miles on the farm road were uneventful until a sharp turn in the road led to another battle scene. The farm road, blocked by a pair of German Panzer tanks and two armored vehicles, had dead bodies lying scattered all around. Karl found it necessary to drive into the field to get past the scene. After driving past the tank, he got out to relieve himself. He saw Russian tank tracks in the soft soil at the side of the road. They reminded him of when he'd first seen the drawing of a Russian tank tread. He recalled sketching an improved tread; lighter and stiffer, it grabbed the snow and soil better, required less milling and machining, and won kudos from Lutz. Karl never knew SS Waffen General Field Marshal von Schultz once visited the Ravensburg factory with Lutz to meet 'whoever it was who designed the new tread.'

Karl approached one of the tanks and put his hand on its barrel. The metal felt cold. "It's been at least a day since this machine saw battle," he remarked aloud. From the scene, Karl was relieved knowing the Soviets had advanced further north toward Berlin. *Heading south makes the most sense. This scene validates my decision.*

He climbed back in the car. His nerves had been on edge all day, focused on following the path out of Berlin. After feeling the tank's cold metal, he grabbed a cigarette. He struck the match and let the sulfur burn off – then lit the cigarette and took a deep drag. And then another. It took only a few moments for the nicotine hit to work its magic. When the cigarette was finished, Karl lit a second one from the first and pulled Plan C from its envelope. He examined the three maps closely, giving more attention to the route through the Swiss mountains and into Italy. When he turned the car back on, the gas gauge showed less than half full. *With the gas in the trunk, I can drive another few hours before refueling.*

Satiated by the nicotine, Karl decided to grab another pack for the next part of his journey. He leaned back, reached into the backseat and tugged his duffel bag into the front passenger seat. In pulling his bag up front, he exposed Traudl's duffel bag and pocketbook. *It probably fell from her shoulder when Gunsche yanked her from the backseat. Too bad for her!*

"Let's have a look to see if she had any cigarettes." Shoving aside his duffel bag for the moment, Karl scrounged around in Traudl's duffel bag. Next he opened her pocketbook. "Hmm, no cigarettes, but what do we have here?"

Inside was a thick roll of money, bound tightly in a rubber band. Unrolling it, he discovered American $50 and $100 silver-certificate bills. He counted it quickly; $3,000 in all.

Looking further, he found a leather purse. Unsnapping its metal clasps, he found five gold bracelets – two narrow and three wide. He examined each one carefully. An inscription on one of the wide bracelets surprised him. Then Karl opened a smaller purse with a similar clasp. Inside, four gold rings shone brightly; two were wedding bands, one had a medium-sized brilliant diamond, and the other had a gorgeous setting showcasing three large diamonds across the middle, with two smaller diamonds on each side.

"Hmm. I'm guessing these belonged to Eva. Wow! Fortune smiles on me again!" he crowed. "Thank you very much, Adolf and Eva. And thank you, Traudl, for your carelessness."

He dug a final time, a little deeper, into the smaller purse, and retrieved a green velvet drawstring pouch. Inside he found white stones – uncut diamonds! He counted them – thirty-three. Karl shook his head, took a deep breath and let it go slowly. He leaned back and lit up another cigarette. Taking the two thin bracelets from the bag, he put them in his pocket and stuffed Traudl's handbag into his duffel. Next, he went back through her duffel bag. At the bottom he found German marks scattered inside her clothing, and fancy, see-through lacy black undergarments. *I bet those were Eva's.* Then voicing his surprise aloud, Karl crowed, "I can't believe what that silly secretary left behind. It's worth a fortune!"

Karl emptied the bracelets, rings and diamonds from her bag and tucked the goods away in his duffel bag. He lighted another cigarette, looked at the map again and drove away. He continued to follow the roads highlighted by the yellow crayon. The names of the towns in the order in which he should travel were printed in order on the side of the map.

At the top of the map, the words "DO NOT DEVIATE FROM THE ROUTE" in bold letters, ordered him to remain on the designated escape path. The route took him south, then west, then south again to Stuttgart. Turning toward Stuttgart would be good, as it allowed him to eventually head south – to Katrina and his child in Langenargen.

He read a second note at the top of each map page. "Red dots along the route are vetted safe houses. – Approved by SS Officer J.C. Hockemeier."

Karl smiled. He was surprised to learn Hockemeier had responsibility for vetting safe houses for Plan C. The two had met in SS Officer training and worked Kristallnacht together, ransacking the butcher shop, then cutting wires at the city's telephone exchange where Hockemeier had once worked setting up countrywide telephone network connections. After that night, Karl lost track of the smiling companion who'd given him the nasty nickname "Butcher."

His first stop would be at the safe house in the hamlet of Beelitz. Karl considered what he'd say to people at these houses; he decided on, "Der Führer is following in a second group of four people; he'll be along in twelve to eighteen hours."

He also mulled what to say if asked about rumors of the Führer's death. He practiced aloud, saying, "News of Der Führer's death is a lie, fabricated and spread purposely by the SS to enable Der Führer to escape to freedom and someday return to restore Germany to greatness.

"I can assure you our leader is alive and well. I am responsible for making safe the path for Der Führer. Tell no one he is coming! You'll be honored by his presence and a small sum of money when he arrives tomorrow."

Karl's strong desire to make the right decisions and right moves kept him constantly re-evaluating. This predisposition arose from childhood chess games with his grandfather; he had to play skillfully to earn a win. His grandfather's strict training served him well these last ten years, where his success was achieved by constantly looking for weak points in production activities and people's skills and characters. He realized Plan C was well developed after all, and for a good reason.

I'm surprised at the encirclement of Berlin by the Soviet Army, and its ability to push so fast into Berlin's central district. Our defenses collapsed so quickly. We failed to resupply our soldiers. Thankfully, our German spy gave the senior SS generals and von Schultz the insight they needed to develop the plan to extract Hitler from Berlin and bring him to safety. But I still don't understand why Plan A wasn't executed a week

ago. Perhaps some SS officers wanted Hitler to die there at the Chancel-
lery? But did he really die there? Was that body really Adolf? Something
is askew; the man's body I saw – it was lying on its side – and it had a
bullet wound in the back.

The thought had troubled Karl since he'd driven away from the
Chancellery – but he suppressed the image. His subconscious at work,
now he finally wondered what really happened.

Looking again at the highlighted route, he recognized the Russian
troops' movement north removed most of the danger. He'd be challenged
not by tanks and fighting soldiers, but by peacekeepers – small groups of
enemy troops left behind to stabilize the recently captured areas. *I'm now*
more likely to encounter Americans and other enemy forces rather than
Russians as I continue south.

He was right. The Allied forces advancing north from Italy, and
east from western Germany, were in a hurry to get to Berlin. He knew
Allied soldiers were tough fighters, but unlikely to kill for the sake of
killing. Reports said Americans were compassionate and took prisoners
whenever they could. The Red Army, however, was still upset by the
Wehrmacht's fierce invading attacks that killed millions of Russians –
especially during Operation Barbarossa and Operation Citadel at the Battle of Kursk, where 8,000 tanks from both sides squared off.

Karl felt relieved at no longer being responsible for bringing the
Führer to safety. He still found it unbelievable that Hitler had poisoned
his bride and then shot himself. He shook his head. The whole situation
at the Chancellery and bunkers still made no sense.

Maybe the scene was staged by Gunsche, Kempka and others.
Perhaps another SS officer also was chosen to transport Hitler. Maybe it
was Eva's body brought out in the wool blanket, but not Hitler's. And
maybe the valuables – the money, jewelry and diamonds given to Traudl
– were part of the hoax to make people believe they were dead.

Still curious, Karl concluded whatever happened was now behind
him. *My focus now is to stay alive and return home for Katrina, my child*
– hopefully my son – and my parents.

CHAPTER THIRTY

Johannes Wolff

Further south, Karl entered a hamlet with a dozen houses that backed up onto farmland on each side of the road. His keen eyes detected movement ahead. Another 200 feet along, he noticed a German soldier standing motionless in a doorway, hiding in plain sight. Karl slowed and peeked to the side. The badge on the soldier's shoulder indicated he was a lieutenant.

As Karl slowed to a stop, the soldier ran toward the car with his rifle pointed at him. Karl, already holding his Luger, shouted through the window, "Halt. Heil Hitler, Lieutenant."

The soldier slowed his charge and pointed the rifle downward.

Karl got out of the vehicle. "At ease, Lieutenant. I'm a soldier in civilian clothes. Look, I still have my boots on. What are you doing here alone?"

"Heil Hitler. My name is Wolff. Lieutenant Johannes Wolff."

"Heil Hitler. I am Waffen SS Officer Karl von Richter."

"Sir, you're headed south, no? May I ride with you – for our mutual protection?"

"Yes, get in."

Johannes, 30 years old, was tall, with a square face and a high jaw. He had blond hair and blue eyes and pale skin – all distinct Aryan German features Hitler believed to be the pure German race.

"Sir, you are smart to be going south," Johannes said.

"Why is that?"

"The Soviets have already pushed north through here. Their fighting is now directed at the center of Berlin. Later, they will secure the areas north from Berlin to the North Sea. May I have a cigarette?"

Karl nodded in agreement.

Johannes lit the cigarette and took a long, hard drag. "My unit successfully held back the Russians for several hours. Mohnke ordered us to defend Berlin's southern flank, to protect Der Führer's bunker at the Chancellery. Then, two days ago, we heard a rumor Der Führer was leaving Berlin. One of my commanders who knew Mohnke said Adolf is flying away and leaving us to die. Another said he might escape north to the sea – but the Russians will capture anyone headed that way. And if anyone goes west, they'll be captured by Americans. So it's best to head south right now. Besides, I live south of here." His tone turned wistful. "Maybe I finally will get to see my wife after four years. Do you know what has become of Hitler?"

Karl, surprised at the young officer's understanding of the big picture, ignored his question and lit a cigarette.

"Sir, there are still many American and British soldiers to the south. Hiding from them should be easy because of large farmlands. The farmhouses, most of them unoccupied, will be overlooked by enemy troops coming this way."

When they stopped to relieve themselves, Karl offered Johannes a change of clothes. He reached into the backseat for his duffel and pulled forth trousers and a shirt. "Here, these should fit you, although the trousers might be a little short."

Johannes changed on the spot. Karl didn't mention the street clothes and shoes had been intended for Der Führer. They hardly spoke for the next several miles. Eventually, Karl fished to determine whether Johannes knew anything of Hitler's suicide.

"Johannes, what do you know of the Führer's status?"

"I don't know anything. It's why I asked you earlier. All I know is this: My entire unit was lost further north, defending Berlin's southern flank. We had no food the last two days. We were taking our energy pills with the little water we had to keep us going. In the last tank battle, all my men, my closest friends… all died. I feel guilty. Now I'm not sure why we all fought and died if the rumor that Hitler left the city is true."

Karl figured Johannes was describing where he'd seen all the dead soldiers and abandoned tanks on the road thirty minutes earlier.

"We spotted three Russian tanks and soldiers advancing north toward us. As they got closer, our tank fired on the first Soviet tank. The shot knocked its turret off. We all cheered, and it helped us all to fight bravely... at first. After we fired a few more rounds, our Panzer ran out of fuel and became a sitting duck in the roadway. The two remaining Soviet tanks maneuvered for kill shots. One approached from the east, and the other from the south. The tank from the side street blew off our turret. We did everything we could to halt their advance. Some of us began to run out of ammunition for our rifles. But the Russians kept shooting. There were just too many of them.

"Just two minutes before the shooting and hand-to-hand fighting ended, I tripped and fell face down. A second later, my childhood friend was shot and fell on top of me. A minute later, all the shooting stopped. I lay there, under my dead friend, scared, with him bleeding on me. Then, through the corner of my eye, I watched as Russian soldiers walked past with their rifles, randomly shooting to be sure we were all dead. My dead friend on top of me took another bullet. Somehow his body stopped the bullet, and it didn't reach me.

"After the Russian soldiers and their tanks were gone, I pushed my friend off me and started crying. We'd been friends since kindergarten. His death saved my life. I got up and walked to each of my fellow soldiers, but every one was mortally wounded. I felt angry for not having enough fuel or ammunition to fight." He paused a moment and sniffled.

"So now I'm heading home. I'm ashamed and I feel guilty, being the only one who survived the battle. I failed as a unit leader and, deep down, I feel like I'm a coward." Johannes' eyes filled with tears, and they rolled down his dirty, bearded face.

Karl understood Johannes better after hearing his story, concluding he was mild mannered, perhaps a schoolteacher or a clerk of some kind, and forced into military service.

They drove another hour, coming across three more tank battle scenes.

Johannes shared what had happened at each location as they retreated north after each skirmish, holding off the Red Army's offensive push. "Our tanks did well against the enemy, but one by one, we lost tanks and men; eventually, in the last battle, it was our one tank against the three."

Karl decided to share Hitler's status. "I was at the Bendlerblock building this morning, awaiting final orders to leave Berlin. I stopped at the Chancellery and learned Hitler and his new wife committed suicide inside the bunker." He didn't say he'd been assigned to help Hitler escape.

Shocked at the news, Johannes was surprised – and even more impressed to be riding with a senior SS officer who'd had access to the Führer.

Further down the road, Karl asked whether Johannes had anything of value on him.

"I have nothing with me. I saw several gold chalices in a room behind the altar in the Catholic church in the city of Ulm, north of Lake Constance. That back room was a treasure chest. But as much as they were of interest, they were too heavy to carry and of no use in battle. I guess I know where the Catholics got all that money... Luther was right to be upset with the Catholic priests' charging money for indulgences."

Karl replied, "I saw a treasure of gold chalices and silver candlesticks in a sacristy at a Catholic church in Padua, near Venice, a few years ago, but it was impossible to carry the cache with me. There are thousands of assets worth millions of American dollars in Catholic churches – not just in Italy, but all across Europe. I'm sure the lives of many greedy soldiers were lost trying to carry gold items with them during the battles. Johannes, you were smart to leave those items where you saw them."

Karl didn't mention the stash of art and other valuables Germans took from Jews and hid at Hitler's direction. In his brief role with Organization Todt, Fritz Todt had asked him to review and comment on the security of several hiding places, including salt mines and tunnels, especially at the Neuschwanstein Castle where some twenty-one thousand objects confiscated from Jews and former German royal families were stored.

Johannes spoke more about his final battle. "We were worried for weeks about our low supplies of ammunition and diesel fuel for the tanks and armored vehicles. Promises about more fuel and ammunition were never kept. Morale in my unit faded badly, and their will to fight had diminished almost entirely. My soldiers wanted to quit and go home to their wives and children. Some of my men cried at night. It was difficult. I had them all take more pills to keep them engaged, but in the end, we couldn't defend ourselves from the Russians."

As Karl and Johannes drove another two hours, Johannes began shaking. Karl realized the pills he'd mentioned were Pervitin. Marketed as a "pick-me-up" drug, Pervitin was also known as methamphetamine or crystal meth. Almost all the German soldiers in the field were given meth to get them hyped up going into, and during, long periods of battle. It helped them to fight boldly and stave off physical fatigue.

Karl knew the Luftwaffe's pilots and German seamen took Pervitin. Much larger doses were given to German soldiers headed into battle. He'd seen an internal statistic from 1940 stating 35 million Pervitin tablets were sent to the front lines for soldiers in the Blitzkrieg.

The German Army had used excessive amounts of Pervitin as it pushed across France so rapidly against the French Army and British Expeditionary Force at Dunkirk. They'd march long distances and fight hard for up to ten days at a time without normal rest.

Karl had often used Pervitin himself but felt no pity for Johannes for becoming seriously addicted, and for being in withdrawal. He offered him another cigarette and lit one up for himself.

"Johannes, did you know the Führer would take amphetamines, barbiturates and opiates daily? It made him anxious, and his behavior unpredictable, especially these last few months," Karl said, to the other man's surprise, judging from the widening of his eyes. "Ironically, he opposed cigarette smoking. He ran huge public campaigns to discourage the German people from smoking, but he – and the entire Army, Navy and Luftwaffe – used methamphetamines."

Karl's memory flashed to the burning bodies behind the bunker. *That had to be Hitler and Eva. No way the Führer could think clearly enough to put together a hoax. But Erich Kempka told me Albert Speer had made a last-minute visit to Der Führer and was there for ten or fif-*

teen minutes. I wonder what that was about. And how does that fit with what I think I saw?

Karl realized Johannes was beginning to struggle more in his withdrawal. In their small talk, he mentioned he was married but had no children yet. He said he lived south of their position.

The village where Johannes and his wife lived was on the Plan C list of towns. Johannes hoped his journey would end at home with his wife, where they would rebuild their lives, as all Germans would have to do. He expressed a desire to start a family. Johannes was a seasoned combat veteran, with four years under his belt fighting alongside Panzer tanks, but had been shocked by the final battle earlier that day. And his withdrawal from heavy doses of Pervitin made him shake even more.

As they drove, Johannes seemed surprised at not encountering enemy soldiers. Their path made him wonder more about who Karl was, and how his magic map kept them from contact with the enemy. Karl occasionally slowed to look at his instructions outlined on Map #1. Each time he held the map, Karl would notice Johannes stretching his neck to look at it. Karl gave him a look.

Johannes smiled. "This is good. I live straight south from here. It looks like the highlighted path goes through my village. Returning home will be good. My wife will be surprised."

Karl nodded. Returning to their families would be good for all German soldiers. The route highlighted headed to Luddwigsfelde and Trebbin, then westward to the village of Beelitz. A red dot signified a farmhouse on the south side of town where Karl and Johannes would stay tonight.

The note said the owner of the large asparagus farm on Langer Wiesen Weg had a son in the Gestapo and another son, a regular German soldier. According to the note, it was safe to bring Der Führer there to freshen up, eat, sleep and resupply any needs, including gasoline.

When they arrived at the farmhouse, Karl felt it was a good place to rest after a difficult day. The farmer, Hanz Gundlach, greeted the men and brought them inside to meet his wife, Greta. After introductions and the explanation Hitler would be along tomorrow, Karl took advantage of a bath in the house. Johannes, now cold, sweating and shaking, lay on the couch in the living room. Greta covered him with a blanket as his withdrawal symptoms worsened.

Dinner was veal and asparagus served three ways. A dry, homemade Gewürztraminer accompanied the meal. As they ate, the farmer proudly shared he was a Nazi Party member with a low number. He told the story of the day Hitler and several others ran away after the Nazis' first attempted putsch failed. He was arrested the following day, along with the young Adolf. They both were incarcerated briefly, and he was one of several released from jail. He looked forward to seeing Adolf again, and wondered whether Adolf would remember him.

After supper, Karl agreed to a sip of homemade dessert wine with the farmer while Greta cleaned up the dishes. Karl shared his own story about Kristallnacht, setting up gas chambers and ovens at the death camps and ensuring the equipment functioned well. He mentioned the trainloads of Jews, Poles and Slavs coming into the death camps, hailing Hitler's plan to purify Germany of such deplorables. Karl mentioned the Jewish and Communist conspiracy to take over the European economy, and elaborated at great length about attending the Wannsee Conference.

It was a great evening for the old farmer's national pride. Living twenty years in the past in his mind, he threw old barbs at the British and French for the Treaty of Versailles' nasty limitations and financial penalties inflicted upon Germany. He relished hearing Karl's stories of eliminating the Jews from Germany and was excited about Der Führer's arrival tomorrow.

As the evening grew later, Hanz suggested it might be safest for Karl and Johannes to sleep in an old empty corn silo out back behind the house. As the two climbed inside, Johannes shivered badly, clinging to his woolen blanket.

Karl removed his shoulder holster and put his trusted Luger in his hand. Greta brought out a few more blankets and wished them good dreams. Both Karl and Johannes fell asleep within minutes.

Back inside, the old farmer stressed to his wife to have the house ready for Hitler's visit. Adolf, a dozen years younger than Hanz, would grace his farm tomorrow. Hanz and Greta stayed up another two hours. She made dough while Hanz cut apples for two fresh apple pies. Tired from a full day of working the asparagus farm, Hanz went to bed while Greta stayed up to bake the pies.

***

Back in Berlin, it was nighttime as well. Most of the people who had left the bunker earlier in the day were now hiding in the underground subway station or walking along the rails in the pitch-dark tunnels.

One German soldier assigned to the bunker came running up from the rear. "A dozen Red Army soldiers are in the tunnel behind us, headed this way."

The group panicked. Most left the tunnel at the next station and, finding themselves near a brewery, hid within its cellar that night. Their expectation was the Russians would focus on reaching the Reich Chancellery, and they could slip into the general population in Berlin the next morning.

Kempka, after speaking with Karl and leaving the bunkers, failed to hide in the subway like the rest who had left earlier. He and Hitler's secretary Christa Schroeder went to the Bendlerblock building, intending to hide there until dark. They purposely left Hitler's nurse, Erna Flegel, in the bunker to care for a few who had injured themselves in attempted suicides.

While rummaging through the building for food and valuables, they met Hilda, who decided to remain and hide there. The three spoke briefly. Hearing others who left the bunker earlier planned to spend the night in the brewery, they left at dusk, and using back alleys headed to the brewery to access its basement.

After the three left, only thirty minutes passed before twenty Russian soldiers and a Russian tank pulled up in front of the Bendlerblock building.

Using dogs, the soldiers ensured neither people nor explosives remained inside. When the building was declared empty and safe, a Red Army general arrived, and established Soviet military operations.

Almost simultaneously, Russian soldiers patrolling the streets and alleys with dogs spotted Kempka and the two women heading toward the brewery. A Russian unit commander put them in his armored car and drove them to the now Soviet-controlled Bendlerblock for questioning.

Once they arrived, Kempka, now held prisoner, shook his head, disbelieving the turn of events of the last two hours. A Russian general fluent in German placed the three in separate rooms and personally questioned them.

Kempka's girlfriend, the secretary, said she was Kempka's wife, and claimed she, Kempka and Hilda all were cooks at the Bendlerblock. Kempka's rehearsed explanation echoed hers.

When the general questioned Hilda, she initially replied in German, saying she was a cook. But then she began speaking Russian. "I'm the only cook here in the last three months; the other two aren't cooks. The woman is Hitler's secretary, and the man is Hitler's driver."

The Soviet general listened carefully. He sent Kempka for further interrogation and kept the women another hour for further questioning. The secretary remained silent, refusing to answer any questions.

But in that hour, Hilda, still speaking Russian, proved to be an excellent source of information. She explained she'd gone to the bunkers several times a week, to help the two cooks there. She also discussed the sexual advances and activities forced upon her in the SS officers' complex both there in the Bendlerblock, and inside the bunker.

Just before dark, the final interrogation in the commander's office grew more relaxed. Hilda's buxom appearance, her eyes, pink cheeks and bashful look pleased the Russian commander. Taking a strong liking to her, he finally gave her a smile. Hilda smiled, too, not only because of the Russian commander's becoming more friendly to her, but because of what she saw on the large credenza behind him: an empty bottle of Benedictine.

"I will be sending Hitler's secretary along with Herr Kempka to Moscow shortly. As for you, Fraulein Hilda, I'd like you to stay here in the building and continue to cook for us. There's a nice private bedroom upstairs you can use. Perhaps it is an upgrade from where you've been sleeping? I'll also compensate you appropriately. You are safe and under my care now."

Hilda thanked the Soviet commander, then laughed to herself. *How ironic it is to be staying here tonight – and the opportunity to cook for the new general. Thank you, Mother, for teaching me Russian as a child – your native language.* Of course, a knock came at her door later that night, and Sweet Hilda obliged willingly.

***

The next morning, just before daybreak, the old farmer came to the silo. He knew Karl and Johannes needed an early start. The farmer bent down and quietly opened the small door at the silo's base. He reached in and lightly shook Karl's boot, sticking out from under the blanket.

Instinctively, his heart racing, Karl pointed and shot his Luger, even before he knew who it was.

"No!" yelled Johannes, who had already been awake a few minutes. He'd been sitting in the dark, recovered from the demons of his overnight withdrawal.

The old farmer fell over backward on the ground, face up, just outside the tiny silo door. He was dead.

Karl pushed the farmer's legs away as he crawled outside, stood and looked at the old man. "He shouldn't have grabbed my foot like that."

"Karl, all he did was touch your boot."

"Yes, too bad."

Greta heard the shot and came running. She saw her husband lying on the ground and started screaming. "Hanz, Hanz! Get up, Hanz!"

She dropped to her knees, bent over his body and started to shake his shoulders, as if to wake him. She grabbed his torso, clutched him to her chest and rocked back and forth. "Hanz, please don't go without me. Hanz, don't go, don't leave me alone."

Johannes crawled out of the silo and, still on his knees, looked up at Karl, standing over the farmer and his wife, in his tall black boots. Stunned at what had just happened, he suddenly saw the emotionless Karl in a different light.

Just then, the early morning's cloud-covered sky briefly brightened, and a rooster crowed.

Unfazed at having just taken a man's life, Karl donned his shoulder holster, returned the gun to its place, and turned to Johannes. "Get your things, Johannes. It's time for us to go."

Last night, the proud Nazi farmer had filled Karl's car and the five-gallon tanks with gasoline. As they drove away, Karl believed with the gasoline refill and spare gas cans, he should be able to cover a long distance today.

Meanwhile, Johannes, looking back, saw Greta, still draped over her husband, crying and rocking his body. Crushed by the scene, a hint of fear entered his mind. *Karl is a heartless killer.*

With a quick look to the side, Karl saw Johannes' anxiety. With one hand holding the steering wheel, he leaned over, grabbed and yanked the other man's shirt collar, pulling him face to face.

"Listen, Johannes, how you think and feel, and every little thing you do – beginning right now – is a matter of life and death. Wake up to your new reality. The war is over, but you're not home yet. If you want to see your wife, be smart."

CHAPTER THIRTY-ONE

Crossing the Elbe

It had been a tough night for Johannes. Coming down from the methamphetamine wasn't easy, and he'd been sick to his stomach as he woke. Now after seeing what had just happened, his emotions felt raw. He didn't know what to say as they left the farm, and so figured it was best to say nothing. With Karl being an SS officer, Johannes had believed he would be a good companion. Now, after the unwarranted shooting, he decided to run away tonight, after Karl fell asleep.

Karl told Johannes today's goal was to get to Wittenberg by late afternoon, cross the Elbe River just after dark and either stay there or continue to a safe house in Eutzsch if it wasn't too late.

Johannes perked up. He wanted to say he didn't live far from Eutzsch, but remained quiet.

As they began their journey, the overcast sky lightened further as the sun rose. A hint of sunlight wanted to break through the clouds, but within an hour, the sky darkened beneath heavy clouds that threatened rain. Another hour passed and it began to pour. They continued along farm roads parallel to main roads, but those filled with water in low spots and became muddy. Up to now they'd avoided the enemy and remained undetected, and the path highlighted in crayon was working. But the mud made driving a challenge. Karl feared they could get stuck, so he turned onto the main road. Both recognized the need to be more alert for any traffic. Johannes looked ahead, using the binoculars.

Reports at the Bendlerblock four days earlier mentioned a large tank battle between the Wehrmacht and Red Army in Wittenberg. The small town had two bridges crossing the Elbe. One was for vehicles; the other, a railroad bridge. Karl anticipated the recent battle might have destroyed one or both bridges. If the vehicle bridge was out, they would have to abandon the car, cross the river somehow and find another vehicle to continue their journey. He didn't like the idea of leaving six filled gasoline containers behind. He hoped the bridge was still standing and unobstructed, and they could drive across. He held positive expectations but concluded it might be hard to reach the next designated safe house tonight.

Another hour south they came upon a huge cornfield. In the open field, three German tanks sat beside three Soviet tanks. All six were burnt; three had their turrets blown off. Karl commented to Johannes it must have been a nasty battle. Dead German and Russian soldiers lay scattered in the cornfield and beside the road. As they drove by the battle scene, they noticed a gravely wounded German soldier propped against a low stone wall. As they drove by, he reached his hand out, pleading for help. Karl saw the soldier but continued on.

How ruthless not to stop!

Seeing his traveling companion cringe, and reading his thoughts, Karl said, "Johannes, he will live, or he will die. Either way, he would be a drag for us. You want to see your wife, right? Then we must keep moving."

It had rained on and off most of the day. And now, as nightfall approached, the bleak, soggy day grew dark. Karl reflected on the nasty day. Moments later, a strong wind began to blow, and the clouds parted, revealing a full moon. It cast long shadows across the road, and within minutes the two could see the silhouette of Wittenberg.

As they turned and drove along a street called Angerschanze, the street along the river's edge, they spotted the town's two bridges. They slowly pulled under the steel railroad bridge. Karl parked in the shadows to take a closer look. The wooden-trestle vehicle bridge lay a hundred meters ahead.

Getting out, Karl turned and whispered, "Stay close and keep an eye for any movement. Just point to what you see, and we can decide how to deal with it. Silence is essential to help keep our presence a secret until we know it's safe."

They walked slowly, moving over to several buildings, carefully remaining in the shadows. Karl looked back. Johannes carried a rifle and looked scared. They continued ever so quietly toward the vehicle bridge. It appeared intact and unobstructed.

Johannes lagged Karl by ten feet. A cat unexpectedly jumped in front of Johannes, knocking over a garbage can. Startled by the cat, Johannes tripped and dropped his rifle. As it hit the ground, the weapon discharged, creating a flash of light. The bullet hit the steel bridge, and the ricochet echoed loudly.

Karl looked back and saw Johannes on all fours. Karl glanced back around to see if the sound of the rifle had stirred up any movement. The moonlight was just enough to help. He saw nothing.

Johannes awkwardly stood up and stepped from the shadows to retrieve his rifle. Remaining in the moonlight, he took several steps to catch up with Karl when another shot rang out.

Karl turned back and saw Johannes face down with his arms sprawled flat on the ground, dead from a sniper's bullet.

Another sudden shot whizzed past Karl's ear. He dropped and rolled to the base of the building next to him. Warm blood began dripping down the side of his neck. He grabbed a cloth from his pocket and pressed it to his ear, to slow the bleeding. The bullet had sliced his earlobe.

His heart raced. For several minutes, he remained in the shadow, low to the ground, then crawled backward, on all fours. He got into a squat and duck walked to the rear of the alley, where he hid behind a metal trash container. Scowling, Karl clenched his fists; a vein throbbed at his temple. He recently thought how lucky he'd been to skate through this war without getting injured. His lucky streak was broken.

As Karl hid behind the smelly trash, a rat scurried past his feet; the same black cat that startled Johannes chased it. Karl waited, Luger in one hand, and a rag held to his ear by the other. He watched and waited another twenty minutes. It was almost 9. Luckily for Karl, the clouds and rain returned, and it was too dark now for the sniper.

Karl made his way over to Johannes' body; he'd been shot in the neck. Karl figured it was a German soldier in the church tower across the street; there was no reason a Russian marksman would have stayed in the town once the Red Army moved north.

It's too bad he didn't know Johannes was a German soldier.

Karl stripped Johannes' body and carried the rain-soaked clothing back to his car, thinking it could be of use later. Johannes' blood soaked the edge of the shirt's collar, but he threw it into the duffel bag in the car anyway. Karl looked at Johannes' naked body and shook his head as he drove away. He rolled slowly, headlights off, then made a turn onto the bridge, his fingers crossed.

Then he said aloud, "So long, Johannes Wolff. You were a nice companion, but you were weak. You would have failed miserably in SS Officer training."

Except for debris and shell casings, the roadway across the bridge was clear. A German tank sat to the side at one end, its turret farther off to the side of the road. It took less than a minute to reach the other side of the Elbe.

Karl continued south. He drove slowly; it was several more minutes before he turned the headlights on. He felt lucky, despite his bleeding ear.

The winds suddenly brought more clouds. They covered the moon, and it began to rain again.

Karl concluded Johannes had bad luck.

CHAPTER THIRTY-TWO

The Bergwitz Safe House

K arl found his way to Bergwitz and searched for an address next to a tiny lake called Bergwitzee. It was dark now and it took a while before his headlights spotted the vetted safe house. The small garage door was open, so he pulled inside, turned off the ignition and swung the garage door shut. The brief note on the side of the map written by Hockemeier read, "Woman, one two-year-old, one six-month-old infant. Husband serving in the war past four years."

Karl knocked at the front door.

A moment later, a young woman with long blonde hair cracked open the door. Holding a candle, she peeked out.

"I'm expecting several visitors. The others?"

"The others will arrive tomorrow."

"Come in and sit." She put the candle on the table, then lit two more. "Are you hurt?"

He brushed off her concern. "It's nothing."

"Are you hungry?"

When he nodded, she went to the kitchen, poured a glass of fresh milk and began heating up the wiener schnitzel left over from her dinner. After putting it on the table, she sat and looked at him as he ate.

"I'm a forward scout making sure the path is safe for tomorrow's visitors. They will follow within eighteen hours."

"I've been promised money for hosting the visit. Do you have it with you?"

"Here is fifty American dollars; you will be given more money in the morning." The house was small and clean, but bare. His mind flashed to his childhood home, where his mother had knickknacks on every shelf in every room. "Do you know where your husband is serving in the war?"

"His letters said he initially fought on the Western front at the beginning of the war, as far west as Belgium, and then further west toward Paris. Then I received a note saying he was being redeployed to Sicily, as part of a Panzer tank unit fighting to keep Italy free from the invading Americans. But I haven't heard from him in over a year."

Karl knew if he were fighting in Italy, it was likely her husband would not be returning. Just as she finished speaking, Karl heard the cry of an infant. The woman stood.

"My husband has been gone almost five years. He doesn't know we have a two-year-old child and now an infant."

Karl immediately understood. He looked at her long blonde hair as she turned to attend to her infant. Her thin nightgown revealed her shape with the candlelight behind her.

Aroused, he stood and stepped toward her, putting his hand on her hip. She looked up at him. He pressed himself against her thigh, and leaned his head down to smell her hair. Then he ran his hand across her lower back, pulling her toward him.

"Let me take care of the baby first. Then it's your turn."

Her bed was fluffy and comfortable. She was coy, then playful. She reminded him of how Katrina had been that first night and the next morning in her apartment.

Karl and Heidi slept deeply that night. In the middle of the night, they woke when the infant cried. When she returned after changing and nursing the infant, they cuddled in the warm bed and enjoyed each other again. Karl enjoyed her fullness and fell back to sleep, but when the baby began whimpering, Heidi got up again.

Minutes before sunrise, Karl had a disturbing dream. Deep, anxious thoughts from the past visited his subconscious. As a ray of sunlight came through the window and landed on his face, he woke, the dream evaporated and he was left with wondering what it was. Then he remembered he was at the safe house, but Heidi wasn't there in bed next to him. He sat up and saw the young mother with the infant in her arms, and a pot of coffee percolating on the stove.

"Here – hold the baby while I start your breakfast."

Without giving him a chance to object, Heidi deposited the baby into Karl's arms. With no prior experience, he fumbled the infant as he tried holding it. She watched and giggled at the strong man's inability to deal with a tiny infant. Giving up moments later, Karl laid the baby on the bed.

Heidi smiled some more. It was the first time in over a year she was feeling satisfied, and it made her happy. She made eggs and toast for breakfast and served him fresh milk along with his coffee. She watched Karl eat as she cuddled her baby.

Karl had seen Heidi's small, economical car parked in the garage when he pulled in last night. He thought about it as he ate and decided he wanted her car. Before he mentioned a trade, he pulled out the roll of American dollars and gave Heidi the $200 in cash promised by the SS officer who vetted her and the house.

"Heidi, I want to trade cars. My car is slightly older than yours but has been driven only four thousand miles. I have a long journey ahead of me, and your car is more economical. I'd like to give you my Mercedes plus three hundred American dollars to trade vehicles."

Heidi needed the cash and accepted Karl's offer.

"And here's an extra hundred dollars for your warmth and for my satisfaction in bed last night. You are beautiful and a wonderful lover."

She stepped closer, kissed him on the lips, then opened her blouse. "Do you really have to leave now? Please stay."

Her offer was tempting, but he had to get on the road. Karl stepped back from Heidi and shook his head.

"I need to leave."

Focused on heading south, Karl moved the gasoline containers into the trunk of the smaller car. As he did, a plane flew overhead; then two more flew by. He recognized them as American transport planes. *The American and British troops are being redeployed to Berlin for the final takeover. That troop movement north is good; it means the fighting infantry units are being moved away from where I'm headed, exactly as Johannes had suggested.*

When he finished moving the gas cans, Karl closed the trunk.

Heidi approached the car; she'd just braided her long blonde hair and looked so young and fresh and beautiful. "Are you sure there isn't anything else I could do for you before you leave?"

"Heidi, you were terrific last night. I need to leave now. I'll miss you. Here, I have something special for you to remember me by."

He reached into his pocket, pulled out a thin gold bracelet and handed it to her. "Keep this to remember me; it's pure gold."

She got on her tiptoes, reached up and hugged him tight and gave him another kiss on his lips. Karl was feeling a strong connection to the attractive young woman – a feeling that he hadn't felt in a long time. It aroused him. Staying another day – or another few hours – crossed his mind.

He opened Heidi's car door and put the maps on the passenger seat. He threw his duffel bag into the car, then he grabbed some of the clothing from Traudl's duffel bag.

"Here, you might be able to use the fancy clothing and pocket-book inside."

He threw his bag with the roll of American cash, the remaining bracelets, the uncut diamonds, foreign currencies and a French passport identifying him as Pierre Louis Boucher on the backseat. Last night he'd thrown Hitler's fake French passport, along with the other passports for Eva, Otto and Traudl, into Heidi's fireplace.

He took a deep breath, released it, turned the ignition and let the clutch out. He was all set to continue the journey to his parents' home in a fuel-efficient car.

As Karl pulled away, Heidi looked on from the doorway, the baby in her arms. She didn't wave. As her car disappeared, she walked back into her bedroom, put the baby in its crib. She opened her drawer, pulled out the photo of her husband and placed it on her dresser.

When my husband returns, from the war, I won't have to explain about sleeping with the SS officer last night. But how will I explain how I've given birth to two children in the last three years when he's been gone the last five?

Johannes surely won't be pleased with what I've done.

CHAPTER THIRTY-THREE

Bonjour, Monsieur

The morning was brighter than yesterday; the sun wanted to break through the cool, foggy mist that hung amid the forest treetops.

Today's goal was to pass Leipzig using the farm roads on the west side, then continue passed the town of Schleiz. *If all goes well, I'll arrive in Munchberg around dark.* Karl remained curious as to his path the first day when he headed south and then so far west to Beelitz, but he trusted Hockemeier's good judgment.

Two hours into his drive, Karl stopped to relieve himself. Not yet finished, he heard the rumble of a tank. Turning, he saw dozens of U.S. troops, led by a jeep, rounding a bend in the road. He berated himself for having foolishly stopped in an awkward location that afforded him no foresight. They were only thirty yards from him. They seemed in a hurry, with not one but three tanks and a fuel truck right behind them. The four American soldiers in the jeep spotted him at the side of his car, as he zipped his pants. The encounter was inevitable. Karl swallowed hard.

As they approached, he saw the unit commander in the open jeep beside the driver. In the rear, a radioman sat next to a standing soldier manning the machine gun mounted on the back of the jeep. They pulled up and stopped beside the car as Karl put both arms in the air.

The driver addressed him in German. "*Hallo, schonen tag.*"

Karl replied in German, "*Danke und guten tag.*" He continued in German. "I understand German, but I am a Frenchman and, as such, can we please speak in French if I am to be questioned?"

An American soldier fluent in French was called up to the jeep as it pulled to the side.

The soldier came forward and said, "*Bonjour, monsieur.*"

Karl replied in French, "*Bonjour, monsieur. I am a French busi-nessman in the dry-goods business and became stranded in Germany when the war started. I've hidden in farmhouses, barns and hay lofts, staying out of sight, and trying to stay alive. I've eaten little and lost much weight during that time. You'll want to know Soviet tanks and foot soldiers passed me in Beelitz and Trebbin going north toward Berlin two days ago. After not seeing anyone, I thought it would be safer now to begin my travel back to Paris. Do you know whether the Wehrmacht occupation of my beloved homeland France is over?*"

While they were speaking, the radioman in the back of the jeep received a call. He leaned forward, relaying news to the commander.

"Okay, that's enough. Tell Frenchy we need to leave and head to Berlin. Tell him *bonjour* and good luck finding his way home."

The soldier informed Karl it was now safe for him to head back to France.

Karl blessed himself as a Catholic would, then said loudly, "*Bon-jour! Vive la France! Vive l'America!*"

The U.S. troops continued north, and Karl watched closely as three M18 Hellcat tanks rumbled past. He knew from briefings in Berlin these machines could reach 60 mph on paved roads. *What fantastic-looking machines – and huge guns. Not as big as ours, but they certainly can outmaneuver our larger Tigers and Panther tanks. No wonder the Americans are winning.*

Congratulating himself over how his encounter with the Ameri-cans had gone, Karl drove away with renewed confidence.

Twenty minutes later, the French interpreter told the U.S. Com-mander in the front seat of the jeep, "Chief, I needed to talk to that Frenchy guy some more. I think he was a Nazi soldier."

"Why do you say that? The Nazis are in Berlin right now, defend-ing old man Adolf."

"Did you notice his boots?"

"No, and stop your complaining, Kilgore. If he had boots on, he probably took them off a dead Kraut. Anyway, we have way more im-portant things to do than picking up a lone Nazi here and there."

Karl had only driven two more miles when another column of five American tanks and some 200 American troops approached. This time he pulled over and stood on the edge of the open car door, waving and shouting, "*Vive la France. Vive l'America. Vive la France. Vive l'America.*"

They were in a hurry and couldn't care less about him.

Karl smirked and spoke aloud. "Impressive. Ten more fast tanks headed to Berlin. It's so ironic. Der Führer could've been hiding behind the car; or, if he had shaved, Adolf could have stood next to me, right here, waving and shouting '*Vive l'America!*' and they'd have driven right by!"

He got back in the car and drove away.

My Führer, my Führer! You should have waited for me. Had General von Schultz done his duty instead of drinking Benedictine and playing with Hilda, all would have turned out differently. But now fate is smiling on me today! C'est la vie!

He chuckled, thinking himself clever for his use of the French phrase.

CHAPTER THIRTY-FOUR

Still Heading South

When dusk arrived, Karl was less than a mile from the next safe house.

He drove down the street leading into the village of Zeitz, and felt confined. The side streets were narrow, the houses too close together for his comfort. Karl slowed, approaching the safe house, and looked in the window. Several people sat inside, speaking loudly and drinking beer.

He decided to drive on. He used the remaining twilight to go further, and he was prepared to sleep in his car. The map showed another red dot in the village of Oettersdorf, several miles ahead and another in Munchberg, about ten miles further along.

Driving became slower as darkness fell. Karl decided to stop at the safe house in Oettersdorf, near Schliez, owned by an elderly couple, Kurt and Heike Ziegenbauer. As his surname indicated, Kurt owned a small herd of goats and made soft cheese, while his wife, Heike, said to be a second cousin to Adolf, knitted and sold sweaters.

The couple welcomed Karl warmly, but as he walked inside, they looked outside for the additional people. Karl explained Adolf and his entourage would be along in sixteen to twenty-four hours.

They said, "We had expected six visitors, based on what Herr Hockemeier said."

The Ziegenbauers relaxed at Karl's explanation that the others, including Hitler, would show up tomorrow.

Heike suggested Karl wash up for supper. When he returned, a plate with veal, vegetables, potatoes, salad and fresh goat cheese sat on the table waiting for him. Karl devoured everything, some extra meat, and finished a full bottle of Gewürztraminer. Then he asked for more meat and potatoes.

Heike said, "Wonderful! It will be a little while. Go have a seat on the couch and relax."

While waiting for another serving, he looked at the red-and-white gingham tablecloth, and the living room's decorations. It reminded him of his parents' home, including the chessboard set up and ready for play. He remembered playing chess with his father and grandfather on Sunday after dinner. The Ziegenbauers even had an old mandolin like his grandfather's.

Karl relaxed and warmed up on the soft couch. He was headed home, home to his parents, no longer running to escape. Then Katrina and his child came to mind. He tried to recall his child's birth date but couldn't. Then his thoughts drifted to Katrina. He wondered if she would be more relaxed this time on his return home. Then his thoughts drifted to Heidi and he wondered who the better lover was, her or Katrina. Heidi was certainly more willing and relaxed – and a bit more aggressive. Now he wished he'd stayed an extra day with her.

Growing sleepy as his mind darted from thought to thought, Karl slipped into a sleep. Within moments his subconscious flashed back to a death camp event, like his recent daydream. In his dream he recalled the first day he had become temporarily in charge of initiating the process of emptying Jews and Slavs from boxcars. The dream scene seemed strikingly vivid and alive.

A swastika-marked German steam locomotive pulled six boxcars stuffed full of undesirables, mostly Jews and Slavs. The engine slowed and, releasing its steam, came to a stop. Two guards pulled hard and slid the first boxcar's large cattle doors open. The prisoners stepped hesitantly out onto the platform, and then were directed down a long ramp. Many were crying, and those who weren't already, began to cry as the men and women were separated. All were led to the newly expanded holding area. They stood in grassy areas next to each other, separated by a chain-link fence. They were moved along again, suitcases, coats and other belongings taken from them. Next, their shoes were removed. Further along a narrowing chute, they were herded into another area, stripped naked on a concrete pad and forced to stand in the brutal summer heat before being directed to another holding area.

Twenty yards out, the wave of an SS officer's hand meant the furnaces in the crematoriums would soon be ready, and the next step of the process could now begin.

The first groups of naked men and women were forced by armed SS guards to enter two rooms, side by side. They were told they would have their hair deloused and get showers. At the doorway, seeing shower heads attached to the plumbing pipes, a group of about 80 men willingly stepped inside. They stood, naked, some embarrassed and crying, some welcoming a shower. The doors behind them closed and they waited for the showers to begin. Suddenly some began gagging. Then more gagged. Toxic gas, not water, spewed from the shower heads. Then they all began coughing, gagging and choking. The first to succumb fell to the ground; one by one, others fell on top of them. In an adjacent room, mothers, sisters, daughters and grandmothers met the same fate.

Twenty minutes later, the SS guard observing the horrible deaths through a small window gave the 'all clear' signal. Everyone was dead. The poisonous gas was shut off and vented from the ceiling of the killing room. Then a dozen Slovak slave laborers wearing gas masks entered the room, lifted the corpses onto steel-wheeled carts and rolled the carts through a corridor into the next building, the crematorium with its gas-fired ovens.

Karl watched the entire process that day, first from the train platform and then through the small glass window. As the bodies fell and were carted from the room, he felt a friendly slap on the back by Fritz Todt, who was there watching with him.

"Karl, your suggested design changes to add the metal rails in the concrete floor, allowing the bodies to be moved more efficiently into the crematorium were excellent," Fritz praised him. "We've cut the time for the removal and transport of the bodies into the furnaces to less than a quarter of the time originally planned. And your idea to put shower heads with false plumbing into the killing room saved time by encouraging the deplorables to get inside more quickly. Great thinking, Karl. I'm sending your name to headquarters in Berlin; you deserve a medal."

After Fritz complimented Karl, they went back outside to watch three more boxcars of Jews and Slavs get emptied into the holding area and go through the same process.

When the next boxcar opened, it was all women. As they stepped onto the platform and down the ramp, Karl recognized one. It was Ruth Steinberger, a young woman from his hometown. Karl and Ruth grew up and played as youngsters, attended high school together, and even skied together a few times. Her father, Franz Steinberger, a big man like Karl, worked in the Ravensburg factory as a foreman for Otto. Some mothers in the primary school occasionally joked with Valentina and Ruth's mother at how much alike Karl and Ruth looked.

Valentina knew exactly why.

Karl was shocked, seeing Ruth among the group of women. At first, he couldn't understand why Ruth was even in the boxcar. Then he remembered Ruth was a Jewess. Her Jewishness never meant anything to him, nor did it even enter his mind. And unknown to anyone else, he and Ruth had spent a long evening together one warm summer's night, tucked away on his grandfather's boat docked in a small slip on Lake Constance. They were 16. For both, it was their first sexual experience.

Within minutes Ruth and the other women had their belongings removed, and were stripped of their clothing. Karl was deeply affected at seeing someone once close to his heart about to be gassed to death, more efficiently and easily moved to the furnace.

Suddenly, she looked up. Their eyes met.

Ruth screamed, "Karl, Karl! Karl, help me, please."

Karl saw her, and he heard her. He looked away, then walked away and lit a cigarette. Ruth's face and outcry haunted Karl the rest of that day, the remainder of that week. That warm, humid summer night with Ruth was a deep, memorable experience, tucked far away in his mind, never to be forgotten. And seeing Ruth that day, among the naked women being herded into the gas chamber, affected him far more deeply than he realized. Karl's hard shell was pierced that day.

Karl snapped out of his brief unconsciousness state when Heike put another heaping plate of food on the table and called his name. Then Kurt brought Karl another bottle of his homemade white wine.

Karl finished the food in no time, and the second bottle of wine as if it were water. He thanked Heike and got up to stretch.

Heike told him to go back and sit on the couch again. A minute later, she served him a huge piece of apple strudel and Kurt laid a few more pieces of wood across the andirons.

Peering into the fireplace, Karl became sleepy again. His eyes closed. *The war is over. I must return home. I did what was asked of me in my role as a Waffen SS officer. I helped to eliminate as many Jews as possible because they spoil our pure Aryan heritage. That is what was asked of me, and that is what I did. What is done is done. The German people are better off for what we have accomplished. And Germany will rise again.*

Karl fell asleep on the couch and Heike lay one of her knitted wool blankets over him, then headed to the kitchen to clean up. She told her husband she would stay up another twenty minutes to make dough for more apple turnovers tomorrow, for when Cousin Adolf arrived.

The next morning, Karl arose early. He wrote a note thanking Heike and Kurt and left without breakfast.

The next two days, he followed the route highlighted on Map #2, and then Map #3. But for each of the next two nights, when he drove by the safe houses, they had more people inside than the notes indicated. So he slept in Heidi's car those nights.

On the sixth day, Karl drove further south than expected, and as the darkness fell, a heavy fog developed. He had traveled beyond Pegnitz to the small village of Hainbronn. With difficulty, he eventually found his way to the safe farmhouse at the end of Echen Weg, next to a newly planted field. As he pulled up to the house, he peered through the fog and saw a dozen deer nibbling grass at the edge of the field. The deer looked up but ignored him.

The farmhouse was dark. Karl went to the side door and knocked. An old, bent-over man came to the door. Karl said he was Der Führer's forward escort and was immediately welcomed inside. The old man woke his wife and told her to warm up some food for their guest. Again, dinner consisted of veal, vegetables and mashed potatoes. The evening was a virtual repeat of a few nights earlier. He devoured the meal and drank more homemade dry Gewürztraminer. Then he had a huge second helping and fell sound asleep.

The next morning, Karl woke early and walked around the farmhouse before the farmer and his wife were up. He spotted a small, clean 1934 Opel Blitz truck parked in the barn. It was a model just like his father's truck. He looked inside. It had low mileage, was in terrific shape, and the keys were in the ignition.

Karl believed the small one-and-a-half-ton truck would offer a better ride than Heidi's small car. And if he were stopped, he could say he had dropped off some merchandise. He pulled Heidi's car next to the barn, transferred the gasoline cans into the truck, made certain he had his envelope, duffel bag and everything else of importance.

Karl felt he deserved a nice truck for his wartime service. But to be nice, he put $100 on the driver's seat, along with the keys to Heidi's car. Then he got in the truck and headed down the driveway.

Hearing his truck start, the old farmer came running out the door, wondering why Karl was driving away in it. He yelled and yelled, but Karl never looked back.

Appreciating the full tank of gasoline, as Karl headed toward his hometown, he admired the beautifully knitted wool blanket that lay on the passenger seat.

CHAPTER THIRTY-FIVE

Returning to Ravensburg

I t was another full day of driving, and another night sleeping in the truck, before Karl finally arrived in Ravensburg late the next day. As he drove on the main street leading to the factory, he noted almost every building along the street – as well as the buildings alongside the railroad – was heavily damaged if not completely crumbled. Debris strewn all over the streets made driving next to impossible. He surveyed damage caused by American bombing raids that would take the town years to recover from.

He drove a bit farther and saw the Ravensburg foundry, milling and machining factory ahead. Bombs had hit each of its four long buildings; the newest assembly building, built after he entered the Waffen SS, was flattened.

Karl pulled over, got out of the truck and carefully climbed over several bent steel beams to get inside to take a better look. Both hundred-ton overhead cranes had crashed to the ground and were twisted wrecks, having fallen from perches along the rails atop the high columns. One crane's main hook lay on the floor, still attached to a ladle that had held molten steel. The ladle had tipped on its side, the steel long since cooled into a perfectly smooth lava flow across the foundry floor. Molds lay scattered across the floor from the explosion. And the furnace chamber, broken in half, lay on the ground.

He saw two bodies face down on the floor, their torsos and legs encased forever by the molten flow that hardened into steel. Karl felt himself cringe. *The molten metal must have splashed onto the nearby workers. What a terrible way to die!* He glanced at a tiny scar on his left hand, where a burbling drop of 2500-degree molten steel had splashed on him more than a decade earlier. That single drop had caused him days of agony.

He stared at the bodies, then turned away and lit a cigarette. He took a couple of long, deep drags. Within a few moments, the nicotine arrived in his brain and satisfied his dependency.

I recognize him. He drove Father to the foundry daily after he returned to work. His face. He must have been in agony when the metal poured over his body.

He took another drag.

What a mess! How many lives were lost here? They were all hard workers, good men. Many were fathers of my friends in Friedrichshafen.

He continued to walk through the factory floor, seeing dead bodies scattered about.

The destruction of this highly productive factory is such a waste! How could the Americans do something so terrible?

Karl continued his walk, entering the milling and machining area, and saw more dead bodies. From the decay and the stench, he estimated they had lain dead at least three weeks. Then he saw Ruth's father, Franz Steinberger, dead on the floor next to a milling machine. Karl paused. *There's something about this man I can't explain. He sometimes smiled at me. It made me uncomfortable. I could never put my finger on it.*

Then he recalled seeing Ruth naked at the death camp. *Father knew Ruth's father was Jewish. How, then, was Ruth sent away?*

Karl never knew Ruth had left town to attend school in Leipzig in 1934. In 1937, at 23, she eloped, marrying an older professor. In 1938, after the Kristallnacht pogrom, Ruth's husband openly discussed his anti-Nazi sentiments. The Gestapo picked him up and sent him away, accused of being a communist. Ruth hid for years in a Leipzig home's attic with six other Jewish women. They all were picked up by the Gestapo when a 14-year-old boy, a member of the Hitler Youth organization, snitched and revealed their location.

Karl wondered if his father had been hurt or killed in the bombing. Covering his nose, he stepped over and past a grouping of dead of bodies and strewn metal parts to the middle of the building, then climbed the bent and broken stairway to his father's office. Located in the middle of the building, the second-floor view enabled the plant superintendent to oversee the workers below from one end of the factory to the other. Otto typically would limp down the stairs and walk around the factory several times a day, to see to it that production maintained a good pace. When the annex was built to handle assemblies and subassemblies for Panzer IV tanks and other armored vehicles, Otto hobbled even farther.

Karl carefully walked up the fractured stairway and looked in the empty room. The plate-glass windows on all four sides were shattered. He breathed a sigh of relief at not seeing Otto or Monika as victims.

Coming back downstairs, Karl ducked his head into the general foreman's office directly below, not realizing Otto had been demoted and moved to the lower office. On the side wall he saw a pinup-girl calendar from 1944 and another beside it, turned to March 1945. Each day was crossed out at midnight by the office manager on the midnight shift. The last date crossed out was March 11. Karl figured the facility was bombed March 12, about seven weeks earlier – no wonder the bodies smelled so badly. He wondered where his father and the other survivors were.

Outside, a stockpile of colorful high-pressure gas cylinders lay scattered on the ground like a bunch of crayons.

Karl thought back to his apprentice days, shuffling the Linde gas cylinders in and out of the factory, allowing the workers to use oxygen and acetylene torches to trim hardened metal slag leaked from molds.

Through a collapsed wall, Karl saw the remnants of the 3,000-gallon liquid-oxygen tank that had sat beside the building. A spark from the bombing must have caused it to rupture. The liquid oxygen had no doubt vaporized, accelerating nearby flames, creating a huge fireball and inferno outside and inside the building.

Much of the nearby steel was melted into globs from the heat of the inferno.

I remember Father telling me about having led a project in his early days to inject oxygen into the furnaces to increase the temperature inside. It made the furnace temperatures rise quickly, so the process to smelt the iron ore was faster and more complete. Now all his ideas and hard work are destroyed.

Returning to the truck, Karl took a last look at the buildings along the main street. *So much damage. How could the Americans do this to our town?*

CHAPTER THIRTY-SIX

Arriving in Friedrichshafen

K arl drove on toward his parents' home on Lake Constance. He wondered how they were doing. *Time has slipped by quickly. Hard to believe it's been eight years and three months since I joined the SS. And despite my years of traveling as a Waffen SS officer through Germany, Italy, France and Belgium, I can't believe I've been home only once to my parents' and to see Katrina.*

As Karl arrived in town, most of the shops were closed or vacant. Seeing the empty streets seemed strange. He drove another half mile and arrived at his parents' home. The sun was setting over the Bodensee – a sight he hadn't seen for many years.

He went to the door and knocked, expecting to be greeted with hugs and kisses as a hero returning from war, but there was no response. He knocked again, then jiggled the handle. Finding it unlocked, Karl let himself in. The house was cold and quiet. With the twilight fading, he lighted candles on the table and the mantel. The table was set with his mother's favorite red-and-white gingham cloth, two plates, forks, knives, his father's beer stein and a wine glass for his mother. The kettle sat on the stove. Wood was piled next to the fireplace, but the ashes were flat. He could tell the last fire wasn't recent.

Karl walked, holding a candle, examining each room. *Mother's Fabergé Easter egg is missing, and all her knickknacks are gone. What's happened? Where can they be? It's as if they are gone. Completely gone away from here. Grandfather's mandolin is gone from the corner in the living room. Even our family Bible is missing from the bookshelf.*

Karl paused and opened the family Bible in his mind's eye. He recalled his von Richter family heritage on the initial foldout pages. He recalled the stories told to him as a boy about the Duchy and Kingdom of Wurttemberg – how knights in shining armor once rode throughout the kingdom, protecting it from foreign invaders. He flashed back to when he first began working on the tanks in the factory. He once daydreamed the Panzer tanks were horses that belonged to the knights of the duchy and kingdom.

Still holding the candle, he walked out back. His father's garden tools to plant spring cold-weather vegetables leaned against the wall of the house, but the ground had not been turned over for planting.

Karl knew as U.S. soldiers made their way north from Italy, through Switzerland and into Germany's southern cities, they'd go house to house in every village, to remove any Wehrmacht soldiers still in hiding. *My parents are civilians and shouldn't be missing from their house.*

He went back inside for another look. Maybe he could find a clue to where they might be. As he walked room to room, he became anxious for their whereabouts.

Father and Mother knew how important the family Bible and Grandfather's mandolin are to me. They must be at my house, with Katrina and our son.

Karl climbed back in the truck and headed toward Langenargen . It was dark, but he knew his way. It was just over five miles further south along the shore, just past Montfort Castle. He was excited at the thought of surprising them all by rushing through his own front door. He drove past a wooded area, then a small farm on the right. He made a right turn, passing a small cemetery, then turned onto Saint Anna Street. His house was just ahead, a short walk from the water. As he arrived, his heart beat fast. He drove up and saw no lights in the house. He knocked; the door swung open slowly. As it did, the hinge creaked loudly.

Karl stepped inside. It took a moment for his eyes to adjust and realize the house was empty. He grabbed the candle from its wall fixture, lighted it and, as at his parents', began walking room to room. Cobwebs hung from the kitchen's light fixture, wall candle fixtures and across the fireplace mantel. He scanned the room again and figured it had been vacant a year or longer. His old shirts and pants hung in the bedroom closet, but nothing else. No pictures of Katrina, nor of the child. Nothing on the walls, no evidence Katrina had ever lived here. Karl continued to look for any clue of family life. He saw a piece of furniture he'd made when he was a teenager, a two-seat bench. Positioned beneath a window, it had held several houseplants in clay pots. One pot remained on the bench, containing the skeleton of a long-dead plant.

Katrina has convinced my parents to leave town and go with her and our son to her parents' home. Lecco would be a safe place because the American soldiers, especially Italian-American soldiers, would be compassionate to the people there. The southeast end of Lake Como, where it's called Lake Lecco, is quiet. That's probably where they all are. Or perhaps Mother suggested everyone go to the family compound in Botticino. Hmm. Lecco or Botticino?

Karl concluded his family was in Lecco. He could see his father enjoying crusty Italian bread and the tasty sfogliatelle pastries Katrina's father made.

I'll stay here tonight; but before it gets too late, I'll knock on some neighbors' doors. I hope someone knows where Katrina, my child and parents have gone.

He walked up and down the street. Finding all the houses empty, he returned to his truck, grabbing the envelope with Plan C, the maps and his clothing bag. Karl calculated how much time it would take to get to Lecco, but realized he'd lost track of the date. The calendar inside the broom closet was turned to March 1943 and of no use.

It didn't immediately occur to him that Katrina had been gone two years. Then he recalled the calendar in the kitchen storeroom where he'd spent five minutes with Hilda. It had been April 30. He counted the days from leaving Berlin – seven – and figured how much time he still had to find Katrina and his son in Lecco, and then get to the submarine off the coast of Ravenna.

He went outside for wood for the fireplace. The night was chilly, and the sky clear. He could see his breath, and in the darkness with his eyes adjusted, he could see the lake at the end of the street. Back inside, he started the fire, changed into some old clothes and grabbed a woolen blanket to cover himself. Hungry, but warmed by the fire, he fell asleep on the couch.

Sometime around 4, Karl's body temperature rose, and he started to dream. Overheated, he was sweating as a rush of emotions flashed deep in his mind, bringing him to a death camp. He had twice dreamed of the death camps since Hitler's suicide. Each time the dream was clear and distinct. This dream was different, stronger, and had arrived evoking ugly crematory smells.

Karl saw himself inside a boxcar, crowded tightly among Jews and Slavs. German soldiers stood outside with rifles and a machine gun, ready to shoot a lineup of naked men. As the shots rang out, he saw their bodies fall backward into the ditch. Then the naked women, all huddled together and crying, were pushed by the soldiers to the edge of the same ditch. As Karl watched from the boxcar, he saw himself. He was the SS officer ordering the shots to be fired. Then, he saw Ruth, this time standing with Katrina and several others, about to be shot with a machine gun. He tried to yell from the boxcar, "No! No!" but his voice was muted. The shots were fired, and the women fell backward into the ditch. He looked again at the SS officer. It was him, standing there, lighting a cigarette, grinning evilly at the boxcar, and then walking away.

Karl woke up. His face was flushed, his skin hot; he was sweating. The atrocities he'd directed and participated in haunted him. He got up from the couch, stepped outside, stripped off his damp shirt to cool himself and sat on the rear steps. He looked at the stars and wondered. In the distance the bluish glow of morning was rising.

He returned to the couch ten minutes later, covered up and slept another hour before rising.

Karl found another set of his old clothing, changed his pants and shirt, then got in the truck. He had driven only a hundred meters up to Friedrichshafener Street when he saw an old man on the corner, walking slowly. Karl stopped the truck before making the turn.

"Old man, where is everyone? The town is empty!"

"The American Army came through Langenargen and Friedrichshafen four weeks ago, a few days after the factory bombing. Everyone was gathered up and sent to the airfield, where they set up tents. They've been holding and sorting through the villagers one by one to determine who is a German soldier or just a civilian. Those of us who worked in the factory are being set aside and detained in different tents.

"How are you here, then?"

"I hid in a crawlspace under my house."

Believing his parents' house was vacated recently, Karl rethought what had happened to them and Katrina. Maybe they'd been detained at the airfield. He got out of the truck. "Old man, do you know Otto Ulrich von Richter?"

"Why, yes, I knew Otto. He used to live up the road on the lake in Friedrichshafen. I worked at the foundry with him years ago."

"Do you know where Otto and his wife Valentina are? And the woman who lived here?"

The old man tilted his head downward briefly, looking sorrowful. "Otto and his wife are dead. Valentina died from pneumonia just before Christmas in 1941."

He paused momentarily, saddened by his recollection. "Otto died of a heart attack at the end of the next summer. Yes, that was 1942. He died in his office at the foundry, late at night. He was found the next morning by his secretary. Some said Otto and Monika had been fooling around, and the affair broke his wife's heart. But Otto was a good man and he would never do something like that. After his wife died, work became challenging for Otto. The pressure became unbearable for every-one there, especially when he was demoted. American airplanes dropped leaflets all around Friedrichshafen and Ravensburg, saying our factory should stop producing war machinery, and we should leave the buildings because they'd be bombed soon. Many stopped going to work and hid as rumors spread that the American Army was advancing north toward our village. Production slowed and Otto was blamed even more.

"Most people thought Otto died of a broken heart after Valentina passed. But we knew he was heartsick after hearing his son, Karl, was killed in the spring of 1942, fighting in the war."

Hearing his parents were dead, Karl's eyes started to fill with tears. He turned away to repress his emotions, and instead lit a cigarette. Then he turned back toward the man. "Old man, did you know Otto and Valentina's daughter-in-law? Her name was Katrina."

At the question, the old man took a closer look at Karl's face, this time from a different angle.

"I remember you. Yes, you're Karl, Otto's son. You're alive. It's me, Wilhelm Muller. You worked at my side as an apprentice on a milling machine. Yes, you were a teenager."

"I remember. What happened to Katrina?"

The old man paused. He remembered Karl's excitable temper, and how he was once a victim of Karl's verbal assault for working too slowly. What had become of Katrina was not coming to him right away.

Annoyed at Wilhelm's inability to remember, Karl grabbed him by the back of his neck, pulled out his Luger and pointed it at the man's face. "Listen, old man. Where did Katrina go?"

He looked up, rattled and barely able to speak. "Oh yes, you're asking about Otto's daughter-in-law. She and her baby, yes. She was pregnant and the child arrived just after Otto died. Otto would have been so happy."

"Old man, the child. Remember the child. Was the child a boy or a girl?"

"Her child was cute – a plump little boy – yes, yes, with blue eyes just like his beautiful mother. My wife knew her. They... they walked the baby carriage... they, yes, they'd go together down to the water. It was so sad. Three months... yes, three months before Otto died, there were changes in the factory. Production slowed because the leaflets scared many of the workers, then your father was removed as the plant superintendent. He was demoted and made assistant to a Nazi politician who was put in charge. The Nazi knew nothing about production. Things got much worse – yes, right after the Nazi took Otto's place. People left. The Nazi made several bad decisions. The workers who remained hated him and decided to make him fail. They all slowed down. All the deadlines were missed. Otto tried to get things running right, but things were a mess. Everything fell apart, yes, it all fell apart... in just three months. Then Speer came and held a meeting in the office with the Nazi. Otto was blamed for everything that went wrong. The Nazi even said Otto had purposely undermined his position by causing many of the deadlines to be missed on purpose and told people to leave. Otto would never do that.

"That night... yes, that same night, Otto died of a heart attack at work. Then his daughter-in-law, pretty Katrina, quit her job as a nurse. No, I remember, yes, she had a big job at the hospital, and she left town with her little baby boy. She left without saying goodbye to any of us. My wife and other women were brokenhearted when she was suddenly gone.

"They said, yes, they... they said Valentina and Otto's deaths were because you weren't here. They all said 'Karl should have stayed to run the factory'. Even the factory workers said you should have stayed. Yes, Karl, if you had stayed to help your father in the factory, everything would have been different. Yes, you should have stayed, and not gone off to war.

"Then everyone, yes, everyone thought you were dead... because you never came home to see your parents or your wife, not even during the holidays. Otto once told me your beautiful wife and your mother were extremely upset. They never got any letters from you. Otto, yes, he knew you were alive and traveling all over Germany all the time. He heard about your evil deeds at the death camps from different SS people who inspected the production at our factory.

"Otto told me all about you. Your father... yes, your father never approved of what you were doing to kill the Jews and the others. He wanted you to fight the English and French, yes, fight them with our tanks and guns, not commit genocide, gassing people to death. But he really wished you had stayed."

Karl shook the old man again, squeezing his neck even harder. "Shut up, old man! That's enough and that's all yesterday. Where did my wife and my son go? Are you listening to me? Where did they go?" He cocked the trigger on his Luger and put the barrel against Wilhelm's forehead.

"No one, no one knows where they went. She just left with the little boy. Imagine, yes, the two of them with blue eyes. One evening after work, my wife sent me to your house to look for your wife to take their walk. The baby carriage was outside and her car was missing. My wife went inside, said she saw a map on the table, yes, a road map to Milan or Bergamo or Brescia or Verona. I swear, Karl, I can't tell you anything else. You should… yes, you should have been here for your parents, for your beautiful wife and son… and for the factory and the workers. Shame on you Karl. Yes, shame on you."

Enraged, Karl loosed his grip on Wilhelm's neck and threw him aside. Already unsteady on his feet, the old man tripped and fell face forward to the ground, severely bloodying his face and hands and catching a mouthful of sandy dirt.

Angry and anxious, Karl climbed back into the truck. As he reached to start the vehicle, he thought he heard the deep rumblings of slow-moving tanks in the distance. He paused to listen more closely.

They're rolling this way, toward Langenargen. Karl looked at Wilhelm lying on the ground, bleeding, let the clutch out and drove back north to his parents' home, to hide from the advancing Americans. He recalled a small addition his father had built with a narrow hiding space between two walls. *I'll be safe in there.*

He parked behind the house and hurried inside. Sliding the secret wall panel to the side, he stepped into the slim space and pulled the panel shut. It seemed much tighter than when he would sometimes hide while playing games as a youngster. Fifteen minutes later, he heard the American tanks growling outside along the street.

As he stood silently inside the false wall, his nose pushed against a wooden stud, Karl hoped the soldiers wouldn't feel the truck's hood, undoubtedly still warm. Then he remembered – the envelope with maps and directions was on the front seat!

The front door's hinges squeaked as it swung open. An American soldier stepped inside and walked around, inspecting each room. He was within a foot of Karl, hidden behind the false wall when he turned to address another soldier at the door. "Leo, it looks okay in here. Let's catch up with Ted and the others and get back to the airport. I think we've identified everyone now that we have that old guy Wilhelm with us. He must have taken a bad fall. He's confused and might have a loose screw. He's saying there's some bigshot Nazi SS officer driving around town."

Karl waited another five minutes, then slid the panel to exit the space. As he moved, a rusty nail tore through his shirt and stabbed his chest. He tipped his head down just enough to look and cut his cheek on another rusty nail. He wiped the blood from his cheek, then headed out the back door. Karl saw dust still lingering in the air from the American tank column as it headed to the airfield.

"Obviously, they didn't feel the hood or look inside the truck," he mused. "I can't believe I was foolish enough to leave everything lying on the front seat! But my good luck continues."

Karl headed back toward Langenargen, remembering to gather extra clothing at his house for the trip to Italy.

He decided to trade vehicles again. Last night he'd seen a two-door 1938 Mercedes-Benz 170 B Kubelwagen cabriolet in the driveway next door. He presumed the owner was being held by the Americans at the airport detention center. Boldly, he went inside the neighbor's house, found the car keys, and in turn, hung the Opel truck keys on the same hook. He felt it was a fair trade. The car would be more economical for heading into Italy.

He started the car; the gas gauge said full. He transferred the five cans of gasoline and put an empty cardboard box into the backseat. Then he went back to his neighbor's house, grabbed all the dishes and glass-ware, and threw them into the cardboard box, purposely breaking them.

I'll use these broken home goods as my cover story if I'm stopped. I'll need to travel on main roads through the valleys ahead, and at some point, my identity will be questioned by the American occupiers. I'll say I'm a traveling home-goods merchant, returning to France when the war began. I was caught in Germany and hid for several years. Now I am returning home to southern France through Italy with these broken dishes and glassware. That explanation and my French passport should suffice.

A minute later, Karl rolled down the street and headed toward Lecco. He reflected on what Wilhelm had said about his parents' deaths, the workers' leaving, the ultimate failure of the Nazi plant superintendent to manage the factory's production schedules, and how all the blame had inappropriately fallen on Otto's shoulders.

My parents are gone. Why did Father think I had died? And what really happened to cause Mother such heartache?

CHAPTER THIRTY-SEVEN

Lecco

Karl's head was spinning again; he was thinking constantly. But now he was sure Katrina and his son were at her parents' apartment at the south end of Lake Lecco.

Long before railroads existed, Lake Lecco's water flowing south carried farm products and grapes grown on hillsides, over 75 miles to the Po River, and then further east to Venice and cities on the Adriatic Sea.

Karl headed to southern Germany, then into Feldkirch, Austria. It was his first target town, according to his map. The next town he targeted was Schaan, in Lichtenstein, then Landquart, Davos and Saint Moritz in Switzerland. The Benz enabled him to make good time through Gordona and Bellano in Italy. It would be a full day's journey of about 170 miles to Lecco.

Lecco isn't an industrial town. It should have been spared bombing by the Allies. Still, if flatbed railcars in the Lecco train yards had gathered tanks and artillery after the defeats at Anzio and Rome, for transport back to defend Germany, American air reconnaissance would have bombed the area. *I'll see what happened when I get there.*

As he drove through the mountains, Karl thought more about the maps, raw diamonds, rings, the four remaining gold bracelets and cash.

It's been eight days since I left the bunker. That leaves nine weeks to get to Ravenna. If I can reach Lecco, pick up Katrina and my son, I should get to the U-boat within the allotted time.

Knowing the Blackshirts mentioned in the escape plan reportedly were still faithful to the Axis, he realized they'd be waiting for Hitler and his entourage. *Even if I veer off the path and take an extra week or two to pick them up, I'll still be well within the ten weeks.*

Then Karl thought about South America, the *de facto* hiding place discussed by so many SS officers. Every conversation praised the continent for its beautiful, shapely women; clean, sandy beaches in Rio de Janeiro; the high pampas region and wine-growing areas of Argentina and the mountainous coast of Chile. The SS officers even joked about an annual reunion on a beach called Ipanema if things went wrong with the war.

By now every German military officer must be scrambling to get out of Germany, one way or another. Things are probably still going badly in Berlin, and the Führer's suicide will bring about catastrophic changes for decades.

If only he'd escaped by plane and flew to South America. Who knows how things would've gone for him in Brazil or Argentina? Maybe he could have reconnected with SARGO, and rejuvenated the Nazi party. I'm sure Otto Skorzeny and his group made it out in time. Skorzeny is more likely the one to pull our SS people back together in Brazil.

He drove further and wondered again whether Hitler's death had been a hoax. *Could that be his reason to not fly from Berlin?*

Eva's death was real. I recognized her before I poured that can of gasoline on the bodies. But was that really Hitler I saw burning in the pit? I'm not sure, because the face was blown off – and I saw the bullet in the back. That made no sense.

Maybe there was another plan. Is it possible I was delayed on purpose? Was my arriving late part of the setup for the hoax? Did Adolf keep a double in the bunker? Or better, did Speer have a doppelganger arrive through the underground tunnel? Perhaps Adolf killed Eva, shot his double with a silencer, and then Speer helped him get into the tunnel from the deep bunker and exit to the south – after all, only Speer and Todt knew about it.

***

Karl remembered drinking with Fritz Todt one night several years earlier. They were drunk and Fritz unexpectedly spilled the beans about a long escape tunnel from the Führer's soon-to-be-built bunker.

He reminisced now about the details. "No way, Fritz! That's really interesting."

"Yes. Last year my military engineering company completed the design for a second bunker, deeper than the one there now. It will be called Der Führer's bunker. Adolf directed me to design a tunnel leading away from that new bunker. And unknown to anyone but me, two of my engineers recently finished managing construction of a five-hundred-meter underground tunnel. The next part of the plan comes in two years, when the Führer's lower bunker is completed. The end of the fifty-five-foot-deep tunnel sits only twelve feet from the edge of the future Führer-bunker walls. The tunnel will be connected to the Führer's bunker once it's completed.

"But, Karl, my friend, that's not the whole story. Hitler's final request to me was to have my two engineers and the dozen tunnel workers killed once the project was completed. I followed his orders a month ago," Todt revealed. "It was brutal. I'd never done anything like that. So right now, only Adolf and I know the exact location of the tunnel, its entrance and exit points. No one on Hitler's staff knows, not Himmler, not Göring or Bormann. Not even Goebbels."

Karl recalled being astonished at the news of the tunnel, especially about the murders of the engineers and the construction team. *I think Todt said too much to me that night.*

Knowing the secret made Karl uneasy, realizing he could be in jeopardy. Then, only a month after their conversation, Todt died in a plane crash. Rumors circulated that an SS member placed a bomb on board in a small briefcase and caused the plane to explode in midair. *Some said it was a power play by Albert Speer, because only a few days later, Speer – Hitler's personal architect – became Germany's Minister of Armaments. He immediately completed the final design of the Führer's bunker and started building it.*

Yes, Hitler and Speer were remarkably close. As Hitler's personal architect, Speer had to know about the escape tunnel and its location. When I saw Gunsche at the bunker the other day, he said Speer was the last person to visit Hitler, and Hitler had asked that they be left alone for a while.

Maybe the Führer's suicide was a perfectly carried-out hoax by using a doppelganger, then Adolf left through that tunnel with Speer's aid. I wonder if Hitler is hiding in another bunker somewhere. Or maybe he's already south of here, using a different set of safe houses on his way to Ravenna ahead of me. My last guess... it's my buddy Hockemeier, with star-studded credentials similar to mine, who's leading Der Führer to freedom.

Karl's hypothesis had merit. It was technically possible. Right now, Albert Speer and Hitler were the only two people alive who knew about the 500-meter tunnel. Everyone else had been purposely killed .

***

Over that past week, as Karl suspected might happen, almost every person who had worked in the bunker and who traveled north and hid in the subway station and the brewery basement was arrested. All were interrogated about the details of the events leading up to the suicides. Many of them, who learned Hitler had passed on flying out of Germany, wanted to escape to Bremerhaven on the north coast. But Plan B became a failure because it was shared with so many. During the interrogations, the Russian commander learned of the existence of the U-boat off the coast of Bremerhaven. Orders were dispatched to the Russian Navy. But it was the British Royal Air Force that found the XXI and destroyed it as it left Bremerhaven bound for Norway, its first stop before going on to South America. Fortunately for Karl, and good thinking by von Schultz, a different U-boat was positioned off Ravenna.

Meanwhile, Hilda began directing a new kitchen staff as more Soviet military officers were stationed inside the Bendlerblock building. She'd played the game well in the last few years, and was on her A game once again. The Russian commander doing the interrogations quickly put on ten pounds. He ate well, and slept better, each night, thanks to Sweet Hilda.

***

In the last week, Karl had traveled back roads and made contact only with people at safe houses. He remained consistent, saying a small entourage would be along within 12 to 15 hours. Hitler's suicide – or his make-believe suicide – still wasn't known as he drove south into Italy. Lack of electricity eliminated radio as a source of information through-out the country. Karl had to move quickly and take advantage of Black-

210

shirt contacts who still believed Hitler might arrive within 24 hours of his visit. Thankfully, no one in Berlin knew about Plan C. In the last few months, it always seemed Hitler would somehow fly from Berlin. And Plan C seemed so ridiculous. But it could be Plan C, or a variant of it, was the route for Adolf to follow once he left the tunnel. Karl believed even more now Der Fuhrer's death was a hoax. *If Hitler and Hockemeier arrive in Ravenna before I do, what do I do? I need to hurry.*

Then he moved on to another concern. *Why did Katrina take my son and leave Langenargen? She had a good job and was making good money as a nurse. Her life was stable, and she was under no pressure. Where has she gone with our son? She wasn't a threat to the enemy, being married to me. Oh, uh. We never did get married. Maybe Father told her I was dead, and since we weren't married, she left.*

His thoughts turned to their future.

When I find her, we'll marry and I will have three more children. No, five more. I have money and diamonds to make her happy. I'll teach my sons many things. They will be the generation that makes Germany great again.

Oblivious to all else, he focused on finding Katrina and his son. He needed them more now, after losing his parents. He changed his route to go farther west from the yellow-highlighted path on the map. With no safe houses along his route, it would be risky. His "French merchant escaping Germany" story should be accepted, especially since he had plenty of cash for a room. His remaining concern was passing American checkpoints, and the northbound American 5th Army.

CHAPTER THIRTY-EIGHT

La Bella Panetteria

Karl arrived in Lecco late that evening. He drove a few blocks before recalling Katrina's parents' street name and address. He knew their bakery was called La Bella Panetteria, but when he arrived at the address, he noticed the name on the overhead sign was different.

He wondered why.

Her parents' third-floor apartment was two buildings away. He grabbed the duffel bag. While walking to the apartment he decided to stay the night with her parents. They'd leave first thing in the morning. It would give them plenty of time to reach the U-boat. *Tonight, I'll have a piece of her father's bread and dip it in some of his red sauce Katrina boasted about.*

Karl opened the door and climbed the steep, dark staircase.

Out of breath before he reached the third-floor landing, he took a deep breath, only to realize how badly the common toilet in the hallway stunk.

Only a few feet ahead, apartment 3B was the one on the left. Karl finally relaxed, believing Katrina and his son were safely inside.

He knocked.

As the door opened slightly, a young teenage girl in a nightgown peeked out.

He didn't recognize her. Instantly frustrated, Karl pushed hard at the door, breaking the small chain to the door frame. The door swung wide open.

"Where is Katrina? What's going on?" he demanded.

Frightened at the sight of the big man, the girl stepped back.

As she did, her grandmother stepped toward Karl.

The nonna said fiercely, "No one named Katrina lives here. Who are you?"

"What are you doing in this apartment? It belongs to the baker Dino Amorino and his wife, Lucia. What happened to them? Why aren't they here?"

"We purchased this apartment a year ago. We moved in after Dino and Lucia were shot and killed. Nazi soldiers believed American spies were hiding in the back of Dino's bakery at night. One night, about three a.m., the Nazis rushed in, firing machine guns, expecting to find and kill American soldiers. Instead, they shot and killed Dino and Lucia as they prepared dough for fresh bread and pastries for the morning.

"Everyone heard the shooting. All the neighbors went outside and saw what had happened. The Germans realized their mistake and, within five minutes, came back and set off a bomb, starting a fire. They claimed it was a gas-line explosion, but the neighbors all knew what they'd done. Our neighbors saw them leave, as well as a few Blackshirts. And one of the Blackshirts, who knew Dino and Lucia, was crying, ashamed of what had happened.

"Lecco has not been the same since," the nonna added sadly. She took a brave step toward Karl, who stood just inside the doorway. "So, whoever you are, we have no idea who this Katrina is, and you have no business here. You need to leave."

Karl didn't care about Katrina's parents. His brain paused to soak in the bad news that Katrina and his son weren't there. Then as his 6-foot 2-inch frame towered over the tiny nonna, he looked past the old woman and eyed her attractive granddaughter, in her thin nightgown. It crossed his mind to have his way tonight with the mature-looking teenager.

Just then, the girl's mother stepped out from behind a curtain, wielding a single-barrel shotgun. She advanced toward Karl and cocked the trigger. "You heard my mother. Leave now or I'll shoot you. We don't want any trouble. You have five seconds, or I *will* shoot. Five... four... three...."

At "two," Karl stepped backward through the doorway, then to the stairway and down the old worn steps to the narrow lobby. He peered through the glass door and saw the street wet from rain. He stepped out-side, looked both ways and walked back to the Benz parked in front of the bakery.

Suddenly a flashlight beam, from about a hundred feet ahead on the sidewalk, shined on him. An American soldier called out in Italian, "Who goes there?"

Holding the duffel bag over his head to protect him from the rain, Karl dropped to the ground behind his car. Releasing the bag, he shoved it under his car and rolled sideways to the other side of the narrow street.

He heard footsteps of two people running toward him.

Soaking wet, Karl stayed low and tiptoed down the alley. Then he stepped into an alcove and squatted behind a trash can. Drawing his Luger, he held his breath.

Two soldiers ran down the alley, passing within three feet of him.

It began to pour heavily. As he waited in silence to see whether they'd come back that way, he wondered why he had run. His passport identified him as a legitimate French businessman. It was in the bag on the ground, at the rear of the vehicle – as were all the papers, bracelets, rings and cash.

He thought about the shooting of Katrina's parents in the bakery and how stupid the German soldiers were for the fire-bombing to cover up their mistake. Now his next stop would be in Brescia, and up the hill to Botticino and the DiBotticino Stone Works. *Katrina and my son must be there with Mother's family.*

His mind skipped back to Berlin. *The Russians must be in control and occupying central Berlin by now. I wonder which SS officers made it out of the city. By now, the news of Hitler's death is probably being broadcast around the world.*

Just then the soldiers walked past him again, headed back to the street. He waited what felt like another hour before exiting the alley. Re-turning to the car, he grabbed his bag and climbed into the car to change into dry clothing.

The shirt he grabbed had blood on its collar. At that moment he reconnected with Johannes Wolff. Karl then remembered the letter J hanging over Heidi's dresser while in her bed. He made the connection to Johannes and realized Heidi wouldn't have to explain her having two babies in his absence.

He rested an hour, then drove from Lecco under the cover of the dark rainy night. A few miles farther along, finding a spot off the side of the road, he pulled over. The pelting rain on the car's roof soothed him, and he slept without dreaming for six hours.

As the dawn sky brightened, Karl woke and started the car. The gas gauge showed it was low, so he grabbed one of the gas cans. He was pouring the last drops of fuel when three American jeeps drove by. He gave them a wave as they continued hurriedly. He emptied the can and noticed the Nazi swastika embossed in the metal, and the words "Berlin-Bendlerblock" painted on the side of the cans. He'd overlooked this up to now, but needed a story about how he had come across five clean, newly painted gasoline cans – or get rid of them.

Karl got back in the car and headed toward Bergamo and Brescia. The journey wasn't long, but avoiding American checkpoints would be difficult. He lingered on the notion of what life might have been like if he'd stayed with Heidi, now knowing her husband, Johannes, wouldn't be returning. For a few moments, his thoughts dwelled on his pleasure with her in bed and her responsiveness. Returning to Heidi crossed his mind.

CHAPTER THIRTY-NINE

The DiBotticino Stone Works

The tiny village of Botticino was Karl's mother's hometown. Valentina had visited her parents, Luigi and Stella, twice a year with Karl. As a youngster it was a fun trip. But as he turned 14, visits to his Italian grandparents seemed like a waste of time. The worst part was all the dancing and singing at family parties. Instead, he saw himself someday working with metal with his father, not rocks like his cousins. During Karl's last visit, the summer before he turned 15, he wished he'd instead gone to the factory to watch white-hot molten metal being poured into molds. When the trips stopped, regrettably, Valentina somehow never again visited her family in Botticino.

Only days ago, I was a key man in the SS, selected to help guide Adolf to freedom. Now, Der Führer's dreams have vanished! What will become of Germany? And what has become of my family – my wife and my son?

Karl saw a small filling station as he arrived in Brescia. It had gasoline, although rationed. He slid the station attendant an American $50 bill, and besides getting the vehicle filled, his five-gallon gas tanks were topped off, as well. The attendant was delighted with his American dollars.

Across the street, several American soldiers stood, holding rifles. Karl kept his head down, avoiding eye contact and pretending he didn't see them. They saw Karl, but he looked like a dusty and tired traveler in a weird-looking car.

After the fill up, he drove for a few minutes and turned up a street leading toward the family stone works. It had been sixteen or seventeen years since his last visit. He drove up the hill, and saw an old lady carrying two bags. Her dress resembled a small tent, and her seamed stockings rolled down below her knees badly squeezed her legs.

He got out of the car, approached her and asked, "*Signora,* where is the home of the DiBotticino family?"

The woman put her bags down and looked at him closely. She noted his tall black boots. He seemed out of place and his Italian wasn't the local dialect. "*Signore,* who are you and what are you doing here?"

"I'm looking for the DiBotticinos' family business."

"*Tutta la famiglia è morta!*" she exclaimed, waving both hands wildly for emphasis. "The entire family is dead. Our lives are ruined. Mussolini ruined Italy, and Hitler has ruined all of Europe. What a terrible mistake Mussolini made to be a friend to Hitler! Those egotistical idiots should go to the deepest part of Dante's hell, and sit next to all the corrupt and power-hungry popes and cardinals, and sinful clergy who take sexual advantage of married women."

Not lacking for words, she continued her rant. "The Jews are beautiful people. My childhood girlfriend was Jewish. I just heard all the Jews on the island of Rhodes all were sent to Germany. Why? They bothered no one. Hitler, his SS soldiers, the Gestapo – and especially all those SS Germans who killed all the Jews in their camps – will burn with the devil in hell for eternity."

She finished ranting, took a deep breath and quieted down. "*Sì,* the DiBotticino brothers' business and their houses… you need to go the rest of the way up the steep hill to their place. But everyone there, except for Vincenzo, is gone."

Over the past eight years, Brescia and Botticino had been rocked by the war. Families were crushed when Mussolini drafted the first groups of men into the Italian Army. Some hillside villagers avoided the conflict by hiding. But when the Italian government had Mussolini step down, Germany stepped in. The Germans swept through Italy, gathering up and conscripting any remaining young men to fight the invading U.S. forces. Such was the fate of the young DiBotticino men.

Thousands of young Italian men who never returned home died along the Gustav Line and other defensive lines the Germans set up. Karl played a role in reviewing these defensive positions years earlier, from

Anzio to Monte Cassino, and the Winter Line. Many Italians were killed fighting north of the Pontine Marshes, along the Via Appia, as the American Army pushed north and then captured Rome.

Leaving the old woman, Karl continued up the steep roadway and arrived in front of the stone works building, partially destroyed by aerial bombing. He looked around and saw an opening that might have been the front door. He climbed over a thick, heavy wooden lintel, the header for the door. For the last hundred years, an elaborately carved wooden door had fit perfectly inside a graceful stone arch. Now the double door lay on the floor, a pile of splintered wooden planks. The family business and its building were in shambles. Statues lay broken, covered in dust. Chunks and small blocks of stone lay tilted atop each other in every direction. As he stepped a little further inside, a few birds fluttered up, causing him to pull his gun. The birds flew around the interior, then swooped down at Karl's head, as if to say, "This is all your fault."

Heavy wooden columns, the parts holding up the roof joists, had snapped and collapsed, allowing the sun's rays to stream down to the floor. What was once a happy and productive place where stonecutters worked now sat in shambles. Bombs intended for the railyard in Brescia had clearly been released too soon by a rookie American bombardier. At least two hit a wall and the roof of the stone works building. A third one destroyed most of the excavating equipment; several others hit the side of the mountain, cascading tons of rocks down onto the stone yard.

An old man gripping his cane stepped from the rubble's dark shadows into the sunlight. He walked carefully past the collapsed roof joists and timbers on the floor. Keeping his balance wasn't easy.

"*Signore*, can I help you?"

Karl didn't recognize who was addressing him. "Old man, my name is Karl von Richter. My mother was Valentina von Richter, who recently passed. I'm looking for my wife, Katrina, and our young son. I'm hoping they're here with our DiBotticino relatives. Perhaps they're staying in one of the nearby family homes."

Karl looked closely at the old man. Besides still having jet-black hair, he saw strong facial features, and a deep cleft in his protruding chin. Karl recalled his grandfather Luigi's face; it had resembled this old man.

Might he be my great-uncle?

The old man sat on a block of stone. "I am deeply sorry to hear about your mother. Your wife is not here. No one is here, except me. All the men in our family were forced to go to war, first for Mussolini, then the rest for Hitler. The Germans told me to stay here when our youngest family men were taken away. The last ones were sent to fight in Anzio. It's been two years now. No one has returned. Not one DiBotticino man has come back. We have lost everyone and everything."

Tears flowed down Vincenzo's cheeks onto his white whiskers. His deep-blue eyes looked exactly like Karl's grandfather Luigi's. They were just like Katrina's blue eyes, too.

"Old man, since you say you've been here all along, has my wife, Katrina, visited with my son? Did they come and stay in a nearby house? Or did they come and leave?"

Before replying, the old man shifted his position on the stone. He swallowed and cleared his throat, but said nothing. But Karl viewed the shifting in his seat and the hard swallowing as body language for being uncomfortable. It was obvious the old man had information, and Karl intended to hear it, one way or another. "Old man, what is your name?"

"I am Vincenzo, your grandfather's brother… your mother's uncle. I'm the eldest of the DiBotticino brothers."

The old man turned and looked over his shoulder, recalling an incident. He turned back and looked at Karl. "I know who you are. I remember you as a child. You were a happy little boy. You came here with your mother several times, first as an infant, and then as a child, and you played among the statues. One day, a statue fell on you when you tried to climb it. And you got a nasty gash in your leg." He pointed. "It happened right over there."

Karl's memory jolted back to the incident. He'd been running, chasing a dog. *I remember seeing statues lined up, and I climbed onto a block of stone, looking for the dog. I lost my balance and fell against a statue. It tipped over and knocked three more over. The last one fell on my leg and I started to bleed. Mother carried me away as she yelled at her uncles for neglecting to watch me. I was just glad she didn't punish me.*

The old man's eyes peered into Karl's. "You speak like a man of high importance who is in a hurry. What has happened to you that you're looking for your wife and child? What have you done that's wrong?"

"Old man, you know I grew up in Friedrichshafen. Britain and France persecuted Germany after World War I with the terms of the Treaty. The world was against Germany. After the Russian Revolution, Jews plotted with the communists to rule the world. Germans had to do something to protect our nation and its pure heritage. I have served as a senior SS officer and have done many good things for Germany. The war is over and I've come to find my wife and son. I believe you know where they are. What information are you holding back from me? Tell me what you know."

Vincenzo pondered for a moment. "My dear great-nephew, you are misinformed by your German leadership! What is a pure heritage? No person, and not one country, has a 'pure heritage,' as you say. Since the beginning of time, all men have migrated from here to there and from there to here. Men have moved all over Europe and the Mediterranean. Even the blood of those who have come from Africa is mingled with our blood. Are we any less for it? Of course we aren't! Don't you see? Our rainbow of skin colors is insignificant. We are all brothers! You've been misled by a power-hungry politician to claim a pure German is above others. Did Adam and Eve live in Berlin, or did they live in Munich, or next door to you in Friedrichshafen? Of course not. Karl, you may have been important recently, but you certainly aren't wise yet. Perhaps my great-nephew should find the truth of his own heritage."

"Uncle, where is my wife? I know you know where Katrina and my son are. You are keeping the truth from me."

The old man's shaky hand gripped his cane as he carefully stood. Karl stepped toward his great uncle and, reaching up, grabbed Vincenzo by the throat with one hand, pulling his gun from his holster. The old man dropped his cane, and Karl's strong hand held him upright.

He threatened his great-uncle again. "You might be my mother's uncle, but you are nothing to me. You know where Katrina and my son are. I can tell by your actions they've been here. Tell me now or I will shoot you and put an end to your miserable life."

Vincenzo struggled to catch his breath as Karl's hand clutched his throat.

Karl saw Vincenzo's pause as the old man's further defiance. He pointed the pistol downward and shot the ground between Vincenzo's feet.

"Go ahead, shoot me," Vincenzo taunted him. "Then you'll never know the whole truth."

"What whole truth? Is there more to finding my wife and son?" Suddenly, getting the old man to talk seemed complicated. Frustrated, he slapped the gun across Vincenzo's face, breaking his nose and slashing his forehead. Red blood ran into his striking blue eyes. Karl loomed over the man. "Shall I hit you again? Tell me! Where are my wife and son? And what is this 'whole truth' you are talking about?"

Vincenzo was bleeding profusely. He didn't believe Karl would kill him, but he felt faint and feared for his life. His blurry vision fixed on Karl. "Valentina's brother knows the truth… and someday you will learn the whole truth." As Vincenzo finished speaking, he passed out.

Karl released his grip and Great-uncle Vincenzo fell backward to the stone floor, striking his head.

He shook his head as he returned to his car. *What is this truth Vincenzo spoke of? Now I need to find Mother's brother. Surely he knows where Katrina is.*

Karl remembered his mother's brother was a Catholic priest. He was supposed to marry Otto and Valentina, but a last-minute meeting at the Vatican prevented him from showing up.

He pulled the folded map from his pocket while descending the steep hill back into town. His next step was to find Uncle Giovanni. He saw the old lady again, walking along the street.

He shouted, "*Vecchia signora*, do you know where the DiBottici-no priest lives? I have a generous donation to give him."

"If you can make a donation to him, make one to me first, and I will be able to remember where he is."

Karl didn't like her snotty response. He hadn't liked her earlier rant against Hitler and SS officers, and now she was about to be a pest again. He got out and reached into his pocket, pulling out an American

$50 bill and the small blue pouch with the loose diamonds. He grabbed a diamond. Then, in front of her, he rolled the diamond up tightly inside the bill.

"*Signora*, here is American money and a diamond. It sparkles like you."

Her eyes opened wide. She took the cash and diamond, and stuck both in her bra. She gushed all she knew. "The DiBotticino priest… that would be Giovanni. He was the monsignor at the New Cathedral next to the Old Cathedral in the center of Brescia. Just over two years ago, he was elevated to bishop by Pope Pius XII."

"So, will I find him there?"

"No. He was our bishop just a few months when the pope called him to live in the Vatican. He was elevated to cardinal about six months ago, and is responsible for the churches, convents and abbeys in Italy's southern provinces. Everyone here in Brescia and Botticino thinks the pope made him a bishop and then a cardinal to get a special deal from the DiBotticino family to help reconstruct the churches and to get some new statues at a discount. But the pope has no idea of the destruction at the family quarry and stone works building. Ha! Now maybe he'll demote Giovanni and send him back here to Brescia once he finds out there are no stone and statue deals to be made."

She continued to chuckle, then added, "But maybe if we are blessed, maybe Brescia will give us a pope someday."

As she turned and began to walk away, Karl pulled his gun and whacked her hard in the back of her head, knocking her to the ground. He rolled her over, reached into her bra and took back the cash and the diamond. *Disrespectful. She was disrespectful to Hitler and Mussolini and to those of us trying to make positive changes in Germany and defeat communism. She's lucky I didn't shoot her.*

Karl returned to the car. He had to find his uncle in Rome. He was sure Giovanni knew where Katrina and the boy were. He repeated aloud what Vincenzo said, " 'And Giovanni knows the whole truth,' whatever that means."

As he drove down the hill toward Brescia, he saw two young men walking up the hill, practically skipping with joy. They stepped off the curb to cross the street as Karl drove by. They looked at him, smiled and waved. He didn't wave back.

After their jaunt up the hill, the two jovial young men arrived at the destroyed stone works building. Crushed at seeing the damage, they stepped inside and saw their great-uncle Vincenzo lying on the floor.

"He's fallen. Let's sit him up," one said to the other.

Pepino picked him up in his arms.

"*Zio! Zio!* It's Pepino and Gianni, your great-nephews!"

Vincenzo barely stirred. He looked at them but remained in a daze. *Is this possible? Are these boys here with me? Or am I in Heaven?*

Pepino and Gianni shook Vincenzo to wake him up, thinking he had fallen and cut himself. Then they said with excitement, "*Zio*, we've returned from Anzio! What a terrible battle. Thank God the two of us were together when we were captured by Americans as the battle ended last June. Rome was captured by the Americans. After interrogating and holding us prisoner at the Ciampino airport these past nine months, they finally let us return home. They believed our story about being forced to fight for Mussolini and then the German army. It's amazing. There were so many Italian-American soldiers! Some of them were born right here in Italy. They sailed with their parents to the United States before the first World War. Some were born in America, but they still spoke Italian, although mostly with southern Italian and Sicilian dialects."

"What's happened to the building? *Zio* Vincenzo, are you okay? *Zio*, wake up! *Zio*, please wake up!"

With the boys' voices fading, and knowing his great-nephews were safe, Vincenzo closed his eyes and stopped breathing.

In a flash, all his brothers greeted him.

CHAPTER FORTY

Finding Uncle Giovanni

Karl drove toward the center of Brescia, planning his next steps to get to Rome and the Vatican. He knew his escape plan needed to change.

If Giovanni knows where Katrina is, I should be able to get her and our son. It'll take a week to get to Rome. Getting back to Ravenna within the ten-week window will be tight.

He'd likely see hundreds of American soldiers in transport trucks, tanks and armored vehicles along the road to Rome. He also anticipated a limited supply of gasoline as he headed further south. With gas economy again in mind, Karl looked for another vehicle. A Fiat would be best, and the extra fuel in the cans would last longer on the journey.

Continuing through Brescia's center, he saw the Old Cathedral, the *Duomo Vecchio*, and the New Cathedral, side by side. The newer one was damaged, probably in the same bombing run that had destroyed the DiBotticino stone works. Ahead on the street were several parked cars. A man was just getting into the Fiat parked closest to him. Karl pulled up as if to park behind it, and purposely struck its rear bumper.

Dressed in a suit, the man got out, looked at his bumper and started yelling and waving his arms. *"Stupido!"*

Karl walked up to the man, then looked down at the small dent to the car's rear bumper. In an instant, he drew his gun and shot the man in the chest. The Fiat owner fell to the ground, dead.

Karl ensured the keys were in the Fiat's ignition. Reaching into the Fiat, he set the gasoline cans upright in the tiny backseat. He took the duffel bags and stuffed them against the cans to hold them steady. Then he put the box of broken dishes and glasses in the tiny trunk, still anticipating being stopped at a checkpoint. He brought along bullets for his Luger but left the rifles behind. As he stepped toward the car's open door, the dead man's shoes caught his eye. Karl took the shoes off the man's feet, tossed them into the car, climbed in and drove away, focused on the quickest route to Rome.

A few miles out of town, He stopped and tried on the dead man's nice shoes. They fit, so he discarded his SS uniform boots. *These shoes feel good... they're broken in perfectly.* He flashed back to the shoes and bags brought to the concentration camps by the Jews and Slavs. As they were forcibly stripped, their shoes and clothes were tossed into piles, to eventually be put into warehouses at each camp, for redistribution some-day among less-fortunate Germans.

As Karl drove south, he was stopped twice the first day by U.S. soldiers. First in Bologna, then in Florence, where he stayed the night, sleeping in the car. The next day, he was stopped late in the afternoon in Montepulciano. He decided to stay there that night after being released from a lengthy interrogation. He was stopped four more times over two days on his way to Rome. His French passport and linguistic skills continued to help him pass as Pierre Louis Boucher.

At the last checkpoint, just north of Rome, he ran into trouble. At the Orvieto checkpoint, an American soldier born in Strasbourg, France, and fluent in English, French and German, picked up on his seemingly phony French accent. The soldier's parents had immigrated to New York City through Paris when he was 16. Karl's French being less than perfect made the soldier curious. He looked at his papers an extra minute and wanted to listen to Karl speak again and more thoroughly. He believed Karl's French sounded more German and guttural than classic Parisian.

Speaking in French he said, "*Pierre, please, again, tell me exact-ly where you are from.*"

Thinking fast, Karl mixed facts with lies. "Ah! I understand your question. My mother was born south of Rome; my father was a French-man from Besançon, France. They met and lived in Besançon, where I was born. We often visited my father's father, in Friedrichshafen. I spent summers with them and learned to speak German fluently as a youngster. When my parents divorced and I remained with my grandfather, a local merchant. My ability to speak German and Italian is why my business as a home-goods salesman traveling between France and Germany is so successful. But I became stuck in Germany in May of 1940, when the Germans invaded France. I've been hiding on a small farm in southern Germany the past five years."

The French-born American soldier then said in German, "I understand your story. What are you doing now, driving south?"

Karl responded again speaking French. "Another good question! My mother's family owned a vineyard. It provided us a generous rental income for her for many years. Antonio Lombardi, the old winemaker, took care of the property, made and sold wine, and sent her the proceeds, less a small percentage for his work. The Grenache, Alicante and Muscato grapes on the property produce a good-tasting blend. The property passed to me when my mother died in 1939. I was headed to the vineyard as the war intensified, and I stayed in hiding in my grandparents' home on Lake Constance. Now I need to check on the vineyard to see if it was damaged by the war, and, if so, what can be done to fix it. I also need to see if the grapes have been harvested these last five years and collect the revenue from old Antonio."

"*Bonjour, monsieur*, you are free to go – and good luck with the grapes. Be sure to bring me some of your wine, should you return this way again."

Karl drove away, continuing toward Rome, surprised the young soldier didn't make him get out of the car after catching his accent. *If it weren't for my confidence and bold lies, I might have been caught with all the goods in my duffel bag.*

The severely damaged roads leading into Rome made driving necessarily slow. Several times as American tank convoys passed him moving north. Karl reached Rome two hours later and decided to have dinner. He spotted a small restaurant and stepped inside, longing for a dish of linguini, meatballs and a glass of hearty red wine.

He was served within a few minutes by a short, old nonna whose smile revealed a missing front tooth. Her chin whiskers made her appearance less appealing. She returned and placed a bottle of chianti, wrapped in raffia straw and sporting dual braided handles, on the red-and-white gingham tablecloth. Then she lighted a candle stuck in the neck of an empty chianti bottle on the table.

As he began to eat, a dozen American soldiers entered and sat at a long table. Several wore head bandages, one using a crutch was missing a leg, another had an arm missing. One was missing a hand, and another wore an eye patch. Despite their injuries, they all were laughing and began singing Italian songs. *These soldiers are lucky to be alive. They probably survived the battles with our brave German troops along the Gustav Line and at Anzio. Maybe they've heard the news and are happy, knowing the war is over.*

Suddenly it grew quiet. The soldier with the eye patch stood and began singing every child's old favorite, "Oh, My Papa." Karl knew it and thought of Otto and his grandfather. Before the soldier finished his singing, Karl, growing emotional, stood and threw an American $50 bill on the table and left. The money was more than enough for the meal he didn't finish.

CHAPTER FORTY-ONE

Alfonso and Gina

K arl drove around for a few minutes before he found what seemed to be a suitable place to stay the night. He went inside and was greeted at the desk. Before paying, he asked the man at the front desk, "Are any women companions available this evening?"

"I'm very sorry, sir, the women who work here are already with British soldiers staying here tonight."

Frustrated, he left and returned to the car. Then he remembered a Blackshirt fellow he'd met four years ago, whose place was a safe house on the east side of Rome. Karl met him in Rome, while advising German generals about their defensive positioning. The Blackshirts had aided the Germans, giving insight into widths of roads and passageways through villages between Anzio and Monte Cassino. Road widths were important for the passage of tanks and vehicles pulling heavy artillery. *If the guy I met is still alive and not being held in a detention camp, I know I can trust him.*

It took Karl twenty minutes to find the place. He knocked, using the old code. The door opened about six inches, and an attractive woman peered out at him.

"*Ciao, signora.* Is Alfonso here?"

"Who is asking?"

"I am an old friend. Alfonso and I worked together several years ago. *Mi chiamo* Boucher, Pierre Louis Boucher."

"No. He's not here." She opened the door a bit wider, looked him over and told him to come in.

"I'm Gina. Sit. *Café espresso? Sambuca?*"

Karl nodded. "*Grazie.*"

As she prepared the coffee, Karl looked around the tiny kitchen. It was a small place. Just past the hanging sheet was the bedroom.

"What's happened to Alfonso? Where is he?"

"He's missing. Gone for over eight weeks now. He was meeting friends in Rome. His friends are missing, too. Other wives haven't seen their husbands either. Maybe they were picked up by American soldiers. All of them were committed to Benito. My Alfonso, and the rest of them, were stupid."

She continued lamenting about the war, the food shortages and complaining how Mussolini lost his momentum as their leader. "Alfonso helped the cause for as long as he could. He was born in Sicily and didn't care about the rest of Italy. Once the British general Mont-something and the crazy American general with the fancy pearl-handled gun made it to Messina, Alfonso said it was all over for the Italians.

"For the last year, my husband has talked about going to a place called Brooklyn and opening a business with his brother Andrea once the war was over. Andrea said they can make a lot of money, selling pizza. Can you imagine just making pizza for a living? I don't know where they get these crazy ideas from. Andrea says, 'Pizza in Brooklyn!' and Alfonso falls for it. I married an idiot! What, or where, is Brooklyn, America, anyway?"

The espresso was ready, and she poured it into a tiny cup. Gina then poured in a little Sambuca to sweeten it. Karl flashed back to his last restaurant dinner with Katrina when they'd had espresso and Sambuca together. As he savored the flavor, he remembered going upstairs to bed with Katrina, and his insides stirred.

Then Gina spoke, jolting Karl from his daydream. "All politicians are stupid, just like my Alfonso. They are showoffs and bullies, and want to be viewed as bold, brave and courageous. They say, 'I will make Italy great!' or 'I will make Germany great again!' Then they lead fathers and sons into war; but, when faced with adversity themselves, few have the stomach for it, and they eventually show themselves as cowards."

Karl saw Gina was up to date on her politics – and her vocal view of many world leaders was accurate. He decided to tell her Hitler had committed suicide. But he decided to tell her nothing about his having been at the bunker, nor anything about his final SS mission to help Hitler escape.

She was surprised to hear the news. "No! Impossible! But thank you! You make my point. Hitler was stupid, too; he was no different than Mussolini. They start something they cannot finish. Mussolini couldn't finish being a leader. And now you tell me this about Hitler – he couldn't finish either. He took the path of a coward because he couldn't face anyone anymore."

She shook her head. It got quiet. He took another sip and looked toward Gina's small bedroom behind the sheet again.

"And so, Pierre Boucher, what is your story, eh? Are you running away from something, or are you running toward something?"

Karl didn't say anything. It was growing late. He was tired and had gotten warm inside from the coffee and Sambuca. His vision of the boxcars briefly reappeared. He again was on the inside looking out. He was in a trance, staring at something far away.

It evaporated in a snap as she said, "Are you okay?" She paused, looking at him closely, then added, "You're not French. You're German, aren't you? I can tell. You were too close to all the killing? Am I right? What is your real name?"

Karl looked up. A ray of late-afternoon sun glinted through the west-facing window, highlighting Gina's face and light-brown eyes. He didn't respond.

"German, when was the last time you slept eight straight hours?"

He still didn't answer. Then Gina poured him a straight shot of Sambuca and pushed it across the table to him. "Here, German. This will help you relax. You need some sleep."

Karl finished the Sambuca and, as she poured another, her long, perfumed hair fell in front of Karl's face. *Hmm. She smells so good. And she's very lonely. It will feel good to satisfy her.*

Within minutes Gina began brushing her thigh up against Karl's shoulders as she went in and out of the tiny kitchen. Karl understood her body language.

She went to the back of the apartment and returned with a bottle of red wine. She poured a glass. He drank it like water; it wasn't long before the bottle was empty. As she went for another bottle, he grabbed her around her waist and pulled her onto his lap. The passionate kissing and grabbing began. Within minutes they were in bed.

Gina wanted him. It was her first sex in months. She enjoyed his aggressiveness. She responded similarly. They fell asleep early and slept deeply.

Karl woke up at 4 with a headache – dehydrated from the dry, homemade red wine. After a glass of water, he went back to bed and lay there, thinking about seeing his uncle Giovanni at the Vatican and hoping to find out where Katrina and his son were. The morning light didn't arrive too quickly because of dark rain clouds. As he lay thinking about everything, Gina woke up beside him. At the sight of him, she rolled her warm naked body next to his.

She put her leg across his thigh. "Good morning, my big German. You were magnificent, and so strong! Would you like espresso now... or perhaps some more of me?" She reached down. "Ah! It seems you are ready for me!"

Anxious for what the day would bring, he ignored her warm hand and chose the espresso.

Gina reluctantly got up and put the tiny *macchinetta* on the stove. "I am lucky to have propane gas because of my husband's connections. We still get deliveries, unlike some others. The delivery people must be indebted to Alfonso and Andrea, the future Brooklyn, America, pizza makers."

She walked to the table with a clean espresso cup.

She put it in front of him, and Karl asked, "Where is the main entrance to the Vatican?"

Gina laughed loudly, and pressed her thigh against his arm as he sat at the table. "So, my big, handsome German, just one night with me and you need to go to confession this morning? I have more to show you. You should wait before you go, so you can confess the rest."

"I need to find a bishop who is a new cardinal. He came from Brescia to the Vatican this past October."

"Ah. You can only be talking about our new cardinal, Giovanni Cardinal DiBotticino."

"Yes, that's him. I need to see him."

"So, Pierre Louis Boucher, I'm thinking you're an important German SS soldier with Italian Blackshirt friends? Am I right so far? And you need to see the cardinal because… why? You did something and now you're sorry… or something happened and you're not happy?"

He was silent.

"My big German, look at me. Relax – you have a new lover! And you slept well last night… why not stay with me another day? You need your rest. The cardinal… he will be there tomorrow, and the next day, and the day after that. We had so much fun last night, German. You pleased me, and I can tell I pleased you. So, stay."

The morning rain cleared, and the sky suddenly brightened with sunshine.

"I need to go."

Disappointed, Gina gave him a hug and a long, deep kiss.

Karl stepped outside. He headed to the Fiat parked around the corner and found it up on cinder blocks – with all four wheels and tires missing.

Livid, he stormed back to Gina's house and banged hard at the door.

She opened it and laughed. "I knew you couldn't leave me so quickly this morning!"

"Gina, the tires and wheels on my car are missing."

"Oops! Wait here, my German. I'll be back in a few minutes."

While he waited for her to return, Karl paced, brooding about the missing wheels and tires.

"Your car will be fixed within the hour. Now, for my reward, you must spend the time with me, here in bed. And when we are finished, the wheels and tires will be back on your car, and you will smile again."

"I'll need my car filled with gasoline. Go make that happen, too."

Gina agreed. She went out again, then returned four minutes later, grabbed his arm and made her way past the hanging sheet to the unmade bed.

When they were finished, they propped themselves against the headboard full of pillows and both lit cigarettes. Karl compared Gina to

Heidi and Katrina. *Gina is very good compared to the younger women.* And then, remarkably, he thought of his first experience with Ruth. It took him far away.

Ten minutes later there came a knock on the door. Gina donned her robe and went to answer it.

"Gina, the tires and wheels are returned, and it's filled with gasoline, as you asked. But I have bad news for you. We just heard Alfonso, his brother Andrea and six others are in an American detention camp in Ciampino. It could be six months to a year before they are released."

Gina scowled. "I knew years ago I had the wrong man. He is so stupid! No. No. It's me. I'm the stupid one. Who wants a man who lasts two minutes in bed, but becomes excited for days about the prospect of selling pizza in Brooklyn, America?"

Hearing the news, Karl dressed again and grabbed his duffel bag. He reached inside for a sparkling stone and two American $50 bills.

"Gina, this is for your warmth. I may be back in two weeks, and if Alfonso hasn't returned, we again can have a few Sambucas and spend more time together."

"I'll be waiting for you, German. Don't forget when you see the cardinal, make your confession. Tell him the bad things you did in the war, and then tell him everything good I did for you. Then say to him, 'Go visit Gina. She wants to make you a happy and satisfied cardinal.' "

CHAPTER FORTY-TWO

Arriving at the Vatican

K arl headed to the Vatican, twenty minutes away. Arriving, he parked on a side street, stowed the cash, rings, bracelets and diamonds in his pocket and walked to the front gate.

Two Swiss guards in colorful uniforms saw him approaching. They greeted him and, showing his fake passport, Karl explained he was a businessman with family ties to the DiBotticino family and to Bishop DiBotticino, whom he understood was there in the Vatican.

The lead guard said, "Do you mean Giovanni Cardinal DiBotticino?"

Karl lied, saying he was unaware of the bishop's elevation to cardinal.

"Yes, seven months ago the pope elevated the bishop to cardinal because of his good works and broad responsibilities throughout the last decade."

The second guard chimed in, quite inappropriately, "Many think our pope is hoping the DiBotticino Brothers will help rebuild many of the churches destroyed by the war."

Karl smiled. *The destruction of the DiBotticino stone works building means no statues or columns will be coming from that quarry in the next few years. And if all the youngest grandsons died at Anzio, perhaps no stone will ever be mined from the DiBotticino quarry again.*

Karl felt like he had played a small part in putting an end to the family's proud name when he smashed his Luger across old Uncle Vincent's face and watched him bleed. He simply didn't care. Karl hated Italians in general, and he hated the DiBotticinos in particular, jealous of their centuries of success.

His only concern now was to find his wife and son. Everything from this point forward needed to focus on finding them and getting to Ravenna and the U-boat waiting off the coast.

The senior Swiss Guard pulled a long rope connected to a bell in an office near the foyer. He then opened the front door, allowing Karl to step into a small, confined space, confronted by another massive set of carved wooden doors. Karl took two steps and one door unexpectedly swung open into a huge foyer with a remarkably high ceiling.

A young seminarian peeked from behind the door. "Good morning. How can I help you?"

"My name is Pierre Louis Boucher. I'd like to speak briefly with His Eminence Cardinal DiBotticino. I have news for him from the family stone works in Botticino near Brescia."

The seminarian bowed slightly at the request. "Yes. Please come in and wait here in the foyer. It will be a few minutes. The cardinal is in prayer."

Karl nodded and accepted the notion of it being a few minutes. The seminarian crossed the large foyer and opened another door, the top half made of beveled glass. It led to a long hallway with several offices on each side. The first door on the right, just past a small alcove, led to the cardinal's office. The seminarian walked down the hall and knocked on the heavy wooden door.

"Enter."

As he stepped inside, the aging gray-haired cardinal arose slowly from the small, padded wooden pew where he'd been kneeling and saying his morning prayers.

"Cardinal, there is a French businessman here to see you."

"French businessman? To see me? What is his name?"

"He says his name is Pierre Louis Boucher. He has news of your family's stone works business in the village of Botticino."

Curious, the cardinal walked to the edge of the doorframe, leaned his head to peer down the hallway and looked through the half-glass door into the main lobby. What little of his face he could see was quite enough to set his heart to racing. His memory flashed back to his meeting with Katrina, and seeing an adult photo of Karl.

Giovanni stepped back and closed his office door slowly, to avoid making any noise. He told the seminarian to stay for a moment.

The cardinal walked behind his desk to shelves containing his personal library. Scanning the shelves, he reached for a book. He opened it on his desk. Inside the front cover were three envelopes. He pulled one out, closed the book and turned to the seminarian.

"Antonio, take this envelope. Deliver it immediately to Sister Maria Cassano, the Mother Superior of the Holy Angels Convent in the Province of Basilicata in the old town of Bernalda. She will answer to the name Sister Maria of the Angels. Tell her I sent you, and say these exact words: 'Karl is in Rome looking for Katrina and the boy.' She will understand and know what to do."

The cardinal stepped back and opened his desk drawer. From it, he removed a piece of parchment with fancy colorful scrolling across the top. He took a pen and dipped it in the ink well, wrote his name and the seminarian's name on the paper, and inserted it into another envelope.

"Take this also. It will allow you to travel to the Convent of the Holy Angels as a papal envoy. Leave immediately. Do not stop for any distraction, except to sleep, and do so only briefly. You must reach the convent as quickly as possible, without delay. Leave through the back doorway of my office. Go now to Father Aldo; he should be downstairs having his breakfast. Show him the note declaring you as a papal envoy. Say it is an emergency and you need to leave immediately. Only take what you are wearing, nothing else. You have no time to pack clothing. Tell Father Aldo to take you by car all the way to the convent in Bernalda. Please God, if the path is clear and the roads allow it, you will arrive there in three or four days. If you are delayed for any reason, you must get past the obstacle. Time is critical. Tell Aldo to bring three containers of extra fuel."

The cardinal reached into his desk a second time. "Here is money for you to use along the way and for your return. Tell Father Aldo you have the money he'll need to buy gasoline along the way. Go now. Hurry."

Antonio anxiously turned toward the door leading to the hall.

"No, not there. I said to go out the back way."

As Antonio exited, the cardinal put the other two envelopes back into the book and left it on his desk. He put on his red zucchetto and buttoned his cassock's red buttons.

The cardinal returned to the doorway and again gazed through the glass pane at his nephew. *I believe Karl was 12 years old the last time I saw him. He's so much taller than anyone in the family! Goodness, has it been two years since Katrina gave up her child?*

He opened the door and, cane in hand, made his way carefully down the hall to the foyer where his nephew paced impatiently. His heart beat faster now than it had when he'd met Pope Pius X, as a seminarian thirty-five years earlier.

This isn't a meeting with my innocent nephew. I'm about to meet a ruthless senior SS officer whose war crimes upon the Jews and Slavs and so many others has been horrific. Nothing will stop a radicalized Nazi officer. This man has neither conscience nor moral compass by participating in genocide. He brutally raped Katrina. I know why he's here. I anticipated this, and the time has come.

Giovanni bowed slightly and lifted his cane to clasp his hands, as though in prayer. "Excuse me for the delay. I was finishing my morning prayers when you arrived. Mr. Boucher, how may I help you?"

Seeing his uncle bent, old and gray, and dressed in the formal garb of a Catholic cardinal, surprised Karl. "Your Eminence, the name given to you upon my arrival was incorrect. I am your sister's son, Karl von Richter."

"Oh, my goodness! Young Karl. Valentina and Otto's son! You've grown into a big strong man. Karl, come follow me. I'm suffering from an old injury from when I was a teenager. My knee is no good anymore and I need to sit down."

Giovanni limped, steadying himself on the cane, as they walked back down the hall and into his office. The cardinal moved behind his desk and sat. "Now, what's this about you being a French businessman, and why are you here?"

"Your Eminence, or should I call you Uncle? As the war is now ending, it is much easier and safer to claim to be a displaced Frenchman traveling in Italy, rather than admitting being a former German soldier who has left the service. The name 'Boucher' has helped me travel as a simple businessman. I was drafted into the service in 1936. Fortunately, I was appointed to a government position, allowing me to avoid the bulk of the conflict as I traveled extensively through Europe."

Giovanni nodded. *This story is a lie so far. What is coming next?*

"As the war began, I married a young Italian woman, and we had a child born in the fall of 1942. Unfortunately, my position during the war years and constant travels took me away from home in Langenargen for the entire war. You may have heard of the recent changes in Berlin, changes that have released me from my responsibilities. Returning home two weeks ago, I learned my mother, your sister, had passed, as did my father. My wife, Katrina and our little boy were gone from our home. By chance, I met an old man who worked with my father. He said Katrina returned to Lecco or Brescia."

Taking it all in, the cardinal played along with facial expressions of sorrow and an attempt to summon tears. He wasn't sure yet what parts of Karl's story to believe.

"Last week I traveled to Katrina's parents' apartment near their bakery in Lecco. I was hoping Katrina and our son would be there, but I learned the bakery was destroyed a year ago. Her parents suffered for weeks and died from burns from misguided American bombing.

"Not finding Katrina, I traveled to Botticino. The stone works building had been destroyed by more American bombs, and I found your Uncle Vincenzo inside. He was lying on the ground, injured and bleeding from more American bombing the day before I arrived. I did everything I could to help him. Before he expired, he said, 'All the DiBotticino men died during the battle at Anzio and in the Battle of Monte Cassino along the Gustav Line.' Then, with his last breath, he said, 'Giovanni knows where Katrina and your son are. He will help you. Giovanni knows the truth.' Then he passed away."

Hearing Karl's unsettling words, the cardinal hobbled around to the front of his desk and sat next to Karl.

Karl carefully watched the prelate's anxious body language: one hand grabbing the desk for stability, and the other rubbing his wrinkled forehead, pondering what to say in response.

Two days earlier, Pope Pius XII and cardinals living inside the Vatican had received a report from a U.S. Army general, fluent in Italian. "Your Holiness, Hitler is dead, and the war will end in the next few days. The American 5th Army is making a final push east, attacking the heart of Berlin. The 157th Infantry and the 45th Infantry battled briefly with the Dachau concentration camp's remaining SS guards, then liberated 30,000 survivors, most of whom are severely emaciated. Sadly, and horrifically, we discovered thirty – yes, thirty – railroad cars filled with dead bodies in various states of decomposition. The people of the town have just buried over 9,000 bodies. I also need to advise you that an American bombing run mistakenly damaged the Duomo in Brescia four months ago. We apologize for that and will compensate the Vatican directly."

Pope Pius turned to Giovanni. "Reverend Cardinal DiBotticino, make sure you handle that."

Giovanni concluded Karl's tale of the damage at the stone works could be true, but that had been over four months ago. If Karl had spoken to Zio Vincenzo, there was no way his uncle would have known to use the term "Gustav Line." Only a high-level German military commander involved in planning Germany's defensive lines would have known that name.

Giovanni stood again, and returned behind his desk, thinking and buying a little time. He had known for years this pivotal moment could someday arrive. He knew when he had helped Katrina give the baby up for adoption, and then helped her enter the convent, those actions would constitute a huge problem if Karl weren't killed during the war.

Giovanni knew from the letters Katrina shared – letters from Karl to his father – Karl planned and directed activities at death camps. The cardinal knew SS officers were the most brutal group in the Nazi regime, strutting around in sleek black Hugo Boss uniforms with tiny skulls.

He also knew Karl would stop at nothing to get information from him. Giovanni prepared for the worst, but hoped to buy time for the young seminarian Antonio and Father Aldo to get to the convent in Bernalda, as quickly as possible, to warn the Mother Superior.

"Karl, Monsignor Paolo Andriaccio is a priest who knew our family. He might have some information regarding where Katrina and your son might be. He is due here tomorrow morning to meet with me, and then we will meet with the pope to discuss the plight of people who fled the southern German and Swiss communities and are exiled in the Milano, Bergamo, Brescia and Verona areas. If you return in the morning around eleven, after the pope and I meet with him, I can introduce you to the monsignor, and he may be able to help. Like so many, it's entirely possible Katrina and your son emigrated to northern Italy, to escape what was happening in Germany but went further east to Padua, Venice or a smaller city."

Karl recognized the old cardinal's uneasy manner: His eyelids fluttered as he spoke, and he swallowed hard while speaking. Giovanni's body language gave a clear signal he knew more than he was letting on.

Karl stood and walked around the room, then came to a stop behind the cardinal's chair and pulled his pistol from its shoulder holster. He pushed its barrel into the back of the cardinal's neck and cocked the trigger.

"Uncle, Uncle. Don't you realize it's a sin for a cardinal to lie – especially inside the Vatican? You know where Katrina and my son are, don't you? Why won't you tell me where they are? What is going on? Are you hiding them? Tell me now or I will shoot you."

"Karl, you undoubtedly are still stressed from the war. The German campaign is over. Please, sit back down, relax. It will do no good to harm me. Let's see what we can learn from Father Andriaccio tomorrow morning. I have some of the finest 1925 French Benedictine here in my credenza, would you like a glass?"

How ridiculous is this coincidence of being offered Benedictine! The suggestion agitated him. *I'll get my uncle to tell me where they are.* He pushed the pistol hard against the back of his uncle's head.

"Uncle, where is Katrina?"

The cardinal kept silent.

Karl stepped around the chair and faced his uncle. Giovanni sat nervously, gripping both wooden armrests. Then Karl put the barrel of the gun against his uncle's thigh.

Looking up at his nephew Giovanni finally said, "Karl, I knew you as an infant when I baptized you in your mother's arms. And I knew you as a happy twelve-year-old, playing soccer, smiling and laughing. You don't want to do this. Be patient and we may find out in the morning where Katrina and your son are."

Karl pushed the gun down hard on his leg, just above his knee. His voice held no warmth. "I will count to three, and I will shoot a bullet into your leg if you don't tell me the truth."

"Ah, truth! So now you want truth! Well, Karl, here's the truth. Listen carefully. Your grandmother, Stella DiVenezia, was the daughter of a Czechoslovakian rabbi. Her original name was Devorah Goldman. Devorah ran away from home to avoid a forced marriage to an older man. She changed her name to Stella. It means your mother, Valentina, was a Czechoslovakian Jew and Italian – and it means I am part Jewish. Your mother never told Otto she was Jewish because she loved him so much. Karl, the truth is you are German, Italian and Jewish."

The words bounced and echoed wildly in Karl's brain. "Uncle, you're lying and spouting this garbage to throw me off their trail. I must be close to Katrina and my son, or you wouldn't be telling me these lies. Are they here in Rome? Are they nearby?"

With the barrel of the gun still in the cardinal's thigh, Karl pushed down hard once more. "Tell me right now where my wife and son are, or I will shoot! Uncle, I have no more use for you."

Giovanni remained silent.

Angered by the lack of a response from his uncle, Karl pulled the trigger, shooting his uncle just above the knee.

Giovanni cringed with pain and fell onto the floor.

Karl intended for the bullet to pass through his uncle's thigh muscle, but it shattered his femur, a fragment slicing his femoral artery. Now only a swiftly applied tourniquet could save his life. Giovanni was quickly bleeding to death.

Karl's voice was filled with malice. "Uncle, tell me now where Katrina and my son are, or I'll shoot your other leg."

Giovanni lay on the floor in severe pain. He reached for the edge of his desk, hoping to pull himself up; instead, he pulled a book onto the floor. Envelopes inside the large book's front cover fluttered to the floor beside him.

Seeing Katrina's name on each envelope, Karl reached down and picked them up. As he did, Giovanni looked up and whispered faintly, "Katrina is no longer yours. She belongs to God."

With those words, Karl's uncle, the cardinal, died.

Monsignor Militano, responsible for statuary, artwork and the historical archive of books in the Vatican, was reviewing budgets in a nearby office when he heard the shot. Confused by the sound, he ran down the hall to see what had happened. He peered inside the slightly open door and was stunned to see Cardinal DiBotticino on the floor in a pool of blood.

Karl, anticipating someone's arrival because of the shot, stepped to the side with the letters. He watched and waited for the door to open.

The monsignor, horrified at seeing the cardinal lying on the floor, rushed in and bent over him. Karl took aim and fired. The monsignor fell dead, on top of Giovanni.

Karl waited another moment, then carefully looked out into the hallway. Seeing no one else, he strode down the hall, envelopes in hand, through the door with its thick beveled-glass pane and into the large foyer. He opened the tall, thick doors and stepped into the small entryway. With one hand on the Luger inside his jacket, he pushed opened the outer door and passed the two Swiss guards standing at attention. Karl was prepared to shoot them both as he left, but fortunately, the distance and heavy doors had muffled all the sounds inside.

"*Bon jour. Bon jour.*"

"*Ciao, Signore. Buon pomeriggio.*"

Karl calmly walked away from the building, got into the Fiat and drove away. The Swiss guards resumed their position guarding the front door, unaware of the two murders inside.

Karl put the letters in the bag. *I'm sure I'll find her now, with these.* Anxious after shooting his uncle, he lit a cigarette. *I don't care about the other cleric, but I wonder about my uncle's comment, "She belongs to God."*

Karl's route leaving the Vatican, and heading out of Rome and toward Bernalda, had him passing by Alfonso and Gina's place. His thoughts returned to Gina and their time together last night and this morning. He toyed with the idea of seeing her again before he left Rome. She was so good. He was twenty minutes into his journey to Bernalda when he thought about the date. *It's only May 14. I have time.* He turned the car around and went back to Gina's.

She was thrilled when he arrived. They spent the rest of the afternoon and evening together. She ordered a plate of osso buco from a local restaurant for her German. Together they drank several more bottles of Alfonso's homemade red, and enjoyed a terrific night together, exhausting each other to sleep.

The next morning, Karl woke with another stiff headache, and left before Gina knew he was gone. He drove for two hours. It was only 8 a.m., but the sun was bright, and it was already a humid 77 degrees. He was extremely dehydrated from all the red wine he drank last night with Gina. Seeing a stream, he pulled over, gulped a few handfuls of water, and took his first break, sitting in the shade of a tree. He opened the envelopes and read the letters. In one, Katrina wrote:

Dear Monsignor Giovanni DiBotticino:
I want to give the child up for adoption, and ask for your help to place the child in a loving home. Next, I want to devote my life to prayer, and plan to enter a convent. I will ask God to forgive the horrific deeds of Karl von Richter, a German Waffen SS Officer, and to forgive me for my strong and inappropriate sexual desires for him.
Respectfully yours,
Katrina Amorino
PS: Here is your nephew's SS photo, which he sent to your sister.

The second page was different, saying *COPY* on top. The letter, by Bishop Giovanni DiBotticino, was addressed to Sister Maria Cassano, Mother Superior, Holy Angels Convent, Via Guglielmo Gioni, Bernalda, Provence of Basilicata. In the letter, Giovanni wrote:

Dear Mother Superior:
I do hereby give permission to Katrina Amorino to enter Holy Angels Convent. As Katrina's dowry to enter, I promise to send 2,500 lire. The money will come from the DiBotticino Brothers Family Trust Fund six months after she is accepted. Thereafter, I

promise to send 250 lire monthly from the same family trust fund while she remains in the convent.

> *Yours truly in Christ,*
> *Reverend Bishop DiBotticino, di Brescia, Italia*

The third page was another letter. It also said *COPY.*

Dear Reverend Father Tommaso Fellini:
> *The infant male child, Bruno Amorino, shall be forwarded temporarily to foster parents in Genoa, and then be sent to Catholic Charities in Brooklyn, New York, as soon as possible, for final placement.*
> *Yours truly in Christ,*
> *Reverend Bishop DiBotticino, di Brescia, Italia*

Karl couldn't believe what he had just read. All three letters were dated two years ago, in the summer of 1943. He shook his head. Aloud, he began speaking to his ghost companion.

"Are these letters a joke? Has Katrina lost her mind? What has happened to this woman? She was so good in bed! Has she denied our relationship and run away? Has she done the unthinkable by giving up our child? My child? How could she? And this all happened... two years ago? That's my son! She had no right to send him away!

"And what was Giovanni saying, about my mother being part Jewish? There's no way I'm part *Jew*! This must all be fabricated. It's got to be an elaborate trick. Yes, a trick or a hoax of some kind.

"I need to find that convent in Bernalda and squeeze the truth out of the Mother Superior. If Katrina and my son are there, I'll go in and drag them both out. She's got to be there. Why else would the bishop be sending DiBotticino Family money to the convent?"

Karl climbed back into the Fiat and headed south. He'd driven another two hours when he suddenly felt exhausted. The temperature outside in the low 90s made the inside of the small car unbearable. He sweated the remaining moisture from his dehydrated body, and his body temperature climbed to a feverish 101°. His mouth felt extremely dry, and dehydration made his head spin. Needing water badly and feeling dizzy, Karl was minutes from heat stroke. Recognizing he was about to pass out, he pulled over and stopped.

While still holding the steering wheel, the image of a death camp came to him again. It was the clearest image yet, and it brought on his strongest anxiety. Karl felt himself inside a boxcar being delivered to the camp. He stood among a hundred men, all Jews, Slavs, homosexuals and other deplorables. He felt himself sweating, pressed tight against other prisoners as they moved, shoved and pushed back and forth within the boxcar. Many cried in fear. Body odors in the boxcar were nasty. Worse, some urinated freely; others lost control of their bowels. Karl tried and tried to push himself to the side of the boxcar for fresh air. Getting to the side, he squinted, peering through the sliding door's slats. Katrina stood, holding a baby. Uncle Giovanni, dressed in a ruby cassock, had his arm around her, protecting her. Valentina stood next to Otto on crutches. To the side of them, Ruth called out, "Karl, come save me. Please, come save me."

Karl pushed and pushed to get out of the boxcar, but his arms were stuck. He could only reach so far through the wooden slats. He tried yelling to them, "Get away! Get away from there."

But though he tried to yell, his words made no sound. He yelled harder; they couldn't hear him. One by one, they each pointed to him and said, "Karl, it's your fault. This is all your fault."

He sat, virtually unconscious, in the steamy car for 20 minutes. Now delusional, his temperature reached a dangerous 104 degrees.

Just then a driver, seeing the stopped Fiat, pulled alongside. He got out and knocked at Karl's window.

"*Signore, signore!* Roll down your windows. It's too hot in there. Are you okay? Wake up!"

Unresponsive, and the knock at the window not waking the man from his daze, the Good Samaritan opened the car door, and Karl suddenly awoke. Still dazed, he found himself with both arms reaching through the steering wheel, his hands across the dashboard, almost touching the windshield.

The man asked, "*Signore,* do you have any water?"

Karl didn't respond.

The man grabbed a half-full canteen from his car. "Here, take this."

Karl pulled his hands back, accepted the offered canteen and took a good long drink, then stepped outside the car. He removed his shirt and poured water over his head to cool off. More alert now, he still felt dazed. He walked around a bit and began to feel better. Two minutes passed before Karl, shirtless, got back into his car and drove off without a word of thanks to the Samaritan.

As the Fiat drove off, the man wondered what was wrong with Karl.

Realizing the gravity of his bad dream, Karl also wondered what was wrong.

CHAPTER FORTY-THREE

Heading to Bernalda

Two years earlier, Karl had been sent to Naples to spend a month training Mussolini's Blackshirts. During the assignment, he had learned more about the geography of Italy, especially south of Rome.

Besides studying road maps to enable German equipment movements, Karl had learned the culture and attitudes of southern Italians, and found them to be far different from Romans, Tuscans or even northern Italians.

Hundreds of years earlier, the city states of Florence, Genoa, Milan, Verona, Venice and the Vatican had become economic rivals. By comparison, southern Italy and Sicily had once been controlled by the ancient Greeks. During that period, beautiful temples were constructed. In the last several hundred years, southern Italian provinces focused on farming and fishing, and their culture was more relaxed.

Karl wasn't happy with the thought of driving into Italy's agricultural deep south. It was too hot and there were too few places to cool off. But right now, he needed to find the convent in Bernalda. As he drove he thought.

The Sicilian Mafia are in a world to themselves, and not to be interfered with. The Mafia didn't even get along with Mussolini's Blackshirts, so I need to pay close attention to how I conduct myself using the Blackshirt contacts as I head into the Basilicata province. The Mafia even could be worse to me, as a former SS officer, than any American soldier would. I'll have to be careful.

Karl recalled what Giovanni had said about his mother's Jewish heritage, and both he and Valentina being part Jewish. Karl rejected the notion of having Jewish blood – and the idea of Katrina's having joined the convent.

Giovanni was just trying to throw me off track. But those letters seem legit. Why did Katrina really go to Bernalda? She's too sexy to be a nun. Maybe it's another man?

Karl traveled inland, south toward Naples and found the roads heavily damaged, especially as he passed the Gustav Line. The bombing by the Americans made it difficult for the Germans to maneuver their artillery north while preparing their defenses at Anzio.

He stopped at the little town of Aquino for more water, then continued to Caserta, where he was surprised and amazed by the grand structure of the Royal Palace of Caserta. He then stopped in the community of Volla, just outside Naples.

Finding what looked like a hotel, he went inside. He was greeted by an old man with a bushy white mustache, smoking the last inch of a tiny, crooked and smelly cigar. Karl asked and was told there was a room upstairs.

Excited to have a guest, Pietro left for a minute and returned with his wife, Patrizia. Immediately taking charge, the old woman told Karl to go out back to wash up and change. He was told to return in ten minutes for supper and to bring his laundry and she'd wash everything.

When Karl returned, Patrizia, who wasn't five feet tall, directed him to the kitchen. He sat at the family table and was given a bottle of Pietro's homemade red wine, a plate with thinly sliced prosciutto, several chunks of soppressata, shavings from a chunk of pecorino and a small loaf of crusty bread with burnt edges. Five minutes later, the wife carried in a dish of homemade linguine covered in olive oil, sautéed garlic and tiny pieces of anchovy.

As Karl devoured it, he remembered his mother making similar noodles, just with oil and seared garlic, when he was a teenager. He also remembered his father getting sick that night. Otto blamed the garlic, and it was never made again.

The next morning Karl rose as dawn approached and grabbed his things off the clothesline, still slightly damp. He left a $50 bill for Pietro and Patrizia and drove away at 5. After a few hours, he saw the Bay of

Naples full of American warships and troop transports from his elevated location near the coast. He knew the cities at the foot of Mount Vesuvius experienced limited fighting because most of the American 5th Army's forces leaving Sicily landed at Anzio to outflank General Field Marshal Albert Kesselring at the Winter Line.

Karl drove through Torre del Greco and then Torre Annunziata and, upon reaching Salerno, saw a small shop and stopped for bread and cheese. He then drove on to Battipaglia and headed east toward Potenza. Hoping to arrive by nightfall, Karl moved along at a good pace on valley roads, but as the terrain grew more mountainous, the steep grades grew difficult for the little car.

Soon the gasoline needle showed less than a quarter tank of fuel remaining, and his gas cans were empty. Karl began stopping in villages and finally found a church with fuel in the tiny village of Vietri di Poten-za. The sacristan, who was happy to help, misunderstood Karl's request. He picked up a two-gallon jug of diesel and approached the car. Luckily, Karl caught the mistake before the man poured the fuel into the Fiat's gas tank.

He stopped at four more churches before he found one that had gasoline. Karl filled the car, and one of his empty five-gallon cans, but there wasn't enough for the remaining tanks. He continued along, hoping to find more gasoline along the road. Before pulling away, he looked at the last map. It stopped there in Naples. He thought he understood the remaining distance to Bernalda, and looked at his watch. It was late. Tired and feeling he'd driven enough for the day, he opted to sleep in the car. He parked in a remote area, not wanting to be disturbed. He ate some cheese and bread and opened a bottle of Greco di Tufo wine he'd bought earlier that day. He finished the bottle and fell asleep.

It was warm that night and the nightmarish dream returned. Karl sweated through his clothes, then woke about 4. He was drenched; even his boxer shorts were soaked. As he changed his clothes, he wondered why the dreams continued, why they were more vivid, and why they kept putting him in the boxcar. He didn't feel guilty – at least not while he was awake. Wondering if something deep inside was bothering him, Karl fell asleep again.

To his surprise, it was bright and sunny and almost 10 when he awoke. After stretching outside the car, he left for Potenza. He expected his progress to be better than recent days as roads improved, but he still had to watch for hazards. He thought on and off about last night's dream.

The last road sign just ahead put him about ten kilometers outside Potenza. While he was reading the sign, his tire hit a chunk of rock and he veered into a long, deep rut. He struggled briefly to steer out of the rut when the right front tire went flat. He stepped out and noticed the small piece of metal in the pothole that slashed the sidewall and tube inside.

Karl kicked the wheel, then opened the trunk, and saw no spare tire. Frustrated, he leaned against the car's hood.

As he looked around, he saw at least a hundred spent artillery shells on the side of the road. On one side two damaged Panzer tanks sat twenty meters off the road: one with its turret blown off, and the other's painted Balkan Cross mostly peeled away from the heat that ravaged the inside of the tank. The image struck him. *Our tanks should have had a swastika on them and not the cross.* A history buff, Karl knew swastikas had once represented symbols of peace and well-being in many ancient societies, thousands of years before they became the symbol of German supremacy.

Distracted by the Balkan Cross and thoughts of the swastika, a thought emerged about what Giovanni had said. *I can't be Jewish. It's impossible. It's bad enough my mother was Italian, but there's no way she was part Jew!*

He had no choice but to leave the car. He checked his Luger, and pushed a few extra bullets, one by one, into its spring-loaded handle. He had space for four new bullets. He'd shot the farmer who yanked on his foot, the car owner in Brescia, Uncle Giovanni and the monsignor who walked into the room. He took the duffel bag with his passport, money, valuables and clean clothing. He shoved the pouch of diamonds into his deep pants pocket and began to walk. An hour passed when an old man, probably from nearby Vietri di Potenza, came along in a small wagon pulled by a donkey, filled with bushels of spring produce. He stopped and offered Karl a ride. The ride on the wagon's wooden wheels was hard and bumpy. Karl felt ridiculous sitting behind an ass, especially when the donkey stopped and lifted its tail at one point to relieve itself. The hot sun beat down on them during the two-hour ride.

When they finally reached the edge of Potenza, the old farmer told Karl he needed to turn right, toward the market, and that the center of town was straight ahead. He pulled back on the leather straps to the donkey's brace, and the cart rocked to a halt. Karl grabbed his duffel bag, jumped down and headed to town, never bothering to thank the farmer, who continued toward the market, to deliver his freshly picked broccolini, broccoli rabe and garlic.

Karl arrived in the center of town near 4 p.m., tired, dusty and hungry. As he looked for a place to stay the night, he got stares from the locals. He was thinking about a place to stay and about finding another car. After speaking to some locals about a hotel, he asked about gasoline. He learned most of the automobiles in town were out of fuel, with gas nowhere to be found. He figured his transportation come morning might have to be a horse or, worse, a donkey. He reasoned if he could find a Fiat without gasoline, maybe he could get a wheel and a good tire, and bring it back to his car stuck outside of town. Maybe he could get a spare as well.

Karl had never been in Potenza, but he knew of two Blackshirt names from when he'd taught a one-month class in Rome. The Germans had sought assistance from the Blackshirts as local guides for knowledge about roads for maneuvering tanks and artillery, fuel and troop transportation. Karl's classes taught them how to communicate with and help the German Army. He pulled the crumpled and slightly torn list from his bag, hoping a Blackshirt on his personal list of contacts might still live in Potenza. He saw a familiar name and felt it was good luck. His newfound optimism shook off his worries regarding the letters about Katrina and his son. He concluded the Jew thing was only a ploy by Giovanni, and a plan by Katrina's family to disassociate themselves from the von Richter family and their pure German ancestry.

Karl spent another half hour walking around town, then found the address of the Blackshirt contact. Karl knocked. The door opened. Karl introduced himself. Gino quickly remembered him from the class. Karl explained about his tire and the car being left behind.

Gino told Karl, "Stay here and have something to eat, I'll be right back."

He went and spoke with two other Blackshirts. They traveled by wagon with two spare tires, and found Karl's vehicle parked just past the mausoleums west of Vietri di Potenza. Replacing the wheel and tire went smoothly, and they put a good spare in the trunk.

When they finished, one headed home in the cart and the other returned in Karl's car. He parked the Fiat behind Gino's house, and let himself in the back door. Karl, enjoying a glass of sweet Moscato dessert wine, was chatting about old war times with Gino when his brother-in-law sauntered in, unannounced.

Reacting to the stranger's sudden appearance, Karl dropped to the floor, pulled his Luger and took aim.

"Whoa! Relax!" Gino shouted. "He's one of us; he just fixed your car. Put your gun away."

Karl scowled. *These Italians are so careless.*

Then, brazenly, the brother-in-law said, "So, Gino says you're the famous SS officer called 'the butcher!' We're honored to have you with us tonight. You have a new wheel and tire, a new spare in your trunk and your gas tank and your gasoline containers are all filled, as well. Now, tell us some of your death-camp stories of eradicating those damn annoying Jews and Gypsies."

Karl gave a nod. *They probably haven't heard about Hitler's death or the end of the war this far south.*

"First of all, your leader, Benito, wasn't a bright military leader. His strategies, and those he surrounded himself with, all failed him. Your best hope was to stay committed to Germany. Next, things have changed in Germany. Hitler has left Berlin and the war will soon be over. I'm a forward scout for a small party of SS officers traveling with Hitler. A strange route was selected to keep the enemy from encountering Der Führer during his escape. Be patient for Hitler's arrival here in Potenza in twenty-four to thirty-six hours. Gino, your home is on a list of places considered as a safe house. Like my arrival, several SS officers will come to you in the dark of night. Be prepared, and don't let your brother-in-law walk in the back door as he did tonight, or he'll be shot."

Then he began filling their heads with stories and ideas. An hour passed when Gino looked at his brother-in-law, winked and politely suggested, "Karl, your travels have been long and hard. Perhaps you'd enjoy a local woman as a companion tonight? It would be our treat."

Karl smiled and nodded in approval, and Gino sent his brother-in-law to fetch the woman. A few minutes later there came a knock, and the door opened.

Karl looked at her from top to bottom. Her unkempt hair, baggy tent-like dress, rolled-down stockings below her knees, and flattened, dirty slippers weren't what he had in mind.

"*Signora*, not tonight. I have a headache from Gino's wine."

He pulled out a $50 bill and handed it to her. She took the money and left. When the door closed, Karl turned and smiled at his host. Gino smiled back, grabbed another bottle of homemade red wine. He brought up a topic Karl enjoyed, by asking whether Italian or German cars were better.

"Gino, of course German cars are far superior. Look at Daimler-Benz, Bavarian Motor Works, Duesenberg and Auto Union. Did you know before the war, Adolf Hitler established a car company? Yes, in 1937 it was renamed Volkswagenwerk. The little cars are Adolf's own design – his dream! He envisioned a network of high-speed roads across Germany called the autobahn, enabling Germans to drive quickly into areas where there were no trains."

Karl ended the evening with an actual headache from the dry red wine. He went to bed and fell sound asleep.

He rose early the next morning with his head still pounding. After some water, he went back through his packet of information. At the back of Plan C were three untitled pages printed lightly in pencil but not over-written in ink. It looked like another alternate plan that wasn't approved because the safe houses south of Rome were never vetted.

The penciled note at the top of the two pages said, "NOTE: If the U-boat isn't in Ravenna, use Plan D." Essentially, it was another fallback plan, taking Hitler all the way south to Taranto and the Isola of San Pietro to leave Italy. This plan's timeframe was sixteen weeks. So, while it had never been vetted, the additional two road maps and the Blackshirt contact list were legitimate. The maps in the packet showed roads in the Province of Basilicata and key roads leading to Taranto.

Karl felt lucky again. *It would be incredible if the U-boat is off the Isola of San Pietro. It would certainly be worth a try after finding Katrina, provided this vague Plan D ever reached the intended U-boat captain.*

All fueled up, with extra gasoline, a new tire and spare, he drove away, his mood again positive.

CHAPTER FORTY-FOUR

The Greenwich Village Soldier

After an hour of driving, Karl was stopped at a dismantled American checkpoint, with everyone gone but for one final soldier making his final stop.

"*Buon giorno, signore!*"

"*Ah! Bonjour, officer!*"

When asked, "May I see your papers?" Karl quickly complied.

As the soldier looked over Karl's fake French passport, he asked, "Where are you headed, Monsieur Boucher?"

"My Italian wife and our baby son were visiting her parents in Lecco when the war began. I sent her a note saying, 'Don't return to our home in France. Instead, go on to Bernalda and stay with your grandparents.' I am going there now and, when the war is over, I will bring them to Brooklyn, America, where we will make pizza. I hear people in America like pizza."

The young Italian-American soldier who stopped him was born in Reggio, Calabria, the toe of Italy, in 1924. In 1928, his parents, Ida and Tommaso Fellini, immigrated to New York City, settling in Greenwich Village, a friendly Italian neighborhood filled with artists, teachers and musicians.

Gregorio had been in his third year at NYU as the war started. A language major with a good ear for dialects, he was purposely stationed at the checkpoint because of his unique ability to pick up dialects and determine whether German soldiers lagged in their retreat from the south end of the Italian peninsula.

"Monsieur Boucher, I see your passport. But your dialect? Where are you really from?"

"Ah! A good question. I am from a tiny town called Briançon in France, not far from the Italian and Swiss borders. I was raised by my grandparents in Zurich before I returned home as a teenager. My mix of French, German and Italian may sound odd to an educated person such as yourself. I was doing business in Germany at the beginning of the war and hid on a farm for four years. When we go to Brooklyn, America – now that the war is over – we will become Brooklyn baseball fans and cheer for Giuseppe DiMaggio."

The soldier laughed. "Giuseppe DiMaggio plays for the Yankees. He enlisted in the Army and, when the war is over, he'll be back playing baseball. By the way, Monsieur Boucher, how do you know the war is almost over?"

"Another good question. I stopped in Rome to see an old friend. He said Hitler is dead, and the war might be over soon. Is this not true?"

"We don't know if he's really dead. The Soviet Army found a tunnel hidden deep under Hitler's bunker. Its entrance was found behind a metal panel and located behind a toilet. When the panel was opened, instead of leading to the normal plumbing, it led to a five-hundred-meter-long tunnel. Some people now think Hitler escaped through it and either headed to the north coast or south into Italy. Anyway, you don't need to know any of that. Good luck in America. When you get there, root for Joe DiMaggio on the Yankees – they play in the Bronx. And if you find your way to Greenwich Village, be sure to visit John's Pizzeria on Bleeker Street and ask for Chubby."

By now, the rest of his unit had driven a few miles away, and the soldier had a jeep to catch up to them. But as he went to let Karl pass, the young soldier thought he heard Karl say, "Achtung."

It was very low and almost under his breath. But the American soldier suddenly had a strong feeling, and said, in French, "Monsieur Boucher, please, just one more thing."

"Yes?"

Then loudly, in a strong guttural German, Gregorio said loudly, "Officer, tell me what it was like in Berlin and working at the death camps. What role did you play?"

Shocked by the unexpected question, Karl swallowed hard.

Seeing his hard swallow, the young soldier said in German, "Get out of the car and raise your hands above your head."

Karl looked at the soldier and complied.

Gregorio began to frisk him and discovered the gun in Karl's shoulder holster.

Knowing he was discovered at that moment, Karl used his full strength and, coming down hard in a chopping motion to the base of the soldier's neck, knocked him to the ground. Gregorio moaned, lying flat on the ground in pain. Karl quickly pulled his Luger while standing over the soldier, pushed hard, stuffing the nozzle deep into Gregorio's neck to muffle the sound, and shot him.

The Army unit, now more than two miles away, never heard the shot. Karl dragged the body over to the bushes. Turning, he gazed enviously at the jeep and its mounted machine gun, but climbed back into the tiny Fiat.

He was young and foolish like Johannes. Challenging me was unnecessary. If only he knew my accomplishments as a defensive analyst in Berlin, and my efficiency improvements at the camps.

He drove away, trying to focus on Bernalda, but thought about the American soldier mentioning how the Russians found an escape door to a tunnel.

It made Karl anxious, and he again doubted Hitler's suicide.

What if it's true – Der Fuhrer's escaping through the tunnel? Speer must have had someone bring a double through the tunnel. The helper held the double at the secret hatchway until Speer's arrival. When Speer greeted Der Fuhrer, he let the double in. Then Speer killed the double with a silencer, while Hitler poisoned Eva. Then Hitler escaped with Speer's accomplice waiting in tunnel. Speer simply left the Bunker as if nothing ever happened.

I'm more certain now, hearing the soldier's comments about the tunnel – there is a second Chosen One! He must have helped the double get in, then waited inside the tunnel to assist Der Fuhrer escape. It must be Hockemeier.

CHAPTER FORTY-FIVE

The Cardinal's Wisdom

It was early May and a number of weeks had passed since Father Luca and Sister Katrina began walking and talking together in the garden – speaking more seriously.

Both had come to recognize they no longer felt forced to remain in their respective roles – and they cautiously hinted at that during their conversations. Instead, they wanted to focus on having new lives – and feelings of having a life together became evident to both. They realized this as they spoke, and their brief looks in each other's eyes confirmed it.

Father Luca made an unexpected visit to Mother Superior's office after morning Mass. He knocked at the open door.

"Come in."

"Good morning, Mother. I wanted to share something with you. There's been a breakthrough with Sister Katrina."

She didn't respond, opting to let Father explain himself further.

"Over the last several weeks, while on our walks, Sister Katrina has shared details of her life before coming to the convent. The circumstances she has endured and the anguish she feels over giving the child up are extraordinary – something few women ever experience. But she seems to be feeling better. Perhaps speaking openly with me has helped her.

"Mother, I need to tell you this. Katrina is such a caring woman, and her heart is so kind." He paused and swallowed. "I must confess to you – I have developed feelings for her."

Mother Superior nodded slowly and thoughtfully.

"Yes, Sister Katrina is truly a kind and caring young woman. I can understand how anyone would appreciate her charitable affection for others, especially the older sisters she cares for here in the convent, day in and day out."

She then paused for a moment as if to emphasize what she was about to say.

"Father Luca, I need to tell you this: It is no coincidence you are here in Bernalda. Cardinal DiBotticino, in his wisdom, sent you here to our parish and convent for good reason. Of course, you are here to care for the parish, the parishioners and their needs, and our convent and all the sisters' needs. But long ago he recognized something in you that was... well, let's say... well... he wrote a letter to me shortly after you arrived. In it he wrote, uh, well, uh, let me paraphrase what the cardinal wrote: 'Somehow, Father Luca Luciano might someday be a match for Katrina, when she realizes she no longer wants to be a nun, and when he realizes he no longer wishes to be a priest.'

"The bishop went on to write that you'd been forced to enter the priesthood by your family, not by your own vocation. He liked you very much and was impressed with your charitable heart. He asked me to keep an eye on you and look out for you. It wasn't long after your arrival, and the arrival of his letter, that it clicked. I reached the same conclusion he did about the potential of a relationship between you and Katrina. Father, I've been pained by what she's gone through. I've prayed for an answer for her, and I feel we have it with your presence."

Father Luca took a deep breath – and let it out slowly. "My goodness! How could the cardinal have seen this so long ago? I'm very taken with what you've just told me. Thank you, Sister."

"Father, let's go to the kitchen and have a cup of espresso. Sister Carmella whispered to me a little while ago that Sister Rita just made fresh almond pignoli cookies. I'm sure they're delightful, and perhaps we can find a little Sambuca for the espresso."

CHAPTER FORTY-SIX

Antonio and Aldo Arrive

Antonio and Father Aldo finally arrived in Bernalda. Their car ride had been a huge challenge, and both were extremely nervous. The papal envoy paper signed by Cardinal DiBotticino helped them secure gasoline from American servicemen at a checkpoint; but the bombed roads, a flat tire and two wrong turns caused them to arrive more than half a day late.

When they parked at Holy Angels Church, the pair walked down the block to the front door of the convent. Father Aldo pulled at the small rope hanging outside the door. A moment later a short nun, not even five feet tall, came to the door. She grabbed a small step stool and peered through the tiny window in the thick oak door.

Seeing what she believed to be two priests, she moved her little step stool, opened the door and welcomed them inside. "Good morning, Fathers. I'm Sister Carmella. How can I help you?"

"We're here to see Sister Maria Cassano, the Mother Superior. We have an urgent message for her from Cardinal DiBotticino at the Vatican. We must get the message to her immediately."

"Yes. Let me go find her. It may be a few minutes."

Sister Carmella scurried to the Superior's office, then ran through the echoing hallowed hallways until she found Mother Superior in the kitchen, chatting with Father Luca over a cup of coffee and freshly baked almond pignoli cookies.

"Mother, Mother! Two priests are in the foyer with an urgent message for you from Cardinal DiBotticino in the Vatican."

"Alright, Sister, tell them I'll be upstairs in a minute."

"How strange," Father Luca exclaimed as Sister Carmella departed. "You just mentioned the cardinal. I wonder what's going on?"

"Father Luca, what you need to do is pray God's will is fulfilled for both you and Katrina. Now, come upstairs with me. I'm curious why the cardinal would send two messengers all the way to Bernalda!"

Mother Superior walked with Father Luca to the foyer. They politely exchanged greetings with Father Aldo and Antonio, and Antonio handed her the sealed envelope.

She opened it, and saw it was written and signed by Monsignor DiBotticino moments after Katrina left the baby with him in Brescia and departed for the convent in Bernalda. The envelope had been stamped, but never mailed.

In the letter, the monsignor said "I anticipate a time might come when Katrina's nemesis Karl may look for her and the child, if he isn't killed in the war. I pray this will never happen, but I want to alert you, Mother Superior, that it is a possibility."

She looked up. "When and where was this given to you?"

Antonio replied, "Four days ago. The cardinal gave it to me in his office at the Vatican. There was a tall man outside his office who wanted to speak to him. He said he had news from the family in Botticino. The cardinal was preparing to meet him, but before he did, the cardinal sent me through his back door with this note. I sensed he somehow spelled trouble for you and the convent."

Mother Superior's stomach turned.

"Father Aldo and I got lost on our way here," Antonio said apologetically. "We made some wrong turns. Even though we had a little head start, we might have lost our time advantage."

She realized from his comment they had little time, if any, to prepare for a visit by Karl von Richter.

She thanked the pair for delivering the message and suggested they walk around the corner to the rectory adjacent to the church for lunch. She said she'd send a sister to fix a meal for them and prepare a room for them for the night.

She turned to Sister Carmella. "Please find Sister Katrina and bring her to my office right away."

CHAPTER FORTY-SEVEN

Karl Arrives in Bernalda

Karl had made good progress driving. He was pleased with the shortcut he took to Bernalda, saving him half a day. He was tired from driving – and perhaps even more exhausted from his constant thinking. When daylight was gone, he slept in the car so as to have only an hour's drive in the morning.

The day had been warm, but to keep mosquitos out, he closed the car windows. He fell asleep quickly and over the next few hours his body began to heat up. Tonight's bad dream arrived just past 3 a.m.

Karl found himself again in the boxcar with other prisoners. The men beside him were all shoving each other, yelling and crying. Looking out the slats of the boxcar's door, he saw Jewish men getting shot by the firing squad and falling backward into a long, deep ditch. Then he heard a single shot and looked down.

Uncle Giovanni lay on the floor of the boxcar, his leg bleeding badly. He looked up and said, "Karl, it's the truth. We both are part Jewish."

Then his mother appeared, standing next to him, saying, "Why would you kill my brother, and why are you killing your people? Karl, you need to know the truth – the truth about Ruth."

Karl felt like he was falling backward. With the sudden feeling of falling, he woke up as he kicked the car's dashboard. He rolled down both windows and stepped outside to cool off. He changed his shirt, then got back in the car. The last dream stunned him. But, still tired, he slept another hour.

Karl was hungry when he woke, and ate the last of the bread and cheese the Blackshirt had given him for his trip. He stretched again in the morning sunlight. He thought again about last night's nightmare and his recent spate of bad dreams.

This morning Karl wondered about Ruth. And for the first time, he wondered if all the destruction caused by the war had been worth it – especially since Hitler's grand plan failed so badly.

Karl continued on his way. The drive was smooth. He noticed a road sign and checked his watch. Bernalda and the convent were now only fifteen minutes away.

***

Meanwhile, as Antonio and Father Aldo departed the convent for the rectory, Sister Carmella left the foyer to find Sister Katrina.

Mother Superior returned to her office. Father Luca, still unsure what was happening, trailed behind. Mother Superior immediately went to a bookshelf; reaching behind a carved wooden statue of St. Joseph, she grabbed a small handgun. She carried it gingerly and placed it in her desk's top center drawer.

Father Luca was stunned, sensing her concern.

"Sister, what is in the letter? And is that a real gun you just put in your drawer? Is it loaded?"

"Luca, according to Cardinal DiBotticino's note, written when he was a monsignor, there might be a day when an angry Karl von Richter will come to steal Sister Katrina away from here. Apparently, he's been looking for her for a few weeks. He found and visited his uncle, Cardinal DiBotticino, a few days ago at the Vatican, and the cardinal immediately sent Antonio and Father Aldo here to warn us. We need to prepare for his arrival – perhaps at any moment."

Just then Sister Carmella returned with Katrina and knocked at Mother Superior's partially open door.

"Come in, come in."

Katrina stepped inside the office and saw Luca at Mother Superior's side.

Immediately anxious, Katrina asked, "Have I done something wrong?"

"No, dear. You've done nothing wrong. You're here because we have something urgent to discuss with you. We just received a note from

Cardinal DiBotticino at the Vatican. He sent a papal envoy with papers to advise me Karl von Richter is looking for you and your son.

"Apparently, he paid a visit to the Vatican a few days ago and questioned the cardinal. The cardinal found an old letter he wrote but never sent to me. He gave it to his two envoys to warn us. We anticipate he isn't far behind them – they arrived fifteen minutes ago. I've asked Father Luca to stay and sit with us, to discuss this matter as we decide how best to protect you."

"Oh, my God. He's coming here! I have to leave. I'll get my things and I'll leave right away."

"Wait, Katrina." Mother Superior's voice calmed her. "You will stay right here. Since the Middle Ages, our cloistered convents and high walls have protected us from intruders. We just need a plan now to best protect you."

CHAPTER FORTY-EIGHT

The Confrontation

As Karl arrived in Bernalda, he stopped and asked an old man in a small, open vegetable stand where the convent was.

The street vendor replied, "The cloistered convent is attached to the Church of the Holy Angels. Go down this street to the end, then make a right and it will be on your right."

***

Karl knew about cloistered convents. Three years earlier, he had been assigned to help flush out a Catholic cloistered convent in northern Germany hiding Jewish women. The local Gestapo received a tip from a local snitch saying many of the women dressed as nuns were Jewesses from nearby towns.

He and his SS team went inside to flush the women out. Upon entering the front door, he saw areas separated by wooden grilles to keep the public from entering where the nuns were located. It only took a few minutes using some equipment to break through the woodwork.

He'd shuffled the women out of the building. He meant to interrogate them and have the Jewish women taken away. But an impasse developed – when no one would answer his questions. Unable to force them to cooperate, and unable to tell the difference, Karl shot two, then sent three dozen to the Ravensbruck concentration camp for women. He packed them into a troop carrier and had the Gestapo take them away.

He didn't know that only three miles away, the truck stopped, and all the women were gassed to death by the truck's exhaust fumes and dumped into a ditch. Many SS officers felt it was a fast and easy method of elimination – and it kept camps from becoming too full.

***

Now Karl was feeling anxious – expecting to run into the silent treatment once again, with Katrina hiding with his son somewhere inside.

He drove around the convent to determine the best point of entry; he sensed Katrina was inside. As he turned the corner, he saw two priests enter the front door. He got a glimpse of one and thought for a moment he'd seen the fellow before, but discounted the idea.

He drove around the block a second time and concluded the high walls made it like a little fortress. He couldn't sneak in a back way, and he knew he couldn't bully his way inside.

Ah! I have an idea. The best way in is to act like a salesman selling something the convent needs, and maybe I can be invited in and get them to open a few doors inside.

Karl pulled around again to the main road, near the entrance to the church. He thought through a possible confrontation and wanted an exit plan. He checked to ensure his gun was loaded, in case he needed to shoot anyone holding Katrina against her will.

He looked up at the neatly spaced windows from the street and wondered where his son might be. He concluded each window was a bedroom and his young son was in a room with Katrina, or in an adjacent bedroom.

He drove around the block yet again, revisiting his entry strategy. Then he saw the two priests walking along the sidewalk, toward the church. Karl remained in his car, watching them. He was sure he'd seen one before... but where?

Just then, another car pulled up and two more priests jumped out. They greeted the two who were walking and the four hugged as if it had been years since they'd seen each other. Seeing the four priests vividly talking and fully engaged, with arms and hands flying in motion, as Italians do, Karl parked and walked down the block. He arrived at the convent's front door, and pulled the white knotted rope, as he'd seen the two priests do earlier.

A bell rang inside. A moment later, impatient, he pulled the rope again. Within seconds, a short little nun opened the door. "Good day, sir. I'm Sister Carmella. How can I help you?"

"*Bonjour*. My name is Pierre Louis Boucher. I'm a French businessman. I have permission, or perhaps I should say, I am directed by the Vatican's own Cardinal DiBotticino to visit the churches and convents here in southern Italy. He's asked me to assist in identifying and resolving their needs resulting from the effects of the war. The company I represent has been vetted and approved by the Vatican. We offer special pricing to Catholic churches for a wide variety of products, but we must act quickly. My time is limited. May I please speak to Mother Superior? I presume she is the head of purchasing in your convent, like the other convents I've already visited."

"Oh yes. Mother always says we need to save money. Come in and wait here in the lobby for a moment, and I will bring you to Mother Superior's office when she's ready. She's in there right now with our pastor, Father Luca."

Karl smiled. As the little sister turned, he ignored her instruction to remain in the lobby, following closely behind her as she walked into Mother Superior's office.

Wow! That was easier than shooting my way in!

As Sister Carmella walked, she noticed the tall man following her. She didn't like that. She'd told him to wait but he ignored her.

Little Carmella rapped at the door four times.

Inside, Mother Superior was surprised to hear the four knocks. It wasn't Sister Carmella's usual two knocks. Rather, four knocks meant a message of concern or a problem. The little nun had suggested the signal last year when she became responsible for answering the front door.

Mother Superior looked at Katrina and Father Luca and then whispered, "God help us. I think he's already here."

"Come in, Sister Carmella."

Sister Carmella opened the door and entered; behind her was the 6'2" German, holding a gun pressed into the little nun's back.

Karl scanned the room, stunned to see Katrina standing to the left of Mother Superior's desk. It was the first time he'd seen her in over four years. She wore a blue habit, unlike the nuns' regular black-and-white habits. The outfit matched her eyes, which were as blue as ever. She had a head covering of some sort, but her dark brown hair was visible and flowed out the sides of her head garment. She looked really good – even in her postulant's uniform.

"Katrina, what are you doing here in this place? Have you lost your mind? And where is our son?"

"He is safe," she replied, her voice steadier than she felt.

"Where? Where is he?" Karl demanded.

Katrina's heart was pounding, and her hands shaking. She never thought the day would come when she would confront Karl. But over the last few years, in the silence of her mind, she'd practiced telling him off a thousand times. She knew it from rote, and as she began to blurt it out, her anger and tone increased.

"Your parents and I expected you home after SS training but you changed after Kristallnacht and disrupting Jewish businesses. We had expected you home at Christmas and you never came. We heard from Wehrmacht generals visiting the factory that you crisscrossed Germany many times. We hoped you'd stop to visit, even for a day or a few hours. You wrote to your father about your building concentration and death camps, killing Jews, Poles, Slavs and Gypsies! My God, Karl!

"When your parents realized what you were doing, they were crushed! They couldn't believe their son would be involved in a massive scheme to murder people. You became a monster, facilitating Hitler's Final Solution – the genocide against the Jews.

"You completely ignored or forgot about me, or both, except that one night when you stopped to see your mother on your way to Italy – then you came to see me for sex. You were drunk, high on amphetamines and you raped me. You held me down as I struggled and said 'No!' You were an animal!

"The child I bore was from that brutal and drunken attack, not from love, as a child should be. You weren't the same man I'd gone to Friedrichshafen to live with. You were a stranger. I didn't know who you had become. And your mother died that same night."

Mother Superior, Father Luca and Sister Carmella were stunned at hearing Katrina call Karl out for his wickedness and horrific attacks on the Jews in the camps, and his brutal attack on her. As her rant escalated, Katrina inched toward Karl.

Meanwhile, little Sister Carmella stepped to the side and slowly backed out of the office. Mother Superior and Father Luca remained to one side, watching the heated exchange.

"Your father heard about your nasty deeds from Lutz, Todt and later Albert Speer when they came to inspect Panzer tank production at the foundry. They would tell him what you were doing, and they'd laugh at your zealous slaughter of Jews in the camps. Your father didn't want to hear it and he stopped telling your mother what you were up to. I watched them both cry, knowing what you were doing.

"Karl, your mother died of pneumonia the night you raped me, and your father died of a heart attack six months later – not at the factory but in his secretary Monika's bed. Your mother lived with that heartache over two years that he was sleeping with Monika. She was emotionally crushed by what you both were doing. It caused her to get sick and she died alone, in the middle of the night, in a cold house – that same night you raped me."

As Katrina continued to rant against Karl, Mother Superior and Father Luca witnessed it all. She then tearlessly moved into a full rage. She yelled louder as she moved even closer, shouting up into his face, and poking her forefinger hard into his chest.

Karl remained still, taking it all in, but his gun now pointed at Katrina.

"When your father died, an SS officer at the funeral told me you were alive, and he went on to tell me more about 'Karl the Butcher,' 'Karl the Brother of the Devil,' 'Karl the brilliant SS officer and military strategist.' He said he visited your father at the factory a month earlier and congratulated him for your reputation as one of the most brutal Waffen SS officers at the camps.

"Then another SS officer told me, 'Karl's experience with the ovens in the foundry made him suggest bigger gas pipes and adding oxygen, to get the furnaces hotter faster to turn the bodies to ashes quicker.' Karl, hearing about details of your actions at the death camps was the last straw – you broke my heart."

He moved back a step, checked on the other two, still pointing his pistol at Katrina.

"Where is my son, Katrina?"

"I'm not done with you. Your Italian grandmother, Stella? Well, her name was originally Devorah, and Stella's father was rabbi Hirsch Goldman. She grew up in Czechoslovakia as Devorah and ran away to Venice where she changed her name to Stella DiVenezia. Do you understand what this means, Karl? Your grandmother was Jewish. Your mother was half Jewish and you're part Jewish.

"But here's the last straw for you: Your mother told me a secret she'd kept from Otto and you all these years. One February night, while your father was away skiing, your mother went to a dance with friends. They had too much to drink and her friends accidentally left her behind. The man who brought her home took advantage of her drunken state and raped her. You came along nine months later, just after Otto left for war. You were a bad memory for your mother as you grew up, because you looked identical to the man who raped her. And Karl, your real father? He was one hundred percent Jewish! He worked at the factory with your father, and he trained you as a teenager. And his daughter? Her name was Ruth. Ruth was your sister. It made your mother sick all those years because you and Ruth looked so much alike, and then your mother heard from other women how Ruth and you spent a romantic night together on your grandfather's boat."

Katrina's volume rose. "And you had the damn nerve to rape me? You bastard! You should die a thousand painful deaths and burn in the deepest depths of hell for what you've done to your own people."

With this last burst of information, and with Katrina shouting so loudly, Karl's anger peaked. He grabbed her by the wrist, twisted it back and pulled her toward him. As he did, he stuck the gun hard against the center of her chest. Then he backed slowly out of the office, pulling her with him. He continued backward down the hall, into the foyer, keeping an eye out so no one would follow them. As they reached the front door, Karl let her go and slapped her face. The blow sliced Katrina's eyebrow, and blood flowed across her eye and down her cheek.

"Shut up, woman! You've had your say. Now listen to me. I've been searching for you and our child for almost three weeks. Hitler is dead. The war is over. You and I and our son have a chance to escape to

South America and start life all over. I have plenty of money. I've been having some bad dreams. I've made mistakes. But the past is behind me now. Now I'm here for you.

"Where is our son? Is he upstairs? Tell me right now, Katrina, or I'll go back inside and kill the others one by one, until you do tell me."

As Karl and Katrina moved out of the office and into the foyer, Mother Superior reached into her desk, grabbed the loaded handgun and then grabbed Father Luca's arm.

"Come with me, Luca. I have a plan."

Pulling Luca along, they exited her office through the back door, hurrying down a long hallway. She opened another door to the narthex of the church, tugging Father Luca out the front door of the church, along the sidewalk and toward the front door of the convent.

Antonio, Father Aldo and the other two priests were across the street, all laughing at Vatican jokes, pope jokes and telling old seminary stories. Intent on each other, they never saw anyone pass them on the other side of the street.

Arriving at the convent door, Mother Superior and Father Luca were breathing hard. She pressed the gun into his hand, saying, "Here. Take this. I'll stand in the middle of the street to catch his attention when they exit, and you do it when he comes out."

" 'Do it'? What?"

"Shoot him! Shoot Karl. Shoot him two or three times – or even four times if you have to."

Father Luca cautiously positioned himself to the side of the oak door, ready to shoot Karl as he exited. Mother Superior stood in the center of street.

Inside, Katrina continued her rant.

"You want to know where your child is, Karl? He's not upstairs. Our son is in America. I sent him away from you. I gave him up because you didn't deserve a child. You will never be a deserving father and you will never have a son. Certainly not *my* son.

"You Nazis killed millions of people with your tanks, guns, planes and bombs. You tortured, and shot, and gassed people to death, reducing them to ashes inside your furnaces. Karl, you deserve nothing

271

good in this life. The only thing you deserve is to sit in the deepest part of Dante's hell for eternity. I came here to the convent to pray for you, but it's over. I'm finished worrying about you and your soul. You aren't worth praying for anymore. Now I deserve a life without you, without the memory of your brutality."

"Katrina, you're all wrong about me," Karl insisted. "I was called to duty. I joined the SS to make my father proud. In the SS, I did what I was asked, to cleanse my country. We needed to stop the communists and Jews conspiring to take over and ruin Germany. I did the things my leader said to do to make Germany great again, for people like you and me, for our child and for future generations.

"Now listen closely. I can take you far away from here. We can start all over. I'll take you anywhere you want to go. But I know you've been lying about our son. You're a beautiful, kind and caring woman. You'd never have the heart to give a child away. I know you better than that. He must be upstairs – in one of those bedrooms. Tell me where he is, and I'll go get him. Then the three of us can leave and go to a German U-boat. One is waiting off the coast. We have two weeks to get there. It will take us to Brazil."

She shook her head. "Karl, you are so wrong. Do you really think killing the Jews has made Germany a better country? Germany has been defeated by the U.S., its allies and the Soviet Union. We heard reports on the shortwave radio. What you've personally done is beyond wicked and evil. I'm done with you. I've been done with you for over three years. I made certain you'd never see your son again, because I gave him to your Uncle Giovanni three years ago. Our baby was sent to America to be safe."

Livid, Karl raised his gun from her chest and pressed it hard on her forehead, pushing her head back.

"Go ahead, Karl, shoot me. It should be easy for you. You're hopeless."

Mother Superior, still standing in the street, whispered loudly to Father Luca, "Something's wrong. They should have been outside by now. Go inside and find out what's happened."

Luca swallowed hard. He wanted to save Katrina's life. He loved her. He moved a few steps closer, kneeling on one knee next to the door, gripping the door handle in one hand and the Beretta in the other. He gently pulled the door handle. As the door slowly cracked open, he heard them still arguing.

"You're lying to me, Katrina," Karl insisted loudly. "I swear I'll kill everyone in this building, and I'll go find him myself! Where is he?"

Karl's back was to the front door. Luca knelt on the step, only six feet away, his hand shaking as he aimed the handgun. Luca leaned a little more, pulling open the door – when the old hinge creaked.

Karl turned. He looked down and saw Luca.

A tenth of a second later, a booming shot rang out. Father Luca fell down the three steps, landing flat on his back, sprawled on the sidewalk.

Mother Superior ran to Luca and grabbed the gun from the fallen priest's hand. Boldly, she pulled the heavy door open, ready to face and shoot Karl herself. She raced inside and saw little Sister Carmella in the middle of the room. Under her arm, a single-barrel shotgun pointed at the floor. She held it comfortably, as an experienced hunter after the kill. A small puff of smoke floated from the muzzle – and the room smelled of gunpowder.

Karl lay on the floor, dead, at the little nun's feet, bleeding from a single shotgun blast to his chest.

Katrina sat crumpled on the floor in shock and crying, her hands covering her blood-splattered face.

Father Luca, who'd fallen backward at the sound of the shotgun, gingerly stood up and stepped inside.

Sister Carmella looked down at Karl's body. "He was a bad man. A really bad, bad man. I slipped out of Mother's office into the hall when Sister Katrina started giving it to him. I heard everything she said – and everything he said. I was hiding in the coat closet, right over there. I saw her yelling and watched him get all riled up at her. Then I saw his eyes get wide open. He threatened to kill everyone in the convent. We know Sister Katrina gave up her son. But he wanted to look for the child and go shoot everyone. I couldn't let that happen.

"I had my shotgun pointed at him through the tiny opening. The end of the barrel fit right on the door hinge. It steadied my aim. Then the front door began to open. I saw Father Luca. Then the door creaked – and the man started to turn his gun toward Father. I shot first. I shot him from inside the closet. He was a bad man. He had it coming. He never even saw me."

"Sister Carmella! My God! What do you mean, *your* shotgun?"

The little nun looked up sheepishly at Mother Superior. "I'm sorry, Mother. Right after you assigned me to be the front-door guard, I told my papa and mama I had an important new job here at the convent. The next week my papa brought my old shotgun to me. I stuck it right there, in the corner of the closet, next to the broom I use to sweep the foyer. It was the same gun I used hunting pheasants with him as a teenager. I've kept that old shotgun loaded in the closet in the foyer for the past two years. It's been ready to protect you and the rest of the sisters from bad people like him. I'm sure glad it still worked." Sister Carmella paused, then added, "He said was going to kill all of us. Now he won't be able to hurt anyone again."

Katrina continued to cry uncontrollably.

A few seconds later, the seminarian and the three priests hurried into the foyer. They huddled in disbelief, staring at the bleeding corpse.

Father Luca knelt to give a final blessing, but he wasn't sure it would help Karl's soul. Three nuns ran into the foyer after the shotgun blast echoed throughout the front of the convent. The oldest of them took off her work apron and covered the body. Another sister put down her apron, to catch Karl's blood spreading across the floor. The third ran for towels.

Mother Superior sat on the floor, taking Katrina into her arms. The last half hour had been traumatic. Katrina was shaking and in need of comfort. Mother Superior motioned to Luca to take her place holding Katrina. He did.

Then Mother Superior got to her feet and turned her attention to Sister Carmella, who was now crying. It had taken a few minutes for the little sister to fully comprehend the outcome, and her role in the shooting.

Five minutes later, the *polizia* arrived. They asked Father Luca questions. Within moments, a U.S. Army jeep with four American soldiers pulled up. Two soldiers came inside while two remained outside. Fluent in Italian, the Army sergeant asked what had happened.

Mother Superior took the lead explaining what had taken place. She mentioned every detail, showed them Karl's loaded Luger, and protecting the little sister, called it the 'convent's shotgun.'

The sergeant told everyone, "Giovanni Cardinal DiBotticino was shot to death four days ago in his office. Another priest was shot there, too. The Swiss Guard put out an arrest warrant for a tall French businessman whom they believed shot and killed the cardinal and the other priest. The Swiss Guard said he was armed and dangerous. They said he might be headed to southern Italy, based on a map they found on the ground with a circle around Bernalda, and two other circles around the city of Taranto and the Isola di San Pietro with the words 'U-boat here.' "

Katrina and Mother Superior gaped at each other at the news of the cardinal's murder. They realized if it hadn't been for his warning, the circumstances could have ended much differently.

One soldier lifted the nun's work apron and glanced at the body. "This man fits the Swiss Guard's description of the man who shot the cardinal and the other priest."

At the news of the cardinal's death, Antonio and Father Aldo wept.

"Cardinal DiBotticino was my cousin," Antonio said through his tears. "My name is Antonio DiBotticino. I grew up in Parma, south of Brescia."

The young seminarian's comments caused Katrina and Mother Superior to look up and take notice of him. That meant he and Karl were distant cousins. Neither mentioned the family tie, nor that the cardinal was Karl's uncle.

One of the American soldiers asked if anyone knew who this man was and why he was there. Mother Superior said the man was Sister Katrina's former husband, whom she'd divorced four years earlier.

The soldier standing guard at the door said, "We were told by the Swiss Guard he was driving a red Fiat. We found such a vehicle parked around the corner., and inside was a duffel bag stuffed with clothing, a passport, some papers and a few maps on the seat. If he's your former husband, Sister, it all belongs to you."

Katrina thanked the soldier as he handed her the items. Not wanting any of it, she passed the bag and papers to one of the sisters in the foyer.

Mother Superior said, "Please send the bag downstairs to Sister Bianca, and put the papers in my office. We will wash the clothing and give them to the poor."

The *polizia* had radioed their local station and a wagon from the mortuary arrived to remove the body. Now considering the case closed, the police left, but the American soldiers remained a few more minutes. Katrina stood, with help from Father Luca, then wrapped her arms around him and lay her head on his shoulder.

Sister Carmella and Mother Superior stood as well. Carmella continued to sob and apologize for what she'd done, as Mother Superior silently thanked God for the little nun's marksmanship. The three sisters who had come to the foyer began cleaning the floor, while everyone else remained silent, stunned and numb, each absorbing the impact of what had occurred in the last hour.

Luca reflected on the incident and his feelings toward Katrina. It felt good to hold her – it felt even better to have her arms around him. Their recent walks had helped them forge a relationship. He'd come to realize Katrina had been running away from something, and the convent was an escape. With Karl's arrival today, and hearing his threats, Luca understood Katrina's pain and sorrow more completely. As devastating as her situation was, he'd just seen the woman he loved finally deal with her antagonist. He admired how she stood up to him, how she told him of his father's disappointment in him, how he had failed his parents. Otto's failed relationship with Valentina no doubt hurt Karl deeply. But hearing how he was not Otto's son, but Ruth's brother – and three quarters Jewish, to boot – had to be devastating. Luca shuddered, recalling the heated exchange.

Karl's mistakes and failings seemed endless. Katrina's heart was so pained by all his wrongs. For her, the series of events and mistakes truly was a litany of sorrows. Luca saw all this and now, more than ever, wanted to be with her, especially having witnessed the emergence of her courage and strength.

As Karl's body was carried out, Katrina took one last look at him. She started crying again on Luca's shoulder.

The American sergeant addressed those remaining in the foyer in broken Italian. "Folks, I forgot to mention this – reports say Adolf Hitler has committed suicide. Russian soldiers found charred remains beside the bunker where he was hiding. German soldiers and staff working there were captured while hiding in railroad tunnels, buildings and a brewery basement. Under interrogation, they revealed plans to help Hitler escape from Berlin, by air and by submarine. No one knows who was supposed to carry out those plans, or where those plans were taking Hitler.

"It remains a mystery why he killed himself if those escape plans existed, and caused a new rumor. Some say the burned male body wasn't Hitler's. Some speculate he escaped through a false wall in the bunker to underground tunnel."

Katrina listened attentively and realized Karl might have been involved in the escape with Hitler, because he had mentioned a U-boat off the Italian coast. She shook her head, realizing Karl must have been given such an assignment.

After the soldiers left, Luca and Katrina went out to the garden. Mother Superior brought Sister Carmella back to her office, where they sat and talked about what had happened. Meanwhile, several sisters on their hands and knees used stiff brushes and hard toothbrushes to scrub the oak floor. They scrubbed and scrubbed until no more blood remained in the woodgrain crevices, and the floor was perfectly clean.

CHAPTER FORTY-NINE

The Duffel Bag

Two hours had passed since Sister Carmella shot Karl. The floor cleaning was just about complete when Sister Bianca, who ran the convent's basement laundry room, found a duffel bag in the "unsorted" laundry bin at the bottom of the three-story chute.

Sister Bianca, a most fastidious woman, was fanatical about her laundry operation. Her singular focus was to perfectly manage the laundry produced by forty nuns. Naturally, she was disturbed to find a large, filthy duffel bag thrown into her laundry bin. As she unzipped it, she was shocked. With her fingertips, she pulled out men's smelly, dirty clothing stuffed inside, then halted when she discovered a navy-blue leather purse and a tiny green velvet bag sitting at the bottom.

Located in the basement and on the far side of the large convent building, she'd missed all the earlier happenings. Now, annoyed and set off at the duffel bag's unexpected arrival – and its unexplained contents, she immediately marched the items upstairs to complain.

The heavy footsteps echoed coming down the hallway moments before Sister Bianca knocked hard, three times, at Mother Superior's office door.

Having heard *that* particular knock previously, Mother Superior responded, "Yes Sister Bianca, the door is unlocked. Please come in."

"Mother, what is going on? I just found this disgustingly dirty duffel bag in the laundry bin. It was filled with smelly men's clothing. There was also a woman's purse and a small pouch tucked under all the clothing. Here they are. This is yours to deal with now. I need to return downstairs – I've started to wash the men's clothing already – in fact, the load may need to be washed a second time using javel water."

"Thank you, Sister Bianca. We had a terrible event happen hours ago. I won't go into the details now, but the bag and its contents belong to Sister Katrina. Thank you for bringing everything up to me. I'll share more about what happened with you and the other sisters at supper."

Grumbling, Sister Bianca left the office in a huff, her nose tilted upward. She resented the disruption of her routine – especially the dirty, stinky load with nasty men's underwear. She also concluded she would have to disinfect the washing machine when the load was finished.

Mother Superior opened the duffel bag, reached deep inside and pulled out the purse and the velvet pouch. She opened one, amazed at its contents. When she opened the other, she almost fell off her chair. She quickly tugged the small rope beside her credenza.

Sister Carmella entered. "Yes, Mother?"

"I trust you're feeling better, Carmella. Please find Sister Katrina and bring her here at once."

Knowing right where to go, Sister Carmella hurried outside to the convent's garden where she found Sister Katrina with Father Luca, walking and holding hands.

"Sister, Mother Superior needs you in her office right away."

Perplexed, Katrina asked Luca to go with her.

Mother Superior had known for months Father Luca was falling for Katrina. She'd seen it in how he looked at her. And from her office window that overlooked the garden, she'd seen them walking more frequently. She had no doubt Katrina was developing feelings for him, too. As she waited, she realized today's events likely would be the catalyst to launch the two. Now there was something else to consider, something well beyond what anyone would expect.

Father Luca in tow, Katrina knocked at the open door and entered the office.

"Sit, my dear. Father Luca, you'll want to sit, as well."

"What is it, Mother? What's happening?"

"First, the papers brought in earlier by the soldier – I've had a chance to go through them. There are two pages with a long list of names in different Italian cities, and several maps, some highlighted in yellow. I've looked them over while waiting for you. They seem to show a route from Berlin to two different locations here in Italy. There was a passport among them, also.

"And the duffel bag brought in by the soldier – it appears there were some items inside besides men's clothing. Sister Bianca brought these up to me."

"Mother, I want no part of any papers, maps, passports, or anything to do with the duffel bag," Katrina insisted, shaking her head. "It's over now, and I want no reminder of that man!"

But Mother Superior persisted. "Katrina, there were a couple of items inside the duffel bag that Karl probably intended for you to have. Here, I want you to open these. You may find the contents of interest."

Katrina frowned but obediently accepted the purse from Mother Superior.

She handed it to Father Luca. "Here, you open it."

Having no choice, he opened the purse. In it he found three wide, heavy gold bracelets. He handed them to Katrina, who looked at them briefly and then handed them to Mother Superior.

"Where could Karl have gotten these? I hope he didn't kill anyone for them."

Luca was wondering as well then Mother Superior spoke.

"Katrina, look closely at the inscription on the inside of this wide bracelet." She handed her the heaviest and widest of the three.

To My Dear Eva, Together forever,
your loving husband, Adolf XO April 28, 1945

"How did Karl get these?" Katrina exclaimed.

"There's a roll of cash in the purse as well. American dollars, Francs and British pounds. There must be thousands just in American dollars. Now look in the bottom of the purse: There are four rings – two wedding bands and two rings with diamonds."

Luca and Katrina gaped in astonishment.

Then Mother Superior handed Katrina the tiny green-velvet bag with its gold braded drawstring. She loosened the drawstrings, opened it and found a handful of medium-size, uncut diamonds.

"Look Luca! These are unbelievable. They must be worth a fortune!"

Katrina poured the diamonds into Luca's open palm. He counted them – thirty-two in all.

Shocked, she stared at the diamonds in Luca's hand, then looked at Mother Superior.

"If what the Italian-American soldier said was true, maybe there was a plan for Hitler to escape through Italy," Luca suggested. "Could it be Karl was with Hitler at some point?"

Then Mother Superior showed Luca the maps and all the names. "Luca, do you think we should give these to the American soldiers who were here?"

He nodded. "Definitely." Then he took Katrina's trembling hand. "But, Katrina, the rest of this treasure belongs to you."

"My children, we'll never know how Karl acquired these things, and it is of no importance to know now," Mother Superior advised them gently. "You must look ahead. It's been a hard day. Luca, please stay for supper. You and Katrina may remain here in my office and eat together. I need to go to supper and share with the sisters what happened today, but I certainly won't mention any of this. Sister Carmella seems to be okay, and she'll bring your supper in when it's ready."

She looked from one of them to the other. "You two have much to talk about. You need some time alone, as well as more time tomorrow to make important decisions. Your lives are about to change. I sincerely believe you should enjoy your lives together as a couple."

Katrina and Luca looked at each other and nodded.

Mother Superior gave her cousin's daughter a motherly hug and a kiss on her cheek, then she hugged Father Luca. She suddenly felt like a mother to her two children.

As she approached the door to leave her office, she turned. "May God bless you both in a happy life together."

As Mother Superior left the room, Katrina held Luca's hand and began to cry. She knew Mother Superior's words were true. Katrina had been falling for Father Luca longer than just two months. She'd thought he was handsome when she first saw him on the altar. Then, one frigid night last winter, she saw him walking outside. She knew then she had fallen for Father Luca. Finally, her deep feelings were confirmed after she shared her innermost anxieties in the confessional. Although she was exceptionally tired that morning from caring for the sick sister all night, she realized she finally had someone to talk to. Perhaps, more important-ly, he was a man she could trust.

As for Father Luca, he'd felt an attraction to Sister Katrina soon after his arrival at Holy Angels Parish, but quickly buried it. He'd hoped his assignment there would further develop and mature his calling to the priesthood. But fate put him face to face with a beautiful woman, and he was immediately attracted to her. He struggled with his feelings each day when he saw her, and he missed her on the days when their paths didn't cross.

Life seemed so good. But was it? For Katrina, there remained an open wound. Her child, little Bruno, was almost three years old. Giving him up was a painful decision. She'd sent him to America for a better life but missed him every day. On one hand, she'd believed it was best to give him a life with a loving family who wanted a new baby they could nurture as their own. On the other hand, she felt she'd made a huge mis-take by giving him up so quickly and going into the convent. She didn't know if she could ever forgive herself for her hasty decision. Although Luca had entered her life – and she felt blessed for that – she remained distraught. Giving up little Bruno was her deepest sorrow; his absence left a huge hole in her heart.

Katrina and Luca sat holding hands in silence, letting the day's events sink in. Then, only a minute after leaving her office, Mother Su-perior returned. She knocked and opened the door in one continuous mo-tion. "I'll be just a moment. There's something I want to give you both."

She went to the credenza behind her desk and reached down for a bottle of red wine called *Amarone della Valpolicella*.

She set the bottle and two glasses on the desk, then retrieved a tarnished brass corkscrew from the same drawer from which she'd pulled the loaded Beretta earlier in the day.

"Here, Father Luca. Use this opener. It was a gift from Katrina's mother when I turned sixteen. Enjoy. Oh, one more little thing. Sister

Bianca found this in the bottom of the washing machine when she was finished today. It must have been in a pair of pants in the duffel bag."

As Katrina took the slim gold bracelet her cousin held out, Luca opened the vintage bottle, and poured the wine. The two smiled at each other.

Minutes later, Carmella brought up their dinner from the kitchen, along with freshly baked crusty bread.

After eating, they continued talking. They knew they were about to make huge life changes. Luca told Katrina he wanted to spend every day and night with her the rest of his life. She told him the same thing.

They finished the bottle of Amarone; it was good. Noticing the time, they stood and readied to part. The two shared a tight hug and their first kiss, long and passionate. Then they retreated to their own rooms, one in the convent, the other in the rectory.

Tomorrow will be a new day – and a new chapter for us, they both thought as they fell asleep before finishing their nighttime prayers.

CHAPTER FIFTY

The Astoria Visit... 1951

*"Adoption is not about finding children for families,
it's about finding families for children."*

– Dr. Joyce Maguire-Pavao, Cambridge, Massachusetts

A fter a sizable donation made by Luca and Katrina Luciano to the Vatican in January 1950, her next letter found its way to the Vatican's newly appointed administrative secretary, Monsignor Aldo, who forwarded it to New York.

In February, a letter postmarked "Manhattan, New York City" arrived at the Lucianos' hillside home in Positano. The letter was from a young, well-connected Italian priest who had just been transferred to the Archdiocese of New York. In the letter, Monsignor Antonio DiBotticino referred Mrs. Katrina Luciano to the Brooklyn Diocese and its Catholic Charities Adoption Services. The letter had a paper-clipped side note wishing her and Luca well.

Excited at the receipt of his letter, Katrina followed up. Another two months passed before she received a letter pinpointing the names of the parents who'd made the adoption, along with their address in Astoria, Queens, New York.

Beginning in the fall of 1950, Katrina wrote a series of letters to Sheila and Joseph O'Sullivan, the couple who adopted her baby in June 1943.

The child was born during the war. His grandparents received word that their son, the child's father, a high-ranking soldier, had been killed in battle. As a single mother, I couldn't support the baby, and gave him up for adoption.

Katrina wasn't specific with dates, where the child was born or any other details in her letter, to avoid curiosity or suspicion. She also explained after giving the child up for adoption, she entered a cloistered convent, eventually left and married a wonderful, gentle and kind man.

In another letter to the family just before Christmas 1950, she wrote:

My husband is traveling to New York City for business meetings this coming spring, the week before Easter. I'd like to join him on the trip and perhaps come and visit you both. And with your permission, perhaps I may briefly see the child. I have no intention of announcing myself to him, but we have 'family memorabilia' from his grandparents that may be of interest to him later in life, especially if he should some-day learn about his being adopted. Surely a visit will calm my soul and reduce my anxiety, constant worries and sorrows for the child.

Very sincerely yours,
Katrina Luciano

PS: With your permission, my husband and I also would like to make a small contribution toward a college fund for the child during our visit.

Sensitive to Katrina's request and still very curious, Sheila and Joseph were taken by the offer to help with a few dollars toward Brian's college fund. Sheila felt if a visit were brief and contained, it would have no emotional impact on young Brian.

The O'Sullivans wrote back:

We are willing to have you come for a brief visit, provided nothing is said about your being the child's mother. We suggest you visit our home on a Tuesday or Thursday, and after school would be best.

Several more polite letters were exchanged. In one, Sheila O'Sullivan wrote:

Young Brian is rather tall, having just turned eight years old. He attends the local parochial school, St. Francis of Assisi, just around the corner. He is bright and is a good student with an A in every subject of his schoolwork and aspect of his behavior. Brian shows an interest in tools on his father's work bench, and picking at his father's guitar.

The last letter contained a few photos of little Brian playing youth baseball on a parish team, and another photo of Brian with his father at a New York Yankees baseball game in the Bronx.

Each letter Katrina received made her heartsick. She vacillated in believing she'd done the right thing. Deep down she still hadn't forgiven herself for giving him up. Her only consolation now was remembering she might have saved the child's life. She recalled memories from the week she stayed with her parents after leaving Germany. Twice during her stay, she helped her father in his bakery in the middle of the night, with Bruno beside her on a table as she made bread dough. After the war, when she traveled to Lecco with Luca, she learned from neighbors about her parents' deaths during the shooting and firebombing of the bakery. The circumstances of their demise crushed her and added immensely to her sorrow. But, had she not given up little Bruno, she and her baby son likely would have remained with her parents, and she might have been helping her father in the bakery when the shooting and firebombing took place.

***

Wednesday, March 21, 1951, a few days before Easter, Katrina and Luca began their two-day journey on PanAm's new Boeing 377 Stratocruiser, from Rome to London, then to Shannon, Gander, then, finally to Idlewild International Airport, at the south end of Queens, New York City. After a smooth overnight flight, they cleared customs in an hour. They exited the terminal, hailed a taxi, stowed their bags and two boxes in the cab and headed north toward Flushing Meadows, the site of the 1939 World's Fair. Twenty minutes later, they arrived in Astoria, a mile west of a small regional airport named after New York's beloved mayor, Fiorello LaGuardia.

From the adoption papers, Sheila and Joseph O'Sullivan knew their young baby was coming from Europe, but they didn't know his nationality. As the adoption neared, they learned the baby was coming from Genoa, and figured he was Italian. When the infant arrived, papers confirmed he was Italian as the name on his original baptismal papers identified him as Bruno Joseph Amorino. But when he arrived, to their surprise, he had sparkling blue eyes. And to fit into their Irish family, they renamed the baby Brian Joseph O'Sullivan. Brian had been a family name, and they planned to call him BJ.

As the Lucianos arrived in Astoria, they asked their cab driver to stop so they could pick up some pastries. He suggested Paul Roettger's German bakery on the corner of Steinway and Ditmars Boulevard.

Luca went inside and bought butter cookies with jelly on top as Katrina, growing nervous and impatient, waited in the cab. Minutes later the cabbie dropped them off around the corner on 39th Street, just off Ditmars. The twenty-minute ride, including the stop at the bakery, cost $4.40. Luca gave the talkative cabbie, a U.S. Army veteran wounded at Anzio, a ten-dollar bill.

"*Grazie tanto!* How do you say... 'Keep the change'? *Signore, por favor?* Uh, please, you... please wait here for us? Not too long. One hour? Please?" Luca asked in his broken English.

"Thanks, mister. Sure. I'll wait. I'll take a short snooze, if you don't mind."

"*Grazie. Qui.* Uh, here. Another ten dollars for you to wait."

"Wow! Thanks, pal. I'll wait all night if you want me to."

They arrived at 2:30 that afternoon, as their last letter from the O'Sullivans had suggested. Sheila was preparing Irish soda bread for their Easter meal, and planned to boil and color eggs with the children later that evening. Joseph had taken the day off from his work at the Fort Pitt firehouse in lower Manhattan, near the Brooklyn Bridge, but helped a friend install a new fuse box install that morning. Like many cops and firemen, he moonlighted to augment his income and add to their Christmas Club account.

Young Brian and his twin sisters were in school. It was the last day before Easter vacation. Their school day was almost over, and the children would be home within fifteen minutes. The O'Sullivans' fourth child, a year-old girl, named Shawn, after Sheila's childhood nickname, was at her grandparents' house next door.

Sheila and Joseph had decided they'd say nothing to Brian or the twins about the Lucianos' visit. They had come to accept the idea of the visit in appreciation for Katrina's interest to see for herself the boy was well cared for. And, frankly, they were enticed by the offer of a college-fund donation. They first believed Katrina's baby might be illegitimate, but believed differently after rereading the first letter in which she wrote, *"the baby's grandparents were told his father died during the war."* In each letter sent by Katrina, she seemed pleasant, and they felt sorry for her misfortune.

Sheila's eyes were glued to the street, and immediately noticed the couple's arrival. She called out to Joseph. He had returned home a few minutes earlier and was upstairs, changing out of his electrician's work clothes.

As the Lucianos emerged from the Checker cab, the driver opened the trunk and retrieved a large box while Luca carried a smaller one to the front door. Katrina took a deep breath and walked to the front door and knocked. Sheila quickly opened the door and, with Joseph at her side, welcomed the Lucianos inside, exchanging polite handshakes. The row house was warm and smelled delicious from the Irish soda bread – a stark contrast to the blustery spring wind and frigid air outside. March was going out like a lion.

Sheila offered Katrina and Luca seats at their worn, green-and-white Formica kitchen table. Joseph pulled out a plastic-covered padded chair for Katrina. She sat and pulled herself in, her hand feeling the sticky metal frame of the seat.

Sheila thanked them for the cookies from Roettger's. Joseph had stopped twenty minutes earlier at the same bakery, and the same cookies already sat on the table, still in the matching white cookie box tied with twine. Katrina apologized for the duplication.

"Oh, that's no problem," Sheila said with a little laugh. "Joseph and the kids will finish all of them tomorrow, if they don't devour them by tonight!"

Despite their pleasant smiles, starting a conversation proved difficult. Katrina took the lead by opening the smaller box they brought. She lifted the lid, then gently lifted the 200-year-old family Bible. The German words for "Lutheran Bible" were embossed across the leather cover.

"Brian's father was from the south of Germany," she explained.

Katrina looked at the O'Sullivans as she spoke. Their facial expressions suddenly showed confusion at what they were hearing.

For the O'Sullivans, the Lutheran Bible and hearing the word "Germany" were a non-sequitur.

Joseph raised his eyebrows, rubbed his forehead and grimaced. "Brian came to us through Genoa and his name on the birth certificate was Italian. What are you saying? Is our son Italian or is he German?"

"Brian's heritage is Italian and German. My heritage is Italian, dating back hundreds of years. My father's people were from Ciampino, just outside Rome, and my mother was from a tiny town called Bernalda, almost at the south end of Italy. Brian's father was from Germany."

Katrina and Luca could tell Joseph felt uneasy hearing about their son's German heritage. Sheila seemed equally anxious. The old German heritage family Bible, meant to be a gracious gift, became a stumbling block. The sudden silence at the table grew uncomfortable, Luca patted Katrina's back; then he gave her a slight push with his hand, meaning, "Keep going with this. I'm here with you. I'm your support."

"How about the… the German part?" Joseph stammered. "Tell us more about that."

"Brian's father's family name was von Richter." Katrina flipped open the Bible to the family history section. "On this page, you can trace the family tree back more than seven hundred years, to the Kingdom and Duchy of Wurttemberg. The von Richter family played prominent roles in the kingdom. Later on, it and several other kingdoms became a unified nation called the German Republic, in the late eighteen hundreds. On this page you can see names of his father, grandfather and great-grandfather, all the way back to the twelve hundreds."

Seeing what seemed like blank stares, Katrina closed the Bible gently, then opened the long, odd-shaped box. It held a black leather case bearing twin latches. She opened the latches and slowly lifted the hinged lid.

"This mandolin was built in the 1860s in Germany. It belonged to Brian's great-grandfather, Kristofer Ulrich von Richter, whose name is in the family Bible. His name is etched on the side. The mandolin was also played by Brian's grandfather, Otto von Richter, and by his father, Karl."

The O'Sullivans remained uncertain. BJ's German heritage had come as a surprise.

Now these two objects – more like old relics – just added to their confusion. Both items made them anxious.

Sheila looked at her watch. It was 2:42. "Our older three children will be home from school soon. I walk them and our neighbor's child to school and she walks them home. Brian's nine now, his twin sisters are almost eight. We had tried and tried to have a child. Our pastor suggested we adopt through Catholic Charities. We submitted all the papers. Then, a week after we were notified a boy baby was on his way here, I learned I was pregnant. It all turned out wonderfully. The three of them are so close. Then, to our surprise, I got pregnant again! Our new baby arrived a year ago. My mother, Ann, lives next door. She's taking care of Shawn this afternoon, so we wouldn't be interrupted."

Just then, the front door flew open with a bang, and the three O'Sullivan children came flying through, with Brian leading the way. Huffing and puffing from running the last block, they stopped for ten seconds, politely said hello to the guests, then each child grabbed a butter cookie and noisily ran upstairs to change.

"The kids have Cub Scout and Brownie meetings this afternoon," Sheila told the Lucianos. "They need to change into their uniforms, and leave right away to get back to their school, around the corner, where the meetings are held."

Katrina felt crushed. Seeing her little boy sail right past her was heart wrenching. Deep down, she had wished her presence would some-how grab the child's attention.

Sheila recognized the disappointment in Katrina's eyes, especial-ly knowing the limited time they would have to spend together. "We'll see Brian when he comes back down in a few minutes."

"Yes, of course," Katrina replied, feeling numb.

Just then, Joseph stood up and shouted, "Kids, let's go! You're gonna be late."

In a flash, the three O'Sullivan children barreled and thundered down the stairs. Brian carried a small wooden car he was planning to race at today's scout meeting.

Tricia and Kathy held their Brownie sashes and asked Sheila for help putting them on.

Then they all grabbed more cookies. As the sashes went over his sisters' shoulders, BJ began looking at Katrina. Her blue eyes caught his attention.

As the children said goodbye to the visitors, Katrina grabbed as much of a look at Brian as she could. Then with his sisters trailing, Brian headed to the front door.

"Goodbye, Brian!" Katrina called.

He stopped and turned back toward her. The twins bumped into him, he had stopped so abruptly.

Then, still looking at the pretty lady, he said, "Did you know you have blue eyes just like mine?"

Katrina smiled. "Yes, I see that!"

He smiled a big, satisfied smile, and his dimples showed.

She stared at BJ's hair and olive skin tone, and the slight cleft in his chin.

He's an Amorino with my father's blue eyes and loving smile – he's not a von Richter. She teared up. Her sorrowful heart hurt.

"Goodbye, lady. I hope you visit us again soon!" Brian said. "We love Duchy's cookies. Oh! Mommy, don't forget. You said we can color the eggs with you when we get home."

BJ flew out the door in a flash.

As their brother ran down the street, Tricia and Kathy hurried to catch up, but couldn't. Nor could Joseph. BJ felt elated – like he was running on air. He was too young and innocent to understand what had just happened. But he felt different. He felt good.

The children were on their way to their meetings at the church hall. As he galloped toward the school, BJ bubbled with excitement for today's Pinewood Derby race. Then he thought again about the lady with the blue eyes.

Outside the house, the cabbie was still sound asleep.

In the kitchen, Sheila turned to Katrina. "Does he look like your husband? We always tell people he's 'black Irish' because of his coloring and because his skin tans so well."

Katrina's smile looked wistful. "Brian looks just like my father, who was pure Italian and had blue eyes."

"Maybe you can tell us more about his Italian side someday? I'm sure BJ will want to know more about his heritage when he's old enough to understand."

Hearing Sheila's comments, Katrina drifted into a few moments of silence.

Luca looked closely at his wife. Seeing her teary eyes, he wished he could assuage her pain. *Seeing and watching her little boy must hurt her so much. Please God, she'll see him again.*

As planned, it was Luca's turn to speak. "*Signora*, we don't want to take up any more of your time, but before we go, we would like you to have these. This first envelope has information about your son's heritage and the towns his families of origin came from. It also has several pages from Katrina, explaining more about who his father and grandfather were, and the kind of work they were involved in before and during the war.

"It's a lot to understand and, frankly, it isn't meant for him to see now. The envelope isn't sealed. You and your husband should read it and then seal it. But hold it aside – until Brian's much older. Perhaps, when he's forty or fifty, he may begin to wonder why his skin tone is different from his sisters', or be curious about his heritage. Save this for him in a safe place until then. But you and Joseph should read it.

"The second envelope contains two checks. One is for twenty-five thousand dollars. Katrina mentioned in a letter last year, we want to finance Brian's college education. This should be enough. Any excess may be used to help him get started in a career or be put toward buying a home. There's a second check, for you and Joseph, in the same amount. It will give you the financial resources to support your family beginning now and for the coming years. Use it any way you see fit. It's our gift to you both for loving and raising Brian."

Sheila, in shock, stared at the Lucianos. Beginning to shake, she clasped her hands together in her lap. "Oh, my God. I don't know what to say. This, all of this, is overwhelming!" She grabbed a tissue and wiped her tear-filled eyes. "I'm so sorry Joey had to leave. I'm sure he'd want to thank you both. I don't know what to say. Thank you so much. And thank you for coming today."

Sheila and Katrina walked to the front door, then hugged warmly, both of them crying.

"I hope your business trip here to New York is successful," she told Luca, still wiping tears from her eyes. "Consider going to the Easter parade in the City this Sunday. Joey always pulls the kids in a wagon in the parade."

She smiled through her tears. "God bless you both. Bye-bye."

Sheila watched Katrina and Luca walk to the cab and knock on the window to awaken the driver. She waved from the front window as the cab pulled away. She had no way of knowing they were headed right back to Idlewild, to board the next plane flying back to Europe in just a few hours.

Sheila returned to the kitchen, poured some coffee, sat and began reading the letter meant for when Brian was an adult. She was only a few paragraphs in when she paused and swallowed hard.

"What is this?" She couldn't believe what she was reading. Then she read it to the end.

Still alone in the kitchen, Sheila exclaimed aloud, "Jesus Christ almighty! Mother Mary of God! Wait 'til Joey reads this!" Then reaching further to the bottom of the envelope, she found two little rocks. "This looks like— why are there pieces of rock salt in the envelope?"

Rush-hour traffic from Astoria south on the Van Wyck to Idlewild was heavy. They hit a snag passing Queens Boulevard. Two cars had crashed up ahead – and one was on fire. The fire truck came up right behind them, pulling over to the car fire. The black smoke smelled like rubber burning under the dented hood. The front car's trunk, crushed in the accident, suddenly flared up as they passed. The traffic jam made Luca anxious about getting to Idlewild on time to catch their flight.

Inside the cab, Katrina ignored the world outside. She was heartbroken and weeping. The last few hours had been filled with so much emotion. It had all exhausted her.

The cabbie, hearing the woman's cries, peeked back to see what was wrong. He wondered what the nice guy could have said to his wife to make her cry like that. Then he saw Luca hold her tightly and kiss the top of her head. It looked like the husband understood the woman's sorrow.

Luca felt the visit with the O'Sullivans had accomplished everything it was intended to do. But now he saw how deeply Katrina was affected by seeing her child. Luca had agreed to the visit and, generously, agreed to make sure the child and the adoptive family were adequately financed. But he completely missed the impact it would continue to have on her – not just for today, but for years to come.

Luca's focus now was on their young and successful business exporting Italian wine. Sales were booming at the Amorino and Luciano Wine Exports Company. For some reason, selling Amarone di Valpolicella in the United States suddenly had become a home run. He smiled, thinking how the most recent sales numbers had continued to rise in the shape of a hockey stick in the last three years. He smiled again as he attributed his wine business' success to that bottle of red Mother Superior gave them in her office to enjoy with their dinner the day of the shooting. He remembered when she winked at him as she left the two of them the second time. She'd told him, "This is good stuff!"

When they arrived at Idlewild, Luca thanked the cab driver, gave him five dollars for the ride and another ten-dollar tip.

They checked in at the Pan-American counter, and twenty minutes later boarded the plane for London. It would be a full week for Mr. and Mrs. Luca Luciano, staying at Brown's Hotel, shopping at Harrods and Selfridges for Katrina, while Luca met with several new wine distributors.

As the plane climbed into the late-afternoon sky, Katrina gazed back across greater New York from her window seat. They turned east over Long Island and headed toward the Atlantic Ocean. In two hours, it would stop in Newfoundland to refuel and continue toward London.

Katrina grabbed Luca's hand and arm. "Deep in my heart, I know I made the right decision for my son. Now I know he'll be fine in New York with the O'Sullivans. They're a good and loving couple. But Luca, if I had known you and I would someday find each other, I'd never have given him up. You'd be such a wonderful and loving father. I'm crushed, seeing my son. Now I'm not sure I should have left that letter with them, about Karl's having been in the SS. The Waffen SS Officer School and those drugs made him evil."

"Hopefully, Sheila and Joe will understand Brian shouldn't read it until he's much older, and maybe they'll decide to never show him the letter," Luca said soothingly. "It's been a long day and now it's time to rest, sweetheart. We'll have dinner in a few minutes. I'll ask for some red wine so we can relax. We have a long night ahead of us."

***

When her husband returned home with the kids, Sheila greeted him with a hug and asked him to join her in their bedroom. "You need to see what Katrina and her husband gave us. After you see these checks, you need to read the letter Katrina wrote about BJ's father. It's crazy."

Joey looked at the checks. He didn't know what to think. He rubbed his eyes and looked again, ensuring he saw where the commas and decimal points were. "Holy smokes, Sheila, this is unbelievable!"

"Joey, if you think *that's* unbelievable, just wait 'til you read her letter. I'll go get you a beer. You're gonna need it."

The late-afternoon daylight was fading and Joey turned on the bedside lamp. He donned his drugstore cheater glasses and began to read the beautifully scripted, multi-page letter. Within moments, he spouted a series of expletives. He had to reread the letter before he fully understood what Katrina had written. Sheila came back into the bedroom with a cold can of Ballantine ale, and sat beside him on their bed. They stared at one another in amazement.

"Sheila, could this all be true? I mean this is… this is like a fake story in the movies. How do we know these checks are real? No one will even believe this."

"I suppose it *is* real, Joey. Why else would she have taken the time to find Brian, come this far and bring the Bible and the guitar – or whatever it is. Brian's eyes are just like hers."

Joey read the letter a third time. Then he saw the two little rocks in the envelope. Putting one to his mouth, he tasted it. It was neither rock salt nor rock candy. He let out a series of obscenities that could be heard downstairs – all untimely as Sheila's mother, Ann, walked in the house with baby Shawn.

The O'Sullivans' Easter weekend was marked with continued anxiety over the Lucianos' visit. The following Tuesday, Joey stopped at the diamond district on Canal Street, near his firehouse. He went to the trusted jeweler's where all the firemen got special deals – the same place where he'd bought Sheila's engagement ring. He showed them the two little rocks. The Russian Jewish jewelers, two brothers who'd left Moscow as teenagers in the 1920s, were amazed at seeing the uncut stones. Respecting Joey and their relationship with the other NYC firemen, they never inquired as to the stones' origin. The diamonds' value came back a few days later, shocking Joey and Sheila.

A month later, the O'Sullivans decided to move to a place in the country where the air was clean, but still close enough for Joey to get to work. They found a new home being built in Staten Island and moved in June, once the school year ended. Joey asked to be reassigned to an active house but was denied and remained assigned to Fort Pitt.

As the years passed, Brian excelled in school. He graduated from St Peter's College in Bayonne, then NYU in Manhattan, and earned his doctorate in European history at Rutgers, where he became a professor in the history department.

Brian initially developed a strong interest in the European Middle Ages from 475 to 1500 AD, but then seemed to focus on events leading up to World War One. He married, and absent of children, traveled quite extensively through Europe. BJ remained close to his parents, siblings, nieces and nephews, seeing them all as often as possible.

His twin sisters became elementary-school teachers and married. His youngest sister, Shawn, became a gym teacher, married and moved to Tottenville, not far from her sisters.

CHAPTER FIFTY-ONE

The Hope Chest

J oseph O'Sullivan smoked two packs of cigarettes a day most of his life, and died in 1980 from lung cancer. He was 56.

His lieutenant's pension and thirty-two years on the job with the NYFD supported Sheila well, allowing her to remain in their Staten Island home, originally purchased with the windfall from Luca and Katrina Luciano.

Thursday, March 8, 2012, was a cold, overcast and blustery day. A sudden but brief snow squall blasted St. Peter's Cemetery near Clove Lake. At 94, Sheila had died of a stroke while driving home from daily Mass celebrated in the tiny chapel at Monsignor Farrell High School.

She was being laid to rest beside her husband in the family plot. Family members, friends of her children and longtime neighbors from Beach and Peter avenues, attended.

Father Gannon, the pastor, presided at the funeral Mass at Our Lady Queen of Peace, and then offered the final graveside prayers. After the burial, the family returned to Nana Sheila's house back in New Dorp.

BJ's twin sisters remained angry. Both blamed Brian for having supported Mother's strong desire to live independently. Sheila drove her old but reliable blue 1972 Datsun 510 with its 234,000 miles every other day to get to their father's grave. It was the car she and Joey had bought when he got the okay to work in Staten Island, and he started driving the rear end of the hook and ladder at the Jewett Avenue fire house. Shawn sided with her brother, supporting Mom's freedom. But right now, independence at 94 didn't seem like such a good idea. Sheila had the stroke while driving. She sideswiped three parked cars and then, careening off them, ran head-on into a moving city bus on New Dorp Lane.

When the siblings arrived at the house, Shawn started a pot of water for tea while the twins set plates and silverware on the table. The kitchen table was filled with cakes dropped off by neighbors. One box contained butter cookies topped with jelly from a local German bakery. Brian commented how they reminded him of Roettger's cookies back in Astoria.

While they waited for the water to boil, Brian found a bottle of Bushmill's 16-year-old single-malt Irish whiskey in the pantry. It had been his dad's favorite, and Brian enjoyed it, too, although his favorite was a peaty, 18-year-old Laphroaig. A moment passed before he realized this was his mother's preferred scotch as he poured from the half empty bottle. The tea kettle whistled as the caterer arrived with lunch. The siblings laid out sandwiches and poured soft drinks for the children.

Tricia turned to her brother. "BJ, did you ever do your ancestry test like we asked? When the three of us did it, we had one sent to your house. Did you send it back in?"

Brian nodded. "Did it a month ago, maybe two weeks after you all did yours. I had the results sent here. I thought it'd be fun to be with Mom when the results say I'm Spanish and Irish. Mom always said I was 'black Irish,' from when the Spanish Armada crashed on the west coast of Ireland in 1588. She said it's why I have dark hair and my skin tans so easily – unlike you three with your red hair and freckles. But frankly, I've wondered for some time now, where, or more precisely, *who* – my blue eyes came from, since neither Mom nor Dad had blue eyes, and you don't find any Spanish folks with blue eyes."

Tricia turned to her sisters. "We need to go through Mom's stuff while we're all here with BJ, and decide before we leave who gets what, like the family photo albums, the framed pictures, her dozens of knick-knacks and Daddy's fire-department memorabilia. I suggest we start with going through her hope chest. Is that okay with you guys? And by the way, I got my DNA test results back last week. I'm ninety-five percent Irish, three percent Scottish and two percent English."

"My report said the same thing," Kathy exclaimed.

"That figures, since you're identical twins," BJ quipped.

"How about you, Shawn? What were your results?"

She shrugged. "I don't know. We were in Boothbay Harbor for a week, and stopped overnight in Ogunquit on the way back, the night before Mom died. I haven't gone through our mail yet. I haven't seen anything about my results."

The siblings left the rest of the family eating lunch and retreated to their mother's bedroom. Meanwhile, the three sons-in-law turned on the television. All had attended the University of Connecticut at Storrs and were hoping to catch the Big East playoff game between Syracuse and UConn at noon from Madison Square Garden.

Brian sat in his father's old recliner while the twins opened the hope chest and, one by one, removed items their mother had saved from their childhoods. They dug deeper and found certificates of baptisms, first communions, confirmations, engagements and weddings for all four of them.

Tricia went to the kitchen for more tea and returned with a large envelope. "Brian, I just checked Mom's unopened mail and found your DNA results. Here, open it . Let's see how much Spanish and Irish you really are."

Brian opened the package, took out the booklet and read his results aloud. "Wow! There's something definitely wrong with my report. It says I'm forty percent German, twenty percent Italian, five percent Czechoslovakian, and get a load of this, thirty five percent Jewish! Ha! That's a huge mistake! Tricia, you should get your money back for my test and this report! It must belong to someone else."

They all laughed at the apparent mix-up and, with that, Brian tossed aside the results and sipped his mom's scotch. His sisters resumed emptying the hope chest. As Kathy reached down to retrieve the last few items, its wood bottom unexpectedly tilted.

"Look, the bottom is rocking a little. It's uneven, like there might be something – yes, there's definitely something underneath. Look from the outside. It's definitely several inches deeper than what it looks like on the inside. Let me see if I can lift the plywood floor up and out. Wow, I've been in here a dozen times in the last twenty-five years and never realized this wasn't its bottom."

Tricia and Shawn looked on curiously.

Kathy couldn't get her finger between the thin lauan plywood and the side of the hope chest, because it fit so perfectly.

Brian went to the kitchen for a long, serrated knife, which he slid down the side, twisted and pulled up. Its serrated blade caught against the edge of the plywood.

Tricia grabbed it and lifted it. "Look! That looks like a musical instrument case! And I wonder what's in that big box." She lifted the case, unclasped the clips and opened it.

"It's a mandolin!" Brian exclaimed. "I bet it's over a hundred years old, from the looks of it!"

Eager for the next surprise, Tricia pulled out the cardboard box; it was heavier than she expected. Looking on eagerly, Brian took another sip of whiskey.

Kathleen, who believed she knew all the family secrets, sat in shocked silence.

As Tricia lifted the box, Shawn lifted off the top, revealing its contents. Suddenly, the four siblings were looking at a dark leather-bound book, five inches thick.

The letters embossed on its leather cover read, *"Unsere Luther-ische Familienbible."*

Brian set down his drink. "Correct me if I'm wrong, but aren't we all Catholic?" He then translated all the German words.

The twins looked at him, then at each other.

Shawn carefully lifted the book and opened its hard leather cover. Inside, the delicate paper unfolded to be four pages wide and two pages long.

An elaborate drawing of an oak tree bore an inscription at the top:
The von Richter Family History
The Duchy and Kingdom of Wurttemberg
Since MCCLXV Anno Domini

The family tree had names of people belonging to the *von Richter family* beginning in 1265 AD, all the way up to the last two entries:
Otto Ulrich von Richter marries Valentina DiBotticino, 1912
Karl Kristofer von Richter, born to Otto and Valentina, 1914

BJ, the retired European-history professor, sat up in amazement. The three sisters turned and stared at him.

"Brian, what in heaven's name is this?" Kathy demanded.

Shawn carefully refolded the pages of the family tree, and turned the next page of the Bible. There, tightly pushed into the binding, was a sealed envelope.

Brian reached over his sister's arm, grabbed the envelope, opened it and pulled out two dozen onion-skin pages. Scripted in beautiful hand-writing by a broad-tipped ink pen, the pages were dated March 1, 1951. The letter started,

To my Dearest Son,
I'm not quite sure how to begin. Many years ago…

Brian scanned the first page silently. His sisters watched him in wonderment. For a few moments, he was confused, thinking it had been written by Sheila. As he continued further down the page, he pensively stroked his chin. His bright blue eyes sparkled as tears appeared. He lay the first page on the Bible, wiped at his eyes and continued reading.

His sisters watched as his expression changed. A few moments later, tears rolled down his cheeks.

"What is it, Brian?" Tricia peered over her brother's shoulder. "What's the letter say?"

When he started reading the third page, Tricia grabbed the first two. As she did, Brian began to cry openly. Kathy and Shawn remained silent, watching now for Tricia's reaction.

BJ's wife, sensing something was happening, entered the room. Brian continued to the next page, read half of it and then stopped.

He looked up at them. "Dear Jesus… Do you remember a visit from a man and lady around Easter when we lived in Astoria …the pretty lady with the beautiful blue eyes? This… this letter… it's from her. She wrote this, and she says she's my birth mother.

"Apparently, Mom and Dad adopted me during the war."

– The End –

Historical Background 1900-1945

T he history of war in Europe is thousands of years old. By the late 1800s, several kingdoms were entering their final chapters, and several royal families had already been ousted. Smaller city -states began to join hands and form countries.

As alliances and treaties developed between and among various countries, a complex set of entanglements formed by the late 1880s.

Eventually during the 1890s, tensions between countries set the stage where almost any skirmish could lead to regional battles or even a broader war between alliances. The assassination of Archduke Ferdinand in June 1914 ignited World War I, as country after country honored treaties and commitments.

The fighting in World War I was harsh. New technology included airplanes, long-range aerial surveillance, improved radio communication, long-range artillery, fast-moving armored tanks and a variety of repeating weaponry. The use of lethal gases and trench warfare took the lives of millions of soldiers from all sides.

As is so often the case, rulers and political leaders used men and war machines as mere pieces in the game of war. World War I, "the war to end all wars" was no exception.

In August 1914, Germany began pushing ground troops east and west. In the East, German troops commanded by Paul von Hindenburg fought Russian troops in the Battle of Tannenberg. Aerial reconnaissance and intercepted radio messages helped Germans capture 125,000 Russian troops after only five days of fighting. On the Western front, Germans engaged the French and British Expeditionary Forces in the Battle of Marne. Both sides made strategic maneuvers, taking advantage of their opponent's weaknesses. Coordinated counteroffensives by the French and English prevented the fall of Paris, causing the Germans to retreat.

German forces re-engaged in the Battle of Aisne in Alsace-Lorraine, in eastern France. Intense fighting along battle lines raged for weeks, while neither side gained ground. Soldiers from both sides dug ditches miles long to fight from and "trench warfare" began. Trenches stretched from Alsace-Lorraine north, almost reaching Belgium and the North Sea. In many places, enemy soldiers positioned themselves only yards away from each other, and fought face to face using bayonets in hand-to-hand combat.

By the end of November 1914, tens of thousands of lives were lost on both sides. As winter arrived, temperatures dropped, and conditions worsened for the fighting soldiers. Water a foot deep sat at the bottom of some trenches, leaving clothing, shoes and socks constantly drenched. Soldiers' extremities were often too numb to walk or pull a trigger. Soldiers struggled climbing in and out of trenches and crawling across snow-covered ground. Making progress attempting to push back enemy lines was impossible at times. Dead bodies of those brave enough to obey the command of "Charge!" littered stretches of land between trenches. The strongest and most physically equipped to deal with the harsh struggles of trench warfare managed best. But physical fitness did not guarantee survival; nor could it deflect the psychological strain of the bombardments and the hand-to-hand killing.

During trench warfare, a notable event occurred late in the afternoon on Christmas Eve 1914. Fighting between enemy soldiers facing each other in nearby trenches slowed. As darkness settled over the battlefield, German soldiers began singing Christmas carols. Soon, the English soldiers responded, singing their own Christmas songs. The singing grew loud enough, allowing each side to hear the other. As German soldiers began singing "Silent Night," British soldiers in nearby trenches began singing the same tune in unison. Soon, soldiers on both sides lay down their rifles, left their trenches and approached one another on the battlefield. Soldiers on both sides were amazed at what was happening.

Eventually, thousands of German and British soldiers greeted each other, hopeful their spontaneous Christmas Eve truce, commenced by the singing of Christmas carols, might end the fighting. At dawn, German and England military commanders heard about the event. They immediately ended the impromptu truce. Shooting resumed and the silent night became a memory to the soldiers.

"The war to end all wars" continued almost four more years.

In September 1918, the German military had lost its will to fight. Germany's ruler, Kaiser Wilhelm, with guidance from his commanders, put an end to the war. On November 11, Germany signed an armistice agreement. On June 28, 1919, Germany signed the Treaty of Versailles with France and Great Britain. The war had caused massive casualties on all sides – estimated at 20 million civilian and military deaths, with another 20 million civilians and military wounded.

In a few short years, the German economy experienced the impact of the harsh terms of the Treaty of Versailles. Indebtedness to repay reparations was substantial, imposing a strong, negative feeling among Germany citizens. As resentment rose in the early 1920s, a young man named Adolf Hitler associated himself with the emerging Nazi Party, as it began fanning the flames of right-wing German nationalism.

In early November 1923, the Nazi Party challenged the German government when 2,000 members marched in protest to the center of Munich. Confronted by local police, the scuffle resulted in the deaths of 16 Nazi Party members and four police officers. Adolf Hitler, wounded during the clash, escaped to the countryside. Two days later, he was found, arrested and charged with treason.

The "Munich Putsch," a milestone in the Nazi party's growth, had failed due to poor planning and misjudgment. However, the broadly publicized insurrection grabbed the attention of German citizens and generated front-page headlines in newspapers across Europe and around the world. A 24-day trial allowed Hitler to present his strong nationalist sentiments. Found guilty of treason, he was sentenced to five years in prison; but through political connections, he was released in December 1924. While in jail, Hitler dictated his thoughts to fellow prisoner Rudolf Hess. The notes became the basis for his book, *Mein Kampf*.

Hitler was 36 years old when the first edition of *Mein Kampf* was published in 1925. In it, he refocused the Nazi Party, suggesting it could achieve political power via propaganda and non-combative methods. Hitler continued to gain popular support, speaking against the Treaty of Versailles' prohibition against Germany's redevelopment of its military, and requirement to pay large financial reparations. In 1927, a second volume of *Mein Kampf* followed, which immediately became the bible of the German National Socialist Workers Party.

An abridged edition called for all Germans to return to their homeland and offered aggressive nationalistic ideas.

The American stock market crash of 1929 also caused financial difficulties for Germany, when calls on international loans helping it to recover from the war were made. Economic hyperinflation led to unrest among Germans, and helped the Nazi Party gain more popular support. Meanwhile, updated Nazi propaganda promoting nationalism and anti-communism gained strength. Germans blamed the Treaty of Versailles for their weak economy more than ever. Suddenly, political maneuvering in the fledgling German congress, the *Reichstag,* became complicated as Germany tried to stabilize itself as a democratic government.

In 1930, Adolf Hitler's increasingly robust and fiery speeches denounced communism and promoted anti-Semitism. The Nazi Party offered German citizens more reasons to support its growth. The Party soon took more seats in the German Reichstag and set up a paramilitary guard called the Storm Detachment or SA. The SA provided protection for Nazi members at rallies and assemblies, and intimidated and disrupted meetings of opposing political parties. It also began to disrupt the lives of Jews with boycotts of Jewish businesses. SA troops, referred to as Brownshirts, developed military titles for members, with ranks later adopted by other Nazi groups. Among the SA was a sub-group called the *Schutzstaffel*, commonly referred to as the SS. The SS was established with a more diabolical purpose. Hermann Göring established the Gestapo in the eastern area of Germany known as Prussia, when the German state police and other political police forces were combined. At the same time in Italy, a group called Blackshirts, reporting to Italian dictator Benito Mussolini, used similar destructive tactics against political rivals.

During 1932, Paul von Hindenburg, president of the German Republic, found it difficult to manage the brewing political storm as the

Nazi Party continued to call for radical changes. To the surprise of many, the Nazi Party lost 34 seats while the Communist Party gained 11 seats in the Reichstag in the November 1932 elections. Despite the changes, no party could form a majority or political coalition to support a specific candidate for chancellor. Former chancellor Franz von Papen, a Catholic, and several other conservative leaders discussed the impasse. Papen then persuaded President von Hindenburg to consider appointing Adolf Hitler as the new German chancellor.

On January 30, 1933, von Hindenburg appointed Hitler in a move to hold off the Communist Party; the decision yielded unintended consequences. Less than two months later, on March 23, the Reichstag passed the Enabling Act of 1933, giving Hitler broad powers to make new laws transforming the young Weimar Republic into a "one-party dictatorship." The totalitarian and autocratic ideology of German National Socialism was in place, and the German Reichstag almost never met again.

Once in power, Hitler countered what he saw as injustices placed on Germany by Britain and France. Hitler also believed Arian Germans were a superior race who should control all of Germany and beyond. He wanted to regrow German territory westward toward France, northeast into Poland, southeast to Czechoslovakia, and eventually east to Russia. These lands historically belonged to Germany, but were given to other countries under the terms of the treaty. He also wanted to make Germany pure by eliminating Jews, Slovaks and others from Germany and any newly acquired territory.

Beginning in 1933, during Hitler's first year in power, Germany experienced a rapid economic recovery from the Depression. He ignored restrictions imposed by the Treaty of Versailles and ordered steps to re-militarize the country. He breached the Treaty first by increasing the size of Germany's armed forces. Hitler ordered volunteer soldiers to drill in secret, with shovels instead of rifles. In 1933 he withdrew Germany from the League of Nations Disarmament Agreement, demanding equality of arms with France and Britain.

In March 1935, he openly announced he would re-arm Germany, in blatant violation of the Treaty of Versailles. Other countries, focused on a post-WWI global disarmament movement, ignored Germany's activities. In June of that year, Britain agreed to a naval agreement directly with Germany, accepting the premise Germany could have a navy 35 percent the size of Britain's Navy. This separate agreement allowed Germany to have more than six battleships; it violated the terms of the Treaty of Versailles and disregarded France's interests. Great Britain's intent was to keep a controlling alliance with Germany. The unintended consequence: It allowed Germany to become a naval power as it built battleships and hundreds of submarines.

In July 1936, Hitler sent air and armored war machines to Spain to assist General Francisco Franco and Nationalist forces in the Spanish Civil War. That provided Hitler's senior military officers the experience they needed for his future war plans. Hitler limited Germany's military activity in the war and urged Mussolini to involve his Italian forces. The three-year Spanish war provided combat experience for in excess of 12,000 German soldiers and officers using the latest air and mobile war machines.

In December 1936, Hitler told his first-line generals to prepare for war starting in three years. In 1937 Hitler began conscripting men into the military. He continued spending huge sums of money building war machinery, including tanks, armored vehicles, airplanes, ships and submarines. He also spent money on the nation's railroad infrastructure and building roadways. Hitler even supported research into a new type of engine that would allow airplanes to fly without propellers. A further development was the design of long-range rockets.

During the mid-1930s, Hitler claimed that a new treaty between France and Russia threatened Germany's safety. His response was to annex adjacent territories. Hitler broke terms of the Treaty of Versailles, moving German troops and equipment into a demilitarized zone called the *Rhineland*. German commanders had orders to retreat if the French Army tried to stop them from invading the area. But to Germany's surprise, France did nothing as 20,000 German soldiers and war machines moved to occupy the area. Following these bold land-grabbing moves, Hitler gained praise and more support from German citizens.

In Austria, an attempted Nazi Party putsch in 1934 failed. Then in March 1938, the Austrian Nazi Party and its SA organized riots as Hitler pressured the Austrian chancellor to declare a political and economic union with Germany. Austria balked and sought help from France and Britain. Sadly, politicians from both countries refused to get involved.

Germany quickly invaded Austria and imprisoned more than 30,000 Austrians. In a referendum shortly after the invasion, 99 percent of Austrians voted "Yes" to *Anschluss*, the official act of being taken over by Germany. But they had no choice. Austrian men, women and military officers were upset. Many attempted to leave the country; some were immediately drafted into the German military. One Austrian Naval officer, Baron Georg Ludwig von Trapp, a highly decorated submarine captain in the Austrian-Hungary Imperial Navy during World War I, took his entire family mountain climbing days after the Anschluss. They hiked far into the Italian Alps, where they hid until WWII ended; then the family moved to upstate New York.

Following the takeover of Austria, Hitler annexed more land. He demanded Sudetenland by threatening war with Czechoslovakia to gain the territory, but Britain and France again broke the Treaty of Versailles, ceding Sudetenland to Germany on September 30. What remained for German expansion was moving into Danzig and the Polish corridor. The Treaty of Versailles was now a useless document, as Britain and France allowed Hitler to act without military consequences.

The next step in Hitler's long-term strategy was an alliance with Communist Russia. His war plan included invading Poland but not to worry about fighting against the Soviet Red Army. While he didn't trust Stalin, he signed a non-aggression treaty with the Soviets to hold them in check.

With their new alliance in place, Hitler continued his aggressive actions in a blitzkrieg of Germany's war machine across Poland in September 1939. Conquering Poland allowed Germany to grow, satisfying Hitler's thirst for expansion and power. His dictatorship from 1933 to 1939 was deemed fruitful in the eyes of the German people. He could now eliminate even more Jews from Europe.

In May and June 1940, the Wehrmacht was on the move again. The German war machine, now fully developed, continued its blitzkrieg style of warfare, racing into Belgium and France.

A year later, on June 22, 1941, feeling militarily emboldened, Hitler set aside his treaty with the Soviet Union and invaded Russia. The Germans launched an aggressive blitzkrieg style attack, eastward against Russia. Military experts consider Operation Barbarossa the largest land-based military attack in history. Almost 3.5 million German soldiers – using more than 3,400 tanks and 2,700 airplanes – blitzed across the border and drove deep into the heart of Russia, knocking the Red Army on its heels. In the first day of the attack, the Soviet air force lost 1,200 planes. The German *Luftwaffe* secured air superiority immediately and severely damaged many Soviet supply lines. Within five weeks, more than 600,000 Red Army soldiers were captured. As December brought winter's cold and snowy conditions, Germany's inability to provide supplies to the front eventually slowed the Wehrmacht's progress. The Soviet Red Army successfully held its defensive line, keeping Germany from capturing Moscow. Red Army tanks and troops led by brilliant commanders from Russia, Ukraine and other areas in the Soviet Union, held their lines and slowly pushed the Germans back. Germany was now fully engaged in battles, fighting on two fronts.

On December 7, 1941, the Japanese, bolstered by success in their war against China, attacked the United States territory, Hawaii, at its Pearl Harbor naval base. Having met regularly with Japan's ambassador to Germany, Hiroshi Oshima, Hitler immediately formed an alliance with Japan and declared war on the United States on December 11. The U.S. immediately positioned itself against Japan in the Pacific, and Germany in Europe, and committed to financial aid, military troops and equipment to its European allies. The United States took broad steps to gather raw materials, and to begin the nation's production of ships, airplanes and mobile war machinery. It trained soldiers for war in the European and Pacific theaters.

In May 1942, the Royal Air Force began its air offensive against Germany with air raids on the continent. In July, American pilots began taking part in RAF raids and sorties – flying from England, across the English Channel and into France and other countries. Meanwhile, a new radio-tracking device called radar was being developed, which enabled England to anticipate Germain air raids.

A year later, Allied forces from the U.S., Great Britain, Canada and Australia landed in Sicily. Under U.S. Army General George Patton and Britain's Field Marshal Bernard Montgomery, the Allies pushed their way to Messina. In their retreat from Sicily, Germany and Italy evacuated some 60,000 troops, 14,000 vehicles, 47 tanks and over 1,000 tons of ammunition from Messina to the mainland before the Allies could stop them. The German command positioned 12,000 troops in Calabria and moved the remaining 48,000 men and virtually all the equipment north, to reinforce their defensive-line positions called the Gothic Line, Winter Line, Siegfried Line, Gustav Line, Bernhardt and Hitler lines across the Italian peninsula.

On August 1, 1943, the American Army Air Force initiated an aerial bombing raid called Operation Tidal Wave. Starting in Benghazi, Libya, 177 B-24s flew to Ploiesti, Romania, where they heavily damaged Axis oil refineries and fuel sources, nicknamed Hitler's Gas Station. In the raid, 53 B-24s and 440 U.S. air crewmen died, and another 300 were wounded. Of the 125 remaining planes, 88 returned to Benghazi and 33 B-24s were forced to land in Turkey, Cyprus and Romania, where 108 U.S. airmen were taken prisoner by German ground forces. This effort initially caused a loss of 40% of capacity and caused interruptions in Germany's fuel-supply chain. Operation Tidal Wave was considered a strategic loss for the allies, but marked the start of difficulties for the flow of fuel to the *Wehrmacht*'s mobile war machinery. Subsequent bombing of strategic German rail lines by the Allies, especially involving tank battles and mass troop movements, proved to be more effective.

During July and August 1943, the German Wehrmacht launched its last major offensive attack called Operation Citadel against the Soviet Red Army. Its second phase expanded its geographic reach, becoming known as the Battle of Kursk, using their newest style tanks, Panthers and Tigers. Considered the largest tank battle in WWII, the Germans had almost 800,000 troops and almost 3,000 tanks; the Red Army involved over one million troops and 3,500 tanks in the battle. Men, long guns and armored vehicles clashed for weeks; during that particular campaign, the German troops went through nearly 500,000 tons of ammunition in two months' time.

As the Red Army pushed back the Germans, Hitler moved his military forces – originally destined to provide support along the Eastern front – to support the fight against the Allies in Italy, by reinforcing their entrenchments in the Italian mountains just before the U.S. and Allied forces landed in Anzio.

In the fall of 1943, the Allies began their battle to liberate Rome. At the same time, the U.S. continued its air attacks, attempting to destroy rail lines the Wehrmacht needed on its multiple war fronts. The logistics of keeping their tanks, halftracks, airplanes and ships fueled became a serious issue recognized by Germany's field generals, but Hitler refused to accept the bad news and advice.

The D-Day invasion of France by the U.S. and its allies in Normandy in June 1944 established yet another front where the German war machine would need to reinforce its fight to hold onto France.

By now, high-ranking German generals and strategists realized they couldn't sustain the fight. They tried to convince Hitler to end the war, but he wouldn't hear it. Frustration over his constant demands and unpredictable decisions led to multiple attempts on his life by German military commanders. One attempt was on July 20, 1944, when several senior-level German officers staged an unsuccessful attempt on Hitler's life during a meeting at the Wolf's Lair. Hitler escaped harm and continued to believe he was destined to win the war.

By December 1944, American and Allied forces had pushed the Germans out of France and Italy. Finally, by spring 1945, American, British and Russian forces pushed Germans most of the way back to Berlin. In March and April 1945, as Red Army and American forces fought their way and advanced toward Berlin, American allies and the Soviets began to free tens of thousands of prisoners from concentration and death camps.

In the final days of WWII, the Soviets arrived first in Berlin and virtually encircled the city. Hitler was said to have been physically challenged from a prior attempt on his life, and mentally challenged due to the drugs he took for pain while hiding in his Führer Bunker. He continued to press his most faithful generals, ordering them to fight to the end, which they did in the Battle of Berlin. Then in the last days, he married –

and then killed – his new wife, Eva Braun. Then he committed suicide. Days later the war officially ended.

***

Numerous reports say Hitler somehow escaped Berlin. Some reports placed him in South America. Other reports said Hitler and several other high ranking SS field marshals fled Berlin to the north and died in the May 6, 1945, sinking of submarine U-3523, a type XXI U-boat, off the Danish coast, when it came under attack by a British B-24 Liberator.

One American soldier, Aubrey Temples, a prisoner of war held on a farm outside Berlin, swears he saw Hitler in a car, as it and several other cars passed the farm in a motorcade on the rural road. The man, from Texas, tells the story in detail on a video recording, insisting he's certain the man he saw was Adolf Hitler.

Many German SS officers quietly found their way out of Germany. Some traveled secretly through Spain and Africa to South America and to Ipanema Beach in Brazil. Many of them wanted to re-establish the Nazi party and, perhaps, even overthrow one or several South American governments. Their interest was laid in the groundwork established by a German Nazi spy, Johannes Siegfried Becker, who began operating in São Paulo, Brazil and then throughout South America under the code name *SARGO* beginning in 1940. Becker encouraged Nazi Party growth, political unrest and revolution in several South American countries. Most of his underground efforts were stopped when his coded information was uncovered by U.S. agents and used against those hoping to overthrow the governments. After the war ended, Becker disappeared.

Otto Skorzeny was another highly decorated Nazi Waffen SS officer. Best known for torturing and killing anti-Hitler conspirators, he surreptitiously directed hundreds of English-speaking German spies clad in U.S. uniforms behind Allied lines. Skorzeny initially gained fame by rescuing Mussolini from confinement by the Italian government in the Abruzzi mountains. Acquitted after the war, he was said to have become a double agent for Israel.

Others Nazi officers with special mechanical or engineering skills were highly prized and brought to the United States or Russia. One such SS German Nazi brought to the United States was Wernher Magnus von

Braun, an aerospace engineer in charge of Germany's rocket-propulsion research and developer of Germany's V-2 rockets used to attack London. Years afterward, von Braun became chief architect of the United States' Apollo Saturn V rocket program that lifted American astronauts to the moon, and launched America's first space station, Skylab. Having lived in several towns in the U.S., von Braun died in Huntsville, Alabama, on June 16, 1977.

Peter J. Marzano

Research Resources

Publications

1) *Brill's Encyclopedia of the first World War*; Leiden, Boston; Brill, 2012.
2) Wikipedia: extensive use and references of events of World War I, World War II, specific facts about battles and events in each war, references to the events leading to each war, events regarding the failings of the Treaty of Versailles and the rise of the Nazi Party.
3) *Soldaten: The Secret Second World War Tapes of German POWs*, by Professor Sonke Neitzel, 2011
4) *Soldaten: Tapping Hitler's Generals: Transcripts of Secret Conversations 1942-1945*, Neitzel, 2013
5) *Understanding World War II Through the Eyes of German Soldiers*, by Professor Sonke Neitzel, 2014
6) Organization Todt: see www.histclo.com/mil/todt ; www.ibiblio.org
7) *Encyclopedia Britannica*/World History/Military Leaders
8) The Battle of Kursk: the largest tank battle in history| HISTORY Channel
9) Erna Flegel – Hitler's Nurse; the Irish Times; www.irishtimes.com
10) Seeing Hitler: WWII Eyewitness Account of Aubrey M. Temples, by Aubrey M. Temples, Lewis S. Robinson III, Editor

Movies

The Last Ten Days — 1955	Hitler: The Last Ten Days — 1962
Hitler: The Last Ten Days — 1973	The Bunker — 1981
The Wannsee Conference — 1987	Conspiracy — 2001
Blind Spot — 2002	Downfall — 2004
Uncle Adolf — 2005	Operation Valkyrie — 2008

YouTube Videos

Operation Barbarossa/YouTube
Airforce Raid on Ploesti/YouTube
Operation Citadel/YouTube
The Battle of Kursk: the largest tank battle in history /YouTube
Mein Kampf: The Secrets of Adolf Hitler's Book/YouTube
Anschluss of Austria – 1938/YouTube
WW2 in Italy – Battle of Anzio | 1944
Operation Valkyrie: The Plot to Kill Hitler/YouTube
Allies Break Through the German Gothic Line/YouTube
Seeing Hitler: WWII Eyewitness Account of Aubrey M. Temples/YouTube

Historical Characters – Alphabetically

German:

Becker, Johannes Siegfried – German Nazi spy who began operating throughout South America under the code name *SARGO* beginning in 1940. He encouraged Nazi Party growth and political unrest in several South American countries.

Bormann, Martin – Deputy to Rudolph Hess; built the Berghof; later became personal secretary and controlled all access to Hitler. Present in the bunker when Hitler committed suicide.

Christian, Gerda – One of several personal secretaries to Hitler.

Donitz, Karl – Commander of the German U-boats and later promoted to Grand Admiral. Surrendered Germany to the Allies.

Eicke, Theodor – An early commander at Dachau, later responsible for expanding and further developing concentration and death camps. He was killed in battle in 1943.

Flegel, Erna – Adolf Hitler's nurse in the bunker.

Goebbels, Joseph – Controlled the Nazi news media beginning in the 1920s. Consistently spread fake news. Promoted Wehrmacht successes on the battlefield. Married to Magda; he allowed his wife to poison their six children then he committed suicide with his wife.

Goebbels, Magda – Wife of Joseph Goebbels. Gave sleeping potion and then cyanide to her six children before committing suicide with her husband.

Göring, Hermann – WWI flying ace who received the Blue Max award; flew with Baron von Richthofen; commanded Luftwaffe; Minister of Economics; senior to all Wehrmacht commanders; became a drug addict after an injury.

Guderian, Heinz Wilhelm – Advocated tank warfare and the architect of the Blitzkrieg; assistant to Oswald Lutz. Spearheaded the Blitzkrieg across France, stranding thousands of English soldiers at Dunkirk.

Gunsche, Otto – Mid-level Waffen SS officer and personal adjutant to Hitler. Carried bodies from bunker. In charge of cremating the bodies of Hitler and Eva Braun.

Hess, Rudolph – Jailed with Hitler after the Munich putsch, wrote *Mein Kampf* as Hitler dictated. Nazi politician became Deputy Führer. Flew to Scotland and parachuted from a plane to negotiate peace with Great Britain. Committed suicide in a prison in 1987.

Heydrich, Reinhard – Assistant to Himmler. Head of the Security Service focused on arresting and murdering Jews. Organized Kristallnacht. Responsible for Einsatzgruppen, which followed the German Army and murdered over 2 million people by mass shootings and gassing – including 1.3 million Jews.

Himmler, Heinrich – Commander of the SS and Gestapo. Administrative leader of the Third Reich. Brains behind effort of Jewish genocide. Allowed some Jews to leave camps before the war's end to negotiate for his self-interest.

Hitler, Adolf – Rogue individual who became leader of the Nazi Party and then Chancellor of the Third Reich. Authored the book *Mein Kampf* while in jail. Megalomaniac. Ordered the murders of millions of Jews and other nationalities. Unskilled military leader who drove Wehrmacht beyond its capacity. Ultimately addicted to drugs, murdered his new wife and committed suicide.

Junge, Gertrud "Traudl" – Personal secretary to Hitler. Married Hans Junge, who later died during the war. Typed Hitler's will and remained in bunker until his death. Died in 2002.

Kempka, Erich – SS officer who served as Hitler's chauffeur. Present at the bunker when Hitler committed suicide.

Kesserling, Albert – General field marshal, one of Germany's most decorated commanders. Career spanned WWI and WWII. He laid the foundation for Luftwaffe; led numerous campaigns in North Africa and spearheaded the defensive campaign in Italy against the invading Americans and the Allies.

Linge, Heinz – Personal valet to Hitler. Present in the bunker, he found Hitler had committed suicide. Responsible with Gunsche for cremating the bodies of Hitler and Eva Braun.

Lutz, Oswald – WWI veteran became WWII German general and oversaw the German military's mobilization in the 1930s. Became commander of all Panzer tanks and troops in 1935.

Mohnke, Wilhelm – Waffen SS Brigade general and adjunct to Himmler leading Wehrmacht actions in France, Poland and the Balkans. Fought in the Battle of the Bulge. Charged with defending the Chancellery in the Battle of Berlin. Led group away from the bunker following Hitler's death.

Schroeder, Christa – One of several personal secretaries to Hitler.

Skorzeny, Otto – Nazi Waffen SS officer who tortured and killed anti-Hitler conspirators. He directed hundreds of English-speaking German spies clad in US uniforms behind allied lines. Gained fame by rescuing Mussolini from confinement in the Abruzzi mountains. Acquitted after the war and is said to have become a double agent for Israel.

Speer, Albert – Hitler's personal architect, who took over for Fritz Todt. Served as Minister of Armaments and War overseeing production of Panzer tanks. Served 20 years in prison after the war.

Suhren, Fritz – Commander at women's camp called Ravensbrück.

Todt, Fritz – Construction engineer who set up "Organization Todt" a construction company turned into a military battalion that built airplane hangars, submarine ports, the Autobahns, defensive pill boxes, death and concentration camps and other German buildings. Died when a plane exploded in mid-air; suspected to have been murdered by Albert Speer.

Russian:

Konev, Marshal Ivan – Ukrainian troop commander; led Soviet Red Army forces in the Battle of Berlin.

Zhukov, Marshal Georgy – Belorussian troop commander; led Soviet Red Army forces in the Battle of Berlin.

Japanese:

Oshima, General Baron Hiroshi – Japanese ambassador to Germany before the beginning of WWII. Educated in Berlin; spoke fluent German. Proposed disintegration of the Soviet Union. Had unparalleled access to Hitler. Used PURPLE cipher machine, broken by American code breakers in 1940. His frequent reports to Japanese superiors gave Allied leaders insight into activities planned by Hitler.

About the Author

Peter J. Marzano is the son of Italian and Irish families, immigrants to New York City in 1908 and 1928 respectively. Born in Manhattan's Greenwich Village, he grew up in Staten Island. After attending Staten Island Community College, Peter worked in construction and eventually migrated into sales with divisions of General Dynamics, United Technologies, AT&T, and an American division of Air Liquid.

His broad business experience spanned 45 years, allowing him to travel nationally and internationally in Europe for work and pleasure while living in NYC; Atlanta, Georgia; Orlando, Florida; Hartford, Connecticut; and Wilmington, North Carolina. His unique skills, knowledge and technical experience allowed him to help customers in a variety of industrial settings.

Father of four and grandfather of eleven, Marzano has been married to his high-school sweetheart, Kathleen (Coyle) Marzano almost 50 years. He is an avid photographer who loves capturing family, friends, outdoor scenery and wildlife. He currently resides in Connecticut.

Litany of Sorrows is his debut novel.

Lightning Source UK Ltd.
Milton Keynes UK
UKHW021824040123
414830UK00011B/963